Donna Alward lives on Canada's east coast with her family, which includes a husband, a couple of kids, a senior dog and two crazy cats. Her heart-warming stories of love, hope and homecoming have been translated into several languages, hit bestseller lists and won awards, but her favourite thing is hearing from readers! When she's not writing she enjoys reading (of course!), knitting, gardening, cooking… and is a Masterpiece Theater addict. You can visit her on the web at DonnaAlward.com and join her mailing list at DonnaAlward.com/newsletter.

USA TODAY bestselling and RITA® Award–winning author **Marie Ferrarella** has written more than two hundred and seventy-five books for Mills & Boon, some under the name Marie Nicole. Her romances are beloved by fans worldwide. Visit her website, www.marieferrarella.com.

Also by Donna Alward

Hired: The Italian's Bride
The Cowboy's Christmas Family
The Cowboy's Convenient Bride

Marrying a Millionaire miniseries
Best Man for the Wedding Planner

Also by Marie Ferrarella

Wish Upon a Matchmaker
Dating for Two
Diamond in the Ruff
Her Red-Carpet Romance
Coming Home for Christmas
Dr. Forget-Me-Not
Twice a Hero, Always Her Man
Meant to Be Mine
A Second Chance for the Single Dad
Christmastime Courtship

SECRET MILLIONAIRE FOR THE SURROGATE

DONNA ALWARD

THE COWBOY'S LESSON IN LOVE

MARIE FERRARELLA

MILLS & BOON

First Published in Great Britain 2019
by Mills & Boon, an imprint of HarperCollinsPublishers,
1 London Bridge Street, London, SE1 9GF

ISBN: 978-0-263-27204-8

0119

MIX
Paper from
responsible sources
FSC™ C007454

This book is produced from independently certified FSC™ paper to ensure responsible forest management.

For more information visit: www.harpercollins.co.uk/green

Printed and bound in Spain
by CPI, Barcelona

SECRET MILLIONAIRE FOR THE SURROGATE

DONNA ALWARD

For Barb—my soul sister.

CHAPTER ONE

March

IT WAS ODD being the person in front of the camera rather than behind it.

Harper McBride smiled once more as she looked around the room, trying to keep her smile genuine, but not quite liking the feeling of being so conspicuous. She was used to being the wedding photographer, in the background and out of the spotlight. Not tonight. The silky dress clung to her curves…what she had of them. She'd always had more of an athletic-type figure and broad shoulders that made buying tops and dresses slightly problematic. The cut of this dress, though…well, it left her shoulders bare, and a slit up the leg to midthigh left her feeling adventurous but also a little awkward.

But it was Adele's wedding day, and Harper was the only bridesmaid, and she'd do anything for her best friend.

Anything. As she'd just proved when she gave Adele and Dan their wedding present. If Harper could help her best friend start the family she'd always wanted, she was all in.

She snagged a glass of champagne from the tray of a passing waiter and took a deep drink. She only had to get through maybe another hour of the dance and she could sneak away, back to her little bungalow and into a pair of soft flannel pajamas. That was how she preferred to spend her evenings, if she wasn't photographing a wedding or special event. Out of the spotlight.

"You disappeared for a while."

A deep voice sounded by her shoulder and she suppressed a delicious shiver. Drew, the groom's brother and the best man. Harper and Drew had walked down the aisle together…and back up again when the I dos had been said, her fingers on his sleeve. Not too tightly, but not too loose, just enough to feel the warmth and strength beneath her fingertips. They'd sat next to each other at dinner, where she'd inhaled his cologne and his warm laugh had washed over her, making her smile even when she didn't quite want to. Drew Brimicombe was sexy and charming—the kind of man she didn't quite trust.

Drew and Dan were similar but also so very different. Accountant Dan kept his hair short and tidy and looked very James Bond in his tuxedo. Outdoorsman Drew, on the other hand, was a few inches shorter, his hair was a few inches longer, and he always seemed to have a little bit of scruff on his jaw. His tux fit perfectly, but there was a roughness to his appearance that was appealing. He wore designer threads as effortlessly as he wore faded jeans and a Henley shirt. Like the ones he'd worn to the rehearsal last night, and her mouth had gone dry just looking at him.

She half turned and smiled at him, her stomach flipping a little. "I went to talk to Dan and Adele on the terrace."

"It's cold outside."

"I wasn't out there very long." She lifted her glass again, hoping she wasn't blushing in the dim lighting. A small band played in the corner, some sort of jazzy blues-type music that made her think of Diana Krall. Drew's hand touched the hollow of her back lightly, and she was ready to move away when she realized he was merely guiding her slightly to the right to make room for a server with a tray of hors d'oeuvres.

His body was too close.

Just when she was ready to say something, he stepped

back. "Sorry about that. She was trying to get through and I could envision a tray of cocktail shrimp going everywhere." He smiled at her, a genuinely friendly smile, but with that edge of ever-present impishness she had to guard against.

"We wouldn't want that," she replied, trying to let out a breath and calm down. For heaven's sake, he was just a guy, and she wasn't truly interested, even if he did fluster her with his sideways smile and twinkly brown eyes. After the wedding he'd be going back to California or wherever it was he called home.

"Hey, Harper?"

"Hmm?" She had been trying to keep her gaze on the band, but when he said her name, she turned back to him and met his eyes. They weren't so twinkly now, but warm and melty. At least that was how they made her feel…

"If I didn't tell you already today, you look killer in that dress."

Heat rushed into her cheeks and she bit back a curse. "Thanks. I clean up once in a while. Even break out the high heels." She tried a nonchalant shrug. "I'm more of a jeans and hoodie person."

"Me, too. But it's nice to get dressed up now and again. Especially for an important occasion like this."

She smiled. "You're right."

"I know." His confidence was at once attractive and maddening, and she snorted a laugh despite herself. When she lifted her head, he was holding out his hand. "Care to?"

He was asking her to dance. Her laughter died a quick death. She was no good at flirting, but even worse when it came to personal space and touching. She never quite knew where to put her hands or where to look. There was a reason why she spent her time behind the camera rather than in front of it. She did a good job faking it most of the time, but inside she was awkward as anything. Always had been.

"I don't really dance." She suspected that she had two

left feet when it came down to it, though it had been ages since she'd tested that theory.

"I don't believe you. Besides, I think it's tradition for the best man to dance with the maid of honour."

She raised an eyebrow. "I'm letting you off the hook."

He still held out his hand. "What if I don't want to be off the hook? What are you so afraid of? I promise I'm well behaved."

She couldn't see a polite way out of it, so she put her hand in his.

He closed his fingers over hers.

Oh, no.

The butterflies in her stomach multiplied as he led her to the parquet and folded her into his arms. His scent wrapped around them, cocooning her in a cloud of masculinity. She took a breath and let it out slowly as their feet began to move.

"This isn't so bad, is it?" Piano and soft vocals swirled around them, lulling her closer to his chest. When she realized it, she shifted back a bit, putting more space between them.

"It's okay," she replied, secretly thinking it was the most wonderful thing to happen to her in months. The last time she'd been this breathless she'd been hiking near Emerald Lake and had caught a shot of a grizzly mom and cubs in the morning mist. It was one of her favorite shots, and she'd framed it and highlighted it in her studio window just off Banff Avenue.

His chest rose and fell as he silently chuckled. "Harper, you are not an easy woman."

She looked up at him, lifting her chin. "I surely hope not."

"I like challenges."

"I'm not a challenge, Drew. And not a trophy."

His eyes lit with a new light. "Thank God. I mean… I like someone who can keep me on my toes."

He tried a small turn and she stumbled a little. His arm tightened around her waist, keeping her upright.

"Careful, or I'll actually be *on* your toes," she warned.

He laughed, once again a warm sound that lulled her closer and made her smile. Damn him. Dan was a great guy, but his brother was all charm. Stupid thing was, Harper figured it was actually genuine, not an act or a cover-up. He was warm and funny and put people at ease.

At least she would be at ease if she weren't so aware of him.

"You're something else, you know that?" he said, softer now, his body brushing hers. Their feet had slowed and their steps shortened, so they were barely more than swaying. Harper swallowed against the nervous lump in her throat. She was so not confident when it came to men. Particularly good-looking ones who said all the right things without trying. They had a habit of turning around and walking away, just when you thought it was safe to believe. To trust.

"Um, thank you?" she murmured, knowing she should pull away, but wanting deep down to enjoy the moment a bit longer.

"I mean it." He leaned back and met her gaze. "Dan told me about how you've been such a good friend to Adele and all the things you did to help with the wedding. I went to your studio the other day, you know. You do some amazing work."

Heat flushed her chest and up her neck. "Oh. I…well. I didn't expect you to say that."

"Your nature photographs are some of the best I've seen. The one of the mama grizzly and her cubs? I love it."

Since it was one of her favorites, too, she smiled, more relaxed now. Talking about her work was much easier than anything overly personal. "I'm pretty proud of that one," she admitted.

"I don't know why you do weddings and stuff, not when you have such a talent for nature photography."

She shrugged. "Weddings are fun, too, you know. There's so much happiness and hope. Besides, weddings and other occasions are my bread and butter. Those bookings keep me in the black so I can indulge in the other stuff. Rent in this town isn't cheap." At least there was happiness and hope for other people. Harper just wasn't sure it was in the cards for *her*.

He nodded. "There. You're more relaxed. I'm not going to bite, you know."

She let out a breath, prepared to laugh a bit, until he added, "Unless you want me to."

The breath whooshed out of her lungs and her feet stopped moving. "Uh. Drew, I..."

"I like you, Harper. A lot."

"You barely know me."

"I'd like to fix that."

Oh God Oh God Oh God.

She decided to be honest. "I'm not good at these types of situations. I don't know what to say and I don't know how to play the game." Besides, being the loser hurt. A lot. And she was under no illusions who'd come out the victor in this match.

He tightened his fingers over hers. "Then I'll be clear." His magnetic gaze held hers. "I'm attracted to you, and I think you're attracted to me, and I'd like to know if you'd like to do something about it."

The answer in her head was *yes*, and it was so disconcerting that she stepped out of his arms as her heart started a strange gallop behind her ribs. Of course her real answer would be no. For one thing, hooking up at a wedding for a fling was not her style. And for another, she'd just offered to be a surrogate for his brother and her best friend. Talk about complicating a situation...

"I think you got the wrong idea," she said coolly. "I like you, Drew, but I'm not interested in hooking up."

He watched her for a long moment. Then his eyes warmed and he gave a little nod. "Then, I'm sorry," he said quietly, "for misreading the signals. And for making you uncomfortable."

But she was uncomfortable, and not really because of him. After all, she *was* attracted, and she'd enjoyed dancing with him and even the bit of verbal sparring they'd indulged in now and again. But it couldn't go any further, and he accepted that, so why was everything feeling so off balance now?

"Friends?" he asked, lifting a questioning eyebrow.

"Of course." She smiled and let out a breath. "It would be nice to be friends, especially if your brother is married to my bestie."

"Agreed." He held out his hand and she shook it, but when his fingers folded over hers, those darned tingles started all over again. It sucked that her body wasn't agreeing with her brain right now.

She pulled her hand away and stepped back. Drew led her to the edge of the dance floor again, grabbed her another glass of champagne and talked to her for a few minutes about her photographs as if nothing had ever happened. Then Dan called him over, he excused himself and, with a small touch on her arm, left her alone.

Alone was what she was used to. And when she wasn't alone she had Adele, and her assistant, Juny, and phone calls with her mom and dad, who were currently living in Caicos, while her dad flew charter planes between islands. She had a good life.

But tonight, being held in Drew's arms…it had been a little taste of heaven. And one she was already regretting passing up.

CHAPTER TWO

May

HARPER HELD HER breath as she sat on the closed toilet in the tiny bathroom at her photography studio. Juny hadn't yet arrived for the day, and everything was still and quiet. Harper had wanted the few minutes of privacy to do the pregnancy test. Now she felt like she might throw up, and it had nothing to do with any potential morning sickness. It was nerves, plain and simple. A lot was riding on these three minutes of pee on a stick.

Two minutes had already passed. One more to go before she could look at the stick and know if she'd be giving her best friend, Adele, good news or bad news.

She desperately wanted it to be good. And yet the idea terrified her, too. Being a surrogate for Adele and her new husband, Dan, was something she'd really wanted to do. Adele had had cancer at a young age and couldn't have children of her own. It had taken eight long years for her and Dan to reconnect and commit to each other, even though they knew they might never have the family they both yearned for. Harper had a completely healthy uterus and no relationship to speak of. There was no reason why she couldn't carry a baby for the woman who'd made such a big difference in her world. The woman who'd made her finally feel as if she had a home and some roots to put down.

But now, with the seconds ticking away, Harper was afraid. Carrying a baby was a big thing. She'd attended medical appointments with Dan and Adele, had combed through research, had sat with her feet in stirrups. There had been little that was glamorous or sentimental about the whole procedure, but it hadn't been frightening.

Until now.

Today, if the plus sign showed up on the stick, there was no going back. She either was or she wasn't. And if she was…she'd be carrying a little human in her body for the next eight and a half months. Her mouth was dry as she tried to swallow. Thank God Adele wasn't here now, waiting. Harper wasn't sure she could have taken the pressure of Adele's heart being on the line while they waited. Better to know now, get her wits about her and decide what to say. The doctor had said this was a long shot, and probably Adele and Dan's only chance at using Adele's eggs. Either way, there would be big news for her friends. Either a second chance or the end of this particular road, and moving on to plan B.

She checked her phone. The seconds ticked down from ten…

But she didn't wait. She reached for the stick and stared at the result.

It was a plus sign.

She was carrying her best friend's baby—the most precious cargo in the world.

July

Summer sun beat down on Drew Brimicombe's head. It had been cool up the mountain, where he'd spent most of the afternoon in an alpine meadow overlooking a turquoise lake. No matter where he traveled, there was something about the Canadian Rockies that beckoned to him and made him feel at home. He'd been here half a dozen times over the past five years, mostly skiing, but now it was different. His brother, Dan, was here, and he was looking forward to some bro time.

And checking out real estate. That was his true reason for the impromptu trip—a tip from a contact about a real estate opportunity. He was always looking at expansion, and this might be his chance to open an Aspen Outfitter store north of the border. He couldn't think of a better opportunity than in the heart of the Rockies. And when one store opened, he was sure others would follow, making his brand North America-wide.

The townsite of Banff was hotter than he'd expected, though, considering how it was nestled smack in the middle of the mountains. He had on his sunglasses but not the standard ball cap he usually wore, and he could feel the heat soak into his scalp. Today had been a light hike, so he'd worn jeans, a T-shirt and a pair of lovingly broken-in boots. Water, a small digital camera, and some trail mix had been in his day pack, but he'd stayed to the marked trail and not ventured into backcountry. Not today. He'd just arrived and had chosen the easy hike to blow off the dust and claustrophobia of travel. Now he'd stop in at Dan and Adele's and let them know he'd arrived before heading to his hotel.

The house was tucked into a little side street, with a simple sign boasting Hawthorne Weddings out front. Adele's business was planning weddings, and one of her clients had been a good friend of Dan's, causing them to meet again after she'd broken his heart years earlier. No one had been more shocked than Drew when Dan had announced they were getting married, but Drew had come to the wedding and it had been clear to see that they still adored each other. Enough that Dan had uprooted his life as CFO of his company and moved here to be with her. Drew shook his head as he climbed the steps to the second floor of the house where Adele and Dan lived. He couldn't imagine doing anything like that. Settling down wasn't even on his radar, let alone leaving everything he'd worked for behind. He'd watched his dad give up dreams and aspirations for marriage and family, and he'd seen the unhappiness in his eyes.

Not that Drew didn't like Adele. He did. And Dan could make his own choices and he seemed to be happy. It just wasn't for Drew. He liked his freedom far too much.

His knock was answered by Adele, whose face lit up when she saw him. "Drew! What on earth are you doing here?"

He grinned. "Surprise trip. Are you surprised?"

"Very." But she smiled back at him. "Dan's going to flip. He was just talking about you last night. Come on in where it's air conditioned and I'll get you something to drink."

He stepped inside and heard another female voice. "Who is it, Del?"

He remembered that voice, sweet and musical. Harper. The maid of honour at the wedding. He'd turned on the charm a little, but she'd made it clear that she wasn't the type for a casual fling so he'd behaved himself.

"A surprise guest," Adele answered as Drew took off his boots. He went into the living room area in his sock feet and saw Harper seated in a plush chair, legs folded beneath her yoga-style, her hair pulled up in a pert ponytail. It highlighted her face and the light smattering of freckles across the bridge of her nose. Beautiful, he thought, but with a definite girl-next-door vibe. He much preferred her natural looks to a lot of makeup and just the right clothes. And shoes. Why women put so much emphasis on shoes, he could never figure out.

"Harper," he said warmly, stepping forward and holding out his hand. "Good to see you again."

She looked surprised at the handshake but put her hand

into his anyway. "You, too." She blinked and met his eyes. "They didn't know you were coming?"

He laughed, then pulled his hand away from her soft, cool fingers. "I didn't even know I was coming. I decided yesterday to take some time off and visit, but I didn't want to call unless it didn't work out on short notice." He wasn't sure how much he wanted to say about a possible land deal. For now it was a bit hush-hush. Besides, he didn't want it to seem like he was bragging—that wasn't his style. So he left it and merely shrugged.

"Oh."

He got the sense she didn't quite approve of his spur-of-the-moment plans, so he added, "I booked a room at the Cascade. No need for Adele and Dan to be inconvenienced by my impulses."

"The Cascade, in high season? How'd you manage to get a room?" Her eyebrows shot up.

He laughed. "I lucked out. There was a cancellation."

Her face relaxed a bit and Adele came back from the kitchen with a couple of beers and a glass of lemonade, which she gave to Harper.

"You don't like beer?" he asked, taking the bottle from Adele and twisting off the cap. "Nothing like it on a scorcher of a day like today."

Her gaze flicked to Adele and then back. "Um, I don't really drink," she answered, then hid behind her glass as she sipped. "Besides, lemonade is perfect."

He took a seat and chatted to Adele for a few minutes, catching up, but in the back of his brain he remembered the wedding and the fact that Harper had indulged in more than one glass of champagne.

Something felt off.

"So what brings you to Banff? It can't only be a visit with Dan."

He smiled at his new sister-in-law, thinking of a way to

divert the conversation. "To see you, too, you know. You're a package deal now. How are the newlyweds?"

Adele's smile was huge, and her gaze flicked to Harper for a moment before shifting back to him. "Oh, we're wonderful. Dan likes his new job a lot, and I'm..." Her smile was radiant. "Well, I'm blissfully happy."

"I'm glad."

"You didn't answer my question, though. What else brings you here?"

He considered for a moment and decided to be honest but downplay his interest. "I'm thinking about opening a store up here, and doing a little recon."

"And you can spend some time with your brother at the same time," Harper added softly.

He met her gaze, felt the jolt right to his toes. She was so pretty. So...artless. At the wedding weekend he'd learned she was a photographer. He remembered seeing her photos and realizing they were as simple and stunning as she was.

"Family's important," he said simply. "I haven't seen mine as much as I might have wanted to over the past few years."

"Dan says you two have always been close."

Harper had been smiling at him, but he dragged his gaze away to look at Adele again. "I'm the baby of the family, but I was the first to leave the Brimicombe family fold. I'd like to be around more, you know?" And look for opportunities. He was always keeping his eyes open. Being sharp was what kept him at the top of his game.

He turned his gaze to Harper. "What about you, Harper? Do you have any brothers or sisters?" Their wedding banter hadn't covered much in the way of personal subjects.

She smiled a little and shook her head. "An only child, I'm afraid. My parents live in Caicos."

"Caicos? Wow. What's in Caicos?"

She grinned. "An air charter service. My dad's a pilot."

"It's a beautiful island."

"You've been?"

He nodded. He'd traveled extensively and didn't have any plans of stopping. Stay in one place too long and he got itchy feet. Luckily, Aspen Outfitters had done well and he could indulge his wanderlust.

Adele's cell rang and she excused herself, leaving Drew and Harper alone. He looked over at her and wondered what was different. Granted, at the wedding she'd been dressed in lovely clothes with her hair and makeup done to perfection, understated but incredibly lovely. Now she was in shorts and a T-shirt with her hair in a simple reddish-brown tail. It was more than what she was wearing, though. There was something about her that drew him in and her skin glowed like she was lit from the inside. And it wasn't the summer heat. The air-conditioning made sure of that.

"You look good," he said, then realized how awful that must sound. "I mean, well."

She laughed a little. "Thanks. I think. I've been busy, but trying to take a little time off for me. It's wedding season, though. I'm booked every weekend from now until Thanksgiving."

"No summer vacations for you then, huh."

"Not really. Weddings really take up an entire weekend, with the rehearsal on the Friday and sometimes a family event on the day following the ceremony. And sometimes couples want engagement pictures, or have an engagement party, bridal shower…"

"They hire photographers for that?"

She waggled her delicate brows a little. "If there's money? Oh, yeah."

"Do you only do weddings?"

She unfolded her legs. "No. I mean, I do things like special occasions, engagement parties, graduations, anniversaries, that sort of thing. I even had a few gigs as prom photographer for a few different schools."

He leaned forward and rested his elbows on his knees. "It doesn't leave a lot of time for your nature stuff, does it?"

She shook her head, the tips of her ponytail touching her shoulders. "Not as much as I'd like. I try to get out of the studio a few times a week and take landscapes and candids."

"Like your mama and cubs photo."

She smiled then, a genuine, happy smile that lit up her eyes. "You remember that piece."

"Of course I do. How you got such clarity with the sun coming up and the little bit of mist on the grass… I don't know how you did it."

She took a sip of her lemonade, then nodded. "The scenery here is so beautiful, and I like experimenting with different filters and lenses. I sell some of my prints, but it's not enough to make a living and pay the rent on the studio. Weddings help me keep the lights on. But that means I don't have as much time as I'd like to explore the other stuff."

Her eyes lit up when she talked about her work. He could relate. There was nothing he enjoyed more than setting up a new store from the ground up. "But as you said, weddings are on weekends. Surely you have time during the week? More than a day or two?"

She laughed, a sound as light as sunbeams. "You mean when I'm not looking after the business side of things, and editing photos? You wouldn't believe how long editing takes."

"I never thought of that."

She smiled. "I try to get out as much as I can, but lately I…"

Her words trailed off and her eyes widened, as if she'd been caught saying something she shouldn't.

"Lately what?"

Her cheeks flushed. "Oh, it's nothing. So you're looking at opening a new store. That sounds exciting."

It was a deliberate evasion and he knew it, but he wasn't going to push for information she didn't want to give. She was a relative stranger, after all, and Adele's best friend. There was no need to be rude or prying. Though he couldn't help but wonder if her glow and now her evasion had anything to do with a new relationship. It shouldn't matter, because she'd already made her feelings clear. But it did. What kind of man could capture the heart of a woman like her? He'd have to be someone special. Drew had definitely gotten the impression that Harper wasn't the type to settle for just anyone.

"It is," he replied, taking a sip of his beer. "Aspen Outfitters would fit in well here, I think, with tourists and locals alike. It's a good market. Besides, I love building a new store. I like the challenge." It certainly beat sitting behind a desk or in a boardroom. With growth came responsibility. He accepted it, but sometimes it weighed a bit heavily.

Adele came back in, bringing a bowl of pita chips and a dish of dip. She put them down on the coffee table. "I'm assuming you're staying for dinner, but I thought you might like a snack for now."

"God, your homemade hummus is to die for," Harper said, leaning forward to grab a chip and scoop it through the smooth dip.

"I laid off the garlic, too. I know it's…"

She didn't finish her sentence.

Drew helped himself. Harper was right. The hummus was delicious, and he wasn't a huge fan normally. "You don't like garlic?" he asked, before popping another chip in his mouth.

"Oh, I like it. It just doesn't like me right now."

He frowned a little. Why would there be a change? Not that it was a big deal. It was hummus, for Pete's sake. But that was the second time one of them had stopped midsentence. He wondered if he'd interrupted something important. Something that was none of his business. He considered leaving, but then knew it would look odd if he left without at least seeing his brother.

They made small talk for a little while, until the door opened and closed again and Dan called out hello.

"We're in here!" Adele called back.

"We?"

Dan stepped into the room and Drew grinned at the look of sheer surprise on his face. He got up and gave his brother a bear hug and received one in return.

Dan clapped him on the back. "What the hell?" He laughed, stepping back. "We weren't expecting you!"

"I know. And I don't have any desire to disturb the newlyweds' love nest. I'm at a hotel."

"Don't be silly. Of course you can stay here."

Drew laughed. "Yeah, well, thanks, but I'm comfortable where I am. You guys deserve your privacy."

That Dan didn't argue further, and Adele blushed a little, told Drew all he needed to know. The hotel had definitely been the right—and most considerate—choice.

"You're staying for dinner, though, right?"

"Sure."

Dan finally noticed Harper. "Oh, and of course you're staying, too, right?"

"Oh." She looked surprised and slightly uncomfortable. "I should probably get back."

"To what? The workday's over. Stay," Adele insisted. "I'm going to grill some chicken and make risotto. I've got falafel I can make for you, unless you want something else."

Right. Drew remembered now from sitting next to her at the wedding. Harper was vegetarian.

"No, no, whatever you have is fine. You know I love falafel. Particularly if you have tzatziki from the market."

"It's settled, then."

"Let me help you in the kitchen," Harper offered, getting up from her chair. When she did, she pressed her hand to her back and stretched.

Once they were gone, Dan undid his tie and took it off, stuffing it in his pocket. He sank into a chair and sighed, then grinned. "It's good to see you, Drew."

"You, too. You guys look really happy. I'm glad."

"We are. Very."

Adele snuck in and handed Dan a cold beer, kissed his head and took off again.

"Did you really just come for a visit? It's unusual for you."

Drew shook his head. "As much as I'd be brother of the year if I said yes, I do have another agenda. Our last few stores are up and running smoothly, and I'm looking at expansion locations again. I got a tip about a property here. But I'm not saying much about it. I'm scouting things out." Of the family, Dan was the only one who knew how successful Drew had become. And they'd talked about keeping it under the radar, even with the family. Drew preferred to keep his life private, particularly his bank balance. Enough people treated him differently. He didn't need it from his family, too.

"You're looking at setting up a store here." Dan's grin was wide. "Cool."

"It's a prime location. I'm here to check out the local competition and see the property. Maybe some other locations if it's not what I'm looking for." He smiled. "And the fact that you're here is a major bonus. We haven't seen each other enough over the last five years."

Dan took a long pull of his beer. "You could have stayed here. I mean it."

"And disturb the newlywed love nest? No thanks. It's as much for my sake as it is for yours." He chuckled and took a drink of his beer, as well. "By the way, is Harper here a lot? I was surprised to find her here when I arrived."

Dan got a strange look on his face. "Oh, she's around quite a bit I suppose."

Drew put down his beer. That made at least four odd looks and a couple of halted conversations. Something was definitely off.

"Okay, I might be totally crazy, but is there something going on? You looked funny just now, and a couple of times Adele and Harper stopped midsentence. Am I missing something?" He frowned. "And if it's none of my business, say so."

Dan hesitated. "Well…it's not that it's none of your business, it's that we haven't said anything to anyone yet."

"About what?"

Dan took a drink of his beer. "Well, you know that Delly can't have kids."

"Y-es," he replied, drawing the word out a bit.

"So when I asked her to marry me, we talked about possibilities. Maybe adoption. Maybe not having children at all, which would have been fine. But at the wedding, Harper told us that she wanted to offer to be a surrogate for us."

Drew's gaze snapped to the kitchen door. He could hear Adele and Harper talking. A surrogate? He'd heard of such a thing but had never met anyone who'd actually done it. "So you're going to do it? But…how? I mean… I'm assuming you're…you know, and are you using her…" He started to stammer. "Okay, so this is actually really awkward."

Dan chuckled. "I know. It was for me at first, too. Adele had some testing done and we decided to try using her eggs. Normally this can be a bit of a long road, but we lucked out on the first try." His smile widened.

Drew stared for a minute as what his brother had just said sank in. *We lucked out on the first try.* "Does that mean… God, Dan, are you saying you're going to be a father?"

He nodded. "And Delly's going to be a mom, and Harper is carrying our baby for us."

Drew flopped back against the cushion of the chair. "Holy mackerel. I did not see that coming. That was fast."

"We haven't told anyone yet, not even Mom and Dad. She's still in the first trimester, and we want to be sure everything is okay. But since you're here…" He leaned forward, resting his hands on his knees. "I've been dying to tell someone, you know?" His grin broadened.

It made sense now. The whole garlic-doesn't-agree-with-me thing and the strange looks and truncated sentences. Drew rubbed a hand over his face and wondered what kind of woman offered to carry a child for a friend. What a huge commitment. What a generous thing. He hadn't realized that Harper and Adele were so close. What the heck was she getting out of it? He didn't consider himself a cynic, but he'd done enough business to know that hardly anyone did anything 100 percent altruistically.

"You okay, bro?" Dan lifted an eyebrow. "You look a little freaked out."

"I'm just surprised. You've only been married since March."

"We didn't want to wait. If it didn't work, we knew it could take time to adopt. I'm telling you, Harper is one in a million. Adele has gone to every appointment so far and soon we get to hear the heartbeat. That's our baby in there, you see? Adele's and mine. We'll never be able to repay Harper for this."

Harper stepped into the living room, her face easy and unconcerned. "Does anyone want another drink?"

Drew got to his feet, his emotions in a bit of a storm as he tried to adjust to the news without being an awkward ass. "Uh, I can get it. You don't need to wait on me."

She smiled softly. "Suit yourself, then. Beer's in the fridge."

He glanced quickly at her abdomen, then back up, his face heating. Harper didn't seem to notice anything and, with a flip of her ponytail, was gone back to the kitchen again.

His brain was a muddle, but he did manage to have one coherent thought as he followed her into the kitchen.

Harper is carrying my brother's baby.

CHAPTER THREE

HARPER KEPT HER hands busy cutting vegetables so she wouldn't have to look up at Drew, who'd come into the kitchen to grab a beer from the fridge. She'd seen the way his gaze had dropped to her belly and back up and the way he'd stood when she came into the room. Dan had told him; she was relatively sure of that. And it was awkward as hell.

She knew there would be some odd looks from people over the next few months, and probably more than her fair share of intrusive questions. She was prepared for that, or at least she was trying to be.

But she hadn't been prepared for Drew.

At the wedding in March he'd been crazy attractive, all sexy smiles and sparkling eyes, but she hadn't been in the mood for a wedding fling, particularly with the groom's brother. It would have been all kinds of messy.

Today had been far more awkward because the moment he'd stepped in the room her body had reacted just the same way as it had when he'd pulled her close on the dance floor. Her breath had caught and she'd felt that ridiculous butterfly feeling in the pit of her stomach. Forget the tux; Drew Brimicombe in faded, dusty jeans and a well-worn T-shirt was delectable. Add in that rough stubble and the slightly curling tips of his sun-streaked hair and she was a goner.

And she remembered how he'd propositioned her.

Now she was pregnant with his brother and sister-in-law's child and…yeah. Just as she'd thought at the wedding. This would be potentially awkward as heck and his reaction proved it. Not to mention that her attraction to him hadn't exactly disappeared.

She should never have agreed to stay for dinner.

"Harper. That might be enough cucumber."

The plate in front of her was rounded with cucumber slices and she realized she'd sliced the whole thing. To cover her embarrassment at getting caught daydreaming, she grinned and popped one in her mouth. "I can't get enough these days," she admitted. "They're so cool and fresh."

"Well, maybe you could cut some carrot and tomato to go with it?"

"Of course. Sorry. I don't know where my mind went."

Except she knew exactly where it went. With Drew, back into the living room. Or more precisely, back on the dance floor at the Cascade, being held in his strong arms, their bodies brushing.

She was peeling a carrot when she chanced a look up at Adele, who was ladling broth into the risotto. "I think Dan told Drew about the baby," she said.

Adele stopped stirring and stared at her. "You do? Why?"

"The way Drew looked at me when I went back in the room. It was the same look I got from Dan the moment I told you guys I was pregnant."

Adele frowned. "We weren't going to say anything to anyone yet. Not until after..." Adele let the thought trail away, and Harper put down the carrot peeler and went to her side.

"I know you're worried, but we're almost at the end of the first trimester. Besides, he didn't take out a billboard or anything. It's his brother. Who's here in person. Don't be too upset."

Adele let out a breath. "I know. And I don't mean to put extra pressure on you."

"I know that." Harper smiled easily, though deep down she felt as if a whole family's hopes were pinned on her keeping this baby healthy. She didn't want to be responsible for any big disappointments. "You'll feel better when you can hear the heartbeat. It's not long now. Besides, I feel great." Most of the time, anyway. Beyond a bit of fatigue and a few hours in the morning where morning sickness had become an issue.

Adele smiled and nodded. "You're right. Let's finish this up and get dinner on the table. We can eat out on the deck."

Harper finished preparing the vegetable platter, then checked on the chicken and the falafel on the grill. Adele brought out dishes for four and Harper set them out as Adele put the risotto in a bowl and brought out a pitcher of ice water.

The guys came a few moments later, still talking and laughing, and the early evening was more mellow in its heat, providing an easy warmth. Harper poured water in everyone's glass as Adele took the food off the grill, and in moments they were all seated and ready to eat.

Plates were filled, but then Drew lifted his glass. "Adele, I know Dan was supposed to keep it a secret, but I'm over the moon about your happy news." He turned his gaze on Harper, his dark eyes warm. "And you, Harper. What an incredible gift you're giving my brother and sister-in-law. To your happy family," he finished, and they all clinked glasses before drinking.

Harper looked up at him over the rim of her glass. He was watching her steadily, and those pesky nerves started again.

She was pregnant, for God's sake. One of the reasons she'd been so willing to do this now was because she wasn't involved with anyone. And it wasn't like she was thinking about starting something with Drew. He was the baby's uncle, after all. It was just that every time he looked at her she got this silly feeling all over. All she could think of was the cheeky look on his face when he'd said, *"I don't bite. Unless you want me to."*

She looked away and instead cut into her falafel.

Dinner conversation moved on to small talk about work and the summer weather, and the mood was easy and relaxed. Harper had been hungry, and the rice and falafel took away the gnawing sensation that had been bordering on queasy. When Adele asked if anyone wanted tea, the men refused but Harper was more than ready for a cup. "I'll get it, Adele. I know where everything is."

She rose from her seat and tried to ignore Drew's gaze following her as she went to the kitchen. For heaven's sake, she didn't look any different. But his perception of her had changed. That much was clear.

The kettle was on heating and she was reaching for a couple of mugs when Adele came through the sliding doors. "The boys are talking shop," she remarked, selecting a tea flavor from the selection she kept in a box on the counter. "For all Drew's outdoorsman ways, he's a good businessman. When they started talking US versus Canadian tax law implications, I had to bail."

Harper laughed lightly. "It was nice, what he said earlier." She grabbed a mint pouch from the tea box and dropped it into her cup.

"Yeah. It's funny, though. He can't take his eyes off you."

And there went that zingy feeling through her body again. She ignored it and shrugged. "It must seem really strange." She smiled at Adele. "What we're doing is pretty unconventional."

"Are you sure that's all it is? I've known Drew awhile. I mean, we had that break where we didn't see each other at all, but when Dan and I were dating before, I got to know him pretty well. I'd say it's more interested than curious."

"I doubt it. Besides, guys don't find women who are pregnant with someone else's baby all that attractive, you know?"

"Maybe. Still. Did something happen between you two at the wedding or something?"

Harper shook her head and reached for the kettle. She poured water into the cups as she answered, the task allowing her to avoid meeting Adele's gaze. "No. I mean, we danced and stuff, but just your typical best man and maid of honour duties."

Which was an out-and-out lie.

"Well, he seems very happy with what you're doing." Adele reached over and touched Harper's hand. "As we are. We'll never be able to repay you."

Harper smiled and turned her hand over, squeezing Adele's fingers. "So you've mentioned a time or two."

"Sorry. I know I probably go on a lot."

"It's okay." Harper withdrew her hand and dipped her tea bag up and down. "I know you're excited, and I want you to be a part of this pregnancy, every step of the way. It's all good."

Except Adele had a tendency to hover a bit, and Harper wasn't sure how to deal with that. With understanding, surely. She'd rather bite off her own tongue than hurt Adele's feelings. Adele was the sister she'd never had.

They took their tea back out to the deck. The sun had dipped behind the mountains, the air cooling. Once Harper and Adele returned to the table, the discussion morphed into things to do around town, and some of their favorite outdoor activities and spots.

"Of course, Harper has to be extra careful now," Dan said, aiming a smile in her direction. "Precious cargo and everything."

Harper shrugged. "I do, but the exercise is still important. I still love going out in the mornings and getting some sunrise pictures. I can do some cool things with the lighting."

"Surely you don't go alone, though," Adele offered, sipping her tea. "I mean, anything could happen. The wildlife alone..."

Drew stepped in. "I'm sure Harper takes proper precautions. She's not naive, after all. She's been doing this a long time."

She appreciated the support and it annoyed her at the same time, as if he felt he had to speak for her when she could obviously speak for herself. Still, she didn't want to upset Adele and Dan. "I am careful," she replied. "And there's no reason why I can't maintain my regular schedule for months. I do intend to work right up until the date."

"Even wedding bookings?" Dan asked.

She shook her head. "No. I'll book until I hit eight months. I don't want to disappoint any brides. And once the baby is born, I'll take a few weeks off to recover and then get back to it."

Once the baby was born. It was a weird thing to think about. In reality, she was just the incubator. But there was no way she would come through this without having some emotions about it. She was going to feel the baby kick. Bring it into the world. She figured getting back to a regular schedule would be important.

"Still," Adele said quietly. "You won't take any unnecessary risks."

"Of course not." She knew the stakes. She'd willingly accepted them when she'd offered to do this. "I'll be careful, you know that."

The mood had dipped a little, so Harper drank the last of her tea and stood. "And now, I've totally overstayed my welcome. I should get home. Thanks for having me over for dinner...again."

"How are you getting home?" Drew asked.

"Oh, walking. It's not far." She laughed. "Nothing's really far in Banff, you know?"

"I'm going back to the hotel. I'll walk with you, if it's okay."

"Sure, if that's what you want." Harper's place wasn't exactly on the way to the Cascade, but it was only a small detour. She couldn't really say no, not after the nice toast he'd given. But she wondered why he'd want to. She didn't think it was to be gentlemanly. Drew might look all casual and laid-back, but Harper got the impression that everything he did had a purpose behind it.

Dan got up, too, and started gathering glasses. "Didn't you rent a car, Drew? You usually do."

"I did, but it's being delivered to the hotel tomorrow. The one I wanted wasn't available until today. Besides, it doesn't hurt me to walk." He looked over at Harper and smiled. "Not when the scenery is so beautiful."

Harper wasn't sure if he meant the town or if he was turning on the charm like he had at the wedding, so she ignored the comment and made her way to the door.

The night had cooled enough that Harper wished she'd thought to bring a sweatshirt, though her intention had never been to stay this late. Trouble was, Adele was a wonderful cook and Harper got tired of eating alone all the time. Now that she was pregnant, Dan and Adele tended to stay a bit close, but she understood. Adele was understandably living vicariously through Harper's experience.

She hadn't counted on Drew being around, though, or offering to walk her home. She put her hand on her tummy for a brief moment, wondering what he really thought about the situation. It might be a good litmus test to find out how the rest of his family would react when they found out.

She tucked her hands into her hoodie pockets and looked over at him. "So I guess you were pretty surprised by the news, huh?"

He nodded. "Yeah. I mean, I felt something was off, the way you and Adele seemed to talk in abbreviated sentences. So I came right out and asked Dan." He stopped walking and turned to face her. "This is a huge thing. I can't believe they asked it of you."

She smiled then. Was that his issue? In that case, she could set his mind at rest. "They didn't ask. I offered. Actually, I offered on the night of their wedding, not long before you and I danced. Adele is the best friend I've ever had. When I found out that she'd left Dan all those years ago because of her infertility, I knew I wanted to help. I told them that this would be my wedding present to them."

Harper herself was what her mom called a "miracle baby," having been adopted since her mom couldn't have children. Being able to help a family—particularly someone she loved—was fulfilling.

"Carrying a baby is a heck of a wedding gift," he remarked.

She started walking again and shrugged. "It's only for a few months out of my life, so why not?"

She saw him shaking his head out of the corner of her eye. "Not many people in this world are completely altruistic. But I can't seem to come up with a way that this benefits you. I mean, it can't be the money."

"No, you're right. It can't. Legally they're not allowed to pay me and since there's no fee for health coverage… I'm not making a penny off of this, Drew. I hope you didn't think I was."

His brow furrowed. "It crossed my mind for a minute or two."

"Then clearly you don't know me very well."

"I apologize," he said quietly. Then he looked over at her as their shoes made soft footfalls on the sidewalk. "I still find it hard to believe you'd go through something as life-changing as a pregnancy out of the goodness of your heart."

She laughed. "Life-changing as in the morning sickness, weight gain, swollen feet, stretch marks, and other things I have to look forward to?"

Drew's voice was soft and hesitant in the semidarkness. "Well, wouldn't you want to go through those things for your own kid, rather than someone else's?"

"Maybe. Someday." She couldn't keep the wistful note out of her voice but hoped he didn't hear it. *Someday* certainly wasn't today and she wasn't sure it would ever be the right time. She tended to go on first dates, but not so many second or third ones, and she'd never had a real long-term relationship—not that she'd ever admitted that to anyone. She was twenty-eight years old, had had exactly two sexual partners, and wasn't confident that she'd ever have that life-partner-and-kid thing.

She had thought it—once. The attraction had been instant and had swept her off her feet. It had been a magical month of bliss on Caicos, an utter whirlwind that carried her away. Jared had pulled out a ring as they walked the beach beneath the stars, and she'd accepted, a 100 percent buy-in to the fairy tale. A week later he was gone, with nothing but a note explaining he'd gotten caught up in the moment and it had been "fun."

She'd been falling in love and he'd been enjoying falling into bed until he got bored—or scared. Didn't matter which. The end result was the same.

After that horrible pseudo-relationship, she'd vowed never to let herself get so carried away again.

She was far better off focusing on her business. So much so that she was considering using Juny as more than an assistant in order to train her up to take over a lot of the wedding and other photo shoot duties. The girl had a keen eye for balance and showed promise in creativity and innovation.

So she didn't say it out loud but knew deep down that this wasn't altruistic. In her heart she felt it might be her only chance to experience a pregnancy, and then when the baby was with Adele and Dan, she could be Fun Aunt Harper who got to run around in the mountains taking pictures of marmots and bears and elk and all kinds of things.

"You do want kids, then."

His voice interrupted her thoughts and she realized they'd kept walking and were only a block and a half from her house. "Oh. Well, I suppose. If the right guy and the right time were to come around." Standard response.

"How about you?" she asked, wanting to divert the attention away from herself. "Do you want kids down the road?"

He shook his head. "Uh-uh. I don't like being tied down, you know? I've got the business and that's enough. And I can pick up and travel when I want. It's not that I don't like kids. I just like my lifestyle better."

She got that. And she also understood what it meant to move kids from place to place all the time. Her dad had been in the air force and they'd moved frequently when she was little. More than anything she'd wanted to stay in one place and have the same school friends for more than two years in a row.

She rather respected Drew for owning his choice and not apologizing for it. They didn't feel the same way about children, but then, they didn't have to.

"Besides, I have nieces and nephews and apparently another on the way. My parents aren't hurting for grandkids."

Hers were. Though they never said a thing about it. She was an only child. Yet they refrained from any pressure to get married or start reproducing. Instead their conversations revolved around her studio and photography. She really appreciated that.

She paused and pointed at the little bungalow on a corner lot. “This is me.”

“Cute place.”

She laughed a little. “It’s tiny and I can hardly turn around in my bathroom, but it’s mine. I’d rather have a small spot to live and better space for my studio, so…”

“Cool.” They stopped by the walkway leading to her front door and the silence grew slightly awkward.

“I should get in. Thanks for walking me home.”

“No problem. I did have a question, though.”

“Oh?” She turned to look at him, his dark eyes nearly black in the twilight. One thing hadn’t changed about Drew. He was still delicious. There was no sense denying it. But she wouldn’t have to worry about any more propositions. Not while she was pregnant. What kind of guy wanted to date a woman pregnant with another man’s child?

“The next time you go out on a hike, can I come with you? I’m guessing you know some good spots off the beaten track that I don’t.”

She frowned a little. “You realize that when I hike, I go to a spot and then sometimes spend a crazy amount of time waiting, right? For the right light, or to get the right shot. It’s not really a heavy-duty workout. You might be bored.”

“That’s okay.”

“I’m off on Thursday morning and thinking of going to Stewart Canyon early, before the tourists go crazy. It’s not off the beaten track, so to speak, but it’s a nice walk with some good photo opportunities. Have you done the Bankhead trails on other visits? Bear in mind these are easy, popular trails. But they’re interesting.”

“I’m up for whatever. Just name the time.”

“Then I can pick you up at the hotel at six.”

"Perfect."

He gave a wave and started back the way they'd come, whistling lightly. No long look, no hand touch, nothing to suggest this was anything more than platonic and based on mutual interests.

So why was she feeling as if she'd gotten herself into a whole lot of trouble?

CHAPTER FOUR

THE DAY DAWNED CLEAR, but the sun wasn't quite up past the mountains when Drew stepped outside at five minutes to six. He was used to being up this early, either to work or get outdoors. There was a reason why he'd chosen to keep a condo just north of Sacramento. He loved the climate and the abundance of opportunities for outdoor activities in the Northern Californian forests and parks. Hitting the trail for a few hours before starting his workday was a common occurrence.

But he often hiked alone. Today he'd be with Harper, and she'd cautioned him that it wouldn't be high on the physical exertion scale. That was okay. He could do that on his own time. Instead, he was interested in watching her in action—taking pictures, that is. Pretty as she was, he wasn't interested in her romantically. How could he be, when she was carrying his brother's child? He liked her. Had, ever since the wedding. She challenged him somehow, even while being sweet as pie and as unassuming as a daisy nodding in a summer breeze.

He bent to retie his boot and gave a chuckle as he remembered her informing him that she wasn't a challenge or a trophy. That had been the moment, he realized. The moment he'd started to really admire her. The fact that she was also willing to put her life on hold for nine months to give Dan and Adele a baby only raised her in his estimation.

Though he expected if he asked her, she'd deny that she'd put her life on hold at all.

She pulled up in a tidy little SUV crossover, an all-wheel drive that would be handy in bad weather and rugged enough it would tolerate slight off-road situations. He opened the passenger door and slid inside. "Nice wheels."

She was looking a little paler than the last time he'd seen her, her freckles standing out on her nose and her cinnamon hair pulled back in a ponytail. "Thanks. I bought a lease-back so I could get something I could carry equipment in and that would handle some bumps and dirt roads." He'd barely buckled his seat belt when she started down the hill from the hotel.

"It's nice. A little more cozy than my pickup."

"You drive a truck?"

He chuckled. "Yeah. I spend a lot of time in the outdoors, and needed something rugged. Plus, you know, I needed enough room to pack some of that gear that I'm selling."

She made a turn and headed past a sign that said Minnewanka Loop. "Well, I'll say this for you. You believe in your product."

He laughed. "I like to think of it as walking the walk." He looked at her again and frowned. "Are you okay? You look a little pale. We didn't have to go this early, you know."

She kept her eyes on the road. "It's only a little bit of morning sickness. I'll be fine by ten or so."

"That's four hours away." And what exactly did a "little" morning sickness mean?

"Yep." She exited off the highway and started up the left side of the loop. "I'll eat some crackers, drink some water. It will probably only last another few weeks. At least that's what the doctor and all the books say."

He shifted in his seat. He'd missed out on the "peculiarities of pregnancy" conversations with his sisters, since he'd moved away from Ontario. He had no idea how long morning sickness lasted or anything else to do with having babies besides what he'd seen on TV, and that was terrifying enough.

"We could have waited to go later."

She looked over at him briefly. "Oh, no we couldn't." She laughed a little. "In two or three hours the tourists will be out in full force, and I like playing with the early morning light. The nausea is an inconvenience more than anything, and I work through it."

He was glad, too. He wanted to spend the majority of his time today looking around town. In particular, the property that had recently been listed. He'd contacted a real estate agent and was anxious to get a look inside.

He enjoyed the scenery for a few moments, but it wasn't long until she pulled into a nearly empty parking lot. "It's a bit of a walk from here to the trailhead, but it's all easy. Another day I'll take you to my favorite alpine meadow, if you like." She smiled as she took the keys out of the ignition and hopped out of the car.

She was still pale, but it wasn't any of his concern if she thought she was good to go. She knew her body far better than he did, and he'd learned long ago not to presume anything when it came to women's strength and capabilities.

He'd worn jeans and a light windbreaker over his T-shirt. Last night he'd had a quick look at the trail thanks to a Google search and knew he'd be fine without his customary pack of water and snacks. It was less than five kilometers total, and since Harper hadn't mentioned going farther onto the other joined trails, he'd kept it to just the jacket, which he could fold and zip up if he got too warm.

Then he turned the corner by her back bumper and his jaw dropped.

"What the heck is that?"

She grinned up at him, a camera slung around her neck and with a huge zoom lens on it. It had to stick out eight inches, probably more like twelve, and looked heavy as hell. "It's my camera. Wow. We really will be starting at the beginning."

"Ha, ha." He grinned and shook his head. "Seriously, how do you not have neck and back issues carrying that thing around?"

"I would if I did it all the time. And Banff isn't exactly hurting for spa services. I do get a massage now and again." She pulled another black padded bag out of the back and prepared to shift it onto her shoulders.

"No way. I'll carry that."

She lifted an eyebrow. "I carry my own equipment all the time."

"Sure, but seriously, I have nothing and you have a huge camera around your neck."

"Maybe I use it for counterbalance."

He snorted, then grinned. "Maybe you like making it difficult for me."

When she smiled back, his heart lifted. "I consider that a side benefit."

But she handed over the pack, with instructions to be careful because there was equipment in there. As well as her water and cracker stash.

The world was still and quiet as they made their way out of the parking lot and down a trail leading to the Stewart Canyon trailhead. There was nothing Drew liked better than crisp, fresh air and the smell of everything green and alive. It was far preferable to days in his office or shut up in a boardroom. Birds chirped in the trees; jays, chickadees and awkward-looking magpies with their long tails and raucous call. Occasionally Harper stopped, looked above and around her and lifted her camera to take a quick few shots. Warm-ups, she called them, but he doubted she did anything like a warm-up. Those photos were considered and shot with purpose.

They met another couple coming out of the trail, and

they greeted them with a quiet hello. "There've been some bear sightings lately," the man advised. "Trail's not closed, but be on the lookout."

"Thanks," Drew replied, and frowned. He hadn't thought of it before, but Harper went into the mountains alone all the time. There were bears and mountain lions to consider.

"I can see the look on your face," she said, laughing a little. "If you're afraid, there's a can of bear spray in the bag."

He stopped, and there was a look of surprise on her face as he took the pack off his back, opened it and rooted around for the spray. He hooked it onto his belt loop and zipped up the pack again. "Not afraid. Smart. The last thing I want to do is turn a corner and find an ornery mama bear staring me in the face."

She lifted her camera. "It's one reason for the lens," she explained. "I don't have to get too close."

"Lead on, then," he said, but kept the bear spray on his hip. Chances were they wouldn't see anything, but he'd rather be prepared.

It didn't seem to take any time at all before they were at the bridge, a short expanse with the Cascade River beneath. The river ran downstream into Lake Minnewanka, and Harper stopped at the other end of the bridge and started setting up shots. He stayed back and watched, enjoying the concentration on her face, the way she adjusted a setting and tried again, or moved her position slightly. Her colour had returned, giving her cheeks more of a rosy glow, and he thought again how stunning she was. All lean legs and strong shoulders, creamy freckled skin and beautiful eyes that didn't require any makeup to make them brighter.

She stood, stretched her back a bit and sent him a grin so big he was dazzled by it.

She lifted the camera. "Oh, no," he began, lifting a hand, but she balanced the camera on her hand and put a finger to her lips, then looked over his shoulder. He half turned and nearly jumped when he realized a bighorn sheep was on the rock above and behind him, horns curled, face impassive.

When he turned back to face Harper, she was already snapping wildly, her face split with a smile that was pure fun.

He turned around and looked up at the sheep. "Good morning," he said. "Sorry to disturb." Then he backed away and crossed the bridge to join Harper. Maybe she wanted some pics of the sheep without him in them.

He waited quietly, and then the sheep moved on and Harper lowered the camera. "Sorry," she finally said. "I couldn't resist. All of a sudden there he was, standing right behind you, and you had no idea."

"He might have hurt me with those horns," Drew said, teasing.

"More like he wanted the crackers in the bag. Tourists aren't supposed to feed them, but they do. There are so many sheep that they wander through the parking lot all day long. People love it."

"Well, I'm glad I could entertain."

"Speaking of crackers, I could use a couple of mine."

He looked at her and his face blanked with alarm. Her pink colour was now pale and slightly greenish. He rushed to take off the pack but it was too late. She swung the camera around to her back, rushed to the bushes beside the path, and gagged.

Drew wasn't grossed out, but he did feel sympathy. He took out the crackers and a bottle of water and, when she was done, uncapped the bottle and offered her a drink. "Here. You can swish that around and then drink some."

She took the bottle and swished and spit, then held out her hand for a cracker. "Could I have four, please? Now that I've got the dry heave out of the way, I can eat something."

"And so begins my education into pregnancy," he said calmly, handing over several saltines. She bit into one and attempted to smile, but she looked embarrassed. "Don't worry about it," he assured her. "I've seen much worse from dehydration or heat stroke. Do you need to go back or do you want to keep on?"

She ate all four crackers and straightened. "We can go on. It's not that far anyway, and I want to get some pictures of the lake and beach. If we wait, the lake will fill up. It's the only lake in the park that permits motorboats."

"I'm game if you are."

They carried on through the woods, heading toward the lake. Drew admired her stubbornness, particularly since she'd barely eaten anything this morning. He'd at least had a shake and a protein bar before he left the hotel, and he was still hungry. What surprised him even more was when they reached a spot she liked, with a view of the shore, and she stopped and sat down on a large rock.

"Now we wait," she said. "Find a seat."

"Wait? For what?"

She grinned. "For whatever comes our way. Wildlife, a cloud that gives some fun shadows, eagles over the lake… I wait for opportunity, and when it comes, I try not to waste it."

He perched on a nearby stump and watched her adjust her camera settings. Her last words…he understood those. At least the part about not wasting opportunities. He didn't wait for them, though. He went after them. He wouldn't be here otherwise.

But he could be patient. For a while. So they sat in the quiet and waited.

Harper got up a few times and shifted position, snapping pics of the lake. A whisky jack squawked nearby, and she found it and adjusted her lens, stealthily moving and getting the bird from a few different angles before it flew away. She leaned against a tree for a moment, and he saw her brow wrinkle before it cleared. She lifted her camera and focused on the shore of the lake.

He couldn't see what she was taking pictures of, so he got up and moved as quietly as possible to within a few feet of her. What he saw made him catch his breath.

A solitary grizzly was at the water's edge, lumbering along the shoreline. He could see the varied shades of brown in its coat, feet damp from the water, the signature hump on its back, just behind the neck. "Wow," he said, and heard rapid shutter clicking as the bear obligingly turned its head to look over its shoulder and right at them…even though they were well over a hundred meters away, looking down.

She kept shooting as long as the bear was in view, but once it disappeared into the tall grass and trees again, she lowered the camera.

Her eyes shone at him, hitting him square in the gut. So blue, a luminescent shade that reminded him of the aquamarine earrings his mother wore. Her excited energy filled the air around him, making him far more aware of her than he was comfortable with.

"Did you see that? He turned around and looked right at the camera. I got some amazing shots! I can't wait to get back and look at them."

"It was incredible. You're incredible."

The words were out before he could think better of them. Her cheeks flared as she blushed and her lips dropped open a little. He found himself staring at them, wondering how they'd taste. Thankfully, the moment passed and he distracted himself by slipping the pack off his back and reaching for the water bottle. "You should have a drink before we head back. I'm assuming that we're not going farther, considering that there are bears in the area."

With perfect timing, they heard an approaching group

courtesy of the "bear bells" they carried, the tinkling echoing thinly through the trees.

"Thanks," she said, taking the bottle from his hand. She kept her eyes from meeting his as she took the bottle, but she took a healthy drink and recapped it. "There's another bottle in there if you want some."

"I'm fine." He was still unsettled by the moment they'd shared. Sure, he'd been attracted to her at the wedding. But now…she was off-limits. Besides, Harper was the most dangerous kind of woman—one who could sneak past his defenses. She was extraordinary in a most understated, natural way, and if he wasn't careful he'd end up taking a wrong step.

They were quieter on the walk back, a new tension between them that hadn't been there before. Perhaps this hadn't been the greatest idea, even if he had enjoyed the few hours and watching her in action.

Tourists clogged the trail now, too, chatting and snapping pictures while posing in front of trees or the bridge, with the view up the canyon. The sheep from earlier was nowhere to be found, but they discovered several more on their way back to the parking lot, just as Harper had warned. As fun as it all seemed, Drew was glad that they'd gone as early as they had and avoided all the crowds.

She laughed as they neared her car, and he guessed it was because of the look on his face. "You were right," he said, giving a small smile. "This place gets crazy, doesn't it?"

She nodded as she took the camera from around her neck and popped the tailgate. "This place and Johnston Canyon are really popular, but at least here the trail's a little wider. I really was planning a shorter outing today because I have a bunch of editing to do the rest of the day. But later, maybe early next week, I'm going to head up to

Healy Pass and make a whole day of it. It's about sixteen kilometers or so round-trip."

But she didn't invite him along, and he didn't ask. First of all, he probably wouldn't be here next week. And second, it wouldn't do to spend too much time with her. Before he knew it he'd lose his perspective and start something he had no right to start. It was better if they went their separate ways.

He got in the car and put on his seat belt. Instead of going back the way they came, Harper drove around the other side of the "loop," coming out by the pond and picnic area where a few cars of tourists stopped and took pictures of the elk wandering nearby.

"It wouldn't be Banff without elk being everywhere," Harper said, smiling a bit. "You never know where they're going to pop up, either in town or in the fields or roadsides."

"It's like they're part of the scenery," Drew said. "Tell me, do you like tourist season? The town seems awfully crowded."

"It's a resort town, so that's what's expected. But you know, there are places around town that aren't part of the bus tour stops and day trips. There are a few places that are more popular with townies than tourists. And honestly, I mingle with some of the other business owners near the studio. I have my assistant, Juny, who's young and energetic and fun. I have Adele, and now Dan. So no, I don't mind tourist season. It's what keeps me in business, and the studio and shop do better business in the summer." She turned back onto the highway and looked over at him. "Pictures like today? This canyon is a recognizable landmark. If any are worth blowing up, I'll showcase them and sell them to tourists who want to take home a little reminder of where they were."

"And the other shots?"

She grinned. "If any of those bear shots are worthy, I'll mat and frame a couple."

"Like your mama and cubs."

"Which still hasn't sold, but it's good enough I'm not going to give it away."

Good, he thought. As a businessman, he often saw people charging too little for their goods rather than commanding a price that was proportionate with the quality.

She dropped him back off at the Cascade, pulling up beneath the overhang at the lobby doors. "What's on the agenda for the rest of your day?" she asked.

"Heading into town to look into a few businesses." He deliberately kept his wording vague. Other than Dan, no one knew he was looking at a major acquisition, and that was how he wanted it. "I'm going to spend a few days doing that, actually. Maybe there won't be room for another outfitter here, you know?"

"And then?"

He shrugged, his hand on the door handle. "I don't know. There are lots of places in British Columbia I can consider. And northern Alberta…lots of good fishing up there."

He couldn't read her expression, but she didn't look overly impressed. "What's wrong?"

"Is it all about moving around for you?"

"Why not? I'm young and have all kinds of energy for this sort of thing. I love traveling and moving around. And man, the challenge in setting up a new store is really exciting."

"But what about when that stops? When is it enough, and what will you do then?"

It was an odd question, he thought. And it seemed there was something more behind it than plain curiosity.

The words to tell her how successful he was were on the tip of his tongue, but he held back. If he were honest with himself, he felt more like his pre-millionaire self when he was with her. No expectations or trappings of success. An easy hike in the mountains. Jeans and T-shirts and a little dust on his boots. Hell, he hadn't looked at his cell phone since last night, and that was nearly unheard of.

So he kept the words back and shrugged.

"I haven't thought that far ahead. I like my life. I like the challenge and the variety and the ability to move around. I don't see that stopping anytime soon."

"I see."

"You don't sound convinced."

They were idling in the passenger drop-off, but it wasn't overly busy at the moment so he waited for her answer, removing his hand from the door handle and placing it back into his lap. The last thing Drew ever wanted was to feel trapped in one spot. Drew loved his parents, and they'd provided a good, loving home for their children. But sacrifices had been made and resentments had taken root because of it. His dad in particular had sacrificed his dream job for his family, and seeing the defeated look in his father's eyes had stuck with Drew all these years.

Harper sighed. "It's a personal thing for me is all. Travel is one thing, and I get that. Who doesn't love a vacation, going new places and seeing new things? But moving around all the time, that rootless kind of existence? I did that for most of my young life, and it was hard. Really hard. I like having some stability now, is all. But that's my life, not yours." She smiled encouragingly. "Of course you should live yours how you want."

"As should you," he replied. "I guess we're not much alike, are we?"

Her gaze touched his, and that spark sizzled between them again. "No, I guess we're kind of opposite in a lot of ways."

"Except we like the outdoors."

"Except that."

"And the fact that we both love Adele and Dan a lot."

Her eyes warmed. "That, too."

And with that he knew he had to leave. Harper had complication written all over her and as much as he was enjoying this…interlude, he knew it wouldn't last. "I'd better let you get out of here before the next tour bus lands. Thanks for taking me with you, Harper."

"You're welcome."

He got out and shut the door, then lifted a hand as she drove away.

He couldn't let himself think about her or why she'd been bounced from place to place, or how her eyes darkened to nearly sapphire when awareness flickered between them.

He was here for three or four days, tops. Surely he could avoid her for that long, couldn't he?

CHAPTER FIVE

HARPER SAT AT the computer and went over the photos from the morning. There were two that she particularly liked: one of the whisky jack sitting on a spruce branch, and one of the shots of the grizzly looking right at the camera. That had been a lucky, lucky thing and would take only a little editing to make it sing.

Then there were the ones of Drew and the bighorn sheep. She paused over those, unable to suppress a smile as she looked at the one where he'd turned and spoken to the animal, their eyes locked on each other. Then there was another where he was laughing about something and it made her heart give a strange thump. It was unfair he had to be so damned handsome and charming.

He'd been a good sport, too; patient and quiet when he needed to be. And he'd minimized her embarrassment when the nausea had gotten the best of her and she'd been sick.

He was a good guy; she knew that. But that was where it ended. It wasn't just the awkwardness of the situation. It was his whole lifestyle, traveling for work and opening new stores and not being rooted in one place. Nowhere was really...home. That kind of nomadic existence simply wasn't for her.

Home was the one thing she'd always wanted. Not that hers hadn't been full of love; it had. She couldn't have asked for better parents. But the nature of her dad's job had been one of moving from base to base, or being alone with her mom while he was deployed. It had been hard to put down roots, and instead of roots Drew had wandering feet.

Good to look at. Even talk to. Not boyfriend material. In March she hadn't been looking for a fling. She rested her hand on her still-flat stomach. She certainly wasn't looking for one now, either.

Juny came into the back room to grab her water bottle and did a double take at Drew's picture on the screen. "Oh my gosh. Who is that?"

"Dan's brother, Drew. Remember? From the wedding?" Juny had helped her go through the photos, and together they'd chosen the best ones for a portfolio for Dan and Adele.

"Sure, but he was all done up in a tux then, and his hair was shorter. He's hot."

"I didn't think that hot guys were on your radar." She grinned up at Juny, waggling her eyebrows. Juny's girlfriend, Renée, had just moved in with her in an apartment in Canmore.

"Depends on the radar. I can appreciate a fine form, no matter the gender. And Drew Brimicombe is a fine form. I like his outdoorsy look."

"Me, too," Harper replied, then realized she shouldn't have said anything. Juny got a speculative look on her face and pulled up a chair. The bell over the door would ring if someone came into the storefront. There was no way Harper was going to be able to avoid Juny's prying.

"Spill," Juny commanded, and leaned forward, ready to get the goss.

"There's nothing to spill. Like you said, I can appreciate a fine form."

"Yeah, but he's on *your* radar."

"Not really." Harper made sure she flipped through another few pictures. "I mean, he flirts but I'm not really interested. I've got other things going on."

She hesitated after that last bit. Juny didn't know about the baby, but Harper would have to tell her soon. Maybe in a few weeks, when the first trimester was officially over. It felt odd, keeping something that special a secret from the employee she liked so very much.

"Things like what? Wedding season?"

"Sure. It's busy around here, or haven't you noticed?"

Just then the bell rang, announcing a new arrival. "Saved by the bell," Juny advised drily, arching an eyebrow.

"Yeah, yeah," Harper replied, but she laughed a little.

The next few days were busy ones, and Harper spoke only once to Adele and not at all to Drew, not that she'd expected to. She'd had a wedding rehearsal and then wedding day, and on Sunday she'd been exhausted. Monday she had a doctor's appointment in Calgary.

Adele went with her and Dan met them at the office. At a little over eleven weeks pregnant, she was close to being past the first trimester, and she knew everyone would feel some relief. When the doctor put the Doppler against her tummy and moved it around, she flinched a little. Dan and Adele looked so excited and expectant. If something happened and they couldn't find a heartbeat today, they'd be so disappointed.

But it came through loud and clear. *Bu-bump bu-bump* galloped in her ears, much faster than a grown-up heartbeat. Adele started to cry. Dan held her hand. And Harper stared at the doctor, marveling that a little human was growing inside her.

For someone else.

It was right and she was glad of it, but something strange and new blossomed in her chest. Maybe this baby didn't have any of her DNA, but he or she was still a part of her even if she wasn't a part of them. She bit down on her lip and kept listening to the rhythmic sound of that tiny beating heart. She didn't want it to stop.

Dan took out his phone and hit the record button.

"Today we get to hear our baby's heartbeat!" Excitement rang through his voice as he angled the camera at Adele's beaming face and then over at Harper, who felt a little self-conscious with her belly exposed.

But she smiled anyway, unable to resist the joy in the room. The tears on her best friend's cheeks told her what she needed to know. This had absolutely been the right decision.

The doctor took away the wand and Harper suddenly felt bereft. She loved the sound of that heartbeat, a quicker version of her own. It touched her in ways she had expected and yet couldn't possibly anticipate. Everything was suddenly so *real*.

In six months, she would birth this little human and put him or her in Adele's arms.

Was it wrong that she felt the need to hold them close until then? That she should feel so…attached?

"Harper, are you all right?"

"What? Oh, of course!" She put on a bright smile. "I'm so relieved everything is going well, you know?"

The doctor nodded. "It is. Everything is right on schedule. Are you still feeling sick?"

Harper nodded. "Yes, in the mornings. But it's nothing I can't handle. By midmorning I seem to come around okay."

"Okay, but if this goes on for many more weeks, come back in. We can look at some medication. Mostly we need to make sure you and the baby are getting good nutrition."

"I will," she promised. "And I'm eating well, I promise. I've been following a vegetarian prenatal diet quite closely."

The doctor looked at all of them. "Well, you're good for another month. You can make your next appointment at reception if you like. You'll get booked for an ultrasound at that appointment, as well. Have you thought about having an amnio?"

Adele looked at Harper, then at Dan. "I know using my

eggs was possibly a bit risky, but I'm not sure I want to take the chance on anything going wrong. I know there are risks with the amnio, too, and I…" She reached over and took Harper's hand. "I think this whole thing is a miracle and we'll take the end result, even if that means special challenges."

Dan put his hand on her shoulder in silent support.

"Well, there's no need at the moment, and from all indications everyone seems to be doing fine. We'll chat again at the next appointment, unless something comes up between now and then."

The doctor paused to give Harper's shoulder a squeeze and then left the room.

"That was pretty amazing," Dan said, tucking his phone in his pocket.

"I know. But guys…" Harper looked up with a wry smile. "I really want to get this goop off my stomach."

Everyone laughed, and then Dan and Adele left the room to let Harper put herself back in order.

She wiped the gel off with a tissue, but before she pulled up her yoga pants again, she put her palm against her stomach. "I heard you today, little one," she whispered. "We're in this together, you hear? So you stay healthy in there. We're almost a third of the way there."

And if the backs of her eyes stung a little, she'd blink it away and be thankful. She needed to embrace this experience and not hide from it, even though she suspected that when it was all over her heart was going to be a little bit tender.

On Tuesday, Drew showed up at her studio.

"You're still here," she said, her voice friendly as she greeted him in the showroom. "I wondered if you'd headed back to parts unknown."

"Not yet. Actually, I think I've found a location. I spent

most of the day yesterday on conference calls with my executive team. I'm meeting the property owner at three today to see if we can hammer out a deal."

"That was fast." She blinked and stared at him. He'd been here only a week.

"When I see something I want, I don't waste time."

She pondered that. Drew definitely didn't seem like a patient kind of guy. Not necessarily reckless, exactly. But he definitely wasn't the kind of man to sit and wait around for opportunities to come to him. Which was kind of funny, because a lot of her day-to-day existence consisted of just that. Sitting around. She'd learned patience that way, and trust. "Sometimes I think the best plans happen when you're willing to sit in the quiet and wait for them. Like the grizzly the other day."

"Ah, but you still went after it." He put his hands in the pockets of his khaki shorts. "You made a plan and put yourself in the right spot at the right time. That's preparation meeting opportunity."

She laughed. "I know theoretically you're right. I think there's a slight philosophical difference in our thinking. Anyway, that's great, as long as you're happy about it."

He seemed happy. His eyes were lit up and he had an air of confidence and satisfaction that was…well, charismatic. She'd never denied that he was attractive or that she was attracted to him. It was more about choosing not to pursue something that would be short term and not, well, meaningful. No matter how…

Her gaze fell on his lips, slightly parted, an imperfect bow shape that looked utterly kissable.

No matter how sexy he was…or how amazing it might be to be his, even for a moment.

She looked away. Ugh, she had to stop thinking like this! It had to be the hormone surge or something. She was normally far more levelheaded and less obvious. After Jared's abrupt departure from her life, she'd vowed to make sure never to let herself fall until she was sure it was exactly what she wanted. And Drew wasn't it…no matter how alluring he was.

"Did you want to see the pictures from the other day? A few turned out really great." She started to lead the way to the back room. Juny had run out for coffee, but there was no worry about leaving the storefront empty. Foot traffic was light today and the electronic bell would always ring if someone came in.

"I'd love to. Was the bear one good?"

"There were a couple from that sequence that I like a lot."

She stopped by her computer and sat; he leaned over her shoulder, close enough she could smell his spicy aftershave. She inhaled deeply, imprinting the scent on her brain. This really was going too far. Hadn't she decided that they were too different? Opposites might be exciting, but it could also cause a lot of friction.

And why was she continually trying to talk herself out of liking him?

"Wow. I love that one."

She'd pulled up the picture of the whisky jack first, letting the grey-and-white bird fill the screen. "He's pretty, isn't he?"

"Very. That's such a soft grey." He pulled up a chair and sat beside her, leaning over to peer at the monitor. "Know what other bird has a gorgeous grey colour? An albatross. Their heads are amazing. It seriously looks like a watercolour."

"I didn't think they were grey." She spun in her chair to face him, getting a jolt when she realized how close their faces were. There was a half second where he paused, the miniscule flash of time it took to take half a breath, and then he leaned back a bit, settling in his chair a bit more. Heat rushed up her neck.

"There are different species, with slightly different sizes and colourings," he said, moving back into the topic smoothly. "Look up a grey-headed albatross. I saw them on a New Zealand expedition to Macquarie Island."

Of course he had. She'd traveled some and had moved around within Canada a lot, but Drew was a different sort of traveler. He was an adventure seeker. Part of her was jealous that he'd had such trips, and totally envious of the photographic opportunities. Another part was simply curious.

"Did you see penguins?"

He laughed. "Tons. Like this ginormous rookery with thousands and thousands."

She sighed. "That must have been amazing."

"You haven't seen them?"

"Only at the zoo. And once at SeaWorld, when I was a little kid."

"Would you like to?"

She turned in her chair. "Is that an invitation?" At his surprised expression, she laughed. "Just kidding. But yeah, I'd like to. I'd like to photograph tons of different ecosystems. Right now, I'm here, so I'm focusing on my backyard. There's lots to keep me busy."

He sat back in his chair and tapped his lip. "But where would you go if you could go anywhere in the world?"

She thought about it a long time, struggling for an answer. "I've always wanted to go to Iceland. The geography is so unique and I have a secret wish to photograph an Icelandic horse." She met his gaze. "I suppose that sounds silly. But you see…no other horse is allowed on the island. They're incredibly unique and untouched."

But his warm eyes held hers. "Not at all. I wish I could take you on some armchair travel, but that's one place I haven't been, either. Though I've been to Norway."

Of course he had.

"Aspen Outfitters must be doing really well for you, if you can travel so much before you're even thirty."

"It does okay."

It was a rather bland answer, and she puzzled for a moment, but his financial status and how he spent his money wasn't any of her business.

"It keeps you in passport stamps," she said lightly.

He laughed a little. "It does. Last year I went zip-lining in Costa Rica."

Harper's eyes widened. "Zip-lining in the jungle? No thanks. I'm afraid of heights."

"Really?"

She nodded. "Really. I don't even like getting up past the second step on a stepladder."

His eyebrows lifted. "I wouldn't have guessed that. How do you manage skiing, or the gondolas? Surely you've done both, living here."

She smiled weakly, her stomach doing a little nervous flip just thinking about it. "I take deep breaths. I don't look down."

His eyes lit up. "You know, one woman in our group was terrified. She was literally crying on the platform. But she did it—took that step off, and she loved it. Couldn't wait to keep going."

Harper shuddered. "Good for her," she said drily, and then they both burst out laughing.

Now they were sitting there smiling at each other like idiots, and as the moment drew out, she wanted him to lean over and kiss her.

The doorbell sounded out front. "Excuse me for a moment," she said, scrambling to her feet. "I'll be right back."

It was Juny, who'd returned with a coffee for herself and an iced fruit-infusion tea for Harper. "I got them to add a splash of soda water for some fizz," Juny said as she handed over the cup.

Harper thanked her and told her to take the money out of petty cash and then took a deep breath, grateful for the interruption, before going back to Drew again.

"Sorry about that. It was Juny, bringing back some drinks." She took a sip of the cold tea—cranberry and pomegranate from the taste of it—and sighed. It was delicious and refreshing, just what she needed.

"No worries. But I would like to see the bear before I ask you for a favor."

A favor? Curiosity whetted, she resumed her seat and brought up the thumbnails, then picked one of her favorites.

"Oh, man," Drew said, drawing a breath. "He's huge. That's magnificent."

Her heart leaped a little at his praise. "I like the balance of it, and the grey tones of the rocks play with the water and the coolness of the green in the evergreens."

She hesitated. "There are other ones where I'd adjusted the exposure, but I don't like them as well. Even with this one, I considered changing the hues slightly, or playing with the contrast, but I actually like it as is. I just made a few minor tweaks."

He was quiet for a moment. "You're right. The eye's drawn to the bear itself. The rich brown really stands out."

She was pleased he understood. "Now, want to see something fun?"

She scrolled until she got a photo of the canyon, the narrow expanse of water with the forest on either side. She brought up her editing software and made a few clicks. The photo changed and Drew let out a quiet, "Oh, cool."

"Right? It's fun to play with." She'd basically turned her photo into a watercolour painting. "If I change the opacity and contrast a little, the definition of water against the sky is better." She dragged her cursor and watched the shades pop a little more.

"Do you do a lot of editing this way?" he asked.

She shook her head. "Not really. I play with it, mostly. Like…look at this." She opened up a picture of a wild rose. "This is an 'underpainting' feature. What do you think?"

"I think someone could easily go down a rabbit hole of playing with all sorts of photos and wake up a week later."

She giggled. "Pretty much."

"Know how those would look great?"

She frowned. "How?"

"If you took some of your favorites and did them up as greeting cards or postcards in the storefront. You could keep the gallery as is, but add a small section near the counter for cards or smaller photos, perhaps pre-matted."

He wasn't wrong. Except…

Except it felt like commercializing on something that she took very seriously. Reducing it to a short-term consumable that could easily be tossed aside, rather than appreciated and cherished.

But what Drew saw was a business opportunity.

"It's an interesting idea," she offered, feeling the need to toss him a crumb, although she didn't know why.

"I have them now and again. And now…for my favor. Could you come with me this afternoon? I'd like for you to see the building I'm considering. Tell me if there's something I'm missing."

"Why me?"

"Because you have a sharp eye and attention to detail. I went in and saw all the possibilities. But I'd like a second pair of eyes to go through it with me this time, and pick out where I'm going to have issues."

She chuckled. "I am so flattered that you want to use me as a fault-picker."

"No, no, no. Attention to detail, remember?" But he smiled, too. "What do you say?"

"You want to go now?"

"I can have the Realtor meet us there." He hesitated.

"As long as you're not too busy. I know you have your own business to run."

It would be an excuse to spend more time with him. She knew she shouldn't want to, and then wondered why the heck not. Lately her whole life had consisted of work, feeling tired and sometimes nauseated, and no social life beyond Adele and Dan, where again, the talk was always of the baby. As the days went on, she found herself getting more and more attached to the tiny life inside her. So much so that she knew she had to keep her mind on the big picture. Like other parts of her life, and what she was planning to do after the baby arrived and she went back to her normal routine.

None of which she felt she could discuss with anyone, because she had been the one to suggest the surrogacy and she didn't want to appear to be a complainer.

"I can spare an hour or so." Actually, the idea of leaving the studio and walking through town in the sunshine sounded blissful. "Where's the building?"

"Half a block off Banff Avenue, right near the Ptarmigan Inn. I looked at a few other spaces, but none had the square footage I need and the only other one that did wasn't as central."

"Sounds logical. Let me close this down and I'll be right with you."

He went back out to the storefront and she could hear him talking to Juny as she closed her programs and shut down her computer. Deep down she got the feeling she might be stepping into trouble, but she'd been doing the same things day after day for too long. This weekend she'd be at a wedding the whole time. Why not enjoy an afternoon off, particularly in the company of someone as sexy and funny as Drew?

CHAPTER SIX

DREW WAITED FOR Harper out front, and spent his time first contacting the Realtor, then chatting to Juny. She looked cute with leggings and boots and a colourful flowy top of some sort, a pair of dark brown braids touching each shoulder. But when Harper came out from the back room, his breath caught. She was wearing a simple denim skirt and a peasant blouse, little sandals on her feet, and her hair was in what he realized was a customary ponytail. He couldn't tell if she was wearing makeup or not. It didn't matter. Harper was just…different.

He shouldn't be here. She'd said as much when she'd dropped him off the other day. But he couldn't help it. A few quiet hours and the first thing he did was find himself walking toward her gallery, eager to see her teasing eyes and smiling face.

"I'm ready if you are," she stated, slinging a small bag over her shoulder.

"Should I close up?" Juny asked.

"I can come back. You don't have to stay until six."

"It's no trouble. I'm meeting some people at seven, so it works out fine."

"Then sure. Taking a few extra hours would be amazing. Thanks."

Drew held the door for her and they stepped out into the afternoon sunshine. "I parked a half block over, and we can take my ride if you want."

"You did get your rental."

"I did. It makes it easier if I have to run to showings or meetings. But we can walk if you want."

"It's a beautiful day. Let's."

The day was hot but with that crisp-mountain-air feeling. Sidewalks were swept and kept clear, with hanging baskets on the streetlamps and brightly coloured planters outside each business. He looked over at Harper, who'd slid on a pair of sunglasses against the glare. She looked good, but he missed being able to see her eyes.

"Does Juny know?" he asked.

She looked over at him. "You mean about the baby?"

"Yeah."

"Not yet. I have to tell her soon, though. Other than the doctor, you're the only one outside the three of us to know anything."

He felt oddly privileged, even though he knew it was just because he was in town. Plus it made him feel as if they shared a secret.

He heard an odd gurgle and saw her cheeks turn a bright pink. "Did you eat lunch?"

"Not yet, but I thought we had to meet your guy."

"We do. But ice cream." He pointed to the Cows Ice Cream store. "And you need your dairy, don't you? Calcium and all that?"

She laughed. "And fat, and sugar…but I love ice cream. It's one of my secret vices."

"You have more than one? I don't believe it."

Then she nudged him with her arm and he felt a warmth slide through him. He genuinely liked her so much.

"I have many. I keep them hidden."

He looked at her again, gave her an assessing up-and-down glance and shook his head. "Nope. Still don't believe you. You're too sweet."

She barked out an unladylike laugh and he couldn't help but grin from ear to ear. They were still smiling when they looked both ways and scooted across the street to the Cows Ice Cream shop.

It was summer. There was a line.

But he didn't mind. He watched as Harper scanned the flavor menu, her sunglasses now perched up on top of her head. It had been a long time since he'd enjoyed someone's company so much. She wasn't the type to expect expensive and intimate dinners and big romantic gestures. A cone of ice cream, or a walk in the forest… Harper was the kind of woman who appreciated little things.

Lately it seemed that anyone he tried to date within his business circle came with an expectation of… He frowned a little. Status? A certain standard? Whatever it was, it frequently left him feeling like they were interested in what he could provide rather than interested in *him*.

He wanted to think money hadn't changed him, that it had just made things easier. Like this trip. He could stay in a hotel for two weeks at summer rates and not worry about maxing out a credit card. It didn't mean he needed or expected five-star anything. Did he? Had he really changed over the years, as his success had grown?

He thought about his day-to-day life and realized he had lost touch with what it was like to be…well, *normal*, for lack of a better word. Sure, financially he'd found it rougher in those days, but his success came with a price, after all, as much as he downplayed it. And that could be summarized in one simple word: *responsibility*. He was responsible to his shareholders, responsible for the people who worked with and for him. As the man at the top, sometimes it was hard to know whom to trust.

His lifestyle was nice, but being with Harper reminded him of the guy he used to be and had lost a little along the way. Easygoing, laughing more, up for a cone of ice cream as a special occasion.

"I'll have a small Cowconut Cream Pie," Harper ordered, then looked back at Drew. "And what are you going to have?"

Her voice drew his attention back to the task at hand. He really didn't care, but he gave the flavors a cursory glance and replied, "Fluff 'n' Udder."

Harper giggled.

"These names are ridiculous," he said firmly, but his lips twitched. "And I like peanut butter, so hush."

They gathered their cones, Drew paid and they made their way back out into the sunshine again.

The ice cream was cold and rich and delicious, but it also melted fast so they put decorum aside and took substantial swipes with their tongues, catching it before it ran down the waffle cones. Once Harper looked over and snickered, then took her napkin and wiped a dot off his chin.

Their cones were almost gone when she took a bite of the waffle and it left her with a dollop of coconut ice cream on the spot where her upper and lower lip met.

He didn't think, didn't analyze, didn't weigh pros and cons. He simply stepped forward and kissed it off, his lips lingering on the corner of her mouth as she froze in surprise. Then she let out a soft, gentle sigh, and he closed his eyes and slid his mouth ever so slightly to the right, kissing her properly while she responded sweetly, with a hint of hesitation and shyness.

She tasted so good, which had absolutely nothing to do with the ice cream. He lifted his hand and cradled her neck a bit as he briefly deepened the kiss, sliding his tongue into her mouth, and then retreating, aware that they were in the middle of Banff Avenue and that Harper was not likely the PDA type. Neither was he, for that matter.

"Oh," she said softly, and her confused blue eyes lifted to capture his.

"I should probably apologize," he replied, his voice equally quiet. "But I don't want to. Because that was—"

"Please don't apologize," she interrupted. A weak smile curved her lips. "I liked it."

That bashful admission did more to fuel his libido than any R-rated proposition she might have whispered. He looked down and found peanut butter and chocolate ice cream dripping off his fingers. What a dangerous distraction she was turning out to be.

They dumped their cones in a nearby trash can and Harper reached inside her purse for a little pouch of glass cleaner cloths. "They're not perfect, but they should get the stickiness off. I keep them for my lenses."

They wiped their hands and then Drew reached down and twined his fingers with hers. "Are we okay? That was totally impulsive, but I don't want to assume anything."

Her cheeks coloured once more. "We're okay," she answered, giving his hand a squeeze and then sliding her fingers out of his. "It's not like I haven't thought about it." She started to walk away.

He reached out and grabbed her arm. "Since when?"

She spun around and met his gaze with laughing eyes. "Since the wedding. Just because I said no doesn't mean I didn't consider it for five seconds. Or that I haven't wondered."

She did a great impression of having a ton of self-control, but the soft pliancy of her lips and the way she'd sighed had told him plenty.

"That doesn't mean I think this is a good idea, though," she continued, and the buoyancy in his chest took a nosedive. "We're very different people. You're only here for a little while and I still don't do flings. Plus the pregnancy complicates matters."

He wasn't sure how to tell her that if anything, it made

her more attractive to him. Plus she wasn't going to be pregnant forever.

"Because of Dan?"

"You don't consider it odd that we're talking about… us…" She hesitated over the word, frowning. "And that I'm carrying his child?"

A handful of tourists looked their way, and Harper quickened her step so that he had to trot to keep up. Did she even know where she was going?

"It's not like you slept with him."

"No, of course not." She turned and faced him then, the frown deepening until there were matching creases between her brows, right above her nose. "It's still weird."

He wasn't going to argue with her, so he let the topic drop—for now. If she felt it was odd, well, her feelings were her feelings. He had no problem stepping up and taking the lead but he also knew when to back off and listen, so he did. "We need to cross the street again."

"I know."

The real estate agent was already waiting for them, and he opened the door to the building and let them walk in ahead of him.

Drew loved the space, and had from the first moment. Oddly enough, it wasn't the initial property that he'd come to see. That one had been okay, but too warehouse-feeling for his liking. This space was a bit smaller, but it had charm to spare. Wide open, with supporting wood beams, thick crossbeams in the ceiling and a second floor with a loft that overlooked the main level.

"Oh, this is lovely. And prime location. I can't imagine what this would cost you."

He tilted his head a bit and watched her move into the large center space. Not once had she mentioned his financial status, though she must know. She was best friends with Adele, after all. It was refreshing, being viewed for himself and not his net worth. If she wasn't going to bring it up, he certainly wasn't.

"The open concept would work great, don't you think?"

Her voice broke him out of his thoughts. "I do."

She stepped farther inside, went to the middle of the room and turned in a full circle. "Cash and customer service over there." She pointed. "Otherwise, if you have lines, you'll end up blocking access to the stairs. If you intend to use it for retail space, that is."

"I'd like to."

"Then you'll have to have an accessibility plan," she said quickly.

She was right. He hadn't thought of that, but he should have. "It's too good a space to waste."

"I agree."

He let her wander around for a few minutes, and could almost hear her brain turning. The Realtor was smart enough to stand back as well, and sent Drew a quiet smile.

She looked at the front windows and then back at him. "Lose the awnings in the front. It'll hide your window displays, and you want them dynamic and visible. They'd be fine for a café or something, but not Aspen Outfitters."

The Realtor nodded. "I told him the same thing."

"You're looking to buy, not rent, right?"

"That's right. When I decide on something, I go all in."

She lifted her brows. "And what if you lose?"

"I win more than I lose. And I always take calculated risks, not foolish ones."

"In other words, it doesn't happen often."

"Nope."

A smile broke over her lips. "Then why am I here again? Clearly you had your mind made up."

"Because before I leap I always want a second opinion. And you know the area. Do you think the town can handle another outfitter?"

She nodded. "It's a big business around here. Some will still shop in Calgary first, but with a good supply and competition here, you'll probably see increased traffic."

Which was his thinking, too, and he'd run some data as well—annual visitors, local populations, volume on marked trails each year or people using tour companies for backcountry expeditions. Nothing was a sure bet, but this felt good.

"And the upstairs..."

"You know what sells better than I do. You could put clothing up there if you wanted, and create a kind of boutique. But if you want to push it on the lower level, there might be some other department you want to put upstairs." She gave him a nod. "Your people will be able to tell you that far better than I can." She smiled. "My photographer's eye likes the balanced feel of it."

The Realtor looked at Drew, who gave him a brief nod. "You have my offer. It stands."

"And your threshold?"

"No more than ten percent above the initial offer. He knows he won't get full asking price. Even for a prime location like this."

"I'll be in touch."

"Shall we?" Drew asked, sweeping his arm out to the side to invite Harper to join him in the sun again.

"That's it?"

He nodded. "Yep. That's it. Now I wait. It'll be a back-and-forth of offers and negotiations now, but I'm guessing we'll have a verbal agreement by tonight and start the ball rolling tomorrow with paperwork.

"And then what?"

He smiled. "Then it's up to the bank. I'll sign what I need to sign, start putting everything in order and then head back home and get the ball rolling on the whole new-store process." He grinned. "This'll go much faster than when we actually build a store from the ground up. A crew will go in and do the renovations, and then we can start the hiring process and shipping stock. All told…we'll probably open in January, give or take."

She was quiet beside him. "Sorry, are you okay?" he asked. "You got quiet all of a sudden." It struck him that she might not be feeling well. "Is the ice cream not settling well?"

She smiled a little and they kept walking. "Oh, I'm okay that way. The morning sickness is getting a little better. There's really only an hour or so in the morning where I feel awful, and then it goes away. I'm hoping it'll disappear altogether really soon."

"Then why so quiet?"

She pursed her lips as if trying to determine what to say. "Well, truthfully… I've enjoyed today, but I conveniently forgot that you were here such a short time. It's not like it's something I haven't known all along."

"Does that mean you'd like me to stay?" he asked, even knowing he never could. The last thing he wanted was to set up some false expectation that he might. He wasn't the kind of guy to commit to personal relationships, and he would never want to hurt her. Still, he wanted to know the answer. Her opinion mattered, and that was a rare thing for him.

She looked up at him. "If I say yes, don't read too much into it. I know in a lot of ways we're very different, but you like some of the same things I do. And you seem to like me, even though I'm…"

She broke off, her cheeks flamed. He could tell, even in the hot sun, that she was embarrassed. He touched her hand and asked gently, "Even though you're what?"

The answer was a long time coming; they skirted around a group of Japanese tourists and then past a dog walker with five dogs on leashes, all of which were amenable to pats and lots of "good boys." He wondered if she was going to answer at all when she spoke softly.

"I've always been the tomboy type. I'm not curvy or exceptionally pretty, not like Adele. I usually have a hard time making friends. And as much as I know starting something between us would be a mistake, I also know it's been nice to feel…wanted."

An ache settled in around his heart. Harper was lonely, and loneliness was something he understood.

"You can have lots of friends and still be lonely," he admitted. They were walking in the direction of her house, and he didn't mind. The ice cream had kept him from being hungry for a late lunch, and there was nothing in the commercial part of town that he was dying to go to today.

"I can't believe you're lonely," she said, glancing over at him. "You're so outgoing and driven and…"

"And I miss my family a lot. I have friends but a lot of my relationships are ones of utility. It's not quite as charming as you'd think." He paused for a moment, reflecting. The words had just come out, but he realized how true they were. "You know, some of the most genuine, rewarding connections I've made have been through travel. A man who takes you to his village and invites you to dinner with his family. A tour guide who stands on the edge of a volcano with you and ponders life's big questions. As much as I love the business, and I do, don't get me wrong, I do occasionally get lonely."

"Wow. Then let me say you do a great job of covering it with charm and confidence."

"I love what I do and I'm good at it. But it doesn't fulfill every single aspect of my life."

They stopped on the sidewalk outside her house. "Nor should it, really. Not if you want any sort of balance."

She was so right. "Then here we are," he said, "two

very proficient people who love their jobs, who occasionally miss personal interaction."

"This has been an incredibly deep discussion." Her gaze touched his and then shifted to the house. "I have lemonade or some sparkling water if you're interested in a drink. But I understand if you have to keep going."

He held her gaze and smiled. "If it means I can drink it sitting on that porch with you, I'm in."

CHAPTER SEVEN

HARPER'S PULSE WAS drumming rapidly as she poured two glasses of lemonade and carried them out to the front porch. The overhang of the porch roof kept them shaded, but the afternoon was warm and mellow and perfect for sitting and enjoying the weather. That she would be sitting with Drew was what had her in a tizzy.

Because he'd kissed her today, and it had been lovely. Wonderful, even. More tender than she'd expected; gentle and unhurried. They'd had a simple ice cream in the sun and he'd held her hand. She'd had to pull away before she got too used to it, because it made her feel so lovely and special and she didn't want to read too much into anything. Next thing she'd start actually caring, and then have her heart crushed beneath his heel.

She handed him his lemonade and remembered the look on his face when he admitted he was lonely.

"Thanks," he said easily, and they sat on the porch swing together, a good twelve inches between them. He took a sip and leaned back, closing his eyes. "This is perfect. Reminds me of home a little."

Home. There wasn't any compliment that would have meant more to her. She'd been in Banff for several years now; longer than she could ever remember being in one place since she was a little girl. She'd put down her own roots and she loved her little house.

"I'm sure your folks had a much bigger house and yard."

He laughed. "They did. There were four of us kids, and a couple of pets usually. But there was something about it, even in all the chaos, that was calming. I don't know. I guess we always knew we were welcomed."

She swallowed against a lump in her throat. "You're welcome here, Drew."

"Thanks."

He nudged his toe on the floor and set the swing moving a little, a lazy back-and-forth that lulled. The lemonade was cool and tart, the sun warm and lazy, and Harper closed her eyes for a moment, breathing in the scent of a neighbour's fresh-cut grass and the spicy smell of the geraniums in her porch planters.

She opened her eyes slowly and saw Drew grinning at her. "What?"

"You look like you could go to sleep."

"Sorry. I'm really relaxed."

He put his drink down on a patio table and leaned toward her. Her heartbeat quickened, but he didn't touch her. Instead he reorganized the pillows on the swing so she could lean back along the side. "Here. Turn around and rest your head there, and put your feet on my lap."

The accelerated heartbeat made her chest squeeze tighter and she shook her head. "Oh, I'm fine, don't be silly."

"When was the last time you took a few hours off and had a nap? Seriously. I'm going to drink my lemonade and wait for my phone to buzz, so please."

She was tired. Pregnancy had a way of doing that to her and the indulgence was so tempting. "I'm not going to sleep. But it would be nice to put my feet up."

It took only ten seconds for her to put her nearly empty glass on the table, shift sideways and lean back against the plump cushions, and for Drew to settle her feet across his lap, his arm lying casually across her shins. "Better?"

It was more than better. It was heaven.

And then he set the swing moving with his toe, just a

little, and she closed her eyes. The warm breeze kissed her skin; she listened to the birds singing and the wind fluttering the leaves of the trees. Drew's phone buzzed and he shifted a little to respond, but said nothing as her breath deepened. She put her hand over her belly, thinking about the little life inside her that was causing all these changes, and the fact that Drew seemed remarkably unfazed that she was carrying his niece or nephew.

That was her last thought until she woke, her feet still in Drew's lap. He had nodded off, too, his phone still cradled in his hand, and she took a moment to look at him without fear of being caught.

There was so much more to him than she'd imagined. Things that were so good and made her think they had a lot in common, and then things that showed her how different they were. He came from a big happy family; she was an only child who'd been abandoned and then adopted. He had wandering feet; she longed to put down roots. She lived from check to check, putting whatever she could back into her business after paying the rent; he was a successful businessman.

And yet despite his ambition and energy, there were things they had in common, too. A love of the outdoors. Loneliness, sure, but also an appreciation for the people who embraced them and were important, like Adele and Dan. Ice cream and lemonade and quiet afternoons on a front porch now and then. Naps.

His lashes lay on the crests of his cheeks, his lips slightly open. She sighed as she remembered those lips on hers, so beguiling. She was still in awe that he seemed to find her attractive. Most men found her...plain. Or friend material, someone good for a laugh but not as a love interest. Or, like Jared, they found her disposable. Good for a while but not exciting enough to hang on to.

But Drew, with his shaggy hair and dancing eyes, made her feel special.

Maybe she should enjoy that while she could. He'd already said he'd be leaving soon, once the details on the property were signed. He had a number of other stores to run, after all. But for a few weeks…

She closed her eyes again, just for a moment, and let herself imagine what it would be like if this was real life. If he were a husband and she were a wife and this was their baby. And this was their porch and a stolen afternoon together, with the bees buzzing around and the birds singing in the trees. It filled her heart with an ache so sharp she nearly caught her breath.

She wanted that kind of life, and if her past dating history was any indication, she might never have it. She tended to have a lot of first and second dates, but after that either she decided they weren't for her or they moved on. Yeah, she was cautious—who wouldn't be? So when men told her she was "cold" or "too guarded," she figured they weren't willing to put in the effort.

She certainly hadn't come close to anything like she'd had with Jared, and that had been a farce from the beginning. The closest she might get was this moment, right now. The stolen kiss this afternoon and a nap on the front porch in the sunlight. She tucked both memories into her heart for safekeeping.

A snuffle came from the other end of the swing and she opened her eyes again. Drew was waking, his dark eyes slightly unfocused and a sheepish smile on his face. "I guess I nodded off along with you."

"It's cozy. Did you hear from the agent?"

"We're countering. I'm expecting another call soon."

She nodded but still didn't move to sit up. Once she did, the moment would be truly gone. Right now his hand was rubbing absently on her ankle. She wasn't even sure he knew he was doing it, but it felt incredible and she wasn't in any hurry for him to stop.

"Do you find yourself sleepy a lot with the pregnancy?"

She was surprised at the question, and nodded a little. "Yeah. Not bone tired all the time, but there are definitely times when I think I could easily go for a nap. Like today. Why do you ask?"

His thumb rubbed behind her anklebone. *Ahhhh.*

"I might have googled a bit."

She laughed. "Really?"

"Really. After you were sick the other day, I wondered. You women go through a lot to have kids."

"That's…kind of sweet of you."

His thumb stopped circling, but his hand wrapped around her ankle reassuringly. "You're carrying my niece or nephew, and putting your body through all of these changes for someone else. That's pretty damned selfless. I guess I never really thought about the small things that would affect you. What's been the hardest so far?"

She thought about it for a moment, wondering if she dare speak the truth. He was Dan's brother. What if she spilled and he went back to Dan and told him what she said? Trust didn't come easily to her, but she trusted Adele and that was where her loyalty lay.

But she hesitated too long, and he leaned over a little, examining her face. "What is it? Is there something wrong?"

"No, of course not," she replied. "We had an appointment earlier in the week and everything is great. We got to hear the heartbeat."

"I heard!" He smiled and straightened, then his face fell. "You don't look thrilled. What's going on?"

"If I tell you, I'm going to sound like the worst person alive."

"I doubt it. But try me."

She swallowed against a lump in her throat. "I shouldn't be surprised that I feel...attached. I mean, I knew that would happen when I offered to do this. I also thought that I would remind myself that I'm just the incubator, that the baby is Dan and Adele's. Intellectually I know that's true. Emotionally I'm finding it harder than I expected. Hearing the heartbeat made it so real. There's a little human inside of me, Drew, and I find that wonderful and surreal and overwhelming. It's a little odd. I made all these assurances to Dan and Adele that they'd be involved every step of the way, but when we heard the heartbeat and they were celebrating, it was me who felt left out."

She let out a huge breath. "And I'm totally aware how selfish that sounds. Why should I feel left out?"

"Because you're human. I'm sorry, Harper."

"Don't be sorry. Like I said, intellectually, I know this is going to work out how it should—with Dan and Adele having a beautiful baby. But if I feel this attached now, how will I feel when he or she starts kicking? Or when they are born?" She thought about her own adoptive mother and sighed. "My mom always said motherhood was more about heart than biology. I'm finding it hard not to think of myself as a mother. Sometimes I think I need to protect myself from having these feelings somehow."

He didn't say anything, and when the silence drew out, she admitted, "And who knows if I'll ever have my own?"

Drew sat up straighter and puckered his eyebrows. "Why wouldn't you? You're not even thirty yet. You have lots of time."

"Maybe, but call me old-fashioned—I'd like to be settled with a partner before having kids, and that doesn't seem to be on the horizon anytime soon. Hasn't ever been, actually."

"What are you talking about?"

She shrugged, pulled her legs off his lap and sat up.

"I've always been something of a tomboy, you know? And I don't make friends easily. I tend to fade into the woodwork. Which is fine." She tried not to sound defensive; after all, she'd chosen to hold back to avoid getting hurt time and time again when she would inevitably have to move. "I'm just more comfortable behind a camera than in front of it."

"Too tomboyish? A wallflower?" His face had blanked, as if he truly didn't understand. But she knew it was the truth. She still felt all the times that girls had been asked to dances and on dates and she'd been overlooked. Or how her mom had taken her prom dress shopping and they'd bought a beautiful gown, only she hadn't found a date. That marked the one and only time she'd lied to her mom. She'd got ready, let her mom take some pictures at the house, and then had said she was going to a friend's place as several of them were going without dates.

Instead she'd gone to a nearby lake with a book and a stash of sodas in the car. And she'd gone home at nine thirty, telling her mom she'd had a great time, but that she felt a migraine coming on from the lights and music and she was going to bed.

Then Jared had come along, and she'd fallen hard. Only to have her heart spectacularly broken. Was it any wonder she was a bit jaded?

She wouldn't say any of that to Drew, though. There was sharing and then there was oversharing. It was easier to stick to the plain Jane theory.

"I'm an outdoor girl," she explained. "I don't wear makeup much. I don't know, I guess I don't…stand out. I'm kind of invisible. Which is fine—I'm happy not being the center of attention." It had served her well, all the times she'd moved to a new town and been the "new girl."

"But it might be nice to be the center of someone's attention?"

That he articulated it so well caused a pang in her chest. “Well, yeah, I guess.”

“Harper?”

“Hmm?”

He looked her fully in the face. “You’ve got my attention now.”

Oh my. She surely did. He wasn’t smiling, wasn’t cracking a joke or trying to be deliberately charming. He was being truthful and focusing all his attention on her.

“Do you want to know what I see?”

“I’m not sure if I do or not.”

A ghost of a smile flirted with his lips. “I’m going to tell you anyway. I see a woman who is caring and generous. I see someone who is beautiful and doesn’t realize it. Who doesn’t need makeup and who has the sweetest little blanket of freckles over her nose. I see a body strong from walking trails and climbing rocks and streams to get a perfect photo of a baby bear cub. I see that same strong body growing a new life for someone who can’t. Don’t ever say you’re plain or ordinary again.”

Tears burned in her eyes at his earnest words. They weren’t like his compliments at the wedding, engineered to woo and romance. They were heartfelt and sincere and she loved him for them, even if she wasn’t *in* love with him.

His phone buzzed but he didn’t look down at it. He held her gaze until she gave a sniff and a small nod. “That’s the sweetest thing anyone has ever said to me.”

“If that’s true, it’s a damned shame.” He smiled then. “People should be appreciated and told so.”

“How did you get so wise?” she asked, blinking away the last of the moisture from her eyes. She wasn’t going to weep over his sweet words, even if they’d touched her deeply.

“My father. We’re very quick to criticize when someone does something we don’t like. But we hold on to our compliments and praise, and it doesn't make sense." He scowled a little bit, and she wondered if she was thinking about anyone in particular. "It's the biggest life lesson I've taken with me," he continued, "and it's probably the number one thing that's helped me in business, too."

Business. Right. The comparison took a little of the bloom off the rose of his compliment, but it also made her respect him even more. For all his charm, she was starting to realize his success came from a place of very hard work and genuinely appreciating his people. It was an attractive quality for sure. One that spoke of integrity.

"Your phone buzzed, by the way," she offered softly.

"I know. I'll get to it. I want to make sure you're okay first. You're not invisible, Harper. I promise."

Her gaze slipped away and she focused on a bumblebee that was sitting comfortably in the middle of a clump of blue lobelia in one of her planters. His words—*you're not invisible*—left her with an odd feeling of discomfort. Did she want to be invisible? Maybe. And if she did, then how could she really complain about being alone? Deep down, she knew she'd made a habit of pushing people away. If she didn't let herself care too much, then it wouldn't hurt when they inevitably moved on.

"I'm okay. Really. I've just been holding that inside for a while."

"Because you'd normally tell Adele, and this time you can't."

She nodded, an ache around her heart.

"Then I'm glad I was here."

"Please don't say anything to Dan or Adele. They're so excited about the baby and they're my best friends. I wouldn't hurt them for the world."

"Of course I won't. But…" A smile curved his lips as he tapped a few buttons on his phone. "Guess what I have on here?"

She frowned a little, curious. "What?"

He tapped another button and leaned closer to her, smiling. A steady *bah bum, bah bum* sounded from his speakers. Her heart gave a little leap. "You have the heartbeat?"

"Dan sent it to me, dying to share it. And now you can hear it, too."

The steady, quick sounds of the baby's heartbeat filled the air. She knew the recording would end, but the moment it did, it merely looped again so it started over. She put her hand on her tummy, sucked in a shaky breath. "Oh," she said quietly, feeling that same overwhelming awe that had struck her in the doctor's office.

"Pretty incredible, huh?"

She nodded, unable to erase the smile from her face.

"How do you feel?"

Oh, that he would ask. No one else had really thought to. She was emotionally invested; how could she not be? She swallowed against the tightness in her throat and reached for his hand.

"Humbled," she whispered, letting out a breath. "And powerful at the same time. That little heartbeat…that's in here." She withdrew her hand and pointed at her abdomen.

"Pretty crazy, huh?" He let it play again, and she took his hand and placed it on her belly, which had only the slightest little bump. Not even noticeable if you didn't have previous shape to use as context.

His gaze locked with hers. "That's my niece or nephew in there."

She nodded.

"And still so tiny."

"I know. I'm not even showing yet. But this…this made it all real to me. More than an idea, you know? Thank you, Drew. So much."

"I can forward it to you if you want."

"Would you?"

He nodded and handed over his phone, pulling his other palm away from her belly. "Go ahead and program your number."

She did and handed it back, then let out a happy sigh. The afternoon was waning, and Drew checked his phone. "They've countered again. We're making one more counter-offer and if he won't come down, the deal's off."

Her mouth dropped open. "Just like that?"

Drew grinned and shrugged. "He'll come down," he said with confidence. "If he doesn't, he doesn't. I think this would be a great location for our first Canadian store, but there are other spots. I'm not going to overpay for real estate."

"You love this, don't you? The bargaining."

"Kind of. What I really love is taking something from scratch and building it, and watching it all come together."

And then moving on to the next challenge. She couldn't forget that. She'd told him before that she wasn't a challenge or a trophy. Now that she knew him better, she knew he didn't see people that way. But it was how he viewed life. Challenges and adventures. In her eyes, a lot of adventures meant confusion and trying to carve a new spot for herself in a strange place with strange people.

Still, he'd listened to her, and he'd given her the moment she'd missed in the doctor's office. He was a good man. A friend, and those were hard to come by.

"Would you like to stay for dinner?" she asked. "I know you're waiting for another update, and I'm an okay cook… for a vegetarian."

"I'd love to."

"You would?" She looked over at him, surprised. She'd half expected him to decline, since they'd spent all afternoon together.

He laughed. "Don't act so surprised. I'm staying in a hotel. I have to eat most of my meals out or suck up to Dan and Adele." He leaned over a bit, enough that she could smell his shampoo, something outdoorsy and fresh. "Little secret. I'm a decent cook. I can even help."

"Well, all right, then." She grinned and pushed on her knees, getting up from the swing. "How do you feel about pad thai?"

"I have very warm feelings about it, actually."

She grinned and led the way inside, taking her glass with her, and he followed, bringing his own nearly gone and now-warm lemonade. She got them new glasses and poured them each a glass of water, then stood across from him at the kitchen island. "So. Do you want to chop vegetables or tofu?"

Drew slid the knife through the carrots and stole a glance at Harper, who was dropping cubes of tofu into a pan with hot oil. It sizzled and spattered a little, and she slid the pan on the burner to stir the cubes. Water was boiling for the rice noodles, and he watched her move around the kitchen, gathering ingredients for the sauce.

He couldn't believe she ever thought herself invisible. And absolutely couldn't believe that some guy hadn't snapped her up already. Maybe she wasn't the flashiest woman around, and maybe she didn't turn heads on the street. Not because she wasn't beautiful but because…

He suddenly smiled. Because she was a chameleon. He didn't know why, but she blended in with her environment no matter where she was.

"How are the carrots and onions?"

He gave a few more chops and finished up the carrot. "Good. Is this fine enough?" He angled the cutting board for her approval.

"Perfect." She took the board from him and slid the vegetables into the pan with the now-crispy tofu, then went back to work whisking ingredients together for the sauce.

It was a domestic type of scene he was unused to. His "dates" usually consisted of restaurants and plus-one type of events. Definitely not comfy home-cooked meals and lemonade on a swing.

It had been different—once. A few years ago he'd fallen in love but she wanted the kind of life he didn't, and the type of commitment he couldn't give. In the end he'd hurt her, badly, even though breaking it off had been the right thing to do. These days he didn't make promises he couldn't keep. Being with Harper sometimes made him forget that, and he had to keep his guard up when he started feeling too comfortable.

She had him crush peanuts courtesy of two pieces of parchment paper and a rolling pin. In no time at all she'd fixed two bowls, sprinkled his crushed peanuts on top and led the way to the dining table, which was little more than a café table with two chairs in the somewhat small kitchen.

He carried their water glasses, and before long they were seated across from each other and sharing the meal.

She told him about working with Juny and her plans to have her take over more jobs; he shared his ideas for the store and then they both threw around ideas for renovation. He ate the spicy noodles and marveled at the way her eyes shone when she grew animated, or waved her fork around—empty, of course—when she talked with her hands. He refilled water glasses and laughed when she cracked a joke about pregnant womens' bladder capacity. They finished and he helped her load the dishwasher and then wash up the few pots and pans. When he was drying the last dish, her phone buzzed, vibrating loudly against the countertop.

"I'll finish this," Drew said, wiping his hands on the dish towel. "Go ahead and answer it."

She picked up the phone. "Oh, hi, Adele. No, I'm not

busy." She looked over at Drew and rolled her eyes, and he laughed.

But then the humor faded from her face. "Oh. Oh, I see. Okay. Well, if you're ready, of course." She took a deep breath and met Drew's gaze. "Hey, we knew you were going to start telling people eventually. You must be so excited."

There was a long pause where Adele had to be speaking, and Harper smiled a little, and then said, "Don't worry about me. And don't worry about what anyone else thinks, either, okay? Remember how quickly Drew was on board. And you can message me later. Good luck."

She hung up the phone. "Dan and Adele are telling your family tonight and wanted to give me the heads-up."

"Oh. Are you okay with that?"

She shrugged. "Why wouldn't I be? I mean, it was their decision and their baby and it's Dan's family."

"Except you think they'll be skeptical, as I was?"

She laughed a little and leaned back against the counter. "That lasted all of about five minutes. If your family is like you, it'll be fine."

"You're right."

"Do you want some tea?"

It appeared as if she was letting it go, but he could tell she was still a little anxious. He seriously didn't know what to say.

They were halfway through their tea when his phone buzzed. And in the space of two breaths, it went off twice more.

Harper looked over at him. "You should probably check it. You're still waiting for news, remember?"

Funny how he'd nearly forgotten about the real estate offer. His jaw tightened as he reached for his phone. Instead of the agent, it was messages from his two sisters.

At least they seemed excited, with a side order of "OMG can you believe they did this?"

Then came the message from his mother, and it wasn't quite so generous.

His parents were of a more traditional variety, and his mother had tons of questions about "this Harper woman" and what she was after. He fired back a quick response, but he'd honestly hoped for better. His mother, especially, had always been accepting and kind. He understood she was being a protective mom, but he reminded her that she was going to be a grandmother again and that Harper was Adele's best friend and not some stranger.

But it sat wrong with him.

"Your family?" she asked quietly.

"There's no sense lying, is there?"

She shook her head, her gaze steady. "Not a bit."

"It'll be fine. My parents are more traditional, I suppose. It's a generation-gap kind of thing."

"That was the last text, wasn't it?" Her lips tightened, and he was truly angry at his mother for being anything less than supportive.

"Do they think what you thought that first night?" she asked, standing perfectly still in the middle of her tiny kitchen. "That I'm in it for something? That I'm after money or…" She swallowed again.

"I don't know." He figured not telling her would be worse than being honest. "Listen, all she said was to ask if I'd known about this and did I actually think it was a good idea." She'd also asked what kind of woman would agree to carry someone else's baby. He'd bet fifty bucks that her solution would have been to adopt or get a dog, not go through a bunch of medical testing or a uterus-for-rent.

He softened his expression and went to her. "Hey, listen, it's okay. Mom's in shock. No one knew Dan and Adele were even considering such a thing, you know? And the girls…they'll be super supportive. They have kids of their own." He took her hands in his and gave them a little shake.

"Supportive of Dan and Adele. Who knows what they think of me?"

"Within two minutes of talking to you, they'll think exactly as I do. That you're a wonderful, generous, loving person. Mom and Dad will, too. They're good and fair people."

Harper let out a breath. "Okay."

"And besides, you're not doing this for them. You're doing it for Adele."

"Yeah," she said, and she tried a wobbly smile.

"Forget *my* family," he said sternly. "Who do you want to tell? Who do you want to share this news with?"

Her eyes widened. "Oh. Uh. Well, Juny. It's been horrible keeping this from her when she's at the studio all the time."

"Then you should call her. Or invite her over. Who else?"

The tears came back in her eyes and one leaked over her lashes and down her cheek. "My mom. I'm adopted, you see. She'll understand how Adele's feeling and how I'm feeling. It's been so hard doing this without telling my mom."

He led her into the living room and what appeared to be her most comfortable chair. Then he gave her her phone and went back to the kitchen to retrieve her tea. "Here. Have your tea and call your mom." He got a light blanket off the sofa and put it over her legs. "Curl up and be comfortable and celebrate what you're doing, sweetheart. It's a wonderful thing. Don't let anyone take it away from you."

She looked up at him with wide, luminous eyes. "Don't go."

He knew he should, but he nodded. "I won't. I'll go out on the porch and give you some privacy and see where we're at with the building purchase. Okay?"

She nodded. He smiled and started for the hall, when her voice stopped him.

"Drew?"

He turned around.

"Thank you. For this, and for the support, and for being my friend today."

He'd kissed her. Just now he'd called her *sweetheart* by mistake. He was feeling far more than friendly toward her but this situation called for support and not seduction.

"You're welcome," he said simply, and went to the front porch to take care of some business.

CHAPTER EIGHT

HARPER FOUND HIM sitting on the porch swing again, an ankle crossed over his knee as he scrolled through something on his phone.

He'd been right. Calling her mom had been just what she needed. She'd wait and tell Juny tomorrow before work. Maybe she'd take in tea and scones or something. In any case, the news was out, and she was free of any big secret. After Drew's unconditional support and her mother's excitement and love, there was a contentment in her heart that had been missing for most of her pregnancy.

"Did you make the sale?" she asked softly.

He looked up and smiled. "I did. And you look much better."

"My eyes are red from crying a bit."

"Yeah, but you look happier. More relaxed."

She went to the swing and sat down. "I am."

When he opened his arm along the top of the swing, she accepted the invitation and leaned into his embrace. She'd desperately needed the touch of another human being lately, and Drew was warm and strong and reassuring.

"I'm glad. I talked to my mom, too, by the way. And gave her an earful."

Harper pushed against his ribs, moving to sit up. "You didn't. Oh, Drew. I wish you hadn't."

"Don't you worry. I told her that you were a wonderful friend doing a wonderful thing and to insinuate anything more was totally off base. And then I reminded her that this meant another grandchild to spoil and told her to get with the times."

"You played into her weakness."

"Nonsense. I prefer to think that I reminded her of the benefits of this arrangement and that ultimately you were helping her to get what she and Dad want most. Lots of little Brimicombes running around."

"Which conveniently gets you off the hook."

"For the time being. As the one kid with no children, it'll come back around." He chuckled. "Come back here and relax a bit more. I got the building for eight percent over my first offer, and we'll sign the purchase agreement tomorrow."

"That means you'll be leaving soon."

"Oh, another week or so. There's lots to do here. I'm going to hire a local team to do the renos, and it's short notice so a lot of companies are probably already booked for the fall. There are things for me to do here, don't worry."

"I'm happy for you."

"Me, too. When I first got here, I had nothing but expansion on my mind. But coming back home to Canada… it feels really good. I can't lie about it."

She leaned against his ribs and sighed. "I didn't think you wanted a home. More of a home base."

"I was speaking in more general terms. Sacramento is my home base, I guess. I'm not there much."

She smiled against him. It wasn't his fault she'd been bounced around as a kid and had struggled to make friends. Maybe it was easier to move around when you were an adult if you'd had more stability as a kid.

"You're an adventurer at heart," she said. "I love how you own it." Even if it meant he was going to be in her life such a brief time and then out of it again.

"That doesn't mean I don't enjoy days like today, Harper.

It's been very nice sharing it with you. Thank you for going with me this afternoon. For dinner. Heck, for the ice cream."

For the kiss. The words sat on her tongue but she didn't say them.

Drew was leaving soon. The difference between now and her past hurtful encounter was that she knew it and had no unreasonable expectations. She was under no illusions that this was forever or he was The One. There was a certain level of protection in that.

So she tilted her head up slightly and met his gaze, then blinked slowly, wondering if he was interested in a continuation of this afternoon's sweet kiss.

"Harper," he said softly, a note of caution in his voice.

"I know. I know I said no in March. And I'm not looking for a wild and torrid affair. But I don't want to pretend I'm not attracted to you, Drew. I know you're leaving. It's okay."

"Damn," he murmured, lifting his hand and placing it along her cheek. "You don't know what you're asking."

"I'm not asking for anything. I'm saying when your business in town is done, you're walking away and I'm fine with it. Maybe I have been trying too hard to be invisible. You see me, and it makes me…a little bit brave."

Her heart was pounding from the vulnerability in that admission. But then his fingers grazed her jaw and his eyes darkened as they looked deeply into hers.

"Let's go inside," he said, his voice low and rough. "Because if I kiss you, I want to do it right, and not in view of your neighbours."

Her body got a little thrill from those dark and promising words, and she stood up from the swing, her knees shaking a little. She led the way inside, her insides quaking with nervousness and anticipation.

She got three steps inside the hallway when he reached out and grabbed her hand, stopping her. His gaze caught hers, dark and full of purpose in the early evening light. He took a step closer, and another, while an army of butterflies took flight in her belly. Her tongue snuck out to wet her lips…oh Lord, had he just noticed that? One more step and his body was so close to hers that she took a step back and found herself against the wall. The screen door was barely a meter away. Moments ago they'd been mere friends. If he kissed her now—and surely he was going to—it would change everything.

He stepped closer still, so her back was pressed against the wall and his chest and hips lightly grazed her denim skirt and blouse. Her breath came short and fast, her lips parted. And still he held her gaze, darkly, deeply, until his mouth was only a few inches from hers and her lashes fluttered closed.

Like this afternoon, he kissed the side of her mouth first, a feather-soft graze of warm lips to tender skin. She let out a breath and tried hard not to moan in response, but kept her eyes closed, enjoying the kiss with all her other senses. He ran his lips to her jaw, then below her ear, causing a shiver that ran straight down her spine. Then the corner of her eyebrow, the tip of her nose, the delicate dip above her frenulum. "Drew," she breathed, realizing that her arms hung limply at her sides. She wasn't able to do anything right now but *feel.*

But her plea did the trick. He placed his hands on the wall on either side of her head and leaned in, covering her mouth with his, a full kiss that had her body responding automatically with a whimper and her arms lifting to coil around his torso.

Subtle head movements, dips and nips and low sounds of encouragement kept the kiss going for a long, long time. It had been years since Harper had been kissed this thoroughly, if ever. Drew's fit body pressed against hers, all muscled chest and lean hips that translated his desire. But still he kept everything at the kissing stage. It didn't matter. When one was an expert, there was no need to rush to the next level.

"You taste good," he murmured, running his lips over to her ear again. She gasped and he chuckled, low and sexy, by her ear. "Told you I wanted to do it right."

She ran her hand over his shoulder. "You really are an overachiever."

"Thank you." His tongue skimmed along to the curve of her neck and she really wondered how far they could go tonight.

His hand left the wall and skimmed down her neck, two fingertips tracing a trail to her collarbone.

He kissed her again, this time with more urgency, and their bodies responded in kind. When it was clear they either had to stop or take things to a whole other level, Drew backed away, breathing heavily.

"You definitely did it right," she said, her voice low with pleasure. "My whole body is humming right now."

"Be careful saying things like that. I'm likely to ask you to show me where your bedroom is."

"And I'm tempted to take you there."

"But we shouldn't."

"We shouldn't."

A long moment held between them, as if each was deliberating the pros and cons.

"You," he said quietly, "are a very tempting woman, and whoever made you feel otherwise is a damned fool."

"Fools," she corrected, but smiled at him, still feeling rather boneless. "And I might have a hard time believing you, but I believe that you mean it, so that's something."

"You're so confident about everything else. I don't know why you're so sure you're unexceptional. But I have a week or so to try to convince you you're amazing."

And then he did something so unexpected that she

didn't know what to say or do. He stepped forward and placed his palm on her abdomen. "This is amazing. I mean, the sheer biology of it alone is miraculous but that you would do this for another person…you have a huge, wonderful heart, Harper. You do. Don't let anyone make you feel small."

He kissed her again, a small, tender kiss, with his hand still on her stomach.

"You struck me as such a player," she finally murmured. "But you're not. You're an observant, considerate man with a lot of integrity behind all that charm. In another time or place…"

"We might have fallen in love?"

Love. Her heart jolted at even the mention of the word and she took a mental step backward. "Maybe. But not now. Now we…" She couldn't come up with the right words.

"Enjoy each other's company, and accept that when the time comes, we go our separate ways with best wishes and good memories. No regrets."

"You said that so well it makes me think you've done it before."

"I've done it, but it didn't end well," he replied, his gaze serious. "I broke someone's heart and hated myself for it. But I couldn't live a lie, and the kind of life she wanted wasn't for me. I like you, Harper. More than that, I admire you. So maybe we can admire each other for a few more days, and leave things with fond memories. It's all I can offer and you should know that up front."

Why not? she thought. It would be a definite change of pace from her other romantic experiences. She'd lost her virginity when she was twenty-one and tired of carrying the burden of it around, and it had been a mediocre experience and certainly not one with any depth of emotion. Her other partner had been Jared. She'd thought him everything she wanted, and he'd disappeared with barely a "see ya." He hadn't even asked for the ring back. It had been disposable, just like her.

Leaving things with happy, "that one summer" sort of memories seemed pretty attractive.

"Does this mean you want to go with me to Healy Pass on Thursday?"

"I'd love to."

"I'll pack food for the day. You know to dress accordingly. It's a longer hike than what we went on the other day, but ten times as rewarding."

"It sounds perfect."

It really did. And the idea of doing the hike with company, and someone who enjoyed the outdoors as much as she did? Heaven.

"I suppose this means I should go for now."

"You can stay if you want to."

"Tempting as that sounds, I feel like I've already overstayed my welcome. But thank you for dinner, and for everything."

"Anytime." And she meant it.

He let go of her hands and turned to go to the door, but paused when he got there. "I'll pick you up Thursday morning. How does that sound?"

"Perfect."

He was holding open the door, but he let it go and walked back inside, coming over to plant a final kiss on her lips. "That's better," he said, and then went for the door. "See you Thursday."

When he was gone, Harper went into the living room and sat down in her favorite chair. Half of her tea was still in her mug and cold now, but it didn't matter.

The people who mattered most knew about the baby. And Drew had kissed her. Twice. More than twice when she thought about it. And touched her. And he'd been kind and understanding.

Never in her life had she felt so accepted by a man.

"Oh, Harper," she said to herself. "You're going to have to be very careful."

The following morning she told Juny about the baby. For a moment, the younger woman's eyes widened, and then she sat back with a victorious smile. "Okay, so I *knew* there was something going on with you! No Friday night wine and chocolate plans, and no more morning muffins and coffee on Wednesdays. Plus you looked sickly some of the time. I can't believe you didn't tell me."

But she didn't look hurt, and for that Harper was relieved. "I couldn't. We really wanted to make sure I got past the first trimester before saying anything to anyone. The only person who knew was Drew, and that was because he showed up and I was at Dan and Adele's. He kind of guessed something was up and Dan told him."

"Is that why he's been around lately? Are you guys a thing?" She put extra emphasis on the word *thing*.

Even though Harper felt her face heat, she shook her head. "No, we're not a thing. We've hung out a few times over the past couple of weeks, but that's it."

Juny waggled her eyebrows. "If that was it, you wouldn't be blushing."

Would a half-truth suffice? She sighed and relented a little. "Okay, so I'm not blind. He's very cute and it turns out he's quite nice as well, once you get past that veneer of charm."

"I bet."

"Shut up. How are things with you and Renée?"

"Fine, and don't change the subject. I've known you for two years now and I've never seen you blush over a guy.

In fact, other than mentioning the odd one-off date, I don't think I've seen you talk about guys at all."

Harper took a sip of tea, decaf Earl Grey this time since she no longer relied on mint tea to settle her stomach. "I'm not a social butterfly, you know that. My friend circle is pretty small, so it's been kind of nice."

"I'll let you off the hook for now."

"Thank you so much," she replied, sarcasm ripe in her voice but accompanied by a smile. "Have another scone. There's a chocolate chunk one in there somewhere."

"Bless you." Juny rooted around in the bag until she came up with the scone, then broke it in half and gave a piece to Harper. "So how is this going to work with the studio?"

"I'm glad you asked." Harper gave her the rundown on her plans to include Juny in more photo shoots, so that she could take on some of the photography duties as the pregnancy advanced. "I'm not booking anything after New Year's," she said. "I'm due in January, and I don't want to leave anyone stranded. Right now we only have one date in November and one in December, but that'll change. I think you and I should consult together on any late-year jobs that come up and decide if we can take them. But I'm not taking much time off after the baby is born. I'm going to need to get back to work and into a regular schedule."

Juny's dark eyes took on a concerned expression. "Are you afraid, Harper? I mean, you're going through all this and then handing the baby over. I know you said genetically it's Dan and Adele's, but this isn't an easy thing."

Harper nodded. "Yeah, I'm a little afraid. So I don't want to set myself up to mope around after it's over. I'll get to spoil this baby rotten." She put her hand on her tummy. "Anyway, if you're okay with a few extra weekend hours doing events with me, I thought I'd look at hiring someone part time to work the storefront." It would mean being even more disciplined with the finances, but if Juny worked out as Harper hoped, they could take on more bookings in the new year to balance out the extra cost of another staff member.

"I'd love that."

"I can spare some extra equipment for now when we go out together. But if it's a tentative plan moving forward, we can figure it out as we go."

"Sounds fine to me. You can pay me in chocolate chunk scones." Juny brushed some crumbs off her lap.

Then she looked up at Harper and smiled. "I'm only going to say one more thing about Drew. Yesterday, when you came out of the back room and he was waiting, you looked so happy. I've never seen you look quite that way before. Even if you're just hanging out until he goes back to wherever, he's good for you. So enjoy yourself."

The support sent a warm feeling through Harper, and she felt very blessed with her friendships. They weren't great in number, but quality-wise they were top-notch.

"Thanks," she said, trying not to look too happy and sure she was failing. The memory of last night's kiss still made her stomach tangle in delicious knots. "And speaking of, I'm taking him on a day hike up to Healy Pass tomorrow. We'll be out of range so I'll be back in the studio on Friday morning. I have the MacPherson rehearsal on Friday night."

"Sounds fine. Now I'd better get out there and unlock the doors. I sold three of the five-by-sevens yesterday, by the way. Maybe next week you can pick some new photos for prints and we can shuffle some stuff around out front. It's the perfect size for tourists who want something for their luggage."

"I'll pick a few and match some mattes and frames. Which ones sold?"

"One was a Peyto Lake, and I think the other was Bow

Lake. An eight-by-ten of Lake Louise went earlier this week, too."

They were recognizable landmarks, and they did tend to sell well, though Harper knew she had equally good photos of more obscure locations. Maybe there was something to what Drew had said about greeting cards. A good portion of their foot traffic was tourists, and smaller did sell better when it came to transport. It didn't make a lot of sense to turn down an opportunity for sales just because they were a more "disposable" form of her work.

"I'll put some stuff together today and double-check the details for Friday's rehearsal party. Do you want to come with?"

"We close at six. I can meet you after that, if it's local."

"It is."

With the day's plan solidified, Juny went to the store to open and Harper started going through her to-do list. If she were going to be gone all day tomorrow, she had to have things in order today.

Tomorrow. A whole day with Drew in the outdoors. She couldn't think of a finer idea.

CHAPTER NINE

DREW KNOCKED QUIETLY on the screen door. It was only seven thirty, but they had a fun day ahead of them. He couldn't remember the last time he'd looked forward to something so much. Even Dan's "are you sure you know what you're doing" during their phone call last night couldn't put a damper on his good mood.

He'd come up with a crazy surprise for Harper today. Something that would keep Dan and Adele's worry at bay, and give her a special treat.

Harper came to the door, her face bright and cheery. "Good morning. You're right on time."

"I hope so." He slid his pack off his shoulder and put it down in the entry as he stepped inside. Two days ago he'd kissed her brainless in this very spot, and his body stirred with remembrance. Harper did something to him that he hadn't expected. Something wonderful. It was too bad he had to head back to California late next week.

Or maybe not. It would be too easy to get caught up in her and he didn't want to go with any hurt feelings left behind or misunderstandings. On either of their parts.

"I'm just finishing breakfast. Did you have any?"

"I grabbed a breakfast sandwich at the coffee shop." He patted his belly.

She laughed. "I'm just finishing up. Come in and sit down."

He sat at her table while she bit into her egg sandwich. "You want some juice?" she asked. "Milk?"

"Naw, I'm good. I've got a big water bottle." He grinned.

She had no idea that today was going to be more of an adventure than she'd bargained for.

"Me, too, in my bag." She laughed. "You know, there's only a washroom at the trailhead. I'm not sure what's going to happen with my pregnant bladder if I drink that much water over the course of the day."

"I'll stand guard for you," he joked, and was gratified when she grinned around the toast in her mouth, a hint of a dimple denting her cheek.

He watched as she wiped her hands on a napkin and grabbed her glass of orange juice. "You ate a whole sandwich. Morning sickness better?"

"Much," she agreed, and put her plate and glass in the dishwasher. "Mostly now I get the odd wave and it passes. Food's stayed down for five days in a row now."

"That must feel better."

"It does."

He waited while she finished putting her pack together. Right now she wore a light jacket over her T-shirt, with a lightweight hoodie in the pack. Bottles of water, her bear spray and sunscreen all went in the backpack.

"You were planning to carry all that *and* your camera?"

"Pretty much. Slightly smaller lens today, though. My neck and back would kill me if I carried that all day. I'm mostly looking for some meadow shots and panoramas." She looked up. "Wait. You said *were*. How come?"

Dammit. Of course he'd make a slip. He figured he might as well get the ball rolling. "Well, as a matter of fact, I have a bit of a surprise for you this morning."

Her brows lifted. "A surprise? I'm not sure if I like that. I'm not really a surprise kind of woman."

He paused and then went to her and took her hands. "Do you trust me, Harper?"

Confusion mingled with warmth in her eyes. "That's a big question, Drew. Especially for me."

"Then listen to your intuition. What does your gut say? Can you trust me?"

There was a moment's hesitation, and then she nodded slightly. "Yes. For some odd reason, I trust you."

"Then let's put this stuff in my car." He dropped a kiss on her cheek. "You're not going to regret this," he promised.

Harper didn't know if she was going to regret it or not. When she went outside, she stopped short at the sight of his rental. The Range Rover SUV sat square in her driveway. A flipping Range Rover! She looked over at Drew, who wore an amused expression. "Something wrong?" he asked.

"No, nothing." She made her feet move and they stowed her gear in the back. Drew headed east on the highway instead of west. When she opened her mouth to speak, he lifted a finger and shushed her. "Surprise, remember?" he said. "And that means you have to wait. You said you were very patient."

"Not about surprises or not knowing where I'm going," she grumbled, slumping down in the seat that cradled her body perfectly. She trusted Drew, but she'd really wanted to hike up the pass today. With the business being so busy, she didn't get a lot of opportunities and as much as it was fun being with Drew, she didn't want to squander her chance for some new shots for her portfolio.

It wasn't long until she realized where he was headed and her head snapped around to stare at him. "The heliport? Are you crazy?" Her stomach turned over both in excitement and fear. A helicopter? She was a bit thrilled and a lot terrified. "Did I not tell you I was afraid of heights?"

He looked over at her and laughed. "You'll be buckled in and snug as a bug. I promise."

"But..." She bit down on her lip. "I've done enough

weddings and events to know that a tour is really expensive, Drew. And I know the building you just bought came at a hefty price. You don't need to do this kind of thing."

"It's the money you're worried about?" He seemed unconcerned. Amused, even.

It *was* expensive, she told herself. And yes, she was terrified. But why on earth would he spend the money on this sort of thing? This car rental alone had to cost a lot. Was he always this careless with his money? "It seems extravagant," she answered, twisting her fingers together. "We were supposed to hike."

"And we're going to," he said. "We're going to get dropped off, hike, and then get picked up again." He met her gaze briefly before turning his attention back to the road. "This way you get the alpine meadows and panoramic views without having to do all the hard climbing."

She wasn't sure what to think. Was he doing it because he was being overprotective and thought she wasn't capable? How could she voice that without being insulting? It was a generous and fun thing he had planned, but Adele and Dan were already making her a bit claustrophobic with their concern. Surely it wasn't an attempt to impress her. She'd never once given him the impression that her head could be turned by such things.

"I'm still capable of doing the hike, you know," she said. "Not that I don't appreciate the gesture, but I'm in great shape. I don't need to be coddled."

They pulled into the parking lot and Drew shut off the engine, then turned to face her. "So hear me out," he said, resting his left hand on the steering wheel. "I don't know if you realize it, but it's not often that I get a day like we had on Tuesday. An afternoon of simple pleasures like a cone of ice cream and a nap on a porch swing. I liked being with you, and I think you liked being with me, and for once it had nothing to do with who I am or…" He ran his hand through his hair. "Or my bank balance, to be honest."

"Why would I care about your bank balance?" Harper puckered her brows. Sure, he had to be successful to have his stores, but Dan and Adele had never said anything about Drew's financial status.

"Most people do," he admitted. "And a lot of the time personal value is determined by the zeroes after your name. But you don't care, do you?"

"I don't even know how much you make," she replied, not quite sure where this was all going. Was he saying he was rich? After all, hiring out a helicopter wasn't something you did when you lived paycheck to paycheck.

"You really don't," he marveled, a smile tugging at his lips. "Harper, my net worth last year was—"

He gave a number that had her lips dropping open and her eyes widening as she gave a very unladylike exclamation.

He chuckled. "So you didn't know. See? This is why I liked being with you. You accepted me at face value. That doesn't happen much anymore."

She was still reeling from the fact that he was a multimillionaire. Drew never put on airs. He wore faded jeans and T-shirts. Drove a pickup, from what he'd said before. He was…ordinary.

But not, she reminded herself. He traveled extensively. Owned a chain of stores. Could apparently rent himself a luxury vehicle and book a custom heli tour at a moment's notice. And he'd hidden that part of himself from her. She was a little bit hurt by that.

"You should have been honest with me," she said, her lips a thin line. "I don't like being lied to, Drew. Or being made a fool of." God, she'd accused him of being extravagant. She felt so stupid.

"That wasn't my intention at all. I just never know who

to trust. If someone likes me for me or if they're after some sort of advantage. I thought that if you knew about the money, it wouldn't have been the same. It wasn't meant to deceive you, I promise. I wanted to enjoy being a regular guy. The last week or so I've felt like an ordinary guy again. I kind of lost touch with that side of me."

She understood that, even though she was still embarrassed. After all, she had her own trust issues. How could she be angry at someone for dealing with their issues in their own way?

"So why the helicopter? Why now?"

He reached over and took her hand. "Because I like you. Because I have fun with you, and this is top-notch fun. I can treat you to something because I want to, not because you expect it, and there's something cool about that, you know? So please, come with me. Let's fly over the Rockies, go for a hike, eat lunch in an alpine meadow. There's no one I'd rather do this with."

She couldn't say no to him, and she suspected that would prove to be her biggest downfall. "I'm scared of heights."

"You'll forget all about it when we're in the air and you take in the scenery. Plus you can hold my hand." He wiggled his eyebrows.

"You're incorrigible," she replied, but knew she was about to get into a helicopter and face one of her biggest fears.

At least it wasn't zip-lining in the jungle.

The helicopter ride was frightening at first, but once they were up in the air it was like nothing Harper had ever experienced. She thought of her father, who had made a career out of flying, and wondered if he felt this same awe every time he looked out his cockpit window. She and Drew were sitting in the back, headsets on, and before long she had her face pressed to the window as the pilot took them on a tour over peaks and through valleys that made her stomach swoop. Puffy clouds dotted a perfect blue sky and made shadows on the brownish-grey mountains. Turquoise glacial lakes dotted the valleys, mineral deposits creating the vivid colours made brighter by the sun's rays.

"Okay?" Drew asked once, and she nodded quickly. He'd been right, of course. Once in the air, the magnificence of the scenery had chased away any lingering fears. It was amazing! And she never would have done it if he hadn't nudged her out of her comfort zone.

The pilot approached a grassy peak and set the helicopter down with barely a bump. Harper's heart beat fast as she unbuckled her seat belt and Drew helped her out of the aircraft, holding her hand and then reaching for their bags. Together they scurried south, away from the rotating blades, and Drew waved the pilot off. He'd be back in two hours to pick them up. In the meantime, they could explore the meadow and valley, take pictures, and eat the picnic he'd had specially prepared by the Cascade kitchens.

Harper had never felt glamorous before, but she did now.

When the helicopter was gone and her ears stopped ringing, she grinned up at Drew. "Well. I didn't faint."

"You were a trooper. Though I thought you were going to lose your breakfast when we landed. You got pretty pale."

"Funny," she mused. "Way up in the air it seems fine. Get within a hundred feet of the ground and my nerves..." She made a zooming motion with her hand.

"Come on. Let's get your camera out so you can take some pictures."

She opened her bag and took out her camera, attached the lens she wanted and zipped it all back up again. "Ready," she said, with a wide smile.

* * *

They descended a bit into an alpine meadow and Drew caught his breath. It was stunningly gorgeous. An endless blue sky soared above, punctuated with nearby peaks and swooped with green valleys. While the drop-off spot had been solid rock and sparse brush, the meadow was positively verdant. As they ventured along the trail, he spotted the nodding blue heads of harebells and the spiky blooms of red paintbrush flowers. There were glacier lilies and the more vibrant yellow of alpine buttercups.

Harper had stopped and was fiddling with her camera, setting up for pictures. It was breathtaking. "It's beautiful, isn't it?"

He nodded, not saying anything. Instead he reached into his bag and took out his camera. The point-and-shoot eliminated the need for any complicated settings, but the waterproof and shockproof features meant it stood up to the most rugged of his adventures. There was no reason why he couldn't get his own photos, even if they weren't artistic like Harper's.

They each wandered, looking for good vantage spots and unique shots, until Harper made her way over to him again. "Here," she said, and she took her camera from around her neck. "I won't make it complicated for you. It's on auto and all you have to do is turn the zoom in or out, and shoot."

"Harper. This is your camera. I mean, it's like giving a teenager a Porsche and saying take it for a spin."

She laughed. "Not quite. Besides, you'd tell a kid to put on his seat belt and I'm telling you to keep that strap around your neck."

He chuckled. "Yes, boss."

"Now go have some fun."

"You're sure?"

"When I first picked up a camera, I didn't want a long

lesson about what everything meant. I wanted to look through the lens and frame my shot. I wanted to play. The rest came later, when I fell in love with it and wanted to learn how to be better. Today's your day for playing." She touched his arm. Then she leaned up and placed a kiss on his cheek.

He obeyed, because he was amazed at the level of trust she'd put in him, and he was humbled by what she'd shared. His first few shots were of the wide expanse of the meadow, getting a feel for the heavy instrument in his hands.

But then he took pictures of her. Walking down the path, her pack on her back. The way she turned and her ponytail bobbed from the hole in the back of her ball cap. She didn't go far before she found a large rock and sat upon it, taking off the pack and rolling her shoulders. He was patient—he remembered her saying that patience was important—and got what he felt was a perfect shot of her relaxing on the rock, one booted foot on the grey stone, her arms resting across her knee as she took a breather, looking off into the distance.

It had been two weeks and a handful of encounters, and yet…he felt a strange, uncomfortable stirring in his chest. He was falling for her, he realized. And not because she was so pretty or that they had the outdoors in common, though that certainly helped. It was who she was on the inside. Vulnerable and yet trusting. Easygoing and yet with a perfectionist side he saw each time he viewed one of her photos. She had a quick sense of humor and a ready smile, and a bigger sense of adventure than she gave herself credit for. If there was anything that he didn't like, it was that she seemed really insecure about her personal relationships. He supposed being bounced around as an air force kid would do that, but he got the feeling there was something more, too. Something she hadn't shared with him. He could hardly ask her to when they both knew his place in her life was temporary. It wasn't like he'd shared his deepest secrets, either.

She looked over, her eyes shaded by the brim of the ball cap, but her smile bright and warm. When he was with her things seemed to fall into place. Which was weird, because he already had the life he wanted.

Didn't he?

That he questioned it at all troubled him, so he turned away and took a few more photos, focusing on a crown-like peak off to his right.

When he finished, he tried a few close-ups of some flowers, particularly the red paintbrush and the harebells. There were bearberries, too, and birds—so many birds. A grey one that reminded him of the whisky jack but wasn't quite the same. He bet Harper knew.

When he went back to the rock, she was leaned back on it, sunning herself. Even though he knew he shouldn't, he perched on the edge, leaned over and touched his lips to hers.

"Mmm," she hummed, and his blood raced. "Hello there."

"This is a nice piece of equipment."

"I assume you mean my camera," she said, opening one eye as she squinted against the sun.

"Oh, that, too," he replied, grinning.

She pushed up from the rock with a laugh. "You're incorrigible."

"So I've been told already today."

She laughed again. "Are you hungry? We can eat the picnic now if you want."

"I could eat."

He sat down next to her, but first took off her camera and handed it over. She put the cap on the lens and set it carefully beside her, then reached for the pack and the goodies inside. The first thing to emerge was a bottle of water. He uncapped it, took a drink and then handed it over to her.

Her throat bobbed as she swallowed, and then she licked her lips to catch any remaining moisture and he clenched his jaw. Tuesday night had whetted his appetite for her and now he couldn't stop thinking about holding her in his arms and kissing her. He didn't remember the last time a woman had held his thoughts captive quite so readily.

She handed the bottle back and then dug into the insulated pack. "What's in here?" she asked, digging around. She pulled out a package and peered at the label. "Hmm. Smoked turkey and gouda on light rye. Yours?"

He reached for it. "I'm guessing. I have no idea what's in there, so keep digging."

She took out a dish of crudités, and then another with a quinoa and chickpea salad—the vegetarian option—and finally strawberries, raspberries and plump blackberries with crème fraiche.

"Wow," she said, looking at the selections spread out over the rock. "This is amazing."

"I asked for a picnic and we got a feast." He had unwrapped his sandwich, but held it in his hand, forgotten, as he watched her take out a fork for her salad. She fluffed the grains a little bit, tasted and closed her eyes. "Oh, that's lovely."

She was lovely. And she appreciated everything. He loved that about her.

They ate for a while in silence, enjoying the view and the fine weather, a little cooler at the higher altitude but still perfectly comfortable. "It feels like we're picnicking on top of the world," he said, brushing off his hands and reaching for a baby carrot.

"Not quite. But close." She sighed, a happy, complete sound. "We are going to be able to hike a bit, yeah? Before they come back? There's a view from that ridge that I think is going to be spectacular."

"Do you feel up to that?"

"Yeah, I'm fine, particularly since I was saved the climb. Actually, the last few days I've felt great. Adele worries. She'd probably have a bird if she knew I was up here right now."

"She knows." He put down the crust of his bread and looked into her eyes. "I got a call from Dan last night."

"About this?" Her brows puckered above her nose.

"No, something else. But I mentioned today and he asked if I thought this was a good idea."

She hesitated for a moment before speaking again. "You didn't tell me that."

"I wasn't sure if I should. I don't want to make things more tense between you guys, you know?"

She nodded, looking down. "It's not even that it's particularly tense. I'm pregnant, not an invalid."

He laughed a little. "You certainly aren't." Then his smile slipped. "Dan accused me of trying to impress you."

She met his gaze. "Money doesn't impress me, Drew."

"Thank God. And I already knew that. Truly, I did this because I wanted to do something special and fun for you. Not to show off."

When she didn't answer, he reached out and touched her chin with his index finger, nudging a little so she'd look at him.

"What? Don't you think you're worth a little spoiling?"

She moved her head away from his finger and he knew he'd touched a nerve. "I'm sorry. I didn't mean to upset you."

"It's not that. It's more…oh, it's complicated."

"Then we don't have to talk about it now if you don't want." He let the matter go and reached for the dish of berries and the other of cream. He plucked out a raspberry, smeared it with some cream and offered it to her. “Peace offering?”

A smile flirted with her lips. “I can’t resist berries.”

“Or me?”

“Or you. And I’m scared for you to know it.”

He popped the berry in her mouth. “I won’t hurt you, Harper. And I’ll be honest with you. Eyes wide open.”

She chewed the berry and swallowed. “Like you were about being stinkin’ rich?”

He laughed, and the sound carried over the valley. “Touché. I mean, when it comes to us. I won’t lead you on or make promises I can’t keep.”

She avoided his eyes and selected another berry. “I appreciate that.”

They packed up their picnic and shouldered their packs, ready to hike through the meadow to the peaks beyond before looping back again. The incline was only slightly challenging, and the views from the top were astounding. Drew took out his camera and took several pictures, and then watched as Harper worked her magic. She took her time, adjusting her position, working with her equipment, squinting at the light. When she was satisfied, she beckoned him over to where the faint trail met a junction. “This way is to the ridge,” she said, pointing, and he looked at the incline. If she was up to it, he was totally game.

They went only maybe half a kilometer when she stopped, lifted her camera and fired off a quick few shots. “Look at that lake. Isn’t it stunning? Now look at what’s around it.”

He squinted and looked, and she laughed. “Here.” She held up her camera, though she kept it around her neck. “Look to the right of the lake, about halfway up, and use the zoom.”

When he did, he saw a bull elk. “How did I miss that before?”

"It's a ways away, you know." He took a quick picture of the entire lake, and then adjusted to take one of the elk, always aware that they were tethered closely together by her camera strap. She smelled like something light and floral, fresh air, and the light sweat from hiking.

"Harper," he murmured, releasing the camera. He turned her toward him and cupped her face. "Damn," he whispered, and then kissed her. He wanted to do more, so much more, but knew it would be wrong. He was leaving and it would be unfair to her. But he wanted to, so much. She tasted like heaven and felt so alive in his arms. The camera dug into his diaphragm but he didn't care. This place was perfect, the day was perfect, and kissing her right now, with the Rockies all around them, was the most natural and important thing in the world.

She sighed against his lips as the kiss eased. "Oh, Drew. What are we doing?"

"I don't know. I just know it feels good."

She nodded. "Me, too. When you kiss me…"

She broke off, took a deep, wobbly breath.

"What, Harper? What happens when I kiss you?"

"I forget about everything. There's only you and me and all the things you make me feel. I know it's not wise but I can't seem to help myself."

"That's a dangerous thing to say to a man like me."

She looked up at him then, her blue eyes wide and full of wonder. "No, it's not. Because I trust you." She smiled a little. "You said you would never lie to me."

He swallowed tightly and put an inch or two between them. When it came to relationships he wasn't reliable, and the last thing he wanted to do was hurt Harper. She was too special. He knew what a broken heart looked like and he didn't want to be responsible for that again.

"You shouldn't trust me," he replied, his voice rough. "I'm good in business, Harper, but I suck at romance. Lies or not." He remembered the accusations leveled at him over the last few years. Commitment-phobe. Married to his work. "My top focus is Aspen Outfitters. That's not going to change."

"I know." She lifted her hand and ran her fingers over his jawline. "But I also know I trust you because you've been honest about that from the beginning. I'm not asking for more than you're offering, Drew."

But that was the problem. As he kissed her again, he knew he wanted to offer her more than he should. And to do so would only lead to hurt all around.

Maybe Dan was right. Maybe he didn't know what he was doing.

CHAPTER TEN

THEY MADE THEIR way back toward the crest where they'd be picked up again, and Harper paused to catch her breath. There was more going on in her mind and body than simple physical exertion. Right now she was simply full of Drew. The way he looked and felt and tasted. What he'd said and the husky sound of his voice…she was in huge danger of falling for him. There was so much more than charm and charisma. There was a good, strong man beneath that persona. A man who freely admitted that work came before personal relationships, so why couldn't she seem to stay away?

Instead they came to an uneven bit of ground, and Drew held out his hand. She took it, loving the feel of her palm against his.

And when she was over the rocks, she kept her fingers entwined with his. Days. They had only days left to enjoy each other. Why shouldn't they?

She looked over at him and he sensed her gaze and looked back, a smile on his face. Harper felt something expand in her chest that was new and exciting. She rather thought it might be happiness. Did she dare hold on to it, even for a brief time? Her whole life she'd held herself apart from relationships, always afraid of getting hurt when they ended. Until she moved here, and she made a best friend—Adele. For the first time, she was confident that despite any awkwardness now, she and Adele would still be best friends and they'd work their way through the current dynamic.

She wasn't afraid to care for Drew right now. She had no unrealistic expectations. Maybe it was time to live for the moment. Take chances, and live life with a bit of messiness. It had to be better than always being the one behind the lens, watching life happen to other people. She was so tired of being on the outside, even if she'd been the one to put herself there. The revelation was amazingly liberating.

"You're awfully quiet," Drew said, tugging on her hand.

"Walking is good for thinking, and thinking is good for working out problems."

"Do you have problems to be worked out?" They made it to the crest and she leaned back, stretching with her hands on her hips.

"A few. It's more realizations, I guess." Her pulse quickened, a little nervous about what she was going to say. "I think I've spent a good portion of my life avoiding risks. But it's not really living, you know?"

He squeezed her fingers. "Hiding behind your lens?"

She laughed a little. "Maybe. And I got comfortable there. Never letting myself get too close to people because I knew eventually I'd have to say goodbye. But I can't seem to do that with you. I know you're leaving soon. I know this will go nowhere after next week. But if I shut this down…" She caught her breath. "If I shut this down, what's between us, I know I'm going to regret it."

He stared at her for a long moment. "What do you want, Harper?"

Courage began to blossom in her chest, even as the faint sound of helicopter rotors started to pulse through the air. "I want to live. I want to stop playing it safe all of the time. I want to get out of my comfort zone now and again and do something daring."

"You don't call what you're doing for Adele and Dan daring?" Drew lifted an eyebrow.

"Yes and no. I mean, I'm really pregnant. But when this

is over, the whole plan is to go back to my safe and boring life. At first that was all I really wanted, but what if that's not enough anymore? What if I want…helicopter rides through the mountains? Kisses on my porch? Surprises?"

The sound grew louder and she knew she had to get this out before the pilot landed. "The last few weeks, seeing you…it's been good for me. I can feel it. I've been so afraid of getting hurt, but I think what's always made me so cautious is being blindsided."

"What do you mean?"

"I mean, every time I moved, it came out of the blue. My dad would get a change of orders and we'd move. New base, new town, new schools. New teachers, new kids who always stared at the new girl in class. For the first few times, I made good friends, but then it hurt so much to move again and say goodbye. Once I hit nine or ten, I stopped making friends. I understood that I'd have to leave again. By the time I was twelve, I had my first camera, and it became my friend. It never got left behind."

Drew let out a breath. "Jeez, Harper. That sounds so lonely. I was really lucky to have my brother and sisters, you know? And we lived in the same house growing up." He shook his head. "Man. You were lonely and I felt claustrophobic. I love my family, but I couldn't wait to get out on my own. The last thing I wanted was to be stuck in one place."

She squeezed his fingers. "I'm not blindsided this time. Like you said, eyes open." The chopper got closer and the wind started to whip her hair as she raised her voice to be heard. "I'm ready for an adventure, Drew!"

His only answer was a quicksilver smile as the chopper hovered, inching its way toward the bluff. He held her hand tightly as they moved to the helicopter. And when they were buckled up and the chopper lifted off and then dropped over the side to skim down the valley, Harper kept her eyes open and went along for the ride.

Drew put his pack in the back of the car and took a deep breath. He had no idea what to do next. His feelings for Harper were complicated, but he'd felt in control of them. Or at least in control of how the next week would play out. Maybe seeing each other a few more times, enjoying each other's company and a mutual goodbye at the end with no hard feelings.

Today had changed all that.

She hadn't said anything since they'd disembarked. They had maybe fifteen minutes in the car to decide what would happen next. And he knew what he wanted to happen and what should happen.

He should drop her off and go back to the hotel. And yet, he wasn't ready for the day to be over. Harper deserved to be treated like the special woman she was, and he wanted to be the man to do it.

Neither said anything until they got close to the townsite exit. Then Drew looked over at her. "I don't want today to end. Come back to the hotel for dinner."

He had to turn his attention back to the road but he felt her gaze on his face. "To dinner?"

He nodded, glancing over again. "I can take you home to change. It's been too wonderful a day for it to end now."

She sighed. "We could always order a pizza. You don't need to go to all this trouble."

"I want to," he insisted. They slowed for a group of tourists crossing the street. "It's not trouble, Harper. It's a pleasure. I want to spend more time with you. And I want to…to show you that you're special."

"At your hotel."

He understood what she was and wasn't saying. "Yes,

at my hotel. But it doesn't have to be there. I don't want to pressure you into anything."

There was a pause of perhaps two seconds, and then she answered, "The Cascade sounds fine."

And with that admission, the air snapped with electricity and the anticipation of what was to come. What did he do? Charm her over dinner? Drive her home again as soon as the meal was over? Wait for her to make a move? He felt as unsure as a teenager faced with undoing a girl's bra for the first time. One wrong move and it would be all over. Maybe he should just play it cool.

He parked in her narrow driveway and she unbuckled her seat belt. Drew reached over and took her hand before she could take the keys out of the ignition.

"I'm not sure what to say or do right now," he admitted. "This is nerve-racking as hell."

She blew out a breath. "For me, too. But first I have to change into something more appropriate. Do you mind if I have a quick shower?" She pulled her hand away and opened her door.

It helped that she was also nervous. Or maybe it didn't… perhaps one of them being tied up in knots was more than enough. Regardless, he followed her lead and got out of the car, then grabbed both their packs while she got her camera bag. He tried to block out the idea of her under the hot shower spray and instead on the evening ahead… which was nearly as bad.

The day had been warm, but the wind took on a sudden chill as the sun went under a cloud. Drew looked up, surprised to see a wall of clouds closing in.

Once inside the house, Drew put down the backpacks and reached for Harper's hand. "Can I kiss you?"

She blushed prettily, the colour highlighting the freckles on her nose as she nodded. He stepped forward and kissed her, a soft, gentle hello of a kiss that reached in and grabbed him right by the heart with its hesitancy and sweetness.

Leaving her was going to be harder than she knew.

He broke off the kiss. "Go have your shower. I'm starving."

"I won't be long. There are drinks in the fridge if you want one."

He got himself a can of ginger ale and settled in the living room on the sofa while the water ran for the shower. How was this evening really going to play out? There was no question he wanted to kiss her again. But how far did he want to go?

His brother's words rang in his ears: *I hope you know what you're doing.*

He didn't. Not even close.

She came back out a few minutes later, her hair wet and darker than usual, which made her pale skin and blue eyes stand out. She wore a light, floral maxi dress that accentuated her breasts but fell in soft folds to the floor, where her toes peeked out from little sandals. She came to sit beside him and that floral scent that had only been hinted at earlier now filled the air around him. Her shampoo, he realized. Whatever it was, it made his blood stir.

"Feel better?" he asked.

"Much." She smiled softly. "Are you ready?"

"I am if you are."

She got up and put her hand on her lower back.

He rose and reached over, touching the muscles just above her sacrum. "Is your back bothering you?"

"A little. The doctor said it might bother me a bit because my body is changing and tendons and stuff." She laughed a bit, but he stood behind her and used his thumbs to rub on the spot where she'd pressed her hand. Over the years he'd come to rely on a massage therapist a lot to deal with aches and pains after difficult expeditions.

"Oh my God, that feels good," she said, her voice almost a moan as she relaxed beneath his fingertips.

He tried not to react to her words. It was difficult, because the attraction was insane, and having his hands on her was arousing, plain and simple. But this wasn't the moment. This was a time for being caring and helpful. As he massaged a tight muscle, the first rumblings of thunder began.

"Have you tried yoga? Like, a prenatal kind or something? It might help with any stiffness or lower back issues."

"I haven't. I've been so busy that my exercise routine has been walking and getting out for the odd hike."

His thumbs rubbed in concentric circles. "Well, maybe you can look into it. Or go for prenatal massage."

"If it's anything like you're doing right now, that's a brilliant idea," she murmured. "That feels amazing."

You have no idea, he thought, but instead he worked on the tight muscles that she probably overused today in addition to the changes happening inside her body.

Lightning flashed outside the window, followed by a deeper rumble of thunder a few seconds later. "Looks like we're in for some rain," he mused.

"I'm glad we're not in the chopper now." She gasped a little as he touched a particularly tight area.

"Me, too."

After a few minutes she straightened. "Thanks, Drew," she said, and despite the "normal" tone to her voice, there was a huskiness underlying it that lent an intimacy to the moment. "I think that's good."

Maybe, but touching her had been a mistake. He didn't want to stop. Maybe not ever.

Harper grabbed her purse and Drew reached into his pocket for the keys. He didn't know how the evening would end, but as long as he was with Harper, it was bound to be perfect.

* * *

Harper chose to wait in the lounge while Drew cleaned up. Being in his hotel room might be a little too dangerous. She was up for an adventure, but not looking to be totally reckless. Drew was a particularly potent temptation she wasn't sure she could resist.

She was halfway through a glass of sparkling water when Drew reappeared, and she caught her breath.

He hadn't been more than fifteen minutes, but he'd showered and changed into dress pants and a blue shirt, open at the collar but pressed and expensive looking. That women turned their heads to watch him didn't escape her attention, and she smiled up at him as he approached. He was so handsome. And his smile…it warmed her from the inside out, like it was just for her.

"What a transformation," she said, turning to him. "And fast."

"I told you that happens when I'm properly motivated."

They were led to their table in the corner, looking out over the townsite and valley below. At one end of the view, the sun was still shining, but at the other, storm clouds rolled in, dark grey and ominous. As she watched, a flash of lightning forked down from a black cloud. "We're in for some weather," she observed, and the electricity of the storm mirrored the excitement inside her. Today had marked a turning point and it left her feeling off balance but also exhilarated.

"Would you like another sparkling water? A virgin cocktail?"

She turned from the view, scanned the drink menu and looked up at the waiter. "Could I get a Paloma Fizz, no tequila?"

"Of course. And you, sir?"

He ordered a whiskey, neat, and the waiter slipped away.

"Drew, this is lovely. Truly."

"I'm glad. Much better than take-out pizza, don't you think?"

She laughed lightly. "Pizza has its place," she replied, fiddling with her napkin. "But you're right. There's something about being here…the hotel is one of my favorites. The steps and railings are practically works of art." She looked down and softened her voice. "You're spoiling me today."

The waiter returned with their drinks and she took a sip of the rosemary-infused grapefruit soda. The sparkles sat on her tongue for a moment and she sighed, enjoying the setting and the company. Maybe she wasn't high maintenance, but it was nice feeling special and pampered now and again. She looked over at Drew and the curl of attraction wound through her again.

"What?" he asked.

Her cheeks heated. "Nothing." She focused on her menu but felt his gaze on her as she perused the selections. The light through the windows darkened from the storm clouds, and a young man clad in black came around with a lighter and lit the candles on the table. Thunder rumbled outside, a low growl that made Harper glad they weren't outside any longer.

They ordered and the appetizers were served quickly and discreetly. She took one bite of the watercress and endive salad and sighed with happiness at the fruity sharpness of the fig dressing. Drew indulged in escargot, and then they dined on risotto primavera and lobster carbonara. Rain spattered on the windows but then the storm moved off, onward through the valley and toward the foothills.

She was starting to get full when she asked what she'd been wondering all day. "Did you really say Aspen made thirty million last year? Three-zero?"

He nodded. "Yeah. Up from twenty-six and change the year before. We've been seeing steady growth. We also do a profit share with our employees, so twice a year they get an extra deposit into their account. I keep them happy, they keep me in business."

"I really didn't have any idea. Neither Dan or Adele said anything."

"Does it matter?" He took a sip of ice water and watched her steadily.

That question was easy to answer. "No. It doesn't make you any more likable…or unlikable, either." She gave a sideways grin. "I'm just…wow. You really are driven, aren't you?"

He shrugged. "Like I said the other day. Work hard, play hard. Now I have a question for you."

"Sure."

"If you'd known I was a millionaire, would your answer at the wedding have been different?"

She started to laugh, and dabbed her lips with her napkin. She wasn't insulted in the least. "Do I look like the type who would see dollar signs?"

He chuckled, too. "No, but I kind of hoped you were. Because then I wouldn't have taken it so personally."

She lifted an eyebrow. "I'd feel bad, if I thought you really meant that."

His grin grew. "I like how you challenge me, Harper. I like it a lot."

Money really didn't turn her head, but she had to admit that she did see him differently now. Not better, not worse, but just different. He was a millionaire at age twenty-eight with a chain of his own stores. It was difficult not to respect that. It also widened the gap between them significantly. There were months she could barely pay the rent.

But none of that really mattered when they were together. Sure, days like today didn't make him bat an eye, but deep down, Drew was the guy who'd talked to a bighorn sheep and enjoyed a cone of ice cream on a busy street. The one who rubbed her ankle while she slept on a porch swing. Who made her laugh without trying, and made her toes curl when he kissed her.

They ordered dessert—Earl Grey panna cotta for her and chestnut tiramisu for him, and she let the flavors sit on her tongue. "I've never had something like this in my life," she sighed happily. "Today has been…oh, Drew. It's been like a fairy tale. And tomorrow I get to go back to my humdrum life."

It also appeared the storms weren't over. A new front rolled down through the mountains, a wall of foreboding cloud that brought with it unsettling wind and flashes of lightning. Thunder growled and then boomed, close enough that she jumped when it rattled the crystal on the table.

"You should see your eyes," he said, smiling a little.

"I'm very glad we're safe and sound inside." The lights flickered but stayed on. "And you didn't even flinch."

"I love thunderstorms." At her raised eyebrow, he laughed. "We're really different in some ways, aren't we?" He reached over and took her hand. "I know you moved around a lot as a kid. That you had a hard time making friends and establishing relationships. But there's more, isn't there? Something that holds you back."

"Why do you say that?"

"Because it's not friends you shy away from. It's intimacy. Someone hurt you." His gaze locked with hers. "I know because you have the same look in your eyes as someone else did once, when I broke their heart."

The rest of her dessert was forgotten. Whether he'd initiated the breakup or not, he hadn't come out of it unscathed.

And for the first time, she spoke about Jared.

"The truth is, I did meet someone once, and it was one of those crazy whirlwind-attraction deals. I fell like a ton of bricks at the ripe old age of twenty-two. He was hot and funny and sexy and I was really swept away, thinking he could be The One. He proposed, and I was thrilled. We were going to elope and just be crazy. Instead, he broke off the engagement and disappeared. I was heartbroken—and blindsided yet again. Oddly enough, that was when my photography really started to take off."

"Because you kept hiding."

"And damn, but I was good at it."

His thumb traced circles over her hand, and she blinked back a little moisture that had gathered in the corners of her eyes. "I feel so foolish now. But then…it was as if no one thought I was worth hanging around for."

"So what changed?"

"Adele. She's the best friend I've ever had. I've made a life for myself here. I put down the roots I've never really had before, but I'm still not totally happy. I've been so busy trying to protect my life I stopped really living it. I want to start living again, even if it's just for a few weeks." She held his gaze and took a breath. "With you."

The lights flickered again, but his thumb kept circling, the pressure warm and soothing. "As long as you know that I can't stay. That the plan hasn't changed." The smile had slid off his face, and he was as serious as she'd ever seen him.

"Oh, I know that. I'm just tired of denying myself things that make me happy because they might not last forever. That not living, that's pure avoidance."

She turned her hand over and linked her fingers with his. "I'm going to miss you when you're gone. But I want to look back on this time as a happy memory, not another case of me choosing the safe route and missing out."

She'd never considered Drew the kind of man to blush, but right now heat was creeping up his neck and into his cheeks. "Then don't leave yet. When we finish dinner…come back to my room. The night doesn't have to end."

"We don't exactly have time to waste, do we?" Her words came out breathy, as if she'd been walking too fast.

He let out a big breath. "I don't… I just…" His eyes were wide and serious. "Despite what you may think of me, this isn't something I take lightly. Or casually."

"I'm glad." Nerves bubbled, both from anticipation and from anxiety. This was all new territory.

Moments later Drew signed the slip charging the meal to his room, and then held out his hand. "Shall we?" he asked.

She put her hand in his again and let him lead her out of the restaurant. They were going to his hotel room. She wasn't sure what she wanted to happen, but she knew something was going to. She wanted it to.

They rode up the elevator in silence, nervousness flooding her from head to toe. Her sandals made slapping sounds on the hall carpet until they reached his door and he waved his key card over the sensor.

His suite was gorgeous. She'd been in Cascade rooms before, doing before-the-wedding photos and the like, but she'd never been in this one. A massive sitting area was flanked by a dining table and chairs. Off to the left was the bedroom, and she took a few steps toward it, as if drawn by a magnet. The king-size bed was the centerpiece, covered with a fluffy gold duvet. Throw pillows in jewel tones were placed strategically on the bed. The view from the window was staggering in its beauty.

She was here. In his hotel room. The Presidential Suite, wasn't it?

The door shut with a quiet click, and then he was there behind her, his hands on her shoulders as he leaned forward and kissed her hair.

Her entire body went into high alert. When a man like Drew Brimicombe put his full attention on a woman, it was an intoxicating feeling.

"Hi," she said, knowing it sounded stupid, unsure of what else to say.

"Hi." His breath was warm on her neck and goose bumps broke out over her skin. "How are you?"

She bit down on her lip. "Nervous. Afraid of doing the wrong thing."

He turned her to face him. "Nothing you say or do will be the wrong thing."

"Really?" She ran her hands over the soft fabric of her skirt. "I'm pretty sure I can be an idiot very easily. Like today, when you told me you were rich. I felt pretty stupid. This is the Presidential Suite, isn't it?"

That sexy grin crawled up his cheek once more. "I told you I was able to snag a cancellation. It was the only room available."

She shook her head but laughed a little. This whole thing was surreal.

He took her fingers in his. "Harper, I just want you to know that tonight is entirely up to you and what you want. You're in control."

When he said it, she realized exactly how much she'd felt out of control the last few months. Once she'd taken the pregnancy test, her life hadn't really been her own. But this decision was, and it felt good.

Her heart pounded so hard she could feel it against her ribs. Her breath shortened; she had never been one to take the lead in sexual situations. But this time he was waiting, leaving it up to her, giving her complete autonomy. It was a dizzying thought. She reached out and put her hand against his chest, touching him but still keeping him a few inches away. Her heart pounded, from excitement but also fear. "I do want this," she said on a breath. "So much it hurts."

"Then tell me." His thumbs were hooked in his front pockets, and she saw them close tighter over the fabric. "Show me."

She stood on tiptoe and kissed him, softly, slowly, as if they had all the time in the world. When she'd tasted her fill—for the time being—she stood back away from him.

And knew this wasn't the right time, or the right place. She was so close to giving her heart away. If they made love, it would only make things worse. She knew he was leaving. But she was conveniently ignoring the depth of her feelings. Right now, looking up at him, she was perilously close to losing herself.

"It's not the right time, is it?" he asked, as if reading her thoughts.

She shook her head.

He took a big breath and then let it out. "Then let's just hang out. Watch a movie and raid the mini bar for snacks."

Relief flooded through her. "Oh, I've always wanted to do that!"

He laughed, and squeezed her hand. "I just want to spend time with you. In bed, out of it…it doesn't matter. Look at the pay-per-view and pick something out." He gave her a stern look. "No porn. I'm already going to need a few minutes to, uh…"

She burst out laughing. Oh, she could love him so very easily. He was sexy and kind and made her smile all the time.

And when they started the movie and she lay on the bed curled up in his arms, it was the best feeling in the world.

When Harper woke, it was twilight.

She carefully rolled to her side and watched him sleep, his lips slightly parted and his eyelashes on the crests of his cheeks. They were on top of the covers, and the TV was shut off. She must have fallen asleep first. She didn't remember watching the end of the movie. It had been so cozy in Drew's arms.

It had been a perfect day, better than any she could

ever remember. Her heart caught. She couldn't fall in love with him. She'd promised herself she wouldn't. And yet now, watching him sleep, there was an expansive feeling in her chest that told her she was dangerously close to losing her heart.

To the one man who didn't want it. Who wasn't looking for love. *It's okay*, she told herself. *I knew all along he was going. I'm going to cherish this time as a special memory.*

The problem was, she was starting to feel as if she didn't want just memories. She wanted *him*.

A funny sound reached her ears, some sort of music. She blinked and realized it was her phone, which she'd left in her purse. It stopped ringing, but then started again, and with a sigh she slid off the bed and tiptoed out to the living room to grab it.

The display showed Adele's number. She kept her voice low so she hopefully wouldn't wake Drew.

"Hello, Adele."

"Oh, good, you're there. I've been worried sick."

"You have? I didn't answer the first time you called because I was sleeping."

It wasn't exactly a lie.

"But I texted you like ten times."

"Sorry. It was a long nap."

Adele let out a long breath. "Okay. I'm sorry. I knew you'd gone into the mountains today and then the storm blew in and the power went out and I was so worried."

Yes, because clearly she couldn't be trusted to take care of herself. Irritation flared, an emotion that felt out of place. Usually she was so easygoing. What had happened to change that? It couldn't be Adele's hovering; Harper knew her friend was just concerned. There was a lot at stake.

Maybe it was stress. Hormones. Or the fact that Drew's arrival had suddenly made her unsettled and longing for...more.

"I'm fine," she said, as kindly as she could muster. "We went early this morning and were back by late afternoon, before the storm blew in. No worries at all. I got some great pictures and it was good to be outdoors for the day. I needed it."

"And you didn't overdo it?"

Harper pinched her nose, willing herself to be patient. "No, I didn't. We took our time and rested lots. Had a picnic in the meadow at the top. I'm fine. The baby's fine."

Adele's exhale sounded relieved. "And we're still going to do lunch next week?"

Drew called her name and she went to the door of the bedroom, putting a finger to her lips as she met his gaze. "How about Tuesday?" she asked Adele. "Monday I'll be trying to catch up after this week's wedding."

"Tuesday's fine. I miss seeing you, Harper. You haven't even been here for dinner in ages. Not since we had our last appointment."

"I know. You know what summer is like. Busiest time of year."

"You know it." The conversation turned to wedding discussion and Harper rolled her eyes at Drew, eliciting a snort from him. When Adele had finally finished with her story, Harper interjected.

"Adele, I'm still really tired. I'm going to go back to bed. I don't mean to cut this off…" She wondered if her nose would grow like Pinocchio's for lying. But if she said she was in Drew's hotel room, Adele would lose her mind.

"Oh! Of course. I'll text you about Tuesday. And glad you're okay. Stay dry. I'm glad the power's back on."

That was news to Harper, and she let out a breath. "Me, too."

"Oh, one more thing. How was Drew today?"

Funny how she added it on at the very end, as an afterthought. Harper had no doubt that Adele's first priority was making sure Harper was home and okay, but she also knew that Adele would be dying to know about her outing with Drew.

"Oh, fine. I'm sure Dan told you he hired a helicopter. I braved it, even with my fear of heights. So I didn't even have to hike that far." She rolled her eyes at Drew again, and his brown eyes lit up with mischief. "I'll tell you all about it at lunch."

"Okay. Well…talk soon."

Harper hung up and went to sit on the edge of the bed. "Adele was worried. But apparently the power is back on."

He nodded. "You fell asleep. I didn't have the heart to wake you. Then you took me with you." His smile was adorable.

Then he leaned up on an elbow and kissed her, just a simple, sweet kiss, but it caught her by surprise. Then he pulled back, lifted her hand and kissed it. Despite all her best intentions, Harper felt herself make the remaining slide straight into love.

CHAPTER ELEVEN

DREW HELD HARPER'S hand in his and tried not to show that inside he was freaking out.

It wasn't that he wanted her to leave, or that their time together had been a mistake. He was freaking out because for the first time in his life, he wanted to stay somewhere and never leave.

With her.

Her eyes sparkled at him with good humor. There was nothing he wanted more than for her to spend the rest of the night right here, in his bed.

But she couldn't. The very idea made his insides freeze with fear. Instead he looked into her eyes, lifted her hand and kissed her fingers.

He was falling in love. At least that's what he figured it was, because it was unlike any other feeling he'd experienced. It should be impossible to feel terrified and happy all at once. Right now terrified was tangling with desire and he had no idea what to do about it.

"I should probably get going," she said softly, and there was a pause. Was she waiting for him to ask her to stay?

He wanted to. God, did he want to. But he knew it was better for everyone if he didn't. "I suppose you have work in the morning."

"Yeah, and a wedding rehearsal tomorrow night." But her easy words didn't reach her eyes. It wasn't how he wanted their date to end, but sex was out of the question. It wouldn't be fair to either of them. Besides, she had enough complications with the pregnancy in the months ahead.

It had nothing to do with being afraid. Nothing.

"Harper, about earlier… I want you to know that I think we made the right decision. I want to be with you. It's just that if we go all in with this, it's going to make it harder next Friday when I fly out."

She nodded a tiny bit. "Next Friday, then. That's the day?"

"I've got a flight early afternoon, through LA."

"You didn't mention it before."

"It happened yesterday. And today I forgot about it while we were out."

Which wasn't exactly true. He'd remembered but hadn't seen the need to bring it into the conversation. Now it seemed important. To set boundaries where a few hours ago there'd been none.

She didn't say anything, and her thumb stopped moving on his hand. The knot of panic doubled in size.

"Listen," he said softly, pulling his hand away and brushing hair away from her face. "We both know where this is going and where it isn't. I don't want to hurt you, Harper. And I don't want to make false promises." The knot started to actually hurt now. "You told me about the guy you fell for and how much it hurt when he left. I don't want to be that guy. I've been that man before and the last thing I want to do is hurt you."

"You've been honest from the beginning and so have I. I know you're not a forever kind of guy, Drew. I've got my eyes wide open, remember?"

She didn't mean the words as an accusation, so why did it feel that way?

"I know you do. But…and I can't believe I'm about to say this…it might be good for us to use a little bit of caution, at least." He wanted to kiss her so badly right now he ached with it. She looked so soft, so vulnerable, and yet determined, too. He loved that about her.

Love. Exactly the reason he had to go.

She grinned. “I’m already pregnant. We don’t have to worry too much about caution.”

He closed his eyes, trying not to smile at her dry crack at humor. “You’re deliberately misunderstanding me, and that’s okay.” He opened his eyes again. In the dim light through the blinds her eyes seemed dark and grey and her freckles were barely noticeable. He wished he was as adept with a camera as she was. She’d make a stunning photo right now. “I’m going to be back in town now and again, Harper. For the store. To see Dan. I don’t want it to be awkward or worse, tense and angry between us. Does that make sense?”

“Yes,” she breathed, and she blinked a few times. He didn’t see tears, thank God. If she cried he wouldn’t be able to handle it. “You’re protecting yourself.”

“And you.” It was true. Sure, he was panicked enough for both of them, but he also didn’t want to hurt her. “When I go, I want it to be with you smiling. If we play house for the next week, I’m not sure either of us will be able to keep our perspective.”

Her eyes flashed. “Then I’ll go right now, and we’ll let that be it. The perfect ending to a perfect day.”

It was like a punch to the gut, but he answered calmly, “If that’s what you want.”

Silence dropped over the room.

She touched his shoulder. “I’m sorry I snapped,” she murmured. “It’s just that you make me feel…” Her cheeks flamed. “Ugh, this is so hard.”

“I make you feel what?”

“Desirable. Wanted. I haven’t felt that way in a very long time. You can’t expect me to give it up after an hour.” She was bright red now. “I sound like a desperate idiot.”

“No, you don’t. And I’m glad. Because you are wanted. And very, very desirable. That’s what makes this so hard. I’m trying to do the right thing.”

He got up from the bed and reached for his shoes. "Come on. I'll take you home. And we'll both respect each other in the morning."

She laughed a little, and it put his mind at ease.

But when he kissed her goodbye at her door, his heart caught. He was in far deeper than he intended. And he wasn't sure he had it in him to stay away.

Harper didn't see Drew at all on Friday, and she spent the evening at the rehearsal for Saturday's wedding. Saturday she woke early and showered, dressing in a comfortable maxi dress for the day. Some of her more fitted clothing was getting too tight around the middle now as her waist thickened. In another month she'd really be starting to show. She put her hand to her belly and thought about the baby growing there. She hadn't even felt him or her move yet. Sometimes it was hard to believe there was really a baby in there.

At nine there was a knock on the door. She was putting makeup on and had eye shadow on only one eye when she went to answer. It was Drew, carrying a paper bag and holding a tray with cups.

"I brought breakfast," he announced, then stepped inside and gave her a kiss.

"Oh! You didn't need to do that."

"I know. But I missed seeing you yesterday, and you have the wedding all day today, so I thought this might be my window of opportunity. I went out for a morning walk and ended up here."

He looked delicious, as usual. Just jeans and a T-shirt but the way they fit his lean body made her mouth water.

And she did have to eat. Now that the sickness was gone, breakfast was no longer a challenge. She craved it.

"I haven't eaten, so thanks."

"Uh, you're lopsided." He pointed to her face.

"Oh! I was putting on makeup when you knocked. Make

yourself at home and I'll do the other eye." She grinned at him and already her heart felt lighter as she faced the day. She hadn't been quite sure how they'd left things Thursday night, but he seemed his old self. If breakfast was all she got of Drew today, she'd take it. In a heartbeat.

She didn't normally wear a lot of makeup, so it took no time at all for her to brush on her eye shadow, add a tiny bit of eyeliner and a swipe of mascara on her lashes. She went back to the kitchen with matching eyes and found Drew putting breakfast on plates.

"Egg and cheese on sourdough for you, and bacon, egg and cheese on a biscuit for me. And fruit salad."

Eggs. She craved them all the time now. Maybe her body needed the protein. Stomach growling, she sat at the table and reached for her fork, spearing a piece of melon.

"This is beyond nice. And it'll fuel me through the morning, too, until I have time to grab a protein bar or something. I have to grab snacks on the run during the day until the reception, when I can gobble a meal quickly." She took a bite of sandwich, chewed and swallowed. "Juny's started coming with me, too, as my assistant. I'm letting her do more and more. She has a good eye and she can help more when I get closer to the due date."

"Plus it takes some of the pressure off you."

"I'll confess, the last few weddings have been long and I've gotten really tired. It's been nice to have someone help set up and lug stuff from the car rather doing it all alone." She shrugged. "I can do it, but it's nice to work as a team. Sometimes it seems as if I need to be in two places at once."

"Well, you look pretty."

She nudged him. "Thank you, though compliments aren't necessary."

"It's the truth. You always look pretty. Though Dan and Adele's wedding was something else. You looked..." He paused as he searched for the right words. “Like a classic movie star.” He took the lid off her tea and slid it across the table to her. “So, was it as hard saying no to me as it is for me to say no to you?”

She met his gaze. “Is it hard to say no to me, Drew?” She held her breath, waiting for his answer.

“More than you can imagine.”

Her heart expanded. She was glad. It made her feel as if she mattered. That despite her efforts to hide, someone actually saw past the barriers she put up and saw her.

“Then no, it wasn’t as hard for me.”

He burst out laughing. “Cheeky.”

She joined in the laughter. “Naw, not really. It’s just that the guy at the wedding? That wasn’t the real Drew. Not really. I like you better now.”

His gaze warmed. “I like you, too, Harper.”

They were still staring at each other when her phone rang. She reached inside her bag and pulled it out. “It’s Juny.”

Two minutes later she hung up, turning her worried gaze to Drew. “Juny’s girlfriend, Renée, was in an accident. She’s okay, or at least she’s going to be okay, but they’re transporting her to Calgary to the Foothills Hospital.”

“Oh, no.” Drew’s face wrinkled in concern. “Does Juny need anything? Is she all right?”

“She’s fine. She wasn’t in the car, but she’s going to the hospital to be with Renée.”

“Of course. What happened?”

“Juny doesn’t quite know. I wish I could go with her, but I’ve got the wedding.”

“And she was supposed to be helping you today.”

“I can manage alone. I do it all the time.” There was no question of expecting Juny to come to work. Not with something like this. It would be a long day, but she could rest tomorrow.

"I could help you."

She'd picked up her tea, but paused before taking a drink. "You?" She chuckled. "I know I let you use my camera yesterday, but Drew."

"Ha, ha," he replied, but he persisted. "I mean, I can carry your stuff for you. Be your right hand. You need a drink or food or anything, I can help. You were planning on having extra hands today. I'm certainly not as qualified as Juny, but I can take orders."

She was touched by his offer. "You? Take orders? Mr. President and CEO?"

"Yeah, me. Unless you'd rather I not be in your professional space. I understand that."

The idea of him being with her on a job didn't bother her in the least. "No, it's not that. But you'll be bored, won't you?"

"Maybe. Maybe not."

And having someone along to do the heavy lifting did sound wonderful. "Okay, but only if you have something suitable to wear."

"If you'll run me to the hotel, I can be ready in fifteen minutes."

After Thursday night's quick change, she didn't doubt him. "Done."

"Then it's settled. Now eat, and we'll get this show on the road."

They loaded all her equipment in the car and by ten thirty they were on the way to the Cascade for Drew to change. He was back in the promised fifteen minutes, and then it was off to the bride's home in Canmore. Harper looked over at Drew, sitting so calmly in her passenger seat yet again. What was she thinking, letting him come along? It was impossible to pretend that her feelings were anything other than love. She loved him. Was in love with him. Would have taken the whole week to be with him—in all ways—and dealt with the heartbreak at the end. Maybe that was what scared her the most. She wasn't used to such a lack of emotional caution. That Drew was the one being reasonable and thinking long term was a total flip of what she figured was their usual roles.

And it wasn't like he would never be back to Banff again, was it? His store would be here. Dan was here. Just because she'd fallen in love with him didn't mean they had to rush everything.

"Penny for your thoughts," he said, his gaze on her profile.

"We don't have pennies anymore in Canada," she replied. "Remember?"

"Right. Okay, I'll round up. Nickel for your thoughts."

She chuckled and realized how much she'd laughed since he'd arrived in Banff. "You make me laugh, you know that? It's nice."

"Is that what you were thinking?"

"No."

"Do I want to know?"

"I was thinking how nice you look in that colour blue." His shirt was the same colour as the open sky. Now that they were traveling east, the peaks were beside and behind them, with the rolling foothills giving way to a pristine blue without a cloud to mar it.

"It's okay I didn't wear a tie?"

Drew wasn't a tie kind of man. He was the kind who dressed up and then undid a few buttons for a more relaxed look. She loved it. "It's fine."

"So where's this wedding?"

"First we go to the bride's home and take some pictures of her and the bridesmaids and her mom, that kind of thing. Then it's off to the church. We'll get some photos of the groom and his groomsmen there, as they wait in a room behind the sanctuary. I'll set up and take some congregational shots, and then when the bride arrives it's really game on."

She looked over. "Once we get to the church, it all happens rather quickly and with precise timing. If you're there with my bag, it'll help a lot." She smiled. "I even tucked a smaller camera in there for you. I thought you might like to have some fun and take some pictures of your own."

He gaped at her. "Are you serious? I can barely handle my little digital one."

"Yeah, but sometimes there's a candid that turns out great, or that I can edit a bit. You don't have to take any if you don't want to. I know this is my thing and you're not required to get excited about it. But it's there if you want it."

"I'll see. It might be fun."

They arrived at the bride's house, and Harper quickly rounded up the women of the wedding party and organized some shots while Drew got two of the bags from the car. They spent an hour there, getting pictures of the dress on the hanger, the flowers, the bride's mother adjusting her veil, the engagement ring and several of the bridesmaids and bride together. When the posed pictures were done, Drew gathered up most of the gear while Harper snapped candids of the family and friends present. There was one of the bride laughing with her father, and another of the flower girl showing an aunt her new white shoes. Those were the kind of memory photos she loved best.

At one fifteen she let the bride know they were heading for the church.

Set right on Main Street, the church was small and quaint with a white picket fence out front. It was the first time Harper had done a wedding here, and despite the simplicity of it, she knew it would be a favorite. There was something solid and reassuring about the old-fashioned wooden pews and the sturdy pulpit at the front. A slightly faded red carpet led the way up the aisle. The pews sported white tulle bows and flowers as pew markers. She stopped at the top of the aisle and took a quick photo of the empty but waiting church, the scent of lilies and roses filling the air. It was a promise of forever, waiting for the people to arrive and make it a reality.

"We're going to the back?" Drew asked.

She nodded. "Yes. There's a room there where the groom should be. If not yet, soon." A few guests had already arrived but were mingling outside until seating began. "Can you take this stuff back? I'm going to get a few sanctuary shots while it's empty."

"No problem, boss." He flashed her a smile and headed toward the back of the church.

Harper took a moment to stop and absorb the character of the church. There was a peace here, and a level of excitement, too, for the joining of two lives together. Weddings were so optimistic and happy. Before long the seats would be full, and the bride would walk up the aisle in her white dress to meet her husband. They'd make promises. She lifted her camera and looked through the viewfinder. The flowers were so fresh and pretty. She took a photo of the table set up for signing the register, a small plumed pen on top of the linen along with a spray of more flowers. Finally, she turned around at the front of the altar and looked back toward the closed door of the sanctuary. Strong and sturdy, the wood was dark with age and she wondered how many brides had crossed its threshold.

And she took a photo of that, too.

Then she made her way to where the groomsmen—and Drew—waited.

CHAPTER TWELVE

COMING WITH HARPER today had been a mistake.

He'd wanted to spend the day with her and he'd wanted to help since Juny wasn't available. But he'd miscalculated. Being at a wedding with Harper was another thing entirely. All around him were reminders of how the world generally worked. You grew up, fell in love, got married, settled down. Locked in.

The ceremony itself had been intimate and warm, with smiles abounding. He'd watched Harper scoot around the church, taking pictures without ever being in the way, admiring her for that talent alone. He'd stood by her side and endured the after-wedding pictures of the receiving line, and then once again for wedding party and family pictures at the reception venue, a hotel on the outskirts of the town. The relatively small number of guests—under seventy, as close as he could guess—mingled by tents set up outside, sipping glasses of punch and champagne, while Harper took photo after photo of the bride and groom and the special people in their lives.

It made him feel claustrophobic.

"Are you okay?" Harper asked, reaching in her bag for the second camera with a different lens. "It's hot. Is the sun too much?"

"No, of course not. But would you like something to drink? Water?"

"That would be great. The sun is really baking things today."

He escaped to find some water and as a member of the

waitstaff poured two glasses for him, he overheard two people talking a few feet away as they sipped pink punch.

"Oh, yes, they've bought a house, only a few blocks from Pat and Susan. Pris is going to substitute teach for now, and Rob's got his job at the insurance company."

Drew dug in his pocket for a tip for the bartender.

"They thought about moving to Calgary, apparently, but she wanted to stay close to her parents."

"It's so good they've both got work. I know Pris doesn't want to wait for a family, either."

Drew's throat tightened and that knot of panic centered in his chest again. This was literally his worst nightmare. Working in insurance? Living two blocks from his in-laws? Tied down with babies?

He grabbed the glasses from the counter and headed back to where Harper was taking photos of the bride and groom alone now that the family obligations were over. When she finished the current pose, she took a moment to have a drink while the bride stood and fluffed out her dress.

"Oh, that's good. Thank you."

"You're welcome."

Her smile was sweet as she looked into his eyes. "This is the nicest wedding. They're so in love. And that little church…it was perfect. I love intimate weddings like that."

"It's definitely beautiful," he agreed, but his jaw was tight.

"Are you okay?"

He pasted on a smile. "You already asked that, and of course I am. What happens after this?"

She took another drink and handed him the glass. "We'll take a few more of the bride and groom alone, and then the reception is mostly informal. More of a garden party sort of thing, with a few speeches later on." She sighed. "And no dance. The happy couple are leaving on a honeymoon tonight, so they're going home to change and get a ride to the airport."

She put her hand on her belly. "I'm not sorry. It means my day will be over before seven, rather than nine or ten."

He put aside his own discomfort and put his hand on her arm. "Is there anything I can do?"

She shook her head. "No. Give me fifteen minutes and we can get something to eat. Then I'll snap some candids, and ones of the speeches."

"Okay."

He stood back while she went to the couple and they decided on a few more shots with the mountains in the background. He watched as she took a few of the couple walking away, and then one as the groom scooped the bride up in his arms.

He could imagine scooping Harper up like that, and hearing her laugh as she settled in his arms.

Invisible walls began closing in. What was he doing? He shouldn't be here. He should have done what Dan had said and stayed away from her from the beginning. But how could he have known that actual feelings would get in the way? That she'd be different? The trouble was, this was the kind of life Harper wanted. Settled. A routine. Babies. The whole white-picket-fence deal. He'd been able to tell when she'd talked about wanting them someday and the look in her eyes when she'd confessed she thought this might be her only chance. She wanted children and she should have them. God, they had really been fooling themselves, acting like this thing between them didn't matter. That they could come away unscathed.

Finished for the moment, he helped Harper gather the camera bags and they made their way to a small table on the perimeter of the eating area. Harper looked like she'd gotten a bit of sunburn, so he told her to stay at the table and he'd bring back food. He returned with a plate for each of them containing finger sandwiches, scones, little pots of jam, and something called clotted cream.

"I looked for vegetarian options," he explained, putting her plate down. "I found cucumber and watercress and a couple of cheese kinds. And scones, of course."

His own plate contained slightly heartier choices: sliced chicken and salmon, along with the same assortment of scones.

"It's perfect. Just what I need." She let out a sigh of relief, but Drew realized he hadn't brought them drinks.

"Do you want tea? Or sparkling water or something?"

A server passed by with a tray of dirty glasses and overheard. "Can I bring you both a beverage?"

What he really wanted was a beer. Instead, he asked for another glass of champagne, the only alcohol that seemed to be available. Harper asked for sparkling water and then picked up a sandwich.

He ate, too, but didn't really taste the food. He wanted to go, to escape, but also wanted to stay for her. What he really wanted was to be chilling out on her front porch in a pair of jeans, a cold beer and a soft breeze. This wasn't the place for him, for them. He and Harper focused on the moment, not on forever. They weren't dresses and dainty things posing as sandwiches. They were lemonade and lazy naps on a swing and…

Maybe this wasn't really love after all. Maybe he was simply caught up in it, in her. An infatuation. Enjoying playing hooky from work and getting out of the rat race.

Yeah. That had to be it. It was the only thing that made sense.

Harper got up to get dessert, a selection of things she called petit fours and Madeleines…it all sounded French and fancy to him, though they tasted fine.

"You look like you'd rather have a steak than that canapé," Harper said, and he realized he'd been zoned out for a few minutes.

"Yeah. This isn't really my style."

"Weddings come in all shapes and sizes," she responded. "Last year Adele did one that used dog sleds to transport everyone to the ceremony location. Dan and Adele's was at the Cascade, I've done ones in people's living rooms, on riverbanks…and in a kayak." She looked up at him and laughed. "The thing is, everyone has to do what's right for them and what they want. A garden party on the lawn is not my idea of the perfect reception—for me."

She looked out over the assembled group. "This is pretty and all, but I'm lower maintenance than that. I loved the little church today, with close friends and family. Then something informal, like spaghetti and salad around a big table with lots of laughter. I want my wedding to reflect how I want to live my life. Fully."

The noose tightened, because as much as he wanted to run, he also didn't want any other man giving that life to her.

He was saved from answering by the emcee, the best man, standing up to the mic. Harper slipped out of her seat and got her camera ready, moving to the back of the tent for a good vantage point.

He needed to let her go. And didn't want to. But it was for the best.

Harper had no idea what had gotten into Drew today, but he hadn't been himself since the ceremony. The sun was in her eyes as they headed into town, and she put the visor down as she squinted. "Do you want to come over?" she asked quietly.

"I should probably go back to the hotel. I've got a lot of work to do tomorrow."

She glanced over at him. "Tomorrow is Sunday."

He met her gaze briefly and swallowed.

"I don't know what happened today, but something did," she said, her voice a little stronger. "So if you want to go back to the hotel, it's fine."

He sighed. "When a woman says it's fine, I know it's anything but."

She looked over again. "I'm fine, really. But I don't think you are."

And she wasn't really either, but she hadn't withdrawn today as he had. Something was going on in his head. She'd hoped they would end up having a fun day together. After all, weddings were romantic.

Maybe that was the problem. She stared at the road ahead and reminded herself that just because she'd fallen for him didn't mean he felt the same way. She was certain he liked her a lot. And their chemistry was off the charts. But she wasn't totally naive. She knew that chemistry wasn't love.

Instead of turning up the hill to the hotel, she pulled into the parking lot for Bow Falls. There were still a few cars in the parking lot; as long as there was light there'd be a few people looking at the water rushing over the falls, but the crowds of the day had dissipated.

"I don't want to have this talk at the passenger drop-off," she said quietly, killing the engine.

"Harper, I… Dammit. I don't know what to say."

"Maybe you can start with what happened this afternoon. We went to the church and you were fine. Headed to the reception and suddenly you didn't seem to know what to do with yourself. You didn't smile, didn't say much. And I don't know why. Did I do something?"

"No!" He was so fast to respond that she knew he meant it, and she gave a little sigh of relief. He sighed heavily. "I was fine until I went to get the water for us, you know?

And I heard a couple of ladies talking, and it made a few things clear for me, that's all."

"Some random women you don't know said something at a wedding and you achieved sudden clarity?" She tried to lighten the mood, but her joke fell flat, instead sounding sarcastic.

He looked over at her. "Harper, we want different things. We know it, and we've chosen to ignore it. But we shouldn't have. You were right at Dan and Adele's wedding. Flings are a mistake."

She tilted her head, examining him. "You know, we talked about all this. You're leaving next week. You have your life and I have mine, and we made any decisions based on that. So what the hell changed?"

He was quiet so long she felt tears prick the back of her eyes. All she'd wanted was to enjoy the week. To spend time with him while she could. To feel cared for and desired. She wasn't sure what changed but it was hard to believe it happened because of two random strangers.

"So what did they say?"

"What?"

"The women. What did they say?"

"Harper…"

"I know you don't want to have this conversation, but I care about you, Drew. And you care about me. I know you do." He had to, because she'd told him things she hadn't told anyone and she couldn't believe that he would be callous after that.

"I do. God, Harper, so much. And that's the problem." He turned and looked at her, his dark eyes tortured. "I can't do this. I can't be with you and be casual about it, and I can't offer you more. I can't do *this*."

She felt as if she'd been slapped. "I never asked you to 'do this.' Whatever 'this' is."

"I know that." His voice raised a bit, and then he let out

a huff of air. “I know that. And yeah, we talked about it. But talking and doing are two different things. I’m leaving to go back to California in a few days.”

“That hasn’t changed.”

“Harper.”

“I know. I’m putting you on the spot. But I’m feeling…” She struggled to find the right words, and then knew what the sinking feeling in her stomach was. “I’m feeling blindsided all over again. *It’s not you, it’s me* right? That’s what you were going to say? Thanks for the fun but see ya?”

“You knew this was going to happen.”

“But not now. Not…yet.”

She wouldn’t cry. She wouldn’t. But she’d felt so alive the past few weeks. He’d made her laugh. Challenged her. Kissed her in the middle of the street and bought her ice cream. She’d seen the pictures he’d taken on top of the mountain. Of her. Almost all of her.

Light began to glimmer, along with a little hope. “Do you love me, Drew?”

His lips dropped open in surprise. “What?”

“Do. You. Love. Me.” She said each word deliberately. “Is that what has you running?”

He swallowed, his throat bobbing, while her heart beat crazily in her chest. “No,” he whispered, the word filling the car with finality. “And today I realized you will always be the woman who wants to put down roots. To have the place to belong you never had. That’s not me, Harper, and I can’t lead you on and let you pretend it is. I’m always going to be the one who needs to keep moving. I can’t be fenced in.”

“Why? What scares you so much?”

He didn’t answer, and she knew he wasn’t going to, either. It was what it was and nothing she said would change it.

“Those women…the bride wants babies right away.

They're buying a house two blocks from her parents and he's working for an insurance company. My God, that's my worst nightmare."

Anger started to seep in past the confusion and hurt. "Did I ever say I wanted any of that?"

"No, but you do want roots. You made that clear. Your life is here. You finally have a home."

"And would living here be so bad? You'd be close to your brother. In the mountains. You'd have a store here."

She took a pause and added, "And I'd be here."

"So you do want it, even if you didn't say it."

"Maybe," she shot back. "But I knew you didn't. So I never brought it up. I feel like you're blaming me for something I didn't even do."

The interior of the car went silent and they both stared out the window. Yes, she'd fallen in love with him, but she'd never made any demands. She'd known better. And instead he'd turned around and ruined what might have been a few wonderful last days together.

That was what she'd wanted. No unrealistic expectations. But a perfect week of happiness. Something to show her she was worth it. Instead she got this. Excuses because he was afraid.

She turned in her seat and looked over at him. For years she'd closed herself off from feeling. Don't get wrapped up in someone and they can't hurt you. She'd done it as a girl with friends. As a teen and then a young woman with relationships—she'd always been the first to leave or break it off so she was in control of the hurting. Jared's abandonment had only confirmed that philosophy.

But that was over. It wasn't living. She'd started to learn with her friendship with Adele, and maybe it was the emotions stirred up by the pregnancy or just her time with Drew, but she wasn't going to close herself off anymore. She was going to feel, dammit.

Feel everything. Even when it hurt.

"If this is it, Drew, then I'm going to be honest with you. I think you're being a coward right now. I think you care and you're running scared. Or maybe to you I'm not worth it. I know how I feel. You told me that I wasn't plain or ordinary. That I was kind and generous. You made me feel like I could finally step out from behind the lens and be me. And you made me fall in love with you. I'm not afraid to say it. I thought I would be, but I'm not anymore." She took a big breath. "I love you, and I never once considered asking you for more because it would mean asking you to stop being you. So don't put this on me, okay? If you want to be done, say so. I never put any pressure on you for more and we both know it."

His jaw tightened and silence dropped like a hammer in the car. She knew he couldn't say those words back. The longer he was silent, the more horrible it became. Finally he was able to form a few words. "I think I should go back to the hotel now. I can walk back if you don't want to drive."

That was it? She said I love you and she got nothing? Worse than nothing. She turned the key in the ignition and the engine came to life. "I'll take you." Inside she was crumbling, but only a little. Not because she was wrong, but because she was sad that this was the way it was ending. He wouldn't even talk.

The drive took about a minute and a half, but it felt much longer as neither of them spoke on the way. She parked in the passenger drop-off and left the engine running, though she put the car in Park.

"Harper… I didn't want it to end like this. I swear I didn't. I thought I could do this week and just walk away. But it's not fair. Not to you, not to me. We were fooling ourselves, you know? I don't want this to end with you angry with me."

She looked over at him, frustrated and sad and disappointed and a lot of other emotions she couldn't sort through yet. "I *am* angry with you, Drew. You were the one who pursued me. Who kissed me. Who made me believe I could step outside myself and take a chance. You whisked me off in a helicopter and took me to dinner and invited me to your hotel room. And now you're the one backing away. I'm disappointed. Not because we're over, because I always knew we would be. But because you freaked out at a stupid wedding and did it this way."

"I don't want it to be like this. I want us to part with a smile and good wishes. Please, Harper. Understand I'm doing this because I don't want to hurt you."

She felt a trembling start inside and braced herself against it, wanting to be alone when the crying started. "It's too late for that," she answered, staring at a nick on the leather of the steering wheel.

He cursed beneath his breath, then undid his seat belt.

He was leaving. Walking away, just like everyone else. Not the way they'd agreed, but on his terms, because once again she didn't matter. Not enough. Fool me once, shame on you. Fool me twice...love had made a fool of her again. And still, she couldn't bring herself to regret it.

Her breath caught in her chest, strangling her.

He got out, then looked inside at her, his eyes sad and lips drooping. "I'm sorry, Harper, I really never wanted to hurt you. I think this is for the best. Like ripping off a Band-Aid."

For him. And that was fine. She'd relied on herself for a long time, and she'd do so again.

"Goodbye, Drew," she said, a hitch in her voice.

After a long moment, he sighed. "Bye, Harper."

He straightened and shut the door. For one prolonged second, she hesitated, wanting him to open the door and say it was all a mistake. That he loved her, too, that he was sorry for being afraid and a jerk and that he wanted to go home with her and make everything right.

But that wasn't Drew. It never had been, and she knew it, so she resolutely put the car in gear and pulled away.

And she didn't look in the rearview mirror, either.

CHAPTER THIRTEEN

DREW HAD ASKED Dan to drive him to the airport. There was no reason to stay in Banff any longer; any business with the building purchase could easily be handled from Sacramento. He'd been staying mostly to handle things in person and be close to Harper, but now he knew it was time to go.

Dan pulled up to the hotel entrance and got out of his car. "Hey, brother. This is everything?"

He tended to travel light. There was one suitcase, and his backpack that doubled as a carry-on. "This is it. Thanks for the lift." He'd had his rental picked up last night. And he could have hired a car service, but he felt the need to see his brother before leaving again.

"No problem. I'm going into the office a little later, is all."

Drew had found an earlier flight even though it wasn't as convenient a route. The sooner he got back, the better. He could get his life back to normal.

They loaded his bags and then headed toward Calgary. A light mist was falling, giving the day a grey, dismal feeling. Drew seemed to remember high school English and something about rain and sad bits of stories being pathetic fallacy. Whatever. She'd called him a coward and maybe she was right. But mostly he figured she represented everything he didn't want for himself. This was for the best.

Except he couldn't stop thinking of the words she'd said. *I love you* had come out of her lips and had rattled him right to his shoes. Because being with her was the closest he'd ever come to uttering those same words.

I love you didn't mean enjoying each other for two weeks. It meant a much bigger investment and much bigger stakes. And for all his success, Drew knew one thing. He took only calculated risks. This one had volatility written all over it.

"You're awfully quiet."

"Just thinking of everything I have to do when I get back."

"Hmm."

"Hmm?" Drew looked over at his brother.

"What happened between you and Harper? Because something did, didn't it?"

Irritation flared, and Drew's lips thinned. "So what if it did? Harper's her own woman."

Dan's brows knit together. "She is, and that's your way of telling me to mind my own business. Except Harper is my business, in a way."

"No, she's not." Drew remembered all of Harper's frustrated sighs and irritation blossomed into indignation. "You might have a baby in her belly, but she's not yours to command, brother."

Dan's lips dropped open. "Holy hell. Where did that come from? Did I say I wanted to 'command' her? And there's no need to be so crude. She's our surrogate. It's not like I slept with her, for God's sake."

Drew tried to get a rein on his temper. Only part of it was Dan; he was also mad at himself for being an idiot. For starting something in the first place. He'd been a fool, thinking he could do something like that and come away unscathed. Because even though leaving was the only solution, he still knew he'd hurt her, and that had been the last thing he wanted. This was exactly why he didn't do relationships.

When Drew didn't answer, Dan let out a slow breath. "Harper is Adele's best friend. So yeah, I'm a bit protective."

"Oh, come on, Dan. You weren't anything like this at the wedding and I made no secret of flirting. The difference now is that she's carrying a baby for you and somehow that means you and Adele have felt like you have a say in everything she does."

"If you mean I didn't want her to get hurt when you left, you're right. We all knew you'd be picking up and leaving again, whenever the fancy struck you."

That stung. It made him sound unreliable, which he wasn't.

"It's more than having to do with me." He tightened his fingers into fists, trying to measure his words better. "All of a sudden you guys were watching what she ate and where she went and if she was okay going on a hike she's done a zillion times. For God's sake, do you think she'd be careless or take unnecessary chances? But all you guys do is hover. And I know this is important to you. This is your baby and a bit of a miracle. Harper gets that, too. But I've watched you guys over the last few weeks. You treat her like you don't trust her, or you act like she isn't even there."

Dan's face was blanked with surprise. "That's not true."

"She's carrying this baby, Dan. It's part of her. She gets attached, too, you know. All this is happening to her, but sometimes you leave her out of the equation. She told me about the day you heard the heartbeat. She was really moved by it, and you and Adele acted as if she wasn't even there. Like the sum total of her purpose was her uterus. And she's more than that. So very much more."

She was everything. He swallowed thickly.

Silence overtook the vehicle, and Drew wondered if he'd pushed his brother too far. When he finally chanced a look over at Dan's profile, he saw his brother's throat bobbing as if he was trying to swallow a lump the size of an egg.

"We got too caught up in ourselves," Dan finally whispered.

"Well, do better. She's given up a lot to give you this gift, and I know the baby is important, but you guys seem to have forgotten all the other good things about her. Do you ever talk about anything other than the baby when you're together?"

Dan's cheeks coloured. He looked over at Drew. "Are you in love with her?"

It was Drew's turn to swallow. "No," he lied softly. "And even if I was, she needs someone better than me. She wants a home and stability and someone like you, Dan. Who'll be willing to stay in one place and settle down. That's not me. It wouldn't work and we'd only end up hurting each other."

More silence, and then Dan spoke up. "You know, at one point Adele and I nearly didn't get back together. It wasn't until I realized that I would do anything to see her happy that it all came together. You're putting her feelings first, Drew. That sounds like love to me."

Drew scoffed, hoping his big brother was wrong. "After a few weeks? Please. Anyway, I've got to get back to run my business. Plus I have a trip booked at the end of August. There's a lot to do between now and then. I can't lounge around a resort town indefinitely."

He knew he sounded churlish, but he couldn't help it. He believed only about half of what he was saying and he was pretty sure Dan wasn't buying it all, either. But it didn't matter. He was getting on that plane today and they would all get back to normal.

Except he couldn't forget how she'd looked the night before last when she'd dropped him off at the hotel.

I love you, and I never once considered asking you for more because it would mean asking you to stop being you.

So don't put this on me, okay? If you want to be done, just say so. I never put any pressure on you for more and we both know it.

He did know it. And it was why he felt so crappy. She'd accepted him as he was, without reservation, even after all her hurts and insecurities.

And he'd done nothing but blame her for hers.

She was better off without him.

January

When the pains started, Harper was at the studio, editing Juny's photos from a New Year's wedding.

When her water broke, she was back at home, thinking the contractions had been more Braxton Hicks, and she'd made herself a bowl of vegetable soup and a grilled cheese sandwich for supper. The moment it happened she'd had a fleeting bit of panic, and then she'd picked up the phone, called Dan and Adele, and prepared for the trip to the hospital. The wait was nearly over, and soon she would have the baby and put her in Adele's arms and go back to her previously scheduled life.

For a moment, emotion washed over her and she wanted to cling to these last moments, despite the pain, despite the discomfort of the last few weeks of pregnancy, despite everything. She and this baby had made a nine-month journey together. It was nearly over and to her surprise, she wasn't quite ready. She ran her hand over her engorged stomach, memorizing the hardness, closing her eyes and imprinting this moment to keep close to her heart for always. "I love you, little one," she whispered. "You're gonna see your mama and daddy soon. But I'm always going to be here for you, you'll see."

And then her body took over and she couldn't think of

anything except breathing through the contractions as she waited for Dan and Adele to arrive.

The drive to the hospital was a blur, though she felt a moment of thanks when she realized the flurries of earlier had stopped and the roads were clear. Dan drove and Adele sat in the back with her, holding her hand, watching her closely and timing contractions. When a pain hit, they breathed together, and Harper felt tears burn her eyelids.

This was such a huge moment. She'd wanted to do this for her friends so badly, but she'd grossly underestimated how difficult it would be to separate herself from the baby that wasn't hers. In the end, Dan and Adele would go home, a complete little family, and she'd be alone…again.

"You hang in there," Adele soothed, rubbing Harper's hand. "I'm here. You squeeze as hard as you need."

Harper gasped and laughed. "I'll break your fingers. Just keep talking to me. It helps."

"You bet." Adele let out a long breath, and Harper followed her lead. She looked up as the contraction waned and Adele cleared her throat. "Harper…" Her voice was thick. "I know things got a little weird in the beginning, and it seemed I thought more about the baby than I did about you." When Harper started to protest, Adele shook her head. "No, don't say it's not true. Drew said as much to Dan at the time, and brought us to our senses."

At the mention of Drew's name, a familiar pain shot to her chest. She pushed it aside.

"We were insensitive, you know? And excited and scared and overwhelmed. But you… Harper, you're our miracle. You're a part of our family, and you always will be."

Harper sniffled a little and squeezed Adele's hand, gently. "And you're my family, too," she whispered. "The kind you choose, you know? Besides, I forgot all about that months ago. Going through this with you…it's been a blessing and a privilege."

There wasn't much time to talk about it more as another contraction hit, faster than before. They got to the hospital and were taken straight to a room. Nurses bustled in and got her into a gown, hooked up a fetal monitor and checked her progress. With her pains only four minutes apart, things were moving along so quickly she could barely catch her breath.

"You had pains all day, didn't you?" the kind nurse said, reading the results of the monitor.

"They started this morning. I thought they were more Braxton Hicks."

"You should have called!" Adele chided, sitting on the side of the bed and tucking a stray piece of hair behind Harper's ear. Dan stood behind, looking slightly out of place. But Harper knew he wanted to be here and so she sent him a smile.

"You spent most of the day in first stage, I think," the nurse said. "The good news is, it won't be long now."

And it wasn't. Less than an hour later, Isabelle Janice Brimicombe came screaming into the world, much to the delight of her mother and father and Harper.

"We want you to be her godmother," Adele said, once the room had quieted and the three of them were left alone for a few minutes. Adele held the baby in her arms, and Harper felt a rush of emotion she couldn't quite define. Happiness and sadness and fullness and emptiness all at once, but she knew that no matter what, she'd be there for Isabelle, and answering yes was the easiest thing in the world.

"We can never repay you for the gift you've given us," Dan said, his hand on Adele's shoulder. Tears glimmered in his eyes. "Harper, I…" Overcome with emotion, he laughed a little as tears slid down his cheeks. "I have a daughter because of you. *Thank you* hardly seems like anything."

Of course she was happy for them. This was what she'd wanted for Adele. Now Harper had roots in this town because of their relationship. It was her home. There was nothing more important.

Adele handed the baby to Dan and took Harper's hands in hers. "I want you to know," she said quietly, tears clogging her voice, "that you are the sister I never had and always wanted. I love you, Harper. Dan's right. I can never repay you for what you've given us."

She sniffed, emotion getting the better of her. "I feel the same, sweetie. Besides, no repayment is necessary." She gave them a tired smile. "Now, as much as I love you guys, the nurse is going to come back in a few moments, and I'm going to have a shower and put on some pajamas. I'm not sure I need spectators for that." She looked up at Dan, who was staring at Isabelle's face with such awe her heart melted. "The baby will spend the night in the nursery and we'll all go home tomorrow, right?"

Adele nodded. "Yes. Oh my gosh, yes. Home."

The nurse came in with a smile. "Okay, happy family. It's time to get Harper fixed up. You feeling a bit wobbly, hon?"

She nodded. "A little, but I think I'll be fine."

Once Dan, Adele and the baby were ushered away, the nurse gently helped Harper out of bed and to the bathroom and shower. "Take your time," she said, "and go ahead and sit down if you need to. The warm water is going to feel great, and before you know it we'll have you in a comfy bed for a well-deserved sleep."

The shower was already running and Harper stepped inside, holding on to a bar for stability. She felt fine, really. At least physically. Now that the pains were over, she was tired. And the nurse was right. The hot water felt heavenly.

But as she stood under the spray, tears came to her eyes and slipped down her cheeks. Her breath came in sharp gasps and she tried to be quiet so she didn't alarm the nurse, who she knew would be somewhere nearby. But she couldn't help it, couldn't explain it. She cried…for the baby she'd carried, for the baby who was now someone else's, for the one she would probably never have, for the life she was now going to have to go back to, empty and lonely.

And when she had cried herself out, she shut off the shower, and the nurse silently helped her dry and get dressed, not commenting on Harper's blotchy face. Instead she retrieved a tissue for Harper to blow her nose, and got her settled in a wheelchair to take her to a private postnatal room.

The baby was healthy and now it was time for Harper to reset—physically, mentally and emotionally. It was time for her to get back to her own life.

And yet somehow she got the feeling nothing was going to be quite the same.

She was home by three the next afternoon, sitting in the back of Dan's car along with the car seat and a sleeping Isabelle inside. She reached out and touched her finger to the soft blanket keeping the baby warm, her little eyelids nearly translucent beneath the pink knitted cap. At home, Adele offered to help her inside, but Harper smiled and shook her head. "Go home with Dan and Isabelle," she said softly. "I'm going to make some tea, grab a book and rest for a while."

And so Adele and her little family left her just inside her doorway.

Life would return to normal now, she thought. Except it couldn't, because too much had happened for it to look like it had only ten months earlier, before she'd started going to the doctor appointments, before the pregnancy test. She was different now; she could feel it deep inside, like somehow her DNA had changed.

She took exactly two days off work. On the third day she was back at the studio, working at her computer. Not pushing herself, but she needed to get back into a regular routine. She edited and put together packages for clients. Went back to earlier in the summer and pulled up wildlife photos and landscapes, scouring them for ones worthy of showing out front. She came in one day and discovered that her mama and babies grizzly print had sold, but Juny said it was an off-the-street purchase. The sales receipt showed a name and address from Calgary. She was sad to see it go.

She replaced it with the grizzly photo from Stewart Canyon, but in doing so, she went through the photos of the day and caught the ones of Drew and the bighorn sheep. She stared at them for long minutes, wondering what in the world was wrong with her. She was going through the motions. Nothing excited her. The photos of Drew made her sad. She worked each day and then went home and stared at the TV, or went to bed since she always seemed tired. It was like living life in black and white after being in bright, wonderful colour.

She lost her baby weight.

Aspen Outfitters announced a grand opening of the second week of February, right around Valentine's Day, when Isabelle would be a month old. The store sign was installed and Opening Soon banners placed in the windows. Now Harper had a reminder of Drew whenever she walked down Banff Avenue to some of her favorite haunts. She couldn't look at Cow's Ice Cream the same, either.

When Drew left she'd had the pregnancy to keep her going. Now she felt as if she had nothing. Work wasn't the same. She couldn't get up any enthusiasm for their scheduled photo shoots. It seemed as if she was photographing the same things over and over. Home wasn't the same, either. All she'd wanted as long as she could remember was a home of her own. Now she had it…and it wasn't enough.

She'd always heard the saying be careful what you wish for. Now she knew what it meant. If the life she'd created for herself wasn't the answer to her loneliness, what was?

CHAPTER FOURTEEN

DREW HUDDLED INSIDE his coat against the freezing rain that was falling. In just over a week the Banff location was going to open, and the hectic but brilliant finishing touches were under way before the grand opening. Another store would open in Whistler in the summer. He should be happy. Canadian expansion was happening, the business was growing, and he'd had a fantastic trip to Switzerland in September. Life was exactly as he wanted it.

Except he was unhappy, and angry at himself for it.

He jogged to his truck. By the time he got it unlocked and inside, his hair was wet with icy droplets.

He drove by Harper's studio on his way back to the hotel. He'd missed her more than he cared to admit. Nothing had been the same since the summer. For God's sake, he'd gone out on two dates and had found himself comparing the women—unfavorably—with Harper within ten minutes.

Being in Banff only made it worse. Dan was a new dad, proud as anything of his baby daughter, sleep-deprived and blissfully happy. Even looking at the baby reminded Drew of Harper. He remembered the awe on her face when he'd put his hand on her belly after hearing the heartbeat, or the way she'd fallen asleep on the porch swing, peaceful and so very beautiful.

He'd get over her eventually, and it would be easier. Right?

Except he couldn't stop thinking about her. Last night Dan had taken him aside and mentioned how he and Adele were worried about her. "Adele and I think she's feeling very alone right now. You might have broken her heart,

Drew, and now she doesn't have the pregnancy to keep her going. Adele lets her spend lots of time with the baby, and she seems happy, but…"

Drew turned down her street and parked a few houses away from hers. He rested his head on the steering wheel. The idea of actually breaking Harper's heart caused him real physical pain. As much as he didn't want to admit it, nothing had been right since he'd gone home at the first of August. He'd left a piece of himself back in Banff. He had fallen in love with Harper despite his best efforts not to.

And now he had to make a choice. Either keep his distance, or take the few steps to her door and see her once more.

He shut off the engine and let out a sigh. He remembered her saying she was worried about being attached to the baby, about getting too close. If nothing else, he could be a friend and make sure she was okay.

The knock on the door was unexpected. It was past six and neither Adele nor Dan had called to say they were coming over. With the new baby, surprise drop-ins didn't happen as often as they used to.

Juny and Adele and Dan had all expressed concern over her, and she kept answering that she was just bouncing back and a little tired. It was much easier than coming out with the complicated truth—that she was dissatisfied with the life she'd thought she wanted.

Or that she'd let Drew in and got her heart broken. That was a big part of it, even if she wouldn't admit it out loud to a single soul.

She looked through the peephole and her breath seemed to strangle in her throat. Drew, looking handsome as ever, stood in the glow of her porch light in a down jacket, his breath making frosty clouds in the air.

Drew. Out of thin air.

Hands shaking, she unlocked the door and opened it. "Hi," she said, standing back.

"Hi. Can I come in?"

"Too cold to stay out there."

He stepped inside, his gaze sweeping her from head to toe and back up again. "Dan was right," he said, his voice low. "You look awful."

The words were a gut punch but also fired some indignation. "Gee, thanks. Is that all you came to say? I mean, it's a Friday night, I'm off work and I'm allowed to lie around in sweats and a hoodie if I want to."

"Sorry," he answered, and unzipped his coat. Apparently he was planning to stay. She could ask him to leave, but while he'd opened with a negative comment, she was still so glad to see him that she couldn't bear to send him away so soon.

She figured she shouldn't. The truth was she still loved him.

Then it occurred to her what he'd said. "Dan called you?"

He nodded. "Not a call, per se. I'm in town to oversee the opening next week. He might have said something last night after dinner."

All of her feelings bubbled up into her chest and throat, but she didn't say them. Instead she said, "I'm fine. I'm back at work and taking some downtime when I'm not shooting or at the studio. That's it." She did have some pride, after all. Before he'd gone back to California, she'd opened her heart to him. He'd rejected it. It wasn't likely she'd do the same thing again in a hurry.

Even if it was true.

"Dan seemed to think you were feeling down." He hung his jacket over a kitchen chair, looked at her for a minute and then sighed. "Harper, I remember how you were starting to have feelings about the pregnancy. Feeling attached to the baby. You went through all that and it's not surprising that you might be lonely now that it's over. Or…sad." He'd done a bit of googling again. "Like…maybe postpartum depression or something."

Postpartum depression? She gawped at him for a full ten seconds, unable to respond. She had no doubt such a thing was possible; she'd done a fair bit of research herself. But that wasn't what was going on with her. Her dissatisfaction came from wanting more. Because he'd shown her that life could be an adventure and she wanted more of it.

"I'm not depressed," she said firmly. "But you're right. Something changed. And I'm not quite sure what to do about it yet."

"I don't understand."

He looked genuinely perplexed. She went to the cupboard and took out a glass, filled it with water and handed it to him. "Here. Have a drink and sit down."

He did, and she sat in the chair closest to him, with just the corner of the table between them. He took a drink and put down the glass. "What changed? Does it have to do with Isabelle?"

"No, not really." She thought about the little girl and couldn't help the smile that spread across her lips. "She's adorable. And when I see Dan and Adele…it was the right thing, Drew. They're so happy. I'll always have a special bond with Belle. How could I not? But I have no regrets."

He nodded, his eyes sober. "I'm glad. I was worried about that…"

The irritation flared again. "Why would you worry? You left. I haven't heard from you since the summer, even though I know you've been in town. I don't need you to check up on me, Drew. I'm doing just fine."

His jaw hardened. "If that's so, why are Dan and Adele worried about you?"

She tried to sound strong. And she was, really. But this was hard. There were times over the past five months that memories of Drew had kept her going. The times they'd shared had been magical.

He leaned forward. "It's okay to not be strong all the time. I know how much you want a family of your own, and how having the baby must have—"

She pushed away from the table, cutting him off. "You really think this has to do with the baby? I'm proud of what I did. I'm so incredibly happy for Adele and Dan, and yeah, it had its moments but I'd do it all over again. If I'm unhappy, Drew, it's not because of sweet Isabelle. It's because I have a home and a family here, and my own business, and it's no longer enough. And you did that. You took me on adventures and made me want more out of my life. That's my problem. I'm not happy with the life I thought I always wanted."

She met his gaze. "Last summer, I told you I loved you and you ran. That's on you, Drew. And yeah, maybe I wanted to finally have some stability. But you know what? I wasn't running scared." She lifted her chin. "And I'm still not."

He looked so shocked that she softened her voice. "But you still are. I'm not a fragile flower, Drew. But I have changed. And I'm trying to sort out what I'm going to do about it."

"I..." His gaze slid away from her, and then back again. "I didn't know, Harper."

She exhaled through her nose, tried to calm her beating heart. "I know. And yes, you were there for me last summer. Getting over you hasn't been easy, okay?" Seeing him again was going to set her back a few steps, too. "You should probably go."

He got up from his chair and went to her. "Not like this. Not angry. We left last time with you being angry, and I don't like it."

"Why is that, do you think?" She tried to ignore the touch of his warm hands as he reached out for her fingers.

"Because people don't generally say no to me?"

She couldn't help the surprised smile at his honesty and insight. "Bingo. But you can't fix this with your charm."

"Nothing's changed for me, really," he said. "I still…"

But he didn't finish. He didn't need to. She knew he wasn't the staying kind, and she also knew she couldn't force someone to be who they weren't.

"You're really okay?" he asked.

"I will be. I just have a lot of things to figure out. I'm not happy, Drew. But no one can fix that but me. I certainly can't rely on anyone else to fix it for me."

She took her hands away from his. "And you. You're opening up the store next week and Adele says another in the summer in British Columbia. You're getting what you wanted."

"Yeah, I guess I am."

Funny, he didn't seem overly excited about it.

"Well, that's good, then." She smiled. He needed to go. She hadn't lied to him but she certainly hadn't been 100 percent truthful. She still had her broken heart to worry about.

"I'd better go. I'm having dinner with Dan and Adele."

"Yes, go. You won't want to be late."

She walked him to the door and held it open as he shrugged on his jacket. He was outside when he turned back and met her gaze.

"Will you come to the opening next week?"

Her heart lurched. "Oh, Drew. I don't think that's a good idea."

"Just think about it, okay?"

"Okay." She'd think about it. And then find a reason not to go. The last time she'd set foot in that space, she'd had one of the best days of her life. She would be fine. But that didn't mean it didn't hurt. A lot.

He turned and left, jogging to his rented truck. She shut the door before he got inside and rested her forehead against the door.

She had to sort things out soon. The status quo wasn't doing her any favors, and seeing Drew only served to show her she wasn't as over him as she thought.

Drew and Dan lingered over a cup of coffee after dinner while Adele took Isabelle for her bath. Dinner had been fine, but now that they were alone, Dan pressed.

"You went to see her, didn't you?"

Drew let out a dry, humorless chuckle. "Is it that obvious?"

"To me it is. You're a wreck. Was it bad?"

"Depends." He took a deep drink of coffee. "She's a strong woman, Dan. She's going to be fine. Stubborn…"

Dan laughed a little. "She's not like other women. She doesn't let you get away with things."

"Not even a little bit."

They sat quietly for a few minutes, the sounds of Adele singing to the baby filtering out to the living room. It created an unfamiliar wistfulness around Drew's heart. "Hey, Dan? Can I ask you something?"

"Sure."

"Do you ever regret that you left your opportunities behind? You were at the top in Toronto, you know? And I know they made this VP position for you, but…you gave up a lot to move here. Your dreams and plans." All Drew could think about was the look on his dad's face whenever he'd turned down a new opportunity. Drew loved his mom, but he had never understood her refusal to let her husband follow his dreams.

"I didn't give up anything," Dan replied. "Not compared to what I'd gained. What makes you ask?"

"I heard Dad and Mom arguing once. He'd been offered

a job that would have been a great opportunity, but Mom didn't want to leave the neighbourhood or put us in a different school. Dad was stuck in that same job his whole life, you know? Locked in because he was tied down…with us."

Dan's face softened. "Drew. You don't blame yourself for that, do you? Because couples…they talk about these things. And they make compromises."

"Yeah, but what if there wasn't a compromise? Because people make ultimatums, too, Dan. I love Mom. She's an amazing woman. But it's always bugged me that she might have held him back from something really great."

"And you don't want that to happen to you."

He let out a relieved breath. "Yes. You get it."

But Dan shook his head. "Sorry, but I don't. It means you're holding your heart back either out of fear or selfishness, and that's not right. Hey, if you're happy being alone, fine. But if you're not, then stop sabotaging good relationships."

Was that what he was doing? Maybe. He certainly wasn't happy. He had been, until…

Until Harper came along and changed everything. Not because he was rich. And his charm didn't work on her, either. She saw past all that and she…

She loved him anyway. She'd loved him even when she had always known he would walk out.

Damn.

"I don't know if I can do it," he murmured, cradling his cup. He looked up at Dan. "I don't know if I have what it takes. I'm not brave like her. Hell, like you." A sideways smile touched his mouth.

Dan laughed. "I'm not brave. Know what it is? It's realizing that life with someone is far less scary than facing life without them. You guys changed each other, and that's pretty amazing. Don't throw it away because of an argument you heard twenty years ago."

When Dan put it like that…

"Better yet," Dan continued, "call Dad and ask him about it. Dad gives good advice."

Drew pulled in a long breath, pursed his lips and let it out slowly, fighting against the wash of emotion. "Yeah," he whispered, suddenly homesick. "He does."

Drew left a little while longer, and once in his hotel room, called his dad. It was late in Ontario, but as always, his parents were ready to chat whenever one of their kids needed them.

"Hey, Dad. I won't keep you long. I just want to ask you a question."

"Sure. Let me go downstairs so I don't keep up your mother."

It took a few moments, then he heard his dad sigh as he sat down in his chair. "What's up?"

"Do you remember, when I was seven or eight, that you had a job opportunity up north?"

"Goodness. Yeah, but that was a long time ago. What about it?"

"Why didn't you take it?"

"Your mother and I didn't want to have to sell the house and move you kids so far. This is a nice neighbourhood. Your friends were here. You were doing well."

Drew stared at the ceiling of his hotel room. "You and Mom decided? Or just Mom?"

He could almost see the wrinkles in his dad's forehead as he answered. "What do you mean?"

"I mean I heard you arguing about it. I know it was a big opportunity for you and she was the one who didn't want to go. And I remember hearing you making comments now and again about being stuck. I guess… I'm wondering if you still resent that. If you wish it had gone differently."

There was a deep sigh. "Drew, sometimes a man weighs

what he wants against the needs of his family, and when you love your family, it's no contest. Family comes first."

"Even to sacrifice your own happiness?"

"Is this a choice you're thinking of making, son?"

Drew covered his eyes with his hand. "I don't know. I love her, Dad. But she wants things…things that I think would make me unhappy. How is that good for a marriage?"

"It's not. But there are compromises, Drew. And when it becomes a choice between keeping or losing the person you love…"

"That's what Dan said."

A warm chuckle came across the line.

"I'll be honest, Drew. Marriage is hard sometimes. It takes work. Sometimes we say things we shouldn't. Sometimes we—and by this I mean I—make passive-aggressive comments about things like lost opportunities. But truthfully, the best opportunity in my life was marrying your mother and raising you kids. I would have been a fool to walk away from it."

"But what if…what if I'm not a good…" He struggled over the word, then forced himself to say it. "A good husband. Or father. Am I too selfish for that? I'm so afraid of messing it up."

"We're all afraid of messing it up. It's an important decision. If you *weren't* afraid, then I'd be worried."

A lump formed in Drew's throat. "Thanks, Dad."

"You're welcome. Settling down isn't a sentence, Drew. It's an adventure. Believe me."

Drew laughed, and after a few minutes more they hung up. He stared at the ceiling again, wondering what he was going to do.

And wondering if anything he said would change Harper's mind.

CHAPTER FIFTEEN

DREW WENT TO Harper's house the next night, feeling slightly sick to his stomach from nerves, but knowing he had to see her and try to make things right.

When she opened the door, he caught his breath. There were no sweatpants in sight tonight. Perhaps she'd just got home from work, because she wore a black-and-white dress and heels, while her hair was up in a tidy topknot.

"Drew," she said softly, but she didn't smile. He missed her smile. Wanted to see it on her lips again.

"You look amazing."

"I had a client meeting at six." She stepped aside. "I'm assuming you want to come in."

He nodded. "Yeah. There were things I left unsaid the other night. Things I didn't realize I wanted to say, you know?"

She kept her chin up, but he saw the flash of vulnerability in her eyes and it both tugged at his heart and gave him a sliver of hope.

"Do you want something to drink?" she asked politely.

"No, thank you." When she would have passed by him, he reached out and grabbed her hand, stopping her progress. "Harper. You said the other night that nothing felt right anymore. That you're dissatisfied and want more. And I'm here to say me, too. It's all been wrong since I left, and I'm here to ask if you will give us another chance."

Wide eyes met his. "What changed? Because the other night you were the same Drew as I remember. Scared to death of settling down and leading a dull life."

He huffed out a laugh. "Oh, Harper. Life with you is never boring. I've been an idiot. Blind, stubborn, scared… but the truth is, I love you. I fell in love with you last summer and it scared the hell out of me. But leaving didn't make the feeling go away. It just made me miserable and took all the pleasure out of the life I used to have. I need you, sweetheart. And I'm still scared but I'm done with running."

He let go of her hand and opened his arms. "And I hope if you do any running, it's to right here. Because I'm not sure I can go on living this way."

Without saying a word, she walked into his embrace, and the moment his arms closed around her, she started to cry. He never moved; he let her cry it out, her hands clinging to his shoulders, his fingers stroking along her hair as he sent up a prayer of gratitude.

Harper breathed deeply and inhaled the scent that was just Drew. He didn't try to shush her, or tell her it was going to be okay. He simply let her be…just as he had last summer when they'd been together. It was one of the things she'd loved about him most. He'd never asked her to be someone she wasn't, and even though he'd walked away, he'd never once expected her to change.

And so she cried, for the heart that had been broken and the emptiness she'd felt in his absence. And when she started to run out of tears, he squeezed her close and kissed the top of her head. "Better?" he asked.

She nodded. "I'm sorry… I shouldn't have bawled all over you."

"It's okay. I'm glad." He stood back and held her upper arms. "I was so afraid you'd turn me away. That I'd messed it up for good."

She shook her head. "I tried to think like you. That maybe no ties, no commitments was the way to go to avoid being hurt. But it didn't work. I couldn't seem to find any joy anymore."

His dark eyes deepened and he took a shaky breath. "It's no guarantee against being hurt. I should know." And his bottom lip wobbled a little bit.

"How do you know?"

He pulled out a kitchen chair and nudged her into it, and then pulled out another and sat knee to knee with her. He took her fingers in his, an anchor in a swirl of emotional chaos. "I know, Harper, because nothing has been the same since I left here. The business is flourishing and I find I don't have the same excitement or passion anymore. It's like there's a puzzle piece missing, and that piece is you. That day at the wedding, I did freak out. I could see this settled and boring life ahead of me if I gave in to my feelings for you. I knew you wanted to put down roots and I couldn't breathe. I was afraid, so I ran, telling both of us it was for the best."

"So you said," she replied.

"Here's the thing. When I was about eight, I overheard my mom and dad having a fight. Dad was always the stable one, you know? Provider for the family. We grew up in the same house our entire lives. And I thought it was great, until I heard that fight. Until I realized how much my father had given up over the years. Opportunities, promotions that would have involved moving…but Mom never wanted to. She didn't want to make us move schools. Didn't want to leave our neighbourhood. And my dad had another opportunity come up and she didn't want to go and he told her he felt stuck in his life. That she and the kids had held him back from reaching his potential."

"Oh, Drew. That must have made you feel horrible."

"I was eight. I felt at least part of my dad's unhappiness was my fault. And I knew, too, that I didn't want to ever be like that. Caught in a rut and unable to get out, resentful of how my life had turned out. I wanted to set my own terms and travel and not be tied down with a wife and kids who I thought would drain me of my energy and passion."

Harper reached out and took his hand. "We really are two sides of the same coin. My mom and dad loved to move around. It was all about the next adventure. But me… I wanted to stay in one place. Make friends for longer than a year or two at a time. Sleep in the same bedroom and live somewhere long enough that I might actually get tired of the paint and want to redecorate it."

His fingers played with hers as her throat tightened painfully. "The truth is…" She met his gaze evenly, and her lip trembled again. "I think I had all these plans to get back to my regular life after Belle was born, and now I am, and I'm not happy anymore. I'm so scared, Drew. If this is all there is, what's to become of me? I wanted roots. My own house. A business. Friends. It was enough. But it's not anymore."

"And you feel empty."

"Yes!" She was so relieved he seemed to understand.

"Me, too," he said. "I called my dad to ask him about that fight. He remembered it, you know. The company had wanted him to transfer up north. It would have meant a big raise. I asked him if he still resented it and if it had always affected their marriage. And you know what he said?"

She shook her head.

"They made that decision together." He let out a breath and shook his head, as if disbelieving. "Oh, there were still times of stress. Dad wasn't always happy at work and it bled over into his home life. But he told me he had no regrets. Now all this time I let that colour who I was and what I wanted. I wasted so much time on something that wasn't even real. I love my life, I do. But since July… I want something more. I need it. Because nothing's been the same for me either, Harper, and I think that's because I fell in love with you, too." He lifted his hand and placed it on the side of her face. "I don't know how we're going to make it work—or if you even want to. But I really, really want to try."

Something that had been missing for months suddenly flickered to life, right in the center of her chest. It was hope…hope at happiness, hope at love, hope at a future she'd given up on.

She was so overwhelmed. But she clasped his hands and bit down on her lip before saying, "I'd like that. A lot."

"Good." He leaned forward and kissed her forehead. "It's gonna be okay now, all right? We're going to figure it out. Together."

She nodded, and then surprised them both by asking, "Can we get something to eat? For the first time in almost a month, I'm actually starving."

His grin lit up the room. "Yes. Whatever you want. We can hit the town and buy lobster and champagne. We can make a grilled cheese sandwich. As long as I'm with you, I don't care what we eat."

"Pizza. I'd kill for one."

Before she could get up and reach for the take-out menus, though, he touched her knee. "I have one more question to ask, Harper. Will you go to the store opening with me on Thursday?"

A little fizz of excitement ran through her veins. "I'd love to. I can't wait to see what you've done with the place."

"That sounds perfect," he answered, and he leaned forward and finally kissed her. Tears burned in her eyes at the sweetness of it, a depth of emotion that was unexpected. It was a hello. It was a confession. And it was a promise to face things together.

Drew didn't think he'd ever been prouder of a store opening. The shelves and racks were stocked, the new manager was circulating and staff was assisting the invited guests and VIPs who'd come in since the doors opened. A bar was set up in a corner and a caterer had hot finger foods that filled the air with rich, savory scents. It looked magnificent, all polished logs and shiny new fixtures and beautiful displays. Harper was beside him in a long skirt and tall brown boots, her hair done in long curls for the occasion, and a bracelet Drew had given her as a gift at her wrist. Dan and Adele were behind them, with little Isabelle in her mother's arms. His family and the woman he loved...his heart was full. Almost.

There was something that he wanted Harper to see, and he'd had his assistant pull a few strings to make it all come together.

He took Harper by the hand and led her to the huge stone fireplace. Display racks and shelving were designed around it, holding an assortment of upscale backpacking supplies. And above the mantel...

He knew when she noticed because she stopped moving and gasped.

"It was you!" she exclaimed, and he turned around. Her eyes shone at him. "The mama bear and cubs. But Juny said it was a guy from Calgary. And beside it...oh, Drew. I love this shot."

The one she'd taken of the grizzly at Lake Minnewanka hung beside the mama and cubs. Beneath was a gold plaque with her name and studio on it.

"You are so talented, Harper." He tugged her close and put his arm around her. "I got one of the management team to buy the print so you wouldn't know it was me. I thought you hated my guts. And last night Juny opened up and sold my assistant the other. I had someone here to hang it at seven this morning. Happy?"

"Thrilled!"

"I know we haven't made any firm plans, but I don't want you to stop doing this. We can make it happen together. Maybe use Banff and your house here as a home base. We can travel and you can take all the pictures you want, on every continent. Juny can manage things here when you're away."

Adele piped up. "You already said she took over in the last few months you were pregnant, Harper. Gosh, it sounds so exciting."

"Here's the thing," he said, and he captured her gaze. "I understand your need for home and stability, and I'll do what I can to give that to you. You tell me what you need." He took a breath. "Because none of this works without you." Now he understood what his father had meant. It was a matter of priorities. And Harper came first. Nothing worked anymore without her.

She stood on tiptoe and kissed him. "What I wanted most was a home and a place to belong. I thought that was a house and a town and the same people all the time. But that's not what home is, is it?"

"It's not?"

She shook her head. "That stupid old saying is true. Home really is where the heart is. And my heart's with you, Drew. That's what's been missing. No matter where we are."

Thank God, he thought.

Adele was sniffing behind them and Dan was grinning from ear to ear. "About time," he said gruffly.

And then Harper reached out and took Isabelle from Adele's arms.

"Oh, my," she said softly, and cuddled the baby close to her neck. She closed her eyes. "What am I going to do if I can't see you every day, huh?"

Drew was damned near crying himself at this point. The scene was so utterly perfect. Why had it taken him so long to figure it out? Now wasn't the time, but when it was right, he'd make sure she had babies of her own to love. Their babies. His sons and daughters.

She opened her eyes and looked up at Drew. "I love you. I never stopped. You're really here to stay?"

"As long as you'll have me."

"Us, too," Dan said. "We're your family. That's what we do."

"Always," Drew assured her, putting his arm around her and holding her and Isabelle close. "A family and a man who loves you desperately. And always will."

If he had anything to say about it.

EPILOGUE

HARPER HAD NEVER seen anything quite like the Thorsmork Valley.

It was cool, and she wore a hat and mittens as well as her jacket and hiking boots as they'd climbed all the way up to Magni and Modi, volcanic craters left behind after 2010's massive eruption.

There were times she'd felt on top of the world in her lifetime, but nothing compared to this.

Drew came up beside her. "Doing okay?"

"Perfect," she replied, catching her breath. "I still can't believe we're here."

The first thing Drew had done when they'd arrived was take her to the famed Blue Lagoon, and they'd spent two days in Reykjavik in luxury, being pampered in a spa and adjusting to the jet lag. This morning, though, they'd stopped at Seljalandsfoss Falls and then on to the volcanic hike. The landscape was different from anything she'd ever seen, majestic and sweeping and so very, very old, like something out of Tolkien or George R. R. Martin's books. She'd stopped often and lifted her camera, in such awe and wonder that she didn't know how she was ever going to process it all.

"I told you I wanted to bring you to Iceland someday. Because neither of us had ever been here. A first for us together, you know?"

She leaned in close to him. "I do know. And it's been more than I ever dreamed possible." In the four months since the store opening, Drew had been true to his word. He'd split his time as much as possible between Sacramento and Banff, and she'd made a few trips south, too. He'd shown her his favorite hikes and spots. But this…this was a big step. Their first expedition together.

And it had been so romantic, right from the beginning. Drew had insisted on deluxe accommodations and amenities. She hadn't ever been treated to such luxury. It wasn't how she wanted to live, but it was darned nice on vacation.

But there was something different about Drew today, and Harper turned to face him. "Are you okay?"

He smiled. "I'm perfect. I think. It'll depend."

"Depend on what?"

He reached into his pocket and dropped to one knee. Ahead of them, the tour guide gave a shout and the rest of their party started to whistle as they clued in to what was happening. Harper's heart skipped a beat as she looked down at Drew, who had pulled a tiny box out of his jacket pocket.

"This is our first trip, and I don't want it to be our last. I want to always be beside you, Harper. I want to love you and be what you need. I want to be your home. I want to explore the world with you, and someday I want to put our little son or daughter in a backpack and go on adventures. If you're up for the adventure, will you marry me?"

There was no other answer she could give than yes. With Drew, she'd learned the meaning of home, and of compromise and of the safety that came from leaning on someone you loved and trusted. "Yes," she said, a laugh of joy bubbling up from her throat. "Yes, I'll marry you. Whenever you say and wherever you want to go."

"We'll make an adventurer out of you yet," he said, sliding the ring over her finger, then standing and pulling her into a bear hug as the tour group cheered loudly.

"You already have," she whispered in his ear, ready to take on whatever came next.

* * * * *

THE COWBOY'S LESSON IN LOVE

MARIE FERRARELLA

To
Glenda Howard,
With Gratitude
For
Continuing To Make
My Dreams
Come True

Prologue

"Are you nervous?"

Shania Stewart's softly voiced question to her twenty-six-year-old cousin broke through the otherwise early-morning silence within their small kitchen in their newly rented house located in Forever, Texas.

Wynona Chee didn't answer her immediately. She was tempted to nonchalantly toss her long, shining black hair over her shoulder and confidently deny the very idea of having even a drop of fear regarding whatever might lay ahead of her today.

Ahead of both of them, really.

But over the course of her young life, Wynona had gone through a great deal with Shania, more than so many women even twice their age. Always close, the cousins had suffered the loss of their parents almost simultaneously. For Wynona, it had been the death of her single mother—she had never known her father—when sickness and heartbreak had claimed her. For Shania, it had come in waves. First, her father had died when a drunk driver had hit his car, then her mother, who had by that time taken in an orphaned Wynona to live with them, had succumbed to pneumonia.

By the time Wynona was ten and Shania was eleven, they did not have a living parent between them. Instead, they faced the grim prospect of being sent off to family care where they would then be absorbed into the foster care system. The latter fact ultimately meant that they would be separated.

The immediate future that faced the two cousins had been beyond bleak at that point.

It was then that they learned the true meaning of the word *hope.* Their late grandmother's sister, Great-Aunt Naomi, came swooping into their lives from Houston like an unexpected twister sweeping across the prairie.

A fiercely independent woman, Naomi Blackwell, a dedicated physician who had never married, had been notified about the cousins' pending fate by the town's sheriff. She immediately came and took the girls under her wing and returned with them to Houston to live with her in her oversize mansion.

Over the course of the next sixteen years, Naomi not only provided them with a home, she also made sure that they both received an excellent education. This helped guarantee that they could go on to become anything they set their minds to.

It turned out that the girls had set their minds to return to Forever and give back a little of their good fortune to the community. After a short attempt to talk the cousins out of it, Naomi gave them her blessings and sent them off.

When they finally returned to Forever, the house where they had spent their early childhood—Shania's parents' house—was gone, destroyed in a fire some eight years ago. Some of the ashes were still there. Consequently, when they arrived back that summer, they moved into a house in town and then set about putting their mission into motion.

Today marked the beginning of their new careers. Shania had been hired to teach physics at Forever's high school while Wynona was taking over a position that had been vacated at the end of the school year by Ericka Hale, the woman who was retiring as Forever Elementary's second/third grade teacher.

"A little," Wynona finally admitted after pausing to take in a deep breath. She could feel her butterflies growing and multiplying in her stomach. "You?"

Shania smiled. As the older of the two, Shania had always felt it was up to her to set the example. But like Wynona, she couldn't be anything but truthful. It just wasn't in her nature.

"I'd like to say no," she told her cousin, "but that would be a lie." Her smile was slightly rueful. "I feel like everything inside me is vibrating to *Flight of the Bumblebee*."

"Really?" Wynona asked, surprised to hear that her cousin was anything but confident. She'd always projected that sort of an image. "But you've always been the calm one."

"Most of the time," Shania admitted. "But I'm not feeling very calm right now, although I guess I did manage to fool you," she told Wynona with a self-deprecating laugh. "Now I guess all I have to do is fool everyone else."

"That's easy enough," Wynona assured her cousin. "All you have to do is channel Great-Aunt Naomi." A fond smile curved her lips. "That woman could make a rock tremble in fear."

Shania laughed. "She could, couldn't she?" A wave of nostalgia came over her as she looked at her younger cousin. "Do you find yourself wishing we were back in Houston with her right now?"

"No," Wynona said honestly. She saw that her answer surprised her cousin. "Staying with Aunt Naomi would have meant taking the easy way. I think we both know that we're right where we're supposed to be just as I know that Aunt Naomi is proud of us for choosing to do this."

Shania smiled in response, nodding her head. "I think you're right." The young woman looked at her watch, then raised her eyes to meet Wynona's. She took in a deep breath. "Well, Wyn, it's almost seven. If we don't want to be late our first day of school, we really should get going."

Wynona nodded in agreement as she felt her butterflies go into high gear. "Okay, Shania. Let's do this."

Chapter One

Clint Washburn wiped the back of his wrist against his forehead while crouching down and holding the stallion's hoof still with his other hand. Seven thirty in the morning and it was already getting hot.

This was fall, he thought. It shouldn't be this hot, certainly not this early in the day. These days it felt as if things were making even less sense than usual.

A movement out of the corner of his eye caught his attention. Clint frowned when he saw the skinny little figure entering the corral. After closing the gate, he was walking toward him.

Ryan.

The boy wasn't supposed to be here. He was supposed to be on his way to school by now.

Clint stopped working on the stallion's hoof. The tiny

rock or whatever had worked its way under the horseshoe, causing the animal to limp, was just going to have to wait until he sent his son on his way.

He squinted. The sun was directly behind the boy, making Ryan's fine features as well as his expression momentarily difficult to see. Clint's frown deepened.

"Shouldn't you be on your way to school by now, boy?" Clint asked.

There was no warmth in his voice, only impatience.

Rather than answer immediately, the small boy looked at his father with wide eyes, his fine, light brown hair falling into his piercing blue eyes. He turned a slight shade of red before answering.

"I...I thought I'd stay home and help you with the horses today."

"You thought wrong," Clint replied flatly. "I don't need your help with the horses. That's what I've got Jake and your uncle Roy for," he reminded the boy crisply, referring to the ranch hand and his brother. "What you need to do is go to school." Shading his eyes, Clint scanned the area directly behind his son. "Lucia is probably looking for you right now. Don't give her any extra work," he instructed his son briskly, then ordered, "Go."

The answer, although not unexpected, was not the one his son was hoping for.

Summoning his courage, Ryan tried to change his father's mind. "But—"

"Now."

A stricken look came over Ryan's thin face. His shoulders were slumped as he turned on his heel and made his way back into the house.

"Kind of hard on the boy, aren't you, boss?" Jake Weatherbee asked. He'd waited until Ryan had left the corral and was out of earshot before he raised the question. "He just wanted to help."

"He just wanted to skip school, like any kid his age," Clint replied gruffly.

"So let him once in a while," Roy Washburn, Clint's younger brother, told him, adding his voice to the argument. "Nothing wrong with that. If you let your son work with you, he'll get to see just what it means to be a rancher. It's what Dad did."

Clint's expression hardened. This was not advice he welcomed. "Dad didn't do anything. He was too drunk half the time to work the ranch. That's why *we* did. The boy has to learn discipline before he learns anything else, not to mention what they can teach him at school." Clint's eyes swept over the two men standing before him. "I want that kid to be able to pick his future, not be stuck with it the way you and I were," he told Roy.

Clint brushed his hands off on the back of his jeans. "Now, if you two bachelors are through debating whether or not I'm raising *my* son properly, maybe you can get back to doing what you're supposed to be doing."

"Didn't mean no disrespect, boss," Jake told him. "I was just remembering what it felt like being the boy's age."

Clint's eyes narrowed. "Maybe you should try remembering what it's like being your age and working for a living." He turned to look at his brother. "Same goes for you."

"Yes, sir," Roy answered with just a slight hint of

mocking in his voice. He turned his attention back to the recently purchased stallion he was preparing to break.

Clint's frown appeared to have been chiseled into his features. He was more dissatisfied with his own behavior than with the behavior of either his brother or his ranch hand. He knew that ultimately, the men meant well even if he hadn't asked for or welcomed their opinions.

Clint blew out a breath. Maybe he'd gone a little too far. "Look, I didn't mean to go off like that," he told Jake and Roy. "I've got a lot on my mind right now and this thing with the boy isn't helping any."

Given a reprieve, Roy decided to take the opportunity to reach his brother. "Don't you think you're making more of this than you should, Clint? At least Ryan was offering to help. He wasn't just running off—"

"Yet," Clint interjected seriously. "But if I don't force him to do what he's supposed to, it's only going to get worse. I've got to nip this sort of behavior in the bud," he insisted. A distant look came into his eyes. It still haunted him. Seven years and the wound still hadn't healed. "I missed what was right in front of me once. I'm not going to let that happen again," he stated firmly.

Roy paused to look at his brother. Though Clint had shut down again, Roy could see the glimmer of pain in his eyes. He knew that he wasn't referring to his son when he talked about missing what was right in front of him. Clint was talking about Susan, Ryan's mother. He was talking about the bomb she had detonated in the center of his life.

He had come home late one evening to find a crying

baby and a note pinned to the sheet in his crib. Susan was nowhere to be seen and he had no idea how long she had been gone. When it finally dawned on him that she wasn't home, he was absolutely devastated. The woman he adored and had been married to for almost two years had left without warning.

The short, terse note she'd left in her wake stated that she realized that she wasn't cut out to be a rancher's wife and even less to be a mother. She went on to tell him that he needed to cut his losses and forget about her.

According to her note, they had never been a proper "fit."

That had probably hurt most of all, the antiseptic words Susan had used to describe what to him had been the most wonderful part of his life.

What he had thought of as his salvation had turned into his personal hell.

From that moment on Clint had sealed himself off from everyone and everything.

He hired someone to care for his house and his son—in that order. He didn't feel that he was up to doing either for a long, long time. To keep from falling into an apathetic abyss, Clint forced himself to run the ranch and to look after the horses that he bought and sold as well as the cattle on the ranch. It gave him a purpose. Otherwise, he felt he had no reason to go on.

Time went on and he made peace with his lot, but he still didn't come around, still didn't reach out to the son who seemed to need so desperately to be acknowledged by him.

While no one could have accused Lucia of being an

outspoken woman, his housekeeper did do her best to try to make Clint open up to the boy, but none of her efforts were successful.

Clint made sure that the boy was clothed and that he always had enough to eat, but that was where it ended. There was no actual bonding between them. If Clint did manage to make it home for a meal—which he missed with a fair amount of regularity—there was no animated conversation to be had at the table. If it weren't for Roy, who lived in the ranch house with them, there would have been very little conversation at all.

On a few occasions Ryan would try to have a conversation with his father, asking him questions or talking about something that had happened in school. Clint's responses usually came in the form of a grunt, or a monosyllabic answer that really said nothing at all.

It was clear that Clint didn't know how to talk to his son, or to people in general, for that matter. The wounds that Susan had left in his heart had cut unimaginably deep and refused to heal. Communication with Roy was generally about the ranch, while his communication with Lucia in regards to Ryan was usually kept to a basic minimum.

In essence, to the adults who dealt with him it was evident that Clint Washburn was in a prison of his own making. The fact that the prison had no visible walls made no difference.

No matter where he went, the prison he was in went with him.

This particular morning, when Ryan walked back

into the kitchen after his father had rejected his offer to help with the horses, Lucia all but pounced on him.

"Where did you run off to?" she asked. The housekeeper, Lucia Ortiz, had made a clean sweep through the house already, looking for the boy who had been placed in her care from the time he was one year old. "If we don't leave for school right now, we're going to be late. Let's go."

Small, thin shoulders rose and fell as the boy followed Lucia out of the house to where her twelve-year-old car was waiting.

"I thought I'd help Dad with the horses," Ryan said in a small voice.

Lucia gave the boy a long look. "Did he ask for your help?" she asked, getting in behind the steering wheel.

Ryan scrambled into the passenger seat, then settled in. He buckled up before answering because he knew that was the proper thing to do.

"No," he murmured.

"Then why did you offer?" Lucia asked, talking to him the way she would to an adult rather than a child. The boy was going through so much; she didn't want to add to that by making him feel that he was being looked down upon. "You know your father has his own way of doing things. Besides, he has Jake and Roy helping him."

Ryan seemed to sink farther into his seat. His voice grew smaller. "That's what he said."

Lucia started up the car. It was getting late and if they didn't leave now, they really were going to be late. Glancing at the boy's expression, she could feel her heart going out to him. There were times that observing the awkwardness between father and son when they interacted was almost too painful.

"See," Lucia said, doing her best to sound cheerful. "You need to wait until he asks."

Ryan pressed his lips together, staring straight ahead. And then he raised his eyes to his ally. "What did I do, Lucia?"

"Do?" she questioned, not really sure what the boy was asking her.

Ryan nodded. "What did I do to make my father hate me?"

She was tempted to pull over and take the boy into her arms, but she knew that he wouldn't welcome that. He wanted to be treated like an adult, so she did her best to oblige. "Oh, *hijo*, he doesn't hate you."

"Well, he doesn't like me," Ryan insisted, hopelessness echoing in his voice.

"It's not that," Lucia insisted. "Your father just doesn't know how to talk to a little boy." *Or to anyone else*, she added silently.

"You do," Ryan said with feeling. "Can't you teach him?"

Lucia let her true feelings out for a moment. "Oh, *hijo*, if I only could. But your father is not the kind of man who would allow himself to be taught by anyone. He doesn't like to admit that he's wrong. He is a very, very sad man."

The expression on Ryan's face was equally sad. "Because my mother left. I know."

Lucia looked at the eight-year-old sharply, caught off guard by his response. "Who told you that?" she asked.

"Nobody," he answered truthfully. "I heard Jake and Uncle Roy talking about my mother, about how everything would have been different if she had stayed with my dad." The look on Ryan's face was all earnestness as he asked, "Did she go because of me? Is that why Dad doesn't like me?"

Not for the first time, Lucia had a strong desire to box her employer's ears. "Oh no, Ryan, no. She didn't leave because of you. Your mother left because she didn't want to live on the ranch. She wanted something more exciting in her life."

"More exciting than horses?" Ryan questioned, mystified that anyone could feel that way. He loved the horses as well as the cattle. Uncle Roy had taught him how to ride when he was barely old enough to walk. The horse had actually been a pony at the time, but it still counted as far as Ryan was concerned. He had loved being on a horse ever since that day.

Lucia looked at him sympathetically. "I'm afraid so."

Ryan just couldn't understand. "But what could be more exciting?" he asked, puzzled.

"That was what your mother wanted to find out." Lucia flashed a smile in the boy's direction. "She didn't realize that she was leaving behind the most exciting part of her life."

Ryan's eyebrows disappeared beneath the hair hanging over his forehead. "Dad?" he questioned.

Lucia bit back a laugh. The boy was absolutely and sweetly unassuming. "No, you."

Ryan frowned at the answer. He stared at the tips of his boots, waving his feet back and forth slightly. "I'm not exciting."

"Oh, but you are," Lucia assured him. "And you're only going to get more exciting the more you learn. For that," she pointed out, "I'm afraid that you're going to have to go to school. Do you understand what I'm saying to you?"

Ryan sighed and then nodded. "I guess so."

The housekeeper caught the hitch in his voice. "Ryan, you're not having any trouble at school, are you?" she asked, peering at his face.

Ryan shook his head. "No."

"None of the kids are picking on you, are they?" Lucia asked. "You can tell me if they are."

"No," he answered, then added quietly, "None of the kids even know I'm there."

Lucia tried something else. "How about your teacher? Do you like her?"

"Yes, I guess so." He shrugged again, then modified his answer. "She's okay."

Because she was trying to get the boy to open up to her, Lucia tried to encourage him to keep talking. "Why don't you tell me about her?"

Looking slightly bewildered, Ryan asked, "What do you want to know?"

Lucia thought for a moment. "Well, to begin with, what's your teacher's name?"

For the first time that morning, possibly that week, Lucia heard the small boy giggle. It was a charming sound, like a boy who adores his teacher.

He grinned as he answered, "Her name is Ms. Chee. She is Native American and used to live right here in Forever when she was a little girl."

"On the reservation?" Lucia asked the boy.

Ryan thought for a moment, as if checking the facts he had stored in his head. And then he shook his head. "No, she said she used to live in a house on the skirts of town."

"Outskirts?" Lucia tactfully suggested.

Ryan's small, angular face lit up. "Yeah, that's it. *Out*skirts. That's kind of a funny word."

"Yes, it is," Lucia readily agreed. She'd heard that the new second/third grade teacher had moved into a house in town. "Did Ms. Chee say why she didn't live there anymore?"

Ryan thought for a moment, then remembered. "Oh, yeah. She said when she came back to Forever, she found out that the house burned down a few years ago. She was sad when she talked about it."

Lucia tried to remember if she recalled hearing anything about a fire taking place near the town. And then a vague memory nudged her brain.

"Was Ms. Chee talking about the old Stewart house?" She remembered that the house had been empty for a number of years before a squatter had accidentally set fire to it while trying to keep warm. The wooden structure had gone up in no time flat. By the time the fire brigade had arrived, there was nothing really left to save.

Ryan nodded. "Uh-huh." He could see his school coming into view up ahead. Growing antsy, he shifted in his seat and began to move his feet back and forth again. "I think so."

Now that she had him talking, Lucia was loath to stop him. "What else did your teacher tell you?"

"She didn't tell me. She told the class," Ryan corrected her.

Lucia had noticed that the boy was very careful about making sure that all his facts were precisely stated. She nodded, accepting the revised narrative.

"Did Ms. Chee say anything else to the class?"

"She said lots of stuff," Ryan replied honestly. "She's the teacher."

Lucia tried not to laugh. "I meant anything more personal. Something about herself."

Ryan thought for a moment. "Just that she liked teaching."

"Well, that's a good thing." Lucia stopped the car right before the school's doors. "Now, go in and learn something."

"Yes, ma'am," Ryan replied dutifully as he slid out of the passenger seat and then closed the car door behind him.

Lucia watched him square his small shoulders before heading to the school's front door. She shook her head and then restarted the vehicle.

The boy had a lot of weight on his shoulders for one so young, she thought. He needed his father. She only wished she could make his father understand that.

Lucia blew out a breath as she began to drive back to the ranch. Maybe someday, she thought. Hopefully, before it was too late.

Chapter Two

Wynona smiled as she watched the children in her combined second/third grade class come trooping into the room. Seeing their bright, smiling faces as they walked in warmed her heart. It was like watching unharnessed energy entering.

Looking back, it was hard for her to believe that these same little people could have actually struck fear into her heart just a little more than a month ago. On the plus side, that feeling had passed quickly, vanishing like a vapor within the first few hours of the first day.

It was true what they said, Wynona thought. Kids *could* smell fear. Conversely, they could also detect when someone had an affinity for them, when that same someone really *enjoyed* their company and wasn't just pretending that they did.

Kids were a lot smarter than they were given credit for. Her own class quickly realized that she was the genuine article. That she wasn't just saying that she cared about them; she really did. And when she told them that she wanted to make learning fun for them, they believed her, even though a few of them, mainly the older ones, had rolled their eyes and groaned a little.

Instead of calling those students out, Wynona sincerely asked them how she could make the experience more enjoyable for them.

Thanks to her approach, within a few days Wynona had a classroom full of students who looked forward to coming to school every day.

But as with everything, Wynona saw that there was an exception. One of her students behaved differently than the others. Ryan Washburn didn't seem as if he was having any fun.

Covertly observing him, she saw that he acted far more introverted than the other students. Whenever her class was on the playground, unless she deliberately goaded Ryan into participating with the rest of the class, the boy would quietly keep to himself, watching the other students instead of joining in whatever game they were all playing.

After watching him for a month, she had to admit that Ryan Washburn worried her. When she talked to him, he was polite, respectful, but there was no question that he was still removed. The calls she'd placed to his home—apparently, there was only a father in the picture—had gone unanswered.

They were almost five weeks into the school year and

she had placed four calls to the man. The man whose deep, rumbling voice she heard on his answering machine hadn't called back once, not even to leave a message. She was going to give the man a couple more days, she promised herself, and then…

And then she was going to have to try something a little more to the point, Wynona decided.

"Good morning, class," she said cheerfully as the last student, a dark-eyed girl named Tracey, came in. Wynona closed the door behind her.

"Good morning, Ms. Chee," her students chorused back, their voices swelling and filling the room rather than sounding singsongy the way they had the first day of class after she had introduced herself.

Instead of sitting down at her desk, Wynona moved around to stand in front of it. She leaned her hip against the edge of the desk, assuming a comfortable position. Her eyes scanned the various students around the room. She was looking at a sea of upturned, smiling faces—all except for Ryan.

"Did you have a good weekend?" she asked them.

Some heads bobbed up and down while some of the more loquacious students in the class spoke up, answering her question with a resounding "Yes!"

Wynona slanted a look at Ryan. He'd neither nodded nor responded verbally. Instead, he just remained silent.

She hoped to be able to draw the boy out by trying to get her students to make their answers a little more specific.

"So, what did everybody do this weekend?" As some of the children began to respond, Wynona held her hand up, stopping the flow of raised voices blending in dissonance. "Why don't we go around the room and you can each tell the class what made this weekend special for you? Ian, would you like to start us off?" she asked, calling on the self-proclaimed class clown.

Ian, who at nine was already taller than everyone else in the class, was more than happy to oblige.

Wynona made sure to get her students to keep their answers short, or in Ian's case, at least under five minutes. She was careful to move sporadically around the room allowing enough children to answer first so that Ryan would feel comfortable when it came to be his turn, or at least not uncomfortable, she amended. She didn't want the boy to feel that her attention was focused on him, even though in this case, it actually was.

After six children had each told the class what special thing they had done over the weekend, Wynona turned toward the boy who was the real reason behind this impromptu exercise.

"Ryan, what did you do that was fun this weekend?" she asked him.

When the boy looked up at her, she was struck by the thought that he resembled a deer that had been caught in headlights.

After a prolonged awkward silence, Ryan finally answered. "Nothing."

"Nothing?" she repeated, searching for a way to coax more words out of Ryan. "You must have done something," she said. When he said nothing in response, she tried again. "What did you do when you got up on Saturday morning?"

"I had breakfast," Ryan replied quietly.

There was some snickering from a couple of the students. Wynona immediately waved them into silence. "That's a perfectly good answer, Ryan. Everyone needs to take in a source of good fuel so that they'll have energy to do things properly. What did you do after you finished breakfast?" she asked patiently.

Ryan licked his lips nervously. "Chores," he finally answered.

"I'm sure your dad appreciated that you did those chores," Wynona told him with feeling. She looked at him encouragingly. "Anything else?" she coaxed.

The boy thought for a moment, as if trying to remember what it was that he did next. And then he finally mumbled, "I went for a ride on Nugget." Exhaling a breath, he stared down at the floor.

"Is Nugget your horse?" Wynona asked, hoping that might get him to talk a little more.

This time, instead of saying anything verbal, Ryan nodded.

There was color rising in his cheeks and Wynona realized that unlike the other children who all vied for her attention and were eager to talk, the attention she was giving Ryan just embarrassed him.

Wynona quickly put an end to his discomfort. "Well, that sounds like a really fun thing to do," she told him. "I loved going for a ride on my horse when I was your age. But I had to share Skyball with my cousin. Skyball was an old, abandoned horse that someone had left to die, but we saved it." She remembered that as one of the highlights of her less-than-happy childhood. Looking back at Ryan, she smiled at him. "Thank you for sharing that, Ryan. Rachel—" turning, she called out to another student "—how about you? What did you do this weekend?"

Rachel was more than happy to share the events of her weekend with the class.

As Rachel began her lively narrative, Wynona glanced back in Ryan's direction. She watched the boy almost physically withdraw into himself.

This wasn't right. She had to do something about it. Wynona was more determined than ever to get hold of Ryan's father and talk to the man. She wanted to make sure that Washburn was aware of the boy's shyness so they could work together in an effort to do something about it. She also wanted to make sure that Ryan's behavior wasn't the result of some sort of a problem that was going on at home.

When the recess bell rang and her class all but raced outdoors to immerse themselves in playing games they had created, Wynona quietly drew Ryan aside and asked if she could talk to him.

Instead of asking his teacher if he had done something wrong, or why he was being singled out, Ryan merely stood to the side and silently waited for her to begin talking.

She wanted to get him to relax, but she knew that wasn't going to be easy.

"Ryan, why don't you come and sit over here?" she suggested, pointing to a desk that was right at the front of the room.

Ryan looked at the desk warily, making no move to do as she said. He had a reason. "But that's Chris's desk."

"I know that, but I'm sure Chris wouldn't mind if you sit there just for a few minutes. He's outside, playing," she reminded the boy.

After hesitating for another second, he finally walked over to the desk she had pointed out. Still hesitating, Ryan lowered himself into the seat as if he expected it to blow up at any moment.

Watching him, Wynona was more convinced than ever that there had to be something wrong, most likely in his home life. Was his father abusing the boy?

Taking care to make and keep eye contact as she spoke, she kept her voice as warm and friendly as she could as she began to talk to the boy.

"I know that I'm still new here at the school, Ryan, but I just wanted you to know that if you have something you need to talk about, or if there's something that's bothering you, no matter how small it might be, I'm here for you."

It was everything she could do not to put her arms around the boy and hold him to her. He looked so terribly vulnerable.

"You can tell me absolutely anything you want." She peered down into his face, trying her best to maintain that eye contact. The boy had attempted to look away, but she wouldn't let him. "Do you understand what I'm saying to you, Ryan?"

Ryan pressed his lips together and nodded, but he didn't say anything.

It was like pulling teeth, Wynona thought. Very elusive teeth.

But she was determined and she tried again. "Is there anything you want to tell me, Ryan?"

Ryan shook his head. "No, ma'am."

His answer was so low, she almost couldn't hear the boy.

She knew that she could only push so much without scaring him off.

"Okay, but if you change your mind," Wynona told the boy, "my offer still stands. And you know where to find me."

Ryan responded to her question in complete seriousness. "In school."

The corners of her mouth curved ever so slightly, but she managed not to laugh.

"Exactly." Wynona glanced at her watch. "You'd better get outside, Ryan. I've used up part of your recess playtime."

He obediently rose to his feet. "That's okay," he told her. "I wasn't going to play anyway."

Wynona took advantage of the opening, hoping to get a better understanding of what was going on in the boy's head.

"Why not? Don't you like to play, Ryan?"

She watched the small shoulders rise and fall in a helpless shrug. "Everybody already picked who they wanted on their side and what games they're gonna be playing," he told her.

She came to stand beside him, trying to convey in

spirit that she was on his side. “Nothing’s cast in stone, Ryan. There’s always room for one more.”

The look he gave her said that they both knew that wasn’t true, at least not in his case. As he began to slip out of the classroom, Wynona called after him. “Would you like to help me put out the books for our reading lesson?”

Sensing that would only put him even further apart from the others, Ryan answered, “That’s okay. I’ll just go outside.”

Watching him go, Wynona blew out a long breath. Granted, she hadn’t been a teacher for all that long, but she could definitely recognize a cry for help when she saw it, even though none of those particular words had actually been spoken.

“Oh, Lord, what happened to you, Ryan?” she murmured under her breath as she observed the boy from the window as he made his way outside.

As she watched, Ryan went to a space on the playground that was totally devoid of any students. It was as if he had voluntarily placed himself in exile.

She needed to do something about this, Wynona thought. She honestly didn’t know what, but there had to be *something* she could do. She couldn’t just stand back and do nothing while she watched the little boy almost wither away and die on the vine.

Over the course of the next two days, Wynona attempted to call Clint Washburn three more times. Each time she called, the phone rang five times and then the call went to his answering machine. She already knew that she was calling a landline. Apparently, Clint Washburn didn't have a cell phone.

He also didn't answer his landline or check his messages, she thought, growing progressively more and more annoyed. Being annoyed was something rare and out of character for her but she was definitely getting there, she thought, frustrated.

When she "struck out" again, waiting in vain for the man to return any of her calls, Wynona made up her mind as to what she was going to do next.

She obtained Ryan's address from the administrative office—a closet of a space, she thought as she walked out—and drove over to Ryan's family ranch.

She knew that this was highly unorthodox, given that they were only entering into the second full month of the school year, but she was out of options. At this point she was dead set on giving Washburn a piece of her mind. She wasn't used to being ignored like this. Especially not when it came to a matter that concerned one of her students.

When she drove her vehicle up to the ranch house that afternoon, Ryan was the first to spot her. The sound of an approaching vehicle had already drawn him to the front window. He was looking out that window when the car pulled up.

The car was unfamiliar to him. The person emerging from it was not.

"It's Ms. Chee!" he all but shouted in surprise. Turning for a split second to look over his shoulder in Lucia's direction, Ryan repeated what he'd just seen. "Lucia, it's Ms. Chee! She's here. My teacher's here!"

Caught by surprise, Lucia quickly wiped her hands on her ever-present apron as she hurried toward the front door. Puzzled, she spared Ryan a glance. "Did she tell you she was coming?"

"No," he answered, his head moving from side to side like a metronome set on high. "She didn't say anything to me about coming here."

"Are you sure?" Lucia prodded. "Did you do something bad in school?"

Even as she asked the question, Lucia was certain that the answer was no. Ryan was the model of obedience at home, but nothing else occurred to her at the moment.

"No," Ryan answered in a small, uneasy voice that said he was wavering in his belief about his own innocence in the matter.

Lucia had reached the front door by now and began to open it.

"Well, she has to have a reason for this visit," Lucia insisted. The next moment the small, dynamic housekeeper was standing on the porch, a one-woman welcoming committee. "Hello, I'm Mr. Washburn's housekeeper, Lucia Ortiz."

Wynona quickly made her way up the steps to the housekeeper. She took the woman's outstretched hand, shaking it.

"Hello, I'm Ryan's teacher, Wynona Chee." She peered over the shorter woman's shoulder, looking into the house. "Is Mr. Washburn around?"

Lucia remained standing in the doorway, making no move to let the other woman in. Her first allegiance was to the family she worked for. "Yes."

Wynona had come this far; she was not about to back off or turn around and go back to town. "I'd like to see him, please."

"He's at the corral," Lucia informed Ryan's teacher politely. "But this is his busy season. He's breaking in the new horses."

From what she remembered, ranchers were always busy, Wynona thought. She hadn't come to discuss what the man was doing; she had come about his son, whose well-being was far more important than any horses or cattle.

"I'm sure that's all very important," she told the woman, "but what I have to say to him is far *more* important." She glanced over her shoulder. "Just point me in the right direction and I'll be out of your hair," she promised the housekeeper.

"Maybe you should wait in the house," Lucia tactfully suggested. "I can bring you some tea to drink. Or perhaps you'd rather leave a message for Mr. Washburn and he'll get in touch with you."

Right, because that had worked out so well, Wynona thought. "Sorry, but I did and he didn't so now we're past leaving messages and waiting politely. I need to speak to him now." She looked down at Ryan. "Ryan, can you take me to where your dad's working?"

Torn, it was the moment of truth for Ryan. Hesitating, he wavered for just a second and then he chose his side.

"Okay," he said, taking her hand. "Follow me."

Chapter Three

Taking a momentary break, Jake leaned against the corral fence. That was when he saw her, a tall, willowy woman with jet-black hair. She was dressed in jeans, boots and a work shirt. And she was heading straight for them.

"Hey, don't look now, boss, but from the looks of it, there's an angry lady coming your way," Jake alerted Clint. "And if you ask me, it looks like the lady's loaded for bear."

Roy was already looking in the woman's direction and she had his complete attention. "I don't care what she's loaded for as long as she brings it my way," Clint's brother declared wistfully. "Who *is* she?" he asked, intrigued. "I don't remember ever seeing her around before. I would have remembered that face," Roy assured his brother and the other man.

Jake hadn't taken his eyes off the woman since he'd first spotted her.

"Yeah, me, too." He glanced toward Clint, who was still working and hadn't bothered to look at the interloper. "You know her, boss?"

"Whoever she is, Clint, she's got your boy with her," Roy added, still not looking away.

"What the hell are you two going on about?" Clint demanded shortly.

He'd been up early, going between the stable and the corral, and working since before his son had gone off to school. He had only spared a minimum of time for the cattle today. He was in no mood for guessing games, or unannounced guests. He just wanted to finish what he was doing and get in out of the sun.

"I don't know about Jake, but I'm talking about the prettiest sight I've laid my eyes on in a long, long time," Roy answered.

Exasperated, Clint dropped what he was doing and finally looked up just as the angry-looking young woman stepped up to the fence. Rather than ducking between the slats the way he would have expected her to do, he saw her climb up and then over the fence, jumping down on the other side as if she'd been doing it all of her life.

He was aware that his son was taking all this in with awe. If he didn't know any better, he would have said that the boy had the makings of a crush on this woman.

"Which one of you is Clint Washburn?" Wynona asked, walking until she was right in the middle of them.

Clint noted that both his brother and Jake would have

been more than willing to say they were, but since he was standing right there, they couldn't. Both looked in his direction.

"I am," he told her, taking off his work gloves and shoving them into his back pocket. "Can I help you?" he asked. His tone of voice clearly indicated that there were a great many other things he would have wanted to do first before turning his attention to whatever it was that this woman had come to see him about.

Wynona did a quick scrutiny of the man. He had broad shoulders and a small waist. His dirty-blond hair could have used a haircut, but it was his attitude that really needed work. The man was just as unfriendly as she had imagined he'd be.

"I'm Wynona Chee," she informed him, introducing herself. And then she added, "I'm Ryan's teacher," in case he hadn't listened to any of the multiple messages she'd left—which she was beginning to suspect he didn't.

"Well, Wynona Chee, if you're his teacher, why aren't you at school, going about your business?" Clint asked.

She resented the way he said that, but snapping at the man wasn't going to help Ryan and it was Ryan who was the important one here. So Wynona bit back a few choice words that instantly rose to her lips and kept her temper in check.

"I *am* going about my business," she informed him tersely, ignoring the other two men taking all this in. "Since you weren't returning any of the countless messages I left on your phone, I decided that a face-to-face meeting with you might be the better way to go."

"Oh, is that what you decided now?" Clint asked and she got the distinct impression that he was mocking her.

"Don't mind my brother," Roy said quickly, speaking up. "He gets kind of ornery when he's been working all day. Around here, whenever rattlesnakes take one look at him, they just head the other way."

Clint shot his younger brother a dirty look, which didn't seem to affect the other man at all.

Instead, Roy just shrugged in response. "I just thought she needed to be warned," the younger man told Clint.

At any other time, Wynona might have even been somewhat amused by this exchange between brothers, but she wasn't here to be amused. She was here because she felt that Ryan Washburn needed help in coming out of his shell before that shell wound up setting around the boy permanently, walling him off from everyone around him.

Wynona opened her mouth to state her purpose, then stopped. While Clint Washburn seemed uninterested in what she had to say, the other two men with him appeared to be all ears. She had a feeling that what she had to say wasn't something that Washburn would want the others to hear.

"Is there someplace we could speak privately?" Wynona asked Ryan's father.

Since he could see the woman wasn't going to just leave even if he didn't encourage her, Clint resigned himself to hearing her out about whatever minor, imagined complaint she had come to voice. It was the only way he figured he could get rid of her.

Gesturing around at the vast area surrounding them, he said, "Pick a place."

She felt that he was humoring her, but it didn't matter as long as he listened to what she had to say and, more important, took it to heart.

"How about over there?" she asked, pointing to the far end of the corral, away from the horses and the other two men.

Broad shoulders rose in a careless, disinterested shrug. "Works as well as any other place," he told her in an equally disinterested voice.

As she led the way to the spot she'd pointed out, Wynona noticed that Ryan fell into step right beside her. She didn't want to risk the boy overhearing his father saying something negative about him.

"No, you stay over there for now, Ryan," she instructed the boy gently.

"But you're gonna be talking about me, aren't you?" Ryan asked. It was obvious that he felt that since this meeting was about him, he did have a right to be there.

She had a feeling that he was always being excluded, but this time it was in his best interest.

Wynona did her best to temper her answer. "I'd like to talk to your dad alone first, Ryan. When that's done, you can join us."

Because she took the time to explain this to him first, Ryan felt a little better about having to be left out. Nodding his head, he stopped walking and obligingly fell back.

His uncle came up behind him and put his hand on

the boy's shoulder as Ryan's teacher and his dad kept walking. He waited until they were a little farther away.

"You getting into some kind of trouble?" Roy asked his nephew good-naturedly. He ruffled Ryan's hair with affection.

Ryan turned around to look up at him. "No, sir," he answered solemnly.

"No, I guess not," Roy laughed. "You wouldn't know trouble if you tripped over it." Ryan had always been a good kid, almost too good, Roy thought. A kid needed to get into things once in a while, but Ryan never did. "Why don't you come on back and help me and Jake get the bridle bits ready for those new horses?" he told his nephew.

He'd seen time and again how eager the boy was to help and for the life of him he couldn't understand why his brother kept turning a deaf ear to Ryan's offers. It just didn't seem right, he thought.

Both he and Clint had grown up working around the horses and doing every imaginable chore there was when it came to running the ranch. They'd practically been born in a saddle and it certainly hadn't done them any harm. It had come in handy when their father had totally stopped doing any work on the ranch at all.

Roy had told his brother more than once that working with the horses was good for the boy, but Clint never seemed to hear him.

He shook his head. If Clint kept this up, he was certain that his brother was going to drive a permanent wedge between himself and his son.

Roy certainly hoped that that young, pretty teacher

had better luck talking some sense into his fool brother's head than he did, he thought, looking over toward where the two were standing.

With a shrug he caught up to his nephew and went to rejoin Jake.

"So what's so important that you felt you had to come all the way out here in person to tell me?" Clint asked once they finally stopped walking and Ryan's teacher had turned around to face him.

Wynona got right to it. Hands on her hips, she demanded, "Do you have any interest in your son?"

Clint felt his back going up instantly.

"What kind of a fool question is that?" he asked.

He'd raised his voice, but she wasn't about to be intimidated. "A pretty straightforward one as far as I can see."

His dark blue eyes narrowed. "Then maybe you have blinders on."

Wynona didn't take the bait, didn't get sidetracked by the hostility in his voice and she didn't get caught up in an argument. Instead, in a very calm voice, she told him, "I would still like an answer to my question."

His face darkened like storm clouds over the prairie. "Yes, I'm interested in my son."

She gave him the benefit of the doubt. "Then why didn't you return any of my phone calls?" she asked, her hands still fisted at her sides. "I told you I was concerned about Ryan's behavior."

What the hell was that supposed to mean? "Was he fighting?" Clint asked.

Responding to his tone, she raised her chin defensively. "No, but—"

"Was he failing finger-painting?" Clint asked her sarcastically.

Was he belittling education, or just her? In either case, she could feel her temper rising. "I don't teach finger-painting," she informed him.

The expression on his face was smug, as if he had just won his argument. "I figured that. Maybe you should."

What was that supposed to mean? Wynona wondered. In any case, she wanted answers out of him. She wanted him to verbalize what was going on in his head. "*What* did you figure?"

The smug look on his face didn't abate. "That you were just making lady noises."

"What?" She stared at him incredulously. "Lady noises?" Wynona repeated. What the hell was that—aside from denigrating?

Despite her best efforts, she could feel herself *really* losing her temper. Something about Clint Washburn made her want to double up her fists and punch him *hard*, knocking some sense into that thick head of his.

His attitude reminded her of a few men she had encountered as a student and growing up in two different communities: the reservation near Forever and Houston. More than one of her friends' fathers were painfully distant from their children, concerned only with their own needs. They never once realized the effect that their behavior had on their offspring. She herself never knew her own father.

She hadn't known that there was any other way to behave until Shania's family had taken her in and she saw what a real father was really like. Dan Stewart had been kind and caring, taking care of her the same way he took care of Shania. Though she had known him only for a short time, the man had made all the difference in the world to her.

That was what she wanted for Ryan—before it was too late.

"Yeah. Lady noises," Clint repeated. "You come in, take one look around, unleash your emotions and think you've got the solution to everything. Well, you don't," he told her. "So, are we done here because I've got a ranch to run."

He was about to turn away but she caught his arm and made him turn back to face her.

"No, we are *not* done here," she informed him tersely. "Your son is starved for your attention," she said angrily.

He'd been surprised at the strength of her grip when she'd grabbed his arm. She was obviously not as delicate as she appeared. But that still didn't change the fact that she had no business telling him how to raise his son and he told her as much.

"I'm not going to coddle the kid."

"No one's telling you to coddle him," she retorted, her eyes all but flashing. "I'm just asking you to give him some of your time."

"In case you weren't listening," he informed her, getting to the end of his patience, "I've got a ranch to run."

"Then have him help you," she countered. She knew

of a lot of kids who helped their fathers out on the ranch. Why was he being so stubborn about it? "And talk to him while he's helping."

Clint was getting really tired of having this woman tell him what she thought he should be doing with his son. "Look—"

She anticipated his protest. "Mr. Washburn, I'm not asking you to read bedtime stories to Ryan, although you might give that some thought—" Wynona couldn't help adding.

"You're kidding," he cried, stunned by her suggestion. Nobody read to him when he was a kid. That kind of thing wasn't important in his book.

"No, I'm not 'kidding,'" she told him. "But the point I'm trying to get across to you is that you need to take an interest, a *real* interest, in Ryan. Treat him like a person. Like he *matters*. Talk to him, ask him how he's doing in school, tell him about the things you did when you were his age—"

Clint cut her off. He didn't have time for this. "I don't remember," he snapped.

Wynona's eyes narrowed again as her frustration with this jackass of a man increased. It was obvious that he was stubbornly fighting her on this but she wasn't about to let him win.

"Then make it up!" she cried angrily. Catching herself, she got control of her temper. "The point is communication. Because right now, every day, this boy is slipping further and further away and if you don't try to stop that, to make him feel as if you care about him, he's not only going to wind up being lost to you, he's going to be lost to himself, too."

That sounded like a bunch of garbage to him. "That's your opinion."

"It would be yours, too," she informed him, "if you just stopped and assessed the situation more closely like a father." She had almost said "like someone with a brain" but had stopped herself in time.

Clint waved her away and turned on his heel toward where Jake and Roy were waiting. "I don't have time for any of this psychobabble," he said as he walked away from her.

"It's not psychobabble," she insisted, calling after him. "It's common sense."

"Ha!" Clint countered, but he kept on walking.

He knew if he turned around to say anything more, she'd just drag him back into another argument and he had already wasted enough time on this woman and her crazy theory.

Clint kept walking until he got back to where Jake and his brother were working. Ryan was with them as well and the boy looked up at him the moment he drew closer. Before his son could say anything to him or ask any questions, Clint said, "Go into the house and do your homework."

"I already finished my homework, sir," Ryan told him quietly.

"Then go do something else," Clint ordered, turning back to what he'd been doing before that woman disrupted his day.

To his surprise, Ryan stood his ground.

"Can I help you?" he asked in the same small, hopeful voice he'd used the morning when he had asked the same question.

The word *no* hovered on Clint's tongue and he'd almost said it. But then he heard that teacher's vehicle as she apparently started it up and then began to drive away.

Good. The woman was really going back into town, Clint thought.

But what the woman had said annoyingly refused to drive away with her. It seemed to linger in the air like a solid entity.

Clint frowned as he turned to look at his son.

"Yeah," Clint finally said, reluctantly relenting. "You can help—as long as you promise not to get in the way."

Stunned that his father had actually said he could help, Ryan looked at him, a wide smile spreading out over his small, angular face.

"I promise! Just tell me what to do and I'll do it, Dad," Ryan proclaimed eagerly. "Just tell me," he repeated.

Clint looked down at his son. Despite the boy's eager reaction, Clint couldn't shake the feeling that he had just unintentionally opened up Pandora's box.

Chapter Four

Hearing the front door open and then close again, Shania came out of the kitchen and into the living room. She smiled at her cousin. "You're home."

"What gave it away?" Wynona asked, dropping her purse and briefcase unceremoniously on the coffee table. She dropped herself down on the sofa almost at the same time. Anger had temporarily drained her.

The sarcastic remark was totally out of character for Wynona, Shania thought, so she didn't bother commenting on it.

Instead, she said, "You're usually here ahead of me. If you hadn't turned up soon, I was going to send the dogs out looking for you."

"We have dogs?" Wynona asked.

The sarcastic edge in her voice was beginning to

fade. They didn't have dogs; they shared joint ownership of one dog, a German shepherd named Belle. Belle was more like a member of the family than a pet.

"Okay, 'dog,'" Shania corrected needlessly. "Belle likes to think of herself as a whole army." Because ignoring her cousin's obviously sour mood was not making it go away, she tried addressing it head-on. "Boy, you're certainly being unusually touchy tonight. Something go wrong today?"

Instead of pretending not to know what Shania was talking about, or denying her cousin's assessment, Wynona came clean.

"I tried to talk some sense into a knuckle-dragging blockhead, but I should have realized that my efforts were doomed from the start," Wynona complained. She closed her eyes, trying to center herself.

Coming farther into the room, Shania sat down on the sofa beside her cousin. "I take it we're not talking about one of your students."

Wynona opened her eyes and sat up, glancing at her cousin in confusion.

"My students?" she repeated. "I'd never say something like that about one of the students—"

"Then who are you talking about?" Shania asked.

"Ryan Washburn's father, Clint." Even as she said his name, Wynona frowned. "I went to talk to him today after school."

Shania hadn't heard her cousin mention the man's name before. Was that someone she'd known before they had moved to Houston with their great-aunt? "Why would you do that?"

Wynona's frown deepened. It was obvious she was struggling to get her temper under control. "Because the Neanderthal wouldn't return any of the twelve hundred messages I left on his phone."

Shania smiled. She was accustomed to her cousin's penchant for exaggeration. She didn't do it around anyone else, but Wynona felt comfortable around her and she relaxed the restrictions she imposed on herself when she was within earshot of other people.

"Twelve hundred?" Shania repeated. "That many times, huh?"

Wynona relented. "Okay, maybe it was more like eight."

Shania inclined her head. "A little more manageable number," she agreed. "What kind of messages were you leaving for this unresponsive parent?" she asked her cousin, trying to get a better picture of what had gone on.

"The kind of messages a concerned teacher leaves for the parent of one of her students," Wynona answered. She would have thought that Shania would just naturally assume that.

But Shania was still attempting to piece the story together. She couldn't remember seeing Wynona this angry or incensed before.

"One of the students getting into trouble and the father doesn't want to hear about it?" she asked, thinking of the most logical reason that would set off her cousin this way.

Wynona got up and, still agitated, began to pace around. "Oh, the father clearly didn't want to hear about it, but it wasn't because his son was getting in trouble." She swung around to face her cousin. "Oh, Shania, Ryan is such a sweet, sweet kid. If you saw his face, you'd think you were looking at an angel."

Shania was still feeling her way around this subject. "And he's not a little devil?"

"No!" Wynona cried defensively. "If anyone's a devil, it's that father of his." The moment the words were out of her mouth, Wynona knew she had gone over the line. She shrugged helplessly. "Maybe that's not exactly fair," she admitted.

Shania took her cousin's hand and pulled her back down onto the sofa next to her. "Wyn, why don't you take a deep breath and tell me about this from the beginning?" she suggested.

Belle chose that moment to come walking over to the two women. As if on cue, the German shepherd put her head in Wynona's lap.

"Better yet," Shania said, amending her initial instruction as she smiled at the dog, "Why don't you pet Belle and *then* start talking from the beginning?" She knew the animal had a calming effect on both of them, especially on Wynona.

Because she had never been able to resist the dog from the moment they had rescued the animal from a shelter literally hours before she was slated to be destroyed, Wynona ran her hand along the dog's back, petting her. The dog seemed to wiggle into the petting motion. A smile slowly emerged on Wynona's lips.

Watching her cousin, Shania asked, "You feel better now?"

Wynona was forced to nod. "It's hard to stay angry petting a dog."

"I had a feeling," Shania said. She remained where she was. "Okay, I'm listening. Why were you talking to a knuckle-dragging Neanderthal and how did that wind up making you so late?"

Still petting Belle, Wynona answered the second part of that first. "I'm late because I didn't want to come home angry so I drove around for a while, trying to calm down."

That certainly hadn't worked out well, Shania thought. Out loud she said, "If this is 'calmed down,' I would have hated to have seen you the way you were before you 'calmed down,'" Shania commented. "I don't think I've ever seen you this worked up before."

Wynona could only shake her head, even as she continued to stroke Belle. "This guy just pushed all my buttons."

Well, this was something new, Shania thought in surprise.

"I didn't know you had 'buttons' to push. You were always the calm one," she pointed out. "So just what was there about this student's father that set you off this way?"

Wynona searched for a way that would make this clearer for her cousin. And then she thought of something.

"Shania, do you remember Scottie Fox's father?" she asked.

Hearing the man's name suddenly took her back over the years, to a time when neither of them was a decade old yet. Shania did her best not to shiver as an icy sensation ran down her spine.

"How could I forget?" she cried. "That man almost beat Scottie to death before Scottie's mother and grandfather pulled him off Scottie." The man's name suddenly came back to her. Henry Fox. "Later, Henry claimed that he didn't remember the incident at all. Is—Ryan, is it?" she asked, pausing as she tried to remember the name Wynona had just used.

Wynona nodded. "Ryan Washburn."

"Is Ryan's father like Scottie's was?" Shania asked, appalled.

That had been an extreme case. From what she could see, Ryan didn't have any visible bruises on his body and he had worn short-sleeved shirts.

"No, at least I haven't seen any evidence of any violence, but the man is just as distant, just as removed, as Henry Fox first seemed. Washburn showed more interest in his horses than he did in his son." Wynona looked at her cousin, a feeling of helplessness washing over her. She wanted to fix this. "That boy is starved for affection and attention."

"And you went to tell the dad that he needed to shape up and provide that for his son," Shania guessed.

It didn't take much of a stretch of the imagination for Shania to reach that conclusion. Wynona had always been a softhearted person.

"Well, what would you have done?" Wynona asked.

Shania sighed. With a surrendering shrug of her shoulders she said, "Probably the same thing that you tried to do, Wyn. But realistically, that doesn't change the fact that you realize that you can't change the world."

Wynona never liked being told what she couldn't do. And Great-Aunt Naomi had taught both her and Shania that they didn't have to accept limitations but to reach for the moon.

This, she thought, wasn't quite the moon. But in a way, it was more important.

"I just want Ryan's father to realize what he's losing if he doesn't do something about the way he treats his son," Wynona insisted.

Shania shook her head. "You know, Wyn, I can almost see the words I'm saying to you just bouncing right off your head, never managing to get in."

"I hear you," Wynona protested.

"Okay, then you're just choosing to ignore what I'm saying," Shania guessed with a grin.

Wynona rose to her feet again. Belle fell into place right beside her. The animal was obviously anticipating food coming her way very soon.

"Let me start getting dinner ready," Wynona said, deliberately changing the subject.

Belle became even more animated at the sound of the word *dinner.*

"What makes you think I didn't start dinner?" Shania asked. She managed to keep a straight face as she asked the question.

Wynona slanted a look in her cousin's direction that practically said she had to be kidding.

"I know because the earth is still round and because

the kitchen hasn't gone up in flames yet," Wynona pointed out.

"Very funny," Shania countered. "Well, maybe I didn't start making dinner because I know just how much you enjoy cooking and I didn't want to take that pleasure away from you."

For the first time since she had come home, Wynona laughed. "Okay, we'll go with that."

"Yes, we will," Shania agreed. "Unless you'd like me to return to our previous, unfinished discussion about you trying to single-handedly tilt at windmills and change the world."

Wynona blew out a breath. She had no interest in going back to that.

"You in the mood for chicken or beef?" she asked, going back to the topic of dinner because that was a far safer way to go than resurrecting the aforementioned discussion.

Shania flashed a smile as she looked at her cousin over her shoulder. "Surprise me."

"Okay, one surprise coming up," Wynona declared as she disappeared into the kitchen.

Belle was still following close behind, hoping for a treat—or five.

The truth of it was, Wynona thought as she worked in the kitchen, she welcomed making dinner. She needed something to focus on and cooking really did have a way of calming her. For her it was dealing with the familiar. Shania was perfectly willing to let her take over the kitchen. There was no competition between them, especially not when it came to cooking.

Shania had often said that her cousin could probably whip up better meals with her eyes closed than most people could poring over cookbooks and laboriously following recipes.

The ironic thing was that it had been her aunt, Shania's mother, who had taught her how to cook. Wynona's mother hadn't had a talent for it, but Shania's mother could make three-day-old dirt taste good and she passed on all her recipes, shortcuts and secret ingredients to her. She had been glad to do it when Shania had shown that she had absolutely no interest in cooking and certainly no talent for it.

Looking back now, it amazed Wynona how much she had managed to pick up in the short amount of time she had lived with her cousin and her aunt and uncle before the final tragedy struck.

And, just as in Belle's case, she thought as she put the finishing touches on the mashed potatoes, she and Shania had been just hours away from having their lives dramatically changed forever.

As it turned out, they did have their lives dramatically changed, but for the better, rather than what she and Shania had anticipated was going to happen to them. Their great-aunt had come sweeping in like a hurricane, scooping them up in her wake and bringing both of them to Houston with her. Dr. Naomi Stewart was not the most demonstrative of people, but there was no question in either Wynona's or Shania's mind that the woman had loved them.

That was what she was trying to obtain for Ryan, Wynona thought ruefully. She wanted the boy to feel loved, to *know* that he was loved. Despite what she'd said to Shania about the buttons that Washburn had managed to inadvertently push within her, she didn't think that the man was being remote because he didn't like the boy. She had a feeling that there was something else at play here. Maybe the man didn't know how to relate to his son—or possibly to anyone at all. Not out of spite, but because there was just something that kept him trapped within himself and unable to display any sort of feelings whatsoever.

"Well, if that's the case, Mr. Washburn, you'll be happy to know that help is on the way. Well, maybe not happy," Wynona amended, taking Washburn's disposition into account, "but it's on the way anyway." Finished with the mashed potatoes, she turned her attention to something else.

"Who are you talking to?" Shania asked, drawn by the sound of her cousin's voice and walking into the kitchen.

Startled, Wynona managed to recover quickly. "No one, just seeing how something sounds out loud. I'm working up a lesson plan," she said.

Shania crossed her arms before her chest and gave her cousin a penetrating, knowing look. "Why, Wynona Chee, I've never known you to lie before."

Wynona got her back up. "I'm not ly—okay, so maybe I was just talking to myself," she amended, backtracking.

Shania continued looking at her, waiting for more. "About?"

"Don't you have any lesson plans to work on?" Wynona asked her cousin, wanting to change the subject or at least put this one to rest. "Something else you should be doing instead of eavesdropping on me?"

Shania just continued standing there, smiling as she watched her cousin move about the cozy kitchen. "Nope. Even if I did have a lesson plan to work on, which I don't by the way, this is a lot more interesting." She tilted her head, giving no indication that she was about to leave the room or Wynona. "Something you'd like to share with the class, Wynona?" she asked.

Wynona just went on working. "No, as a matter of fact, I don't."

Shania didn't give up. She and Wynona were in tune to one another the way other cousins weren't. She had a feeling there was something more going on. Wynona had seemed too upset when she'd come home.

She tried another tack. "How about something to get off your conscience?"

"No, again." Wynona stopped moving around the kitchen and fixed a look at her cousin. "Look, Ryan's father just got to me and I'm trying to work that out. I'll be fine by the time we finish eating this meal," she said, nodding at the dinner she was busy preparing for the table.

Shania smiled. She knew when to prod and when to back off and stop pushing. This was one of the latter times. She smiled at Wynona. "You know, you just might have stumbled onto a new way to handle problems—cooking your way into working things through."

"Very funny," Wynona commented drily. And then

she suggested, "Why don't you make yourself useful and set the table?"

Shania was more than willing to comply. "Well, if that's all it takes to be useful to you, you've got it. I'll go set the table."

"Shania," Wynona called after her.

The other woman stopped and turned away from the kitchen cabinet, holding two plates in her hands. "Yes?"

"Thanks."

Shania knew her cousin wasn't referring to her setting the table. She smiled, nodded. "Don't mention it. My pleasure, Wyn. My pleasure."

Wynona laughed as she got back to preparing the chicken. "You certainly have a low threshold of pleasure, Shania."

"Well," Shania replied philosophically, "if you keep your expectations low, almost anything at all will turn out to be a nice surprise, guaranteed to make you happier than you'd thought you would be."

Wynona laughed, "Good philosophy, cousin."

"I always thought so," Shania said cheerfully. "Now, hurry up," she urged, taking out the silverware. "I'm hungry."

Chapter Five

Wynona didn't know exactly what to expect when she arrived at school the next day.

As had become her habit, she had come in early. Trying to take her mind off Ryan and all the different possible scenarios that might have taken place after she had left the Washburn ranch, she moved around the classroom, tidying things up and preparing for that day's lesson.

Despite moving at less than her regular pace, she still found herself with a lot of time on her hands and nothing to do. When her students finally began coming in, she held her breath, watching the doorway.

But unlike other mornings, her attention wasn't focused on the children in her class. It was focused exclusively on Ryan, waiting for him to come in. There was a part of her, she had to admit, that was afraid that her visit to his ranch in order to have things out with his father had ultimately only made things worse for the introverted boy.

If that was the case, she would never forgive herself—after she went back to the man's ranch and boxed the man's ears.

But when the boy came in with the rest of his class and she saw the look on his face, she knew that at least for now, no return visit or boxing of ears was called for. Ryan was smiling, looking a great deal happier than she had ever seen him.

Rather than keeping his head down, Ryan actually made eye contact with her. And when he did, when he caught her looking at him, he smiled wider. It was as if the sun had suddenly come out, casting light on everything in the immediate vicinity right after a prolonged, heavy rain.

Wynona raised her eyebrows in a silent question and the boy's smile grew wider still. Breaking rank before he reached his desk, he came up to her and whispered, "I got to help my dad with the horses," and then just as abruptly he went to take his seat.

She hugged what he had just told her, dying to ask Ryan to elaborate. But she didn't want to embarrass the boy in front of the class by singling him out so she held off until recess.

It was possibly the longest two and a half hours she'd ever gone through.

Once her class began to file out into the school yard,

she waited to see what Ryan would do. As she'd hoped, he hung back for a minute and then shyly, slowly, he made his way over to her. He moved like a newborn colt trying out his legs and learning how to stand for the first time.

Wynona waited patiently. "Is there something you'd like to talk to me about?" she asked, coaxing the words out of Ryan.

The boy's head bobbed up and down enthusiastically. Every part of him seemed so much more animated than it had been up until today.

"Uh-huh! My dad asked me to help with the horses!" he told her again.

Wynona's smile matched Ryan's. "Tell me everything," she encouraged. "What did you do?"

"I got to hold on to their bridles. Not all at once," he said quickly, not wanting her to misunderstand. "I held on to the bridles one at a time."

As she felt everything inside her lighting up, Wynona nodded her approval.

"Very smart," she told him. "If you're holding on to more than one bridle at a time and the horses decide to go in two different directions, you have a problem," she said solemnly.

"Mostly I helped Uncle Roy," Ryan went on. "But at the end of the day, when we all went into the house, my dad said I did okay." He beamed as if his father had just paid him the highest compliment possible. His bright blue eyes were dancing.

It wasn't exactly an avalanche of praise, Wynona thought, but it definitely was a start. Most important, Ryan was happy about how things had gone.

She was careful to sound totally positive about his experience. "That really sounds wonderful," she told the boy. "I'm sure you were a great help. How do you feel about it?"

"Wonderful!" Ryan declared. And then, although he had always been shy and withdrawn around her, Ryan threw his arms around her waist and hugged her, nonverbally expressing all the gratitude and joy he was feeling right at this moment.

After several minutes, he stepped back. "Okay if I go outside?"

"Absolutely," she told him with enthusiasm.

"See you later." Ryan waved as he dashed out into the school yard.

It's a start, Wynona thought. Moving to the side, she watched through the window as Ryan made his way outside where the younger students gathered to play. To her surprise, she saw Ryan approach one of the more quiet students. She obviously couldn't hear the few words that were exchanged, but she got the general gist as she watched the two boys begin to play together.

Definitely a start, Wynona thought as her heart swelled. She couldn't have felt happier than if someone had just told her she was in the running for the Nobel Prize.

Because she wanted Clint Washburn to know the positive effect his action had had on his son—after all, she had let him have it with both barrels when it had involved the negative effect he'd had on the boy—Wynona called Clint Washburn the first chance she got.

After five rings, the answering machine picked up.

She stifled a sigh and almost hung up the phone. But she forced herself to stay on until she heard the tone prompting her to leave a message.

"Mr. Washburn, this is Wynona Chee. Ryan's teacher," she added, then bit her lower lip because at this point the man damn well *knew* who she was. Washburn might be a lot of things but he wasn't an idiot. "I just wanted you to know that Ryan was like a changed boy today. He said you let him help with the horses. I can't begin to tell you how incredibly happy he was."

Every word sounded stilted to her ear. She couldn't seem to convey the really positive note she was attempting to express. She wasn't trying to pat herself on the back, and somehow, congratulating a father for acting like a decent father didn't seem right, either, but there was no way to state what was going on at school today without making it sound awkward.

Aware that she'd allowed several seconds of dead time to go by, she cleared her throat. "Anyway, I just wanted you to know. Bye," she said belatedly.

Hanging up, she realized that she had wound up repeating herself in the short message she had left on Washburn's answering machine.

With a sigh, Wynona returned the receiver to the cradle.

She had gotten her message across and that was all that counted. Maybe if Washburn was made aware of how far a little bit of kindness could go, he'd be more prone to act kindly toward the boy.

At any rate, she had done what she had set out to do. She'd let him know that his son had been a great deal happier today than she'd ever seen him and that was all she was trying to convey to the man.

Wynona forced herself to put the matter out of her mind. Though she was happy about Ryan, he wasn't her only student. She had a classroom of kids to inspire and motivate and she needed to concentrate on them right now.

To her, that was the only way to learn—to turn everything into a stimulating, challenging game whether she was teaching the students math, or reading, or any of the other subjects that she touched on in her daily attempt to turn her students into eager little sponges soaking up the knowledge she was imparting.

At the end of the day, after all her students had cleared out of the classroom and gone to their homes, the euphoria Wynona had felt because of the way that Ryan had behaved was still there. She was still feeling pleased with herself.

She couldn't get over how Ryan's demeanor had been so light, so different than anything she had previously witnessed from him. Wynona felt as if she could probably live off the fumes of that happiness for an entire month, if not more.

Sitting at her desk, she had just finished grading the surprise quiz that she had given today. It was a history quiz and as she reviewed the grades, she was pleased to see that most of the class had done very well.

She was even more pleased to see that Ryan had done far better than he normally did.

Though she knew all about the benefits of positive

reinforcement, it still amazed her that a little bit of positive interaction with his father could have this much of an effect on the boy. It was as if he'd been trapped inside this dark box and all he had needed was this one simple act of thoughtfulness from his father to make him come out.

Wynona stared at the quiz she had just finished grading. Common sense would have dictated that she just hand the quiz back to Ryan tomorrow when she gave the rest of the students back their quizzes.

But right now she felt this strong urge to show Washburn what a little bit of kindness and attention on his part had managed to accomplish in his son's case. Most of all, she secretly hoped that this would encourage the man to continue treating his son this way.

She pressed her lips together as she went on looking at the quiz.

"Let it go, Wynona. Nobody's paying you to be this man's conscience," she murmured under her breath. "Most likely, he'll probably resent you for it. You know what bullheaded men are like."

She wavered over the matter, her good intentions warring with her common sense.

In the end, her common sense never had a chance. Her desire to make sure that Washburn's actions had not been just a one-time thing, or a fluke that the rancher had committed in a moment of what the man would probably think of as weakness, had Wynona making up her mind on what course of action to take.

For the second time in two days, she drove to the Washburn ranch.

* * *

This time, when she arrived, Wynona didn't stop at the ranch house first. On a hunch, she drove her small, fifteen-year-old car toward where she had seen the corral yesterday.

Not wanting to risk spooking the horses just in case Washburn and his hands were working with the animals in the corral, she parked her vehicle about a quarter of a mile away from it.

As she made her way toward the corral, Wynona could immediately make out Washburn. The two other men she had seen working alongside the rancher were with him, as well.

The person she didn't see in the area was the one person she was actually looking for. Ryan was nowhere around.

Her heart dropped.

The next moment Wynona forced herself to rally. She'd been right in coming out, she told herself. This man not only had to be led to water, he also had to be tethered next to the stream and forcibly have his muzzle held right in the water.

As with the first time, Washburn wasn't the first to see her. He was too busy working with one of the horses. It was his brother, Roy, who saw her first.

Roy stopped what he was doing to admire the figure Ryan's teacher cut as she strode toward the corral and them.

"What did you do wrong this time, Clint?" he asked his brother.

Clint didn't even bother looking up. If he stopped

every time one of the other two men felt like talking, he'd told them that he would never be able to get anything done.

So instead, he growled, "What the hell are you talking about?"

Not waiting for an answer, Roy just continued talking. He'd already made an assumption. "Whatever it was, it brought that spitfire of a teacher back, big brother," Roy told him.

Clint didn't have to look at his brother to know that he was grinning ear to ear. He could hear it in Roy's voice.

With a sigh, he looked over in the direction of the ranch house. That was when he saw her. Ryan's teacher, heading straight for them.

For him.

Just like yesterday. It was almost like déjà vu, except that the woman was wearing different clothes than she had yesterday.

He noticed the way she moved in them.

He noticed everything about her.

Muttering under his breath, Clint took off his gloves and dropped them as he headed toward the woman. *Now what?* he wondered, annoyed.

"Need backup?" Jake asked, calling after Clint as the latter strode toward the teacher.

"No," Clint bit off. "You just keep on working," he ordered the ranch hand.

Never taking his eyes off the woman—it both impressed and annoyed him that she met his glare head-on—he cut the distance between them until they were finally facing each other.

"Something else on your mind, *Ms.* Chee?" he asked.

Wynona unconsciously squared her shoulders, bracing herself for a no-holds-barred confrontation. Her eyes continued to meet his.

"Yes," she informed him. "I came to tell you that Ryan has gotten a ten on his quiz."

"A ten?" Clint repeated. He knew his son wasn't a walking brain, but the kid wasn't dumb, either. "That doesn't sound very good."

"That's ten out of ten," Wynona pressed, realizing that Washburn probably thought she meant ten out of a hundred.

The angry crease across his forehead relaxed. "All right, then that's a good grade."

"Yes, it is." For just a split second, Wynona caught herself being distracted by Washburn's chiseled face. There was such a thing as being too good-looking. And this man was. "And I also came to tell you that Ryan was like a different boy in class today. He was actually smiling."

Clint continued to peer intently at her. "And you think that's a good thing?"

Did he actually have to be told that? she couldn't help wondering. "Yes," she said emphatically. "That's a good thing."

"Okay," Clint said, trying to get to the bottom of why she'd appeared on his property and came at him as if she wanted to hang him by his thumbs. "So why do you look like lightning bolts are about to come shooting out of your eyes?"

The rancher was more than six inches taller than she was but Wynona wasn't about to be intimidated or back down. This was important. "Because you obviously thought that treating Ryan like a human being was a one-time thing and you and I both know that it can't be."

He stared at her. "Let me get this straight. You came all the way out here so that you could lecture me again?" he demanded.

Honey. She could catch more flies with honey, she silently cautioned herself. Wynona tempered her voice. "I'm not here to lecture," she answered in a softer voice. "I'm here to beg you."

Clint's eyes narrowed as he continued to pin her in place. "I don't follow."

"Then let me explain." She noted that Ryan's father bristled slightly at her tone. She proceeded carefully. "That little bit of attention you showed your son had a huge effect on him. For the first time since the beginning of the school year, I saw a smile on Ryan's face. Not only that, but come recess time, he actually went out to play on the playground," she told him.

To her surprise, Washburn looked completely unimpressed. "I thought he was supposed to learn something, not play."

"Part of learning is to learn how to play with others," Wynona countered. "My job isn't just to teach reading, math and history," she told him, her voice beginning to rise. "My job is to teach the whole child, to help him cope as he goes on to be a well-adjusted adult."

A look of impatience creased Clint's face. "Adult? He's eight."

"But he's not *always* going to be eight," Wynona reminded him.

Clint made the natural progression. "Nine's not an adult, either."

"No, but it's closer to an adult than eight. See how this goes?" she asked.

He'd wasted enough time arguing with this woman. "What I'd like to see going is you, Ms. Chee, because I have work to do."

He began walking away from her. She was quick to catch up. She wasn't finished with him yet. "Seems like you always have work to do."

"You're catching on," he tossed over his shoulder as he kept on walking.

"Your number-one priority should be your son," Wynona insisted, following him again.

Clint stopped walking and turned to face her, annoyed. "I don't need you to tell me that."

But Wynona didn't back down. "I think you do."

"Don't take this the wrong way," he began, "but I don't really care what you think."

She surprised him by saying, "Fair enough—but don't you care what your son thinks?"

He didn't answer her, but a small voice behind her spoke up. "Ms. Chee, what are you doing here?" Ryan asked.

Turning around, she saw that Ryan was standing right behind her. She hadn't even heard the boy come up.

"I, um, came to show your father your quiz." She

pulled the paper out of her bag and held it up for the little boy to see it. "You got a ten, Ryan. I'm very proud of you."

Ryan took the paper in his hands, his eyes shining. "I got a ten?" he cried, and then he grinned. "Hey, I did. I got them all right!" It was obvious that he was thrilled. He looked up at his teacher and then at his father. "I'm gonna go put this back in the house. Is that okay, Dad?"

Clint nodded. "Yeah, sure. That's fine."

Ryan was almost jumping up and down. "And then I'll come right back to help you like you said you wanted me to."

As she watched the boy dash off, Ryan's joyfully proclaimed words replayed themselves in her head. Washburn had actually asked the boy to help. Just as she had told him he should do. Apparently, the rancher was one jump ahead of her.

More than a little embarrassed, Wynona turned to look at the boy's father.

She cleared her throat and then said, "I guess I owe you an apology."

Chapter Six

Clint allowed his eyes to drift slowly over the length of the woman standing in front of him. He didn't say anything. It was as if he was taking stock of his words, deciding which ones he was going to use. Seconds went by, intensifying the silence.

Finally, he acknowledged, "I guess maybe you do after jumping all over me like that."

By then Roy had obviously decided to join them. He was as curious about things as his older brother seemed to be indifferent to them. Roy had managed to reach his brother and Ryan's teacher just in time to hear the last exchange.

The younger Washburn filled in whatever blanks still existed. "C'mon, Clint, lighten up. Ms. Chee wasn't trying to tread on your toes. She was just thinking of

the boy and putting his best interests
else."

"I was," Wynona said, quick to pick up
"But obviously I spoke out of turn because I w
jumping to conclusions. The wrong conclusions,
emphasized. "After seeing Ryan so happy earlier today, when I came out here just now, it looked like he'd been excluded from the activity that meant so much to him, so I thought—well, I guess you can see why I thought what I did." She looked at him, expecting Washburn to come to the same conclusion that she had.

"Actually, no, I can't," Clint answered flatly. "Maybe because I'm not in the habit of sticking my nose into other people's business."

"Clint!" Roy's admonishment came automatically before he had a chance to censor himself.

Although he was definitely on her side, Wynona hardly took note of Washburn's brother. She was entirely focused on Ryan's father—and doing her best not to lose her temper. Again.

The man had definitely cornered the market in pigheadedness, she thought.

"Your son's welfare *is* my business, in the same way that the welfare of all the other children in my care is my business," she informed Clint icily. Her eyes had narrowed into slits and she had raised her chin pugnaciously.

"Did I miss something here?" Clint demanded. "Aren't you Ryan's teacher, not his social worker?"

The man looked as if he was on the verge of having steam come out of his ears, but she wasn't about to allow him to intimidate her. Angry, she was not about to back off. "We're all our brother's keeper."

"Oh wow, lady. You really are something else, you know that?" Washburn marveled and she didn't have to guess that he didn't mean that in a flattering way.

Shooting Clint an impatient look, Roy took a step forward, moving closer to his nephew's teacher. "I'd like to apologize for my brother."

Clint's dark look shifted toward his brother. "Nobody asked you to speak for me," he informed Roy coldly.

The last thing she wanted was to start something between Ryan's father and his uncle. "That's all right, I should be—"

"Dad," Ryan called out as he returned from the house. "Lucia wants to know if Ms. Chee is gonna stay for dinner. Can she?"

Both Clint and Wynona turned toward the boy and answered his question almost at the same time.

"No!"

And, at the same time, they both saw the boy's face as it fell.

Seeing his obvious disappointment, Wynona felt a sharp stabbing pain in her heart. However, despite the housekeeper's question, she was not about to stay anywhere she wasn't welcomed. It didn't take any sort of advanced degree for her to see that she definitely wasn't welcomed at Clint Washburn's table.

Clint's expression didn't change when he saw the distressed look on his son's face, but that didn't mean that he was unaffected by it. Although he had managed, over the years, to build an almost airtight wall around himself, sometimes that wall got a little fissure and just for a moment, feelings would get through.

Wanting to just drop the matter, for some reason he couldn't begin to fathom, Clint felt compelled to offer a halfhearted explanation to his son. "Ms. Chee's too busy to have dinner with us."

Rather than accept his father's explanation, Ryan looked up at his teacher as if he harbored a slim hope that she would change her mind if he pressed her to explain why she couldn't come.

"Are you really too busy, Ms. Chee?" Ryan asked her.

The wound in her heart grew a little larger. Wynona could easily see having her stay for dinner meant a lot to the boy and although she would have rather walked barefoot over hot coals than break bread with Clint Washburn, he wasn't the one who mattered here.

And neither was she.

Only Ryan mattered and for him, she *would* break bread with his father as long as doing so would bring back that sweet smile to the boy's small face.

Bracing herself for what she knew in her heart was going to be an ordeal, she asked Ryan, "What time's dinner?"

Wynona deliberately avoided his father's penetrating stare.

"Five o'clock," Ryan announced, almost singing out the words. The hopeful look on his face had doubled as he asked again, "Can you stay, Ms. Chee?"

"Well," she replied, this time looking over Ryan's head at his father, "I wouldn't want to intrude where I'm not wanted."

The ball was now in Washburn's corral, she thought, waiting for him to say something.

Clint laughed shortly. "Well, that pony's already ridden out of town," he informed her evenly.

"What my brother's trying to say in his own special way is that of course you're welcome," Roy said, a broad smile on his handsome face. "We'd be honored to have you join us for dinner."

It wasn't easy, but Wynona managed not to laugh. "I don't think that's quite the word that Ryan's dad is thinking right now," Wynona responded. She was talking to Roy but it was obvious that she was looking at his brother.

The corners of Clint's mouth curved ever so slightly in a smile that only had a vague hint of humor underlining it.

"So now you're a mind reader?" Clint asked her.

Wynona's eyes met his. She never wavered. "Doesn't take much reading in this case," she answered.

For his son's sake, Clint preferred to think that the woman was saying his feelings were obvious rather than saying that he was just simpleminded.

Looking at Ryan, he said, "Why don't you take your teacher into the house and keep her company until we're finished out here?"

Ryan looked almost stricken. "But I thought I was going to help you fix the fence," he protested.

Wynona immediately picked up on the boy's distress. "I don't want to disrupt anything," she protested. And then an idea occurred to her. "As a matter of fact, why don't you let me help?" She looked at Clint. "That way you can get finished that much sooner."

"Help?" Clint echoed incredulously. Was she kidding? Okay, so she could climb over a fence better than he would have thought, but now they were talking about basic labor. And the teacher had delicate hands.

"This is the kind of work where you have to get your hands dirty," he told her as if that alone would have her turning on her heel and quickly retreating into the ranch house.

She chalked his insult up to the fact that Washburn wasn't very good at sizing up people. "I'm familiar with work on a ranch, Mr. Washburn," she told him with a smile she didn't feel. "I grew up on one."

Clint looked at her skeptically, but he decided to call her bluff. "All right, pick up a hammer and make yourself useful." He looked at his brother. Since Roy seemed to have appointed himself this woman's champion, he could work with her. "Roy, take her with you and go work on that length of rotting fence over there," he said, indicating the break that they had discovered earlier in the day.

"Sure thing," Roy agreed. He looked more than happy to comply. It was obvious that the thought of having Wynona accompany him while he worked on the length of fence that needed replacing had just brightened his afternoon.

"Don't worry," Roy told her, lowering his voice as they began to walk away. "I won't really put you to work."

"I'm not worried," Wynona told him as she followed

Washburn's younger brother to the section that Washburn had just pointed to. "But I think you missed the point. I offered to help to make the work go faster. I meant that. I don't say things I don't mean."

He couldn't picture her swinging a hammer or using a saw. "Then you weren't just saying that for Clint's benefit? Not that I'd blame you," he said quickly. "My brother's got a knack of really rubbing most people the wrong way," Roy confessed. He stopped in front of a section of fencing that was clearly in need of work. Picking up a hammer, he began removing planks of rotting wood. "But he wasn't always that way."

"Nice to know," Wynona commented.

She wasn't really in the mood to listen to Roy make excuses for his brother, even though that did speak well of the younger man. Spotting a second, discarded hammer on the ground, she got to work herself.

Roy watched her out of the corner of his eye, surprised and amazed. She worked like someone who was used to working with her hands and who could assess what needed to be done without waiting for directions.

He grinned at her. "You really did work on a ranch, didn't you?"

Responding, Wynona grinned back. "I told you I don't lie," she said with a wink. "Now, let's put some muscle into this and see if we can't get finished mending this length of fence before your brother finishes his."

"A competition, huh?" Roy asked. "Well, you won't get an argument out of me," he told her. Roy stepped up his pace.

Pausing just for a moment, Clint watched his brother

and Ryan's teacher working from across the field. The next moment he roused himself and got back to work with Jake as Ryan hovered about, eager to assist in any way he could.

Glancing back across the field, Clint had to admire the woman's tenacity, not to mention her form. From where he was standing, there was something almost hypnotic about the way she swung her hammer and threw herself into her work.

Well, she wasn't afraid of getting dirty, he'd give her that, Clint thought grudgingly. Quite honestly, for the first fifteen minutes he kept waiting for her to throw down her hammer, declare that she was suddenly really tired and walk away from the fence.

But she didn't walk away, didn't stop. She just kept on working and though he hated to admit it, she was actually pretty good at it.

Maybe even better than pretty good, Clint admitted grudgingly, although he made the silent admission only to himself. He wouldn't have said anything of the kind to anyone out loud.

Apparently, he didn't have to, he realized. Ryan was more than happy to make the proclamation for him and anyone else within earshot.

"I didn't know Ms. Chee could fix things," his son said in awe as he looked over to where his teacher was working with his uncle. "I guess she can do just about anything, huh, Dad?"

He wasn't about to validate that sentiment, or to say anything more about the teacher than he absolutely had to. "Hold that steadier," Clint instructed, nodding at the post his son had his small hands on. He'd already anchored the post in the ground. All that was left were the final swings. "I don't want to hit your head by mistake."

"No, sir, I don't want that, either," Ryan answered, turning his attention back to the pole he was holding for his father.

"That's better," Clint commented.

In reality, there was no danger to the boy. He'd safeguarded the pole before he had let Ryan near it. He was allowing Ryan to think he was holding it upright while he drove it into the ground with a sledgehammer so that the boy would feel part of this since it seemed to mean so much to him—as well as to that busybody teacher of his, Clint thought, casting another glance in the woman's direction.

Why the woman felt called upon to horn into his life was totally beyond him. No matter what explanations she spouted, as far as he was concerned it wasn't right for her to come on out here, looking in on him to make sure he was treating his son well.

She didn't know him. The woman had no reason to believe that he had, or ever would, mistreat the boy.

Like he'd ever hurt Ryan, Clint thought angrily. He wasn't that kind of man. But neither was he the kind of man who coddled his son, either. That was against everything he believed in.

Still, he supposed that it wouldn't hurt to teach the boy a few of the basic things, show him how they were done so that he could make himself useful once he got older and actually could be put to work.

Clint slanted another look toward the teacher.

He was more than able to raise his own son without having that woman coming to the ranch to "share her wisdom" with him. Who the hell did she think she was anyway?

"Did I do something wrong, Dad?"

The small, hesitant voice broke through Clint's thoughts, forcing him to push them aside. Replaying Ryan's words, Clint looked down to see that his son was looking at him with wide, fearful eyes.

"Why would you think that?" he asked.

"'Cause you have on your mad face," Ryan answered nervously.

Looking over toward him, Jake nodded. "You do, you know," the ranch hand said.

What the hell was going on today? "What are you talking about?" Clint asked. "Has everyone gone crazy today?"

"If I had a mirror with me, I'd hold it up and show you," Jake told him. "But I don't, so you're just going to have to take it from me. You're scary. Nobody can scowl the way you do, boss. Very effective," Jake commented. "Guaranteed to put the fear of God into all of us when you look like that."

Clint started to say that they were both imagining things but then he stopped. To be honest, he could feel the muscles in his jaw tightening. They only did that when he was scowling.

He took a long breath, then forced himself to relax. It wasn't easy. He'd been so intense for so long that the expression he was being accused of wearing came naturally to him and it wasn't easy just to banish it.

But Clint had no intention of allowing Ryan's teacher to feel that she had somehow bested him, making him do something he hadn't wanted to. Concentrating, he pulled his lips back until they appeared to approximate a smile. His eyes met Jake's.

The latter held up his hands, pretending to take a step back. "That's even worse," he retorted. "Maybe you should go back to scowling."

"No, he shouldn't," Ryan cried, speaking up. He turned toward his father. "You look nice when you smile, Dad. Like you're happy."

"Like a rattler just before he strikes," Jake murmured.

"Rattlesnakes don't smile," Ryan protested, distressed. "Do they, Dad?" he asked the next minute, turning his attention back to the highest authority in his life.

"Not that I know of," Clint said. "Why don't you focus on getting this job done so we can call it a day and finally get something to eat?" he suggested to his ranch hand.

Jake inclined his head as he wrapped his hands around the shaft of the sledgehammer. "Sounds good to me," he agreed.

"And me!" Ryan spoke up, his eyes shining as he added his voice to Jake's.

Clint merely nodded, applying himself to the job at hand. "Less talking, more doing," he told his crew of one and a half.

In his mind, he was already thinking himself past the next few hours, to a time when this meddlesome schoolteacher was finally back in her car and driving back to town.

Chapter Seven

She had a feeling she was going to regret this little venture come tomorrow, Wynona thought. She had used more muscles in the past couple of hours than she had in the last year. Maybe two. Teaching had never really required much from her physically.

She tightened her grip on the hammer that she had been wielding after she had retired the sledgehammer. Her hands were really beginning to ache now, even though she was doing her best not to pay any attention to them as she went on working.

There were times, Wynona had to admit, although only to herself, that she was too stubborn for her own good. But at least in this case, it had all been for a good cause.

She wouldn't have traded the way Ryan looked at her when they finally knocked off for the day for anything in the world. Up until now, she had thought that "literally beaming" was just an expression. But Ryan really *was* beaming.

"You know," Roy said to her as he leaned against the newly fixed section of fence, "they certainly didn't have teachers like you back when I was in school. If they had, I would have been really tempted to stay back in the second grade for at least an extra year—or two."

"Temptation wouldn't have had anything to do with it. You would have been kept back because kids are brighter these days than they were back when you went to school," Clint said as he walked up behind his brother and his son's teacher.

Although he'd addressed his brother, Clint hadn't come over to engage Roy. He was looking over the work that his son's teacher had completed. The truth of it was, he was looking for shoddy work and oversights, something to point out and criticize.

Clint frowned.

There wasn't anything to find fault with. He'd had a feeling that there probably wouldn't be.

Still, he examined the work long and hard, going over it slowly.

He found nothing wrong with it. Because, at bottom, he was a fair man, Clint resigned himself to giving the woman her due.

But glowing words were not his long suit. "Not bad for a teacher," he finally pronounced.

Wynona drew the back of her wrist against her forehead, wiping away the sweat. "Not bad for anyone," she corrected with a toss of her head.

Clint started to comment that she certainly thought a lot of herself, but then he changed his mind. She was right. It *was* a good job for anyone.

After a moment he nodded. "I guess you're right," Clint agreed.

About to walk away, he noticed that Wynona was rubbing her thumbs against her fingers. She probably didn't even realize it, he thought. He was acquainted with that movement. Unlike the rest of them, the teacher hadn't worn gloves while she'd worked.

The palms of her hands had to hurt like hell, he thought.

Roy nodded toward the house. "We'd better get a move on and wash up for supper before Lucia decides that she's being ignored and makes life really hard for us," he advised, changing the subject.

Wynona looked at the younger Washburn. Roy had to be pulling her leg, she thought. She couldn't visualize the housekeeper making any sort of a fuss, much less pitting herself against Ryan's father. The man didn't strike her as someone who had a sense of humor. Moreover, she had a feeling that the milk of human kindness just curdled in his veins.

But she was the outsider here and she wasn't about to say anything that would contradict Roy in any way, so she pretended to go along with the possible "threat" he'd just voiced.

"Then I guess we'd better get moving, right, Ryan?" she asked, smiling down at the boy.

It was obvious that Ryan was surprised to be included in the conversation. Surprised and pleased.

"Yes, ma'am," he responded quickly, "we sure better."

As Ryan shyly slipped his small hand into hers, the pain she felt surprised her. Caught off guard, Wynona winced slightly, but she made no move to break the link between them.

Her palm was throbbing. She was actually getting calluses already, she realized. How did that happen so fast?

"Something wrong, Miss Chee?" Ryan asked, concerned.

"Nope, nothing at all," she assured the boy cheerfully. "I'm just looking forward to eating Lucia's dinner."

The answer satisfied Ryan and he moved faster, leading her into the house and then the small dining area where they took meals in the evening.

Wynona saw Washburn watching her. The man was undoubtedly waiting for her next wrong move, she thought, determined not to make one.

"So, you survived," Lucia declared with an approving nod as she walked in from the kitchen carrying a tureen filled with the stew she had just finished making. "Glad to see that."

She really wanted to run some cold water over her hands, Wynona thought. They were really beginning to sting.

"Where can I wash up, please?" she asked the housekeeper.

"The bathroom is right past the kitchen," Lucia answered. Setting the tureen down, she pointed toward the passageway.

"I'll show you," Clint offered gruffly. The surprised

look on Roy's face didn't go unnoticed, but Clint made no comment as he led the way to the bathroom.

"Thanks," Wynona murmured when they reached what amounted to a powder room. When Clint gave no indication that he was leaving, she told him, "I can take it from here."

Clint ignored the obvious hint. Instead, he moved her to one side. With her out of the way, he opened the medicine cabinet. Taking out a small jar from the bottom shelf, he placed it on the rim of the sink.

"Here, this might help," he told her.

"Help?" Wynona questioned. She had no idea what he was talking about.

"Yeah." Since she didn't seem to understand what he was saying, he explained further. "Rub a little into your hands, especially on your palms. It's something my mother came up with for my father. Back when he used to work the ranch, he'd come home at the end of the day and the calluses on his hands would be bleeding."

"Didn't he have any gloves?" she asked, thinking of what Washburn had said earlier to her about needing a pair of gloves.

"Kept losing them" was all he said as he left the bathroom.

"Thank you," Wynona called after Clint. His unexpected act of kindness had thrown her off for a moment.

She thought she heard Washburn grunt in response but she wasn't sure.

Gingerly opening the jar—right now even the slightest movement was beginning to really hurt—she took just the smallest bit of what looked like off-white salve on her fingertips and gingerly spread it over one palm.

It stung immediately and she sucked in her breath. The pain began to dissipate. Within a minute her calluses were only mildly sore. Encouraged, Wynona repeated the process, spreading the salve onto the calluses on her other palm.

She waited a minute just to make sure that there wasn't some delayed reaction that would cause tears to spring to her eyes, but there wasn't. What she did feel was relief.

Washburn had actually done something kind, she thought in amazement as she walked back into the dining room.

She saw Washburn watching her, a mildly curious expression on his face.

"It worked," she told him.

Immediately curious, Ryan asked, "What worked?"

She took the vacant seat next to the boy. "Your dad gave me this jar of salve to use on my calluses," she told him. "I haven't done that kind of work for a long time and I got calluses almost right away."

Ryan took his teacher's hand closest to him and he gently turned it over to examine. He looked genuinely concerned.

"Oh." He raised his eyes to her face. "Does it hurt a lot?"

"It did," Wynona answered solemnly. "But not anymore, thanks to your dad. My hands look a lot worse than they are," she assured Ryan. She'd heard the sympathy in his voice and she didn't want him to feel bad about her hands. "Besides, a little hard work never killed anyone, right?" she asked.

"Right," Ryan echoed.

Aware that Washburn was studying her—did he expect her to complain? she wondered—she tactfully redirected attention to the dinner in the middle of the table.

"That smells wonderful," she said with enthusiasm, then looking at Ryan's father, she asked, "Can we get started?"

Rather than say anything, he merely gestured at the tureen, indicating that she take the first serving. Instead, she took Ryan's plate and dished out some of the stew onto it before taking some for herself.

It was obvious that Ryan appreciated her attention. Smiling from ear to ear he cried, "Thank you." And then he surprised her by politely waiting until she had served herself before he started to eat.

She couldn't let that pass unnoticed. Raising her eyes to Clint's, she said, "Your son has wonderful manners. You should be very proud of him."

"I am." Clint's staccato tone indicated that he didn't need her to tell him that he should be proud of his son.

Can't win for losing, Wynona thought.

The old adage ricocheted through her head and it was never truer, in her opinion, than it was right now.

Still, all in all, she had been somewhat successful this afternoon. At least she had shown Washburn that she wasn't just some helpless woman who was all talk. She'd done something to back up her words as well as pitch in. That had to mean something.

* * *

Wynona took her leave shortly after dinner was over. She said her goodbyes to the housekeeper, thanking Lucia for a delicious dinner.

Lucia took the words as her due, but then smiled warmly and squeezed her hand. "I hope to see you again."

Wynona merely smiled rather than say anything in response because whether or not she returned wasn't up to her. At least not a third time.

It came as no surprise to her that Clint had made himself scarce as she began to leave. It was Roy who walked her to her car.

"I hope you weren't too uncomfortable at dinner," he told her. "Clint's not exactly at his best when it comes to company."

Wanting to spare Roy, Wynona said, "You don't have to apologize for him."

After all, it wasn't Roy's fault that his brother was difficult, to say the least.

"I kind of feel that I do," Roy told her. When she looked at him, puzzled, he told her, "He wasn't always like this."

Wynona nodded. "So you said."

Reaching her car, she thought that would be the end of it. She opened her car door and got in. But when she went to close the door, Roy put his hand on it, stopping her.

"Is there something else?" she asked Clint's brother.

"Yeah. Ryan wanted me to give you this," Roy said,

handing her something. "You'll probably need to put some more on tomorrow."

He was talking about the salve. Apparently, Clint had put some in a smaller jar for her. The thoughtful gesture doubly surprised her. Looking at the salve, she smiled. "Tell him thank you."

She waited for Roy to withdraw his hand, but he didn't. He continued to hold on to the door. "There's something else, isn't there?"

For a moment Roy looked as if he was going to say no, there wasn't, and just close her door for her. But then he apparently had a change of heart.

"Yeah, there is," he admitted.

"What is it?" she asked when he continued to wrestle with his thoughts.

Looking at her, Roy made his decision.

"Ryan's mother walked out on Clint when Ryan was less than nine months old," he told her.

Whatever she thought Roy was going to say, it certainly wasn't this. The revelation appalled her. "She just abandoned her baby?" she cried, stunned.

Roy nodded. "Yeah. We came home after putting in one of those grueling twelve-hour days and found Ryan in his crib, howling and wet. Susan was nowhere to be found. I can still hear Clint calling her name as he went from room to room. When he picked Ryan up, that was when he saw the note. She'd left it in Ryan's crib."

Roy's face clouded over as he recalled the incident. "The note was brutally short. Susan told my brother that she didn't want to be a rancher's wife anymore. That she wasn't cut out for it, or for being a mother, either." Roy shook his head. "I'm not even sure if she said that she was sorry. What I do know is that she cut out my brother's heart with that note. I saw him change right before my eyes from the fun-loving, hardworking brother I grew up with to this hardened, angry man I barely recognized."

Recalling that day, Roy's face hardened. "Because she had hurt him so badly, Clint just separated himself from everyone. It was like he just couldn't feel anything anymore. There's no other way to say it. I know he loves Ryan," Roy said quickly, not wanting Wynona to misunderstand. "But the risk of being hurt again is just something he can't face. So he doesn't." Letting out a long breath, Roy searched her face as if to see if she understood. "I just thought you should know."

It was a lot to take in. Wynona slowly nodded her head. "Thank you. I appreciate you sharing that with me." Her eyes held his. "For your own sake, I think you shouldn't tell him that you told me. Most men don't appreciate being regarded as vulnerable by other people, especially someone they think of as an outsider."

Roy laughed softly. "You're pretty smart, you know."

She accepted the compliment while making light of it. "That's what it says on my teaching degree," she told the man.

"Ryan's a lucky kid to have you for his teacher," Roy said as he finally closed her car door for her.

"Just doing my job," she replied just before she started her vehicle.

And the rest of my job, Wynona thought as she drove

away from the ranch, *is to find a way to get Clint Washburn to come back among the living.*

For both Ryan's sake and his own, she decided.

"You'll be happy to know that I didn't starve even though you didn't come home to make dinner," Shania informed her cousin playfully when Wynona walked in the door. "When you didn't show up at five, I went to Miss Joan's. She asked after you, by the way and..."

Shania's voice trailed off as she took a closer look at Wynona. There was some dirt on her cousin's clothes that she was certain hadn't been there this morning and Wynona looked worn out in general. "I told her you were fine but I think I was lying."

Her body was really starting to ache now. When she'd crossed the threshold, all Wynona wanted to do was reach the sofa.

Now that she had, she all but collapsed onto it.

"What are you talking about?" Wynona asked, shifting as she tried to find a comfortable position. There really wasn't one.

"Well, for one thing you look like someone rode you hard and put you away wet." Shania was standing directly in front of her now, assessing her condition. "What did you do today?"

"I taught," Wynona answered. Dropping her head against the back of the sofa, she closed her eyes. Her body just continued aching.

"Taught what? Ditch digging 101? You don't get to look that exhausted just from teaching eight-year-olds."

"Eight- *and* nine-year-olds," Wynona corrected, her eyes still closed.

"Oh well, that explains it. Getting those nine-year-olds to listen is like herding cattle—" Shania replayed her words in her head. "Wait, you went out there again, didn't you?"

Wynona opened her eyes. "Went where?" she asked innocently.

"You are many things, Wyn," Shania said, exasperated, "but an actress is not one of them. Now, stop trying to throw me off the track and explain to me why you have this desire to keep beating your head against a concrete wall—because that's what you're doing, you know. Trying to reason with a man who wouldn't know reason if it bit him on the butt."

Wynona sat up, her aches and pains no longer the center of her attention, at least temporarily.

"How would you know what Clint Washburn's like?" she asked defensively.

That was simple enough to answer. "Because you're my cousin and I love you so I asked around."

Now it began to make sense.

"You talked to Miss Joan, didn't you?" The woman who ran the diner—the only restaurant in Forever—for as long as anyone in town could remember had a reputation of knowing everyone's business before they knew it themselves.

Shania shrugged. "I might have."

"Might have my foot. You went to Miss Joan's on purpose to pump her for information," Wynona stated.

"Oh please, since when does anyone have to pump that woman?" Shania asked. "She gives you her opinion whether you ask for it or not."

Wynona sighed. "And what is her opinion of Clint Washburn?" she asked. But before her cousin could answer, Wynona stopped her. "No, don't tell me. She thinks that he's a hard-hearted SOB and she doesn't like him, right?"

Instead of saying yes, Shania surprised her by saying, "Try again."

Wynona's body was really aching in earnest now and she was in no mood for guessing games. She felt her temper slipping away from her.

"Why don't you tell me, then," Wynona retorted, waiting.

"She thinks that he was given a raw deal seven years ago. Miss Joan wouldn't go into details, said that was a private matter for Clint to share when he felt up to it. But she did say that he's sealed himself off because of what happened back then." Shania paused for a beat, looking at her cousin. "Miss Joan told me to tell you to be careful."

Some things never changed no matter how much time passed, Wynona thought. Miss Joan was still dispensing advice even if she wasn't asked for it.

"She has nothing to worry about. I intend to be careful," she replied.

Shania looked at her cousin, a knowing expression on her face. "But you're not going to back off, are you, Wyn?"

"If by 'back off' you mean am I going to stop being Ryan's teacher, then no, I'm not going to 'back off,' Shania."

Shania sighed and shook her head. "That's not what I meant and you know it," she said quietly.

Chapter Eight

Rather than get drawn into an argument or become defensive, Wynona just wearily told her cousin, "Shania, I love you more than anyone else in this world, but right now I am really not in the mood to listen to any lengthy lectures."

Shania held her hands up in a mute protestation of innocence.

"No lectures," she promised.

"Okay," Wynona said, deciding to reword her last statement. "No warnings or 'advice for my own good,'" she told her cousin.

As if on cue, Belle came trotting over to her and put her head on Wynona's lap. The German shepherd raised her soulful brown eyes up to her face.

Wynona smiled at the dog. "This is what I need right now."

Shania laughed. "I don't think there's enough room in your lap for both of our heads, Wyn, but I'll take that under advisement for the next time that I feel inclined to give you a little well-intentioned cousinly advice."

Her eyes closed, Wynona nodded in response. "That's all I ask," she replied as she began to lightly stroke their pet's head.

It amazed her how such a basically simple action could have such a calming effect on both her and the dog, she silently marveled. Too bad Clint Washburn couldn't take lessons from the German shepherd.

The thought made her smile.

After a moment Wynona asked, "Was Miss Joan her usual self?" As she sat there, she continued to stroke Belle. She could feel the dog turning her head into her hand, trying to absorb as much of the stroking as possible.

"You mean did she ask questions?" Shania asked, not sure what her cousin was asking her.

Opening her eyes, Wynona looked at her cousin. They both knew that asking questions was what Miss Joan did. It was as much a part of the woman as the air she breathed. That and, in her own unique way, caring about the various residents of Forever.

"Yes."

Shania laughed to herself. "This is Miss Joan. What do you think?"

Wynona sat up, suddenly alert. "What did she want to know?"

Shania shrugged as she sat down beside her cousin. "The usual. How I was doing. How *you* were doing. Did we find life here disappointing after being in Houston for all those years."

Wynona interrupted her before Shania continued. "And what did you tell her?"

Shania shrugged, as if Wynona already knew the answer to that. "That it took a little bit, but we were adjusting to the change. And I told her that we both enjoyed what we were doing now."

That didn't seem like it would be enough to satisfy Miss Joan. The woman was known to dig deep when it suited her.

"And that's it?" Wynona questioned.

Shania pretended to think for a moment, then said, "I didn't tell her about the dismembered body in your suitcase."

"Say what?" Wynona cried, stunned. Her surprise quickly faded into impatience. "I'm being serious, Shania."

Obviously, Wynona's sense of humor had taken a leave of absence. "You make it sound like there's some big secret we're trying to keep from Miss Joan," Shania said, explaining her flippant remark. "There isn't." With a sigh, she added, "I almost wish there were."

"Why?" Wynona asked, confused.

"Well, for one thing, it might make life more interesting," Shania commented.

Wynona frowned. "Life's plenty interesting just as it is," she told her cousin. She looked at Shania, trying to figure out if there was something wrong.

Shania shrugged, giving in to indifference just for a moment. "If you say so."

"Why?" Wynona asked, looking at her more closely. "You miss Houston?"

"What I miss are activities," Shania admitted. She hadn't thought she would, but she did. Maybe she was just restless, she thought, looking for an explanation. "Houston's not New York, but there were always things to do there. Here," she said, a touch of regret slipping into her voice, "not so much." She sighed. "Not unless you're into watching grass grow."

"It's not that bad," Wynona protested. She pressed her lips together. Had she missed something? "I didn't know you felt that way."

Embarrassed, Shania flashed an apologetic smile at her. "Not usually, just once in a while. I miss going out Friday nights—"

They had gotten caught up in lesson plans and schedules, but that was only because everything was still very new and needed to be worked out. Things would settle down soon.

"We could still go out Friday night," Wynona pointed out.

Shania shook her head. "It wouldn't be the same thing."

She knew what Shania was saying. "I grant you that Murphy's isn't exactly a place that people make plans to visit on their way through Texas," Wynona agreed, "but you can have a good time there. In addition, there's a comfortable feeling knowing that you're safe and that no one wants to take advantage of you."

Everything Wynona said was true, but still… "It's also not exactly earth-shatteringly exciting, either," Shania replied.

Where was this going? "So, what are you saying? You want to go back to Houston?" Wynona asked.

The thought surprised her because she thought that she and Shania were on the same page as to what they wanted to accomplish with their lives. They wanted to give back to the community where they were born. Had she pushed her own agenda on her cousin without having realized it?

Shania sighed. She realized she was being whiny. "No, I just want to complain a little, that's all," Shania admitted. "Forever's a little bit of a culture shock after life in Houston, but you're right," Shania told her. "It is a good trade-off. And I remember that you and I made that promise that one day we'd come back and do some good here. In essence that was payback for the fact that if it weren't for Great-Aunt Naomi, we might have wound up like a lot of those people who were around us while we were little girls on the reservation."

Smiling in earnest now, she turned toward Wynona. "I want to hear all about it."

"Hear about what?" Wynona asked. Shania had changed the subject and Wynona found herself lost.

Belle, meanwhile, had grudgingly moved over to make more room for her other mistress, but she didn't move far. The dog made it abundantly clear that she wanted to remain in the middle of her mistresses since most of her day was spent being alone.

"Just why did you go back to Washburn's ranch?"

Shania asked her. "I thought you said that Ryan's father seemed to come around a little and he let the boy work with him."

"That's just it," Wynona answered. "I went to the ranch because I wanted to tell Washburn how happy Ryan had been in class today. He seemed totally different," she added.

"And?" Shania asked, sensing the situation wasn't as simple as that.

Wynona took a breath. "When I got there, Washburn, his brother and the ranch hand were working on mending breaks in the fence. I didn't see Ryan anywhere," she added quickly.

"And you wanted to know why," Shania guessed.

"What makes you say that?" Wynona asked.

Shania smiled. "Because I know you, Wyn," she told her cousin. "What was his excuse?" she asked. "And did you let him live?"

"Yes." She answered the last question first. "Because he didn't need an excuse. It seems that Ryan had just gone into the house to get something. Washburn had had him helping all along this afternoon."

"All right," Shania said, nodding. "If that was the case, why didn't you just turn around and come home? You obviously stayed. Why?"

"It's complicated," Wynona said, hoping that would be enough.

It wasn't. "I'm not going anywhere," Shania told her, waiting.

Grudgingly, Wynona said, "Because I volunteered to help."

"Help with what?" Shania asked. And then, belatedly, it dawned on her. "Fixing the fence?" she asked incredulously. When Wynona nodded, she could only ask in wonder, "How did that happen?"

"Not really sure." Wynona looked down at her hands. "Now I have calluses on my hands."

Shania got up from the sofa. "I think we might have something in the medicine cabinet for that," she said, beginning to go get it.

"Don't bother," Wynona called after her. "Washburn had some kind of homemade salve to treat that. He gave me some before I left."

"Oh?" Shania's tone clearly indicated that she was intrigued.

Wynona immediately knew what her cousin was thinking. "Don't 'oh' me. He gave it to me because he was feeling guilty about the calluses."

"This from the man who, according to you, doesn't feel anything," Shania said sarcastically.

"I got some insight into that, too," Wynona told her cousin.

Even Belle raised her head, detecting Wynona's shift in tone.

Shania grinned, her previous malaise already forgotten. "Wow, you really did have a productive visit there. What kind of insight?" Shania prodded, curious.

Wynona took a moment to reflect before answering. A great many things had changed in Forever since they had lived here ten years ago. There was a hotel in town now, as well as a law firm. Granted there were only two lawyers in the firm: the sheriff's wife, Olivia, and Miss

Joan's step-grandson, Cash. But those people were new to Forever, as well, although Cash, like Shania and herself, had returned to Forever after a long absence.

The most important change in the town's dynamics, however, was the medical center. Its doors had been closed for over thirty years, ever since the last doctor had left town. It didn't reopen until Dr. Daniel Davenport came to Forever. Opening the medical center's doors had been his way of paying back his late brother. It was the latter who had initially been slated to come to Forever to practice.

Once the medical center's doors were reopened, it slowly drew two more doctors and two nurses to the little town to join in. They had also wound up marrying residents and permanently settling down in Forever.

With such an influx of new people, it wouldn't have surprised Wynona if Miss Joan had missed ferreting out Clint Washburn's story. But she obviously hadn't. She seemed to know the story that Roy had told her in confidence. The woman had just decided that it wasn't her story to tell, beyond warning her to "be careful."

Miss Joan had her own code of ethics, Wynona mused.

Wynona could see that her cousin was waiting for her to tell her what she'd learned.

"Washburn's brother told me that Washburn came home one night to find that his wife had just taken off, leaving behind Ryan. The boy was less than a year old at the time."

"Taken off?" Shania repeated. "Taken off with whom?" she asked.

"With nobody, I gathered," Wynona answered. "Or at least if there was someone, his brother didn't mention it to me. But the upshot of it was that she didn't want to be a mother and she didn't want to be a rancher's wife. She'd left a note stating as much."

"Insult to injury," Shania commented. "That kind of thing is pretty rough on a guy's ego," she said sympathetically.

"Not to mention his heart," Wynona told her. In her estimation, egos really didn't count. It was the heart that did. "From what I gathered, after that, Washburn pretty much just kept everyone at arm's length. He still does."

"And yet he gave you salve," Shania reminded her, smiling broadly. To underscore her point, she fluttered her lashes at her cousin.

Shania was making too much out of the simple act, Wynona thought. "Washburn was just being a decent person," she insisted.

"Which tells you what?" Shania asked, temporarily treating her cousin as if she was one of her science students.

Agitated, Wynona blew out a breath. She knew what her cousin was trying to get across. "That underneath all that barbed wire he's got wrapped around himself is a decent person."

Shania smiled triumphantly.

"Bingo," she declared. "Okay," she said, regrouping. "Now that you realize that, we need to get *him* to realize that."

Shania wasn't the type to just throw words around.

"You're working on an idea, aren't you?" Wynona asked, wondering if she should be bracing herself.

Shania nodded. "Washburn needs to start socializing. Right now, except for his brother and that ranch hand you said is working for him, he's practically a hermit. That's not good for him or for his son."

She already knew that part. "What do you have in mind?" Wynona asked. "Tossing a net over him and dragging him off the ranch to wherever this party of yours is being held?"

Shania hadn't thought out logistics yet. She did now. "We could throw a get-acquainted party at Murphy's," she said, referring to the town's only saloon.

Owned by three brothers, it was run by the oldest, Luke, who coincidentally was married to the town's third doctor. Rather than a bar, the saloon was more like a tavern where family members, even children, were not out of place.

"You still haven't answered how you plan to get him there," Wynona pointed out.

Shania thought for a moment. "From the way you described Washburn, a simple invitation isn't going to cut it."

"I could enlist his brother," Wynona declared.

"And if that doesn't work?" Shania asked, playing devil's advocate.

Wynona grinned. "We could always sic Miss Joan on him."

"I've got a better idea," Shania said, cutting her short.

"Okay, I'm open to suggestions," Wynona answered, waiting.

"*You* invite him," Shania said simply.

Wynona stared at her. "Me? I'm not nearly as good at persuading people to do what I want them to as Miss Joan is."

Shania gave her a knowing look. "It wasn't Miss Joan that he gave that salve to," she reminded her cousin with a smile.

Wynona waved a hand at her, dismissing what her cousin was saying. "That doesn't mean anything."

Shania just continued looking at her. "Doesn't it? You made the man seem like a complete ogre, yet that ogre went out of his way to give you something to help ease the pain you were experiencing from the calluses you got while working on his ranch. That means something in my book."

"You do have a way of twisting things around, don't you?" Wynona asked.

"No, I can just see things more clearly than you do at times," Shania answered. "We complement each other that way," she added with amusement. "I see things you don't while you see things that I don't. It balances everything out," Shania concluded. She let her words sink in, never taking her eyes off her cousin's. "I mean, you won't *have* to try to convince him to come to this party. You can just let him continue living in that solitary prison of his, emotionally removed from his son, his brother and everyone else in the world. After all, we all know you have more than enough to do to keep busy without taking on soul-saving."

"All right, all right. If I invite the man personally,

will you stop trying to bury me in your rhetoric?" she asked.

"Of course I'll stop. If you say you're going to go talk to him, then there's no need for me to go on talking, is there?"

"I should be so lucky," Wynona said with a weary laugh.

"Don't worry. I have a feeling you will be. Once you invite him," Shania added.

Wynona had no idea what her cousin was talking about. But even so, she couldn't help thinking that she had somehow walked into a trap of her own making.

Chapter Nine

In the end, after considering all the various options open to her, Wynona decided that the best way to go about drawing Clint Washburn out and make him at least a little more social was to hold an "Open School Night." This way he couldn't accuse her of singling him out from the other parents. The focus of Open School Night would be the students with the idea of getting the parents involved with the current curriculum.

"Hey, sounds good to me," Shania said when Wynona bounced the idea off her. "I'd take it up with your principal if I were you," she encouraged Wynona.

So she did. Adele Wilson gave it her blessings. The event was scheduled in two weeks to give everyone enough time to make the necessary arrangements at school and also on the home front. It also gave the parents enough time to send back replies to the invitations.

In order to fit everyone into the small school without resorting to overcrowding, it was decided to hold the event over the course of two evenings. Grades one, two and three would come the first evening while grades four, five and six would attend on the following evening.

Wynona got her own students involved by having them make up the invitations that were going out to their parents. Even at this age, there were a couple students who showed real promise when it came to artwork. She encouraged them to help the others.

Responses started to come in almost immediately and continued arriving over the next several days. By the end of a week, everyone had acknowledged and returned the invitations.

Except for Washburn.

Well, she had known that this wasn't going to be easy, Wynona thought. She gave it another day, hoping against hope that Washburn would come around—secretly feeling that most likely, he wouldn't.

When Ryan began to slowly withdraw again, Wynona decided that it was time for her to beard the lion in his den. After school was over and she had finished preparing the lesson for the following day, she rode out to Washburn's ranch.

She spent the entire trip to the ranch giving herself a pep talk.

"You know, to some people, this might be viewed as the definition of harassment," Clint said.

He was facing away from the stable entrance when he said it.

When she had arrived at the ranch, Wynona had encountered Jake first. Looking pleased to see her, the ranch hand seemed to know why she was there. Before she could ask, he directed her toward the stable where Clint was currently working on mending some of the bridles that looked as if they were about to fall apart.

His back was to the doorway and Wynona was trying to find a way to announce herself without startling him. Washburn had caught her off guard with his statement.

Stunned, she came forward. "How did you know I was here?"

"Roy and Jake don't wear perfume," he answered matter-of-factly.

She was about to protest that neither did she, but then she caught herself. The splash of perfume she applied in the morning was so automatic—her one indulgence to femininity—that half the time she didn't even realize she was doing it.

"Very good," she murmured, feeling it best to start out by saying something positive to the rancher.

When Washburn made no response to her comment, she decided she had nothing to lose. She launched into the reason she had come to the ranch, seeking him out, this time.

"I'm here about the invitations that were sent out to the school's Open School Night."

As she spoke, she took a few more steps closer to the silent man.

Turning his head, Clint spared her a single glance,

then went back to focusing his attention on the bridle he was repairing. "Figured you might be."

The man was definitely *not* a sparkling conversationalist, she thought. Taking a breath, Wynona tried again. "You didn't send it back."

"No, I didn't," he answered matter-of-factly.

The man really did require a great deal of patience, she thought, digging deep for hers. Unearthing it was not easy. "Why?" she asked.

His shrug was indifferent. "Figured not sending it would get my message across."

"What message?" Wynona pressed, hoping that it wasn't what she thought it was.

He still didn't turn around to look at her. Instead, he continued working on the worn bridle. "That I wasn't coming."

All right, so it *was* the message she thought it was. But she wasn't about to give up. "Why not?"

This time he did turn around to look at her. There was no warmth in his eyes as he sized her up. "I don't have to explain myself to you."

"No, you don't," she surprised him by agreeing. "But since this does involve your son—and you being the only parent not attending will make him feel like an outsider," she stressed, "I thought I'd come and try to convince you to give up a couple of hours for your son's sake. It's all going to be informal and there'll be cookies," she added quickly, hoping the thought of food might be appealing to him. She was willing to try anything at this point to get Ryan's father to come around.

She should have known better.

"I'm not a kid to be bribed with treats," Clint informed her flatly.

"No, you're an adult and sometimes, as an adult you have to do things you don't feel like doing for the sake of the son you brought into the world," she told him, trying to make him see the harm his nonattendance would do. "Do you want him to feel different because he's the only one whose parent didn't attend Open School Night? Do you have any idea what that feels like when you're a kid?" she asked, passion entering her voice. "It's awful."

Putting his tools down, he faced her squarely. "Oh, and you speak from experience?" Clint asked. It was obvious that he was mocking her.

Instead of flinching, the way he'd expected, Wynona's eyes met his defiantly.

"Yes," she answered with a quiet ferocity, "I do. I know exactly what it's like to be the odd kid out, even in an area where half the kids in school only had one parent."

Clint regarded her with skepticism, but he didn't come out and ask her to elaborate.

She did anyway. To an extent.

"I lived with one parent, and let me tell you, it was hard, especially because she wasn't well." It wasn't something that she usually talked about. Her history was a private matter, even though she and Shania had gone through it together. But if it helped Washburn to understand that his actions could have unwanted consequences, then it was worth it.

He looked at her for a long moment, as if weighing whether or not to believe her. "Kids get what they need from more than their parents. It's different these days," he finally said.

"Not so different," Wynona contradicted. "Kids still look to their parents for moral support. Ryan's no different. He sees you as his first line of defense. And you should be glad of that."

Clint raised an eyebrow. "Oh?"

"Yes, you should," she insisted. "There are lots of parents who only wish they had kids who looked up to them instead of just ignoring them. Your son looks up to you and you don't appreciate it."

Clint looked at her. The impatience etched into his face was not as pronounced as it had been. But his tone wasn't exactly friendly.

"How long do you plan on standing there, yammering at me?" he asked.

Wynona didn't even hesitate. "Until you agree to come."

He believed her. He could see that he wasn't going to be able to finish his work until he gave in. "And that's all it'll take?"

"Yes," she informed him firmly.

His eyes narrowed. He was trying to discern something, she thought, but she had no idea what.

"And if I say yes," he finally said, "are you telling me that you're naive enough to think I'll actually show up?"

His expression was impassive as he spoke. Was he telling her she was a fool to just take his word? But Wynona considered herself to be a good judge of character and that was what she was banking on right now.

"I'm not naive," she told him. "You're a man whose word means something to him. So if you say you'll do something or be somewhere, then you will." She smiled at Ryan's father, confident she was right. "Tell me I'm wrong."

The words hovered on his lips and very nearly came off his tongue. But if they had, if he told her she was wrong, he'd be lying.

Because she was right.

Clint frowned at her. "What I *can* tell you is that you're a colossal pain in the neck."

"I can live with that," Wynona answered philosophically, clearly taking no offense. "So, will you come?" she asked, quickly adding, "It'll mean the world to Ryan."

Shaking his head, Clint blew out an exasperated breath. "Still don't see why."

"Because you're his hero."

Clint waved a dismissive hand at her statement. "Now you're just imagining things."

"No, I'm not. All you have to do is look into Ryan's eyes, Mr. Washburn. Your son wants to be just like you when he grows up," she told him, then challenged, "do you want him growing up to be a withdrawn, uncommunicative man?"

"So now you want me to transform for him?" Clint asked.

"No," Wynona answered honestly. "But you might want to transform for yourself. I think that both you and your son will be happier if you do."

So now she was professing to be able to psychoanalyze him? How did she know what it took for him to be happy? Just who did this woman think she was?

"I'll be happier if you just stop preaching at me and go away," he told her bluntly.

They had circled back to what she'd already told him. "You already know how to make that happen," she reminded him cheerfully, adding, "It's just one evening, Mr. Washburn. I promise you won't regret it."

"I already regret it," he informed her. "And stop calling me Mr. Washburn," he told her. "*Mr. Washburn* was my father, who was a functioning drunk." The memory darkened his face. "My name's Clint."

Well, she was more than willing to oblige him regarding the way she addressed him. Wynona smiled. "Nice to meet you, Clint. So, will I see you at Open School Night?" she asked again.

The woman just didn't let up. "I'm surprised you're not ordering me to be there."

Wynona shook her head. "It won't work that way, remember?" she reminded him. "You have to give me your word that you'll come to the school."

It was obvious that she was waiting for him to do just that. He had a feeling that she was also as good as her word and that she planned to stay right in front of him, talking at him for as long as it took before he cried uncle and gave in. She wasn't going anywhere until he agreed to attend this Open School Night or whatever she called it.

He blew out a long, ragged breath that was all but vibrating with weary annoyance. It really bothered him that she seemed to be able to see right through him like that. After all, the woman hardly knew him.

"All right," he bit off. "You win."

"Win what?" she asked, waiting for Clint to say the words she was waiting to hear.

His eyes narrowed. "Don't push it," Clint warned. She went on looking at him.

"Okay, you win. I'll come to Open School Night," he bit off. Clint tried not to notice that her eyes were sparkling as she looked at him.

"It's next Thursday. Seven o'clock," Wynona told him, just in case he'd forgotten.

"Yeah, I know," he snapped. "It was on the invitation."

If he thought his tone of voice intimidated her, he was wrong. Hearing his response, she looked pleased. "So you did read it."

"I had to know what I was turning down," he pointed out matter-of-factly.

"And now you don't have to," she concluded with a smile. There was no triumph in her smile, just joy. The woman was either a damn good actress, he thought, or she was genuinely verging on sainthood.

"Well, I've taken up enough of your time. I'd better leave you to your work," she said happily, backing away before he decided to change his mind.

He glared at her impatiently. "I would have been a lot happier if you'd led with that," he told her. Murmuring something under his breath, he picked up the bridle again.

"No, you wouldn't have," she answered confidently as she turned on her heel.

The remark irritated him. He didn't care for the fact that she acted like she knew things about him better than he did.

"You're awfully sure of yourself, aren't you?" It was more of an accusation than an observation.

"Only sometimes," she told him honestly. "Only sometimes."

He watched her walk out of the stable. Clint continued to look toward the open door after she was no longer there.

The woman had managed to get to him, to burrow under his skin, creating an itch he wanted no part of. He didn't have time for it and he certainly didn't need the consequences that lay at the end if he followed that itch to its logical conclusion.

For two cents he'd just ignore the fact that he'd said he'd be at the school and just go on with his life as if nothing had happened. But something *had* happened and she was right, damn her. He wasn't the type to go back on his word after having given it, even for something as meaningless as this open school thing.

His word had been extorted from him, but he still had to keep it.

He realized that he'd almost balled up the leather strap he was trying to restore.

Damn the woman, she was undermining his thoughts. He didn't have time for this. Didn't have time to get dragged off to some meaningless session at the elementary school that his son wouldn't even remember.

Maybe he shouldn't have allowed himself to get railroaded like that.

Maybe there was still a simple way out of this if he just—

"I just saw Miss Chee," Ryan said, walking into the stable. He looked up at his father, a mixture of excitement and shyness on his face. "She said that you told her you were going to come to Open School Night." He uttered each word with an aura of hopefulness around it. "She told me that you gave her your word. Did you, Dad?"

"Why do you ask that?" Clint asked. For the first time in a long time, he found himself wondering just what was going on in that small head.

"Because I know if you really did that—if you really gave your word," he explained, "you won't go back on it. So, was she right?" he asked, allowing eagerness to enter his voice. "Did you give your word?"

He couldn't bring himself to lie and rob that look from his son's face. So he didn't. "Yeah, she's right. I did."

What happened next caught him completely by surprise. Ryan was not demonstrative. At least, he had never known the boy to be. He was quiet and obedient but not expressive.

However, this time the boy threw his arms around his waist and hugged him for all he was worth.

Clint hardly felt the actual squeeze. After all, the eight-year-old was small for his age and Clint had had years of hard work to build up his own body so that he didn't feel things like a child's arms. But the *effect* of that squeeze, that spontaneous, gleeful hug that his son had suddenly delivered, well, that was a different matter entirely.

Like an arrow shot from a bow, his son's hug had a direct effect on the leaden part within his chest that had once been a heart.

Clint awkwardly hugged the boy back.

Chapter Ten

Wynona realized that she kept watching the classroom doorway. Given tonight's event, under regular circumstances it would have been normal to look toward the doorway every so often, especially when someone came into the classroom.

But Wynona found herself slanting glances in that direction even when there was no movement in that general area, no indication that someone new was entering the room.

There was a reason for that.

Clint Washburn wasn't here yet.

Open School Night had gotten underway almost twenty minutes ago and the rancher and his son hadn't arrived yet.

Had she misjudged the man after all? Had she placed too much faith in the sanctity of his word?

No, he was going to be here, she silently insisted. She just knew it. Washburn really believed in a code, believed in a time when a man's word actually was his bond, a bond he neither regarded lightly nor broke unless something completely unforeseeable happened.

Had it? she wondered. Had something dire happened that subsequently was responsible for keeping Washburn from accompanying his son to this event?

"Worried?"

Wynona turned around to look at her cousin. Shania had insisted on coming to Open School Night in order to lend a hand in the arrangements as well as to offer her moral support.

Right now Shania was eyeing her knowingly.

"No, it's going very well," Wynona responded, nodding around the room at the clusters of milling students. As if united in purpose, the children were almost all tugging on their parents' hands, leading them from one wall to another as they proudly pointed out their artwork from amid the rest. "Better than I'd hoped, actually," she confessed.

But Shania saw through her cousin's act and her blasé attitude. "He'll be here, Wyn," she assured Wynona in a low voice.

Wynona didn't bother to pretend that she didn't know who her cousin was talking about. A denial would have been childish and dishonest and she had never been anything but honest with her cousin. Ever.

She answered Shania in a tough tone. "He'd better if he knows what's good for him," Wynona retorted.

Shania grinned. "Ah, there's the Wynona Chee that

I know and love," she declared with a laugh. The next moment her smile grew even wider. "And you are living proof that everything always comes to she who waits," Shania concluded.

Wynona stared at her cousin. "What are you talking about?"

Rather than answer, Shania merely pointed behind her, toward the doorway.

Wynona turned her head to see Ryan entering the classroom, his small fingers wound tightly around his father's hand as he led the way into the room.

Wynona hardly felt Shania's pat on her shoulder. The next moment her cousin had made herself scarce, managing to unobtrusively meld into the gathering of parents and children. Leaving her to greet the father and son coming into the classroom.

"You came," Wynona said, addressing the remark to both Ryan and his father as she greeted them warmly.

"One of the horses got loose," Ryan said, speaking up. It was obvious that he wanted his teacher to know why they were late. "We had to get to Flora before the coyotes could find her," he explained, a very serious expression on his face.

"I understand completely," Wynona assured him. "So did you finally find her?" she asked, although she already assumed that they had because the boy didn't seem distressed.

Ryan nodded his head up and down with vigor. "My dad's real good at finding lost animals. Horses *and* cattle," he told her proudly.

"Good thing to know in case I ever need help," Wynona

said. Her eyes shifted toward the silent rancher. "Thank you for coming," she told Clint.

"Had to," he answered simply with a vague shrug of his shoulders. When she looked at him quizzically, he said, "You were holding my word hostage."

"I had nothing to do with it," she told him. "You were the one honoring your word."

Clint merely made an unintelligible sound under his breath in response. Turning his attention to the classroom in general, he asked the teacher, "So tell me, why am I here again?"

She didn't even have to pause to frame her answer. "To see firsthand how well your son is doing," she told him. Gazing down at the boy, she gently coaxed Ryan, "Tell you what. Why don't you take your dad around and show him all your different projects?" Redirecting her attention toward the rancher, she said, "The students spent the entire day getting the classroom ready today." She smiled, oblivious to the effect her smile had on both father *and* son. "I think they're very proud of their work—and rightly so," she concluded.

Wynona could see Ryan's father looking at the various displays. The expression on his face gave her no clue what was going on in his mind so she felt obligated to add, "They all put their hearts into it."

Clint glanced at her. He had a feeling that the teacher was putting him on notice that he was to say nothing but appreciative words when talking about the work on the walls as well as the booklets that had been put together for viewing.

"Did they, now?" Clint asked, his tone giving nothing away.

Glancing around, he zeroed in on the booklet that Ryan had painstakingly put together. It was placed right below some of his artwork. Clint picked up the booklet to take a closer look.

She could see Ryan holding his breath as he watched his father leafing through the booklet.

"They certainly did," she told Clint with quiet enthusiasm that cautioned him to say only positive, glowing things about the pages he held in his hands. Moving closer to the rancher, she indicated the wall with Ryan's drawings. "I think his artwork shows a lot of promise, especially for an eight-year-old." Her eyes met Clint's. "I think your son has a great deal of talent," she said.

Clint stopped flipping through the pages of the booklet his son had put together and looked up, his eyes meeting the teacher's.

It struck him how intensely blue her eyes were. It struck him that she could look into his very soul.

Clearing his throat, he commented, "Not much call for that kind of thing on a ranch."

Wynona glanced to see that Ryan was talking to another student. That, too, was a heartening sign as far as she was concerned. The boy was blossoming, slowly coming out of that shell he'd had around him those first few weeks of class.

Grateful that Ryan was out of earshot and hadn't heard his father's comment, she told the rancher, "Maybe Ryan won't always be on the ranch."

Clint's eyes darkened. He looked as if he was less

than happy at her observation. But she felt she had to at least voice her thoughts as well as give the man something to consider.

Despite the brooding expression on Washburn's face, she pushed on. "When he grows up, he might decide he wants to do something else with his life than be a rancher. I'm not saying that he will," she quickly clarified. "I'm just saying that that door should remain open to him." Her eyes were on his again. "You do want to be fair to your son."

"Did I say that?" he questioned, as if wanting to know if he had given her that impression.

"You don't have to," she informed him. Part of her felt that she might be on shaky ground but she stood on it anyway. "You're a fair man by definition."

Clint made no response. Instead, he studied her in silence for so long, Wynona thought he had decided just to stop talking altogether.

But then he completely surprised her by saying in a grudging tone, "You're good."

For a second she thought she'd either misheard him, or imagined his response. Her eyebrows drew together as she said, "Excuse me?"

She half expected him to just walk away. But Clint didn't walk away. Instead, he explained what he was telling her. "You twist words around, saying flattering things as if they were gospel. You also make a person feel as if he was being extremely unfair if he says anything to contradict you."

He got all that from her simple answer? "I'm afraid

you're giving me way too much credit, Clint," she told him, shaking her head.

Just for a moment the rancher appeared as if he was about to laugh at her. But he didn't. Instead, he responded, "If anything, I'm not giving you enough credit."

Before she had a chance to dispute his answer, Ryan had returned to his side. With a smile on his bright, shining face, the boy was eagerly tugging on his arm, wanting to bring him over to another display.

"Dad, come this way," Ryan urged. "You gotta see this one."

For a second, Clint could only stare at his son. He really couldn't get over the boy's transformation. The difference seemed almost like night and day. His son wasn't the hesitant, quiet, wide-eyed boy he'd always known up until just a few weeks ago. If anything, Ryan was like a whole new person.

The boy's withdrawn, quiet qualities had receded until they had vanished into thin air like vapors that had dried up in the fall breeze. In place of those quiet qualities were traits more in keep with the way a regular eight-year-old boy behaved.

In a way, Clint realized that he could now see himself in Ryan. Thinking back, he had been just like this when he had been Ryan's age.

Except not nearly as eager for parental approval, he recalled.

"I drew this, Dad," Ryan was proudly telling him. Then, in case his father was having trouble recognizing just what it was that he had drawn, Ryan said, "It's a picture of my horse."

"I can see that," Clint answered.

The truth of it was he was rather surprised that he actually *could* recognize what it was, given the usual nature of childish drawings.

All around them there were drawings on the walls that looked more like colorful blobs or slashes of color than anything that was actually recognizable.

Apparently, Wynona was right, Clint thought, grudgingly giving the woman her due. Ryan did have a glimmer of talent when it came to those drawings of his. But he had to admit that he just hoped the boy had talents that lay elsewhere.

Like having a penchant for learning.

That would stand Ryan in good stead as he grew older, Clint thought.

As far as those pictures went, drawing those things wasn't going to lead to anything on its own. It certainly wasn't anything for him to consider when it came to making a living.

Clint hadn't realized that he had been looking up at the drawings for some time until he felt Ryan tugging on his sleeve.

"Do you like them, Dad?" Ryan asked. There was no missing the hope in his voice.

For a second, Clint weighed his options.

"Yes, I do," he finally answered, knowing that his response would make the boy happy. He thought he heard a sigh of relief behind him coming from the teacher.

He had to admit, in an odd sort of way, he did like

the drawing. Or rather he liked that his son could do something that he couldn't. When it came to drawing, stick figures were a challenge for him.

"I'm glad," Ryan said.

Wynona stepped back. Although she would have loved to have accompanied Clint and his son around the classroom, pointing out things and attentively listening to anything the rancher had to say about or to his son, the reality was that she had a great many more parents to talk to before the evening was over. She couldn't very well ignore them, especially after they had come out at her behest.

Slanting a last glance in Clint and Ryan's direction, she forced herself to turn her attention toward the rest of the parents.

Wynona made herself available to answer any questions, comment on any parental observations and in general just share the evening with these parents who had come out to show their children that they supported them and were proud of them.

The evening lasted a little longer than she had initially planned, but eventually, parents began to slowly leave the classroom, their children safely in tow. Almost all of them had a few words to share with her in parting, telling her the same comment in a variety of different ways.

But in essence, what they all told her was that they appreciated that she saw as much potential in their offspring as they did. They told her, in so many words, that they were very glad that she was their children's teacher.

She had to admit that their sentiments made her feel really happy.

And then, out of the corner of her eye, she saw Clint and Ryan leaving. They were going without bothering to say anything to her. She knew she could have hung back, but given the effort she had made just to get the man to come out here, she wasn't about to just stand by and let him walk out.

Instead, she made her way over to the duo before they reached the door.

Getting in front of them, she smiled at Clint and his son.

"Thank you so much for coming," she said, taking Clint's hand and shaking it.

Rather than giving her the brush off, or mumbling, "Yeah, sure," Clint fixed her with a look. "I really didn't have a choice," he reminded her. "Did I?" He challenged her to contradict him.

Which she did.

"Actually, you did," she told him cheerfully. Before he could ask how she had come to that conclusion, she said, "You could have looked for that horse a little longer, then used that as an excuse not to attend the event tonight."

"And be accused of missing your cookies on purpose?" he asked.

There was actually humor in his voice, she thought, pleased.

"I would have set some aside and sent them home with Ryan tomorrow," she told him in the same tone that he had just used.

There was a glimmer of admiration in his eyes. "Got an answer for everything, don't you?"

"Not yet," she said honestly, "but I'm working on it."

"I'm glad we came, Dad," Ryan said, speaking up, then added, reverting back to his shy persona for just a moment, "I'm glad you came."

Taken completely aback for a moment, Clint managed to gather himself together in order to say, "Yeah, me, too." And then he looked at the woman who had all but goaded him into being here. "Me, too," he repeated, this time addressing his words to Wynona.

She smiled at him and he felt something within him responding.

He didn't want to and he didn't welcome the feeling within him, but it was there nonetheless.

Clint took a breath, steeling himself off.

With a nod of his head, he said, "Good night, Miss Chee."

Then, with his hand against his son's back, Clint guided the boy to the door and out into the hallway.

For his part, Ryan turned around and waved at her, beaming like he had just been awarded a lifetime supply of his favorite ice cream.

And while she smiled at Ryan and returned the boy's wave, she couldn't help wondering what had just happened here. At the very last moment, Clint Washburn seemed to withdraw and take ten steps back from where they had just been only a few minutes ago.

Or was that just her imagination?

"You're frowning," Shania whispered, coming up behind her. "It didn't go well?"

"Oh, it went well," Wynona answered. "And then it didn't."

"I don't allow any riddles after seven o'clock," Shania told her. "My mind won't process them after that. Save it until morning."

Wynona was staring in the direction that Clint had taken. "I hope it's gone by morning."

"One can only hope," Shania said just before they closed up the classroom. It just seemed like the thing to say.

Chapter Eleven

There were some people living in and around Forever who considered Miss Joan to be as close to an institution as they could ask for.

Tireless, the older woman—no one really knew how old she was and no one, not even her husband, was brave enough to ask—kept the diner open seven days a week, closing only on Christmas, New Year's and Thanksgiving. On those days the people who had no family found themselves sitting at the table with Miss Joan, her husband, Harry, and anyone else who was alone on that day.

It was also generally believed that if there was anything worth knowing in the town, Miss Joan already knew about it. It wasn't that Miss Joan gossiped. She just had a way of assimilating information before anyone else even knew there was information to be gathered.

When Wynona finally decided to come into the diner to ask Miss Joan what light she could shed on Clint Washburn's self-imposed isolation, she felt rather uncomfortable about it.

She hadn't seen the woman since she had left Forever all those years ago. More important, she hadn't dropped by since she had returned. That made turning up now to ask questions particularly awkward.

As she entered the diner, Wynona tried to think of the best way to approach Miss Joan. Arriving at the diner when she felt fairly certain that it wouldn't be full, Wynona practically tiptoed up to the counter.

The redheaded woman had her back to the door and was, from the looks of it, slicing up the freshly baked peach pie that was sitting on the counter right in front of her.

Wynona pressed her lips together, still searching for the best way to initiate the conversation.

"So are you going to just stand there admiring my hair, or are you actually going to say something, Wynona?" the woman asked, her back still to her.

Wynona's mouth dropped open. It had gone suddenly dry and she was totally speechless as she continued to stare at the woman's back.

The sound of her own breathing seemed to echo in her ears.

Finally, she found her tongue. "How did you know it was me?"

Miss Joan slowly turned around to look at her. Wynona continued to stare. It was as if the woman had somehow been preserved in time. She hadn't aged in ten years.

"I'm Miss Joan. I know everything," the older woman replied simply. And then she added matter-of-factly, "And I saw your reflection in the metal cabinet."

"Oh, thank goodness," Wynona replied with a relieved laugh. "For a second I thought you actually had eyes in the back of your head."

Hazel-green eyes traveled up and down the length of her body slowly, taking complete measure of the young woman before her.

"I never said I didn't," Miss Joan replied quietly.

Finished with the pie, Miss Joan retired the long, thin knife she'd been using, letting it slide back down into the pitcher filled with hot water. She had been dipping the knife into the hot water in between cuts to ensure the pie was cut in clean, even pieces.

"You filled out some since I last saw you," she observed.

Given that her last clear memory of the woman was just before she and Shania had been taken to Houston to grow up there, Wynona could only smile. "Well, it's been more than ten years," she replied, even though she knew that Miss Joan was aware of that fact.

Miss Joan nodded her head, as if silently agreeing with Wynona's response.

"It took you this long to say hello?" the woman asked.

Wynona flushed. "Sorry," she apologized, at a loss as to how to excuse the fact that she hadn't come by even once since she'd returned to Forever. She'd been busy at first and then, the more time that went by, the more awkward just dropping by became.

Until she had a reason.

"Don't be sorry," Miss Joan told her. "Just don't let another ten years go by between visits." She looked at the elementary school teacher knowingly. "I take it you didn't drop by to see if my hair was still as red as you remember." The laugh was dismissive. "Your cousin could have told you that."

Well, nothing had changed. The woman never did stand on polite ceremony or beat around the bush, Wynona thought. Taking a breath, she launched into the reason she had finally dropped by.

"I came to ask you what you know about Clint Washburn," she said honestly.

"Runs a ranch with his brother that their father left them before he could drink it out from under them," she said, reciting the information as if she was talking about the number of eggs that were still in her refrigerator after breakfast had finished being served. Her eyes looked into Wynona's. "You want to know about the wife, don't you?" Miss Joan said.

There was no point in pretending the question surprised her. "Whatever you can tell me," Wynona replied honestly.

Miss Joan took a cup out from beneath the counter and placed it in front of Wynona. Reaching for the coffeepot, she poured the dark brew into the cup. Done, she placed a coffee creamer next to the cup, along with a couple of packets of sugar.

"She ran off, leaving him to raise their son. Kid was little more than an infant at the time. Nine months, if I remember correctly." She shook her head. "Never knew what Clint thought he saw in that woman." She laughed shortly; there was no humor in it. "I guess the poor guy was just looking to have a family of his own." She pressed her lips together, shaking her head again. "Couldn't see past her face, otherwise he would have been able to see how empty she was."

"Empty?" Wynona repeated, trying to understand what Miss Joan was saying.

"The woman had no character," the older woman explained. "No values. Susan's world revolved around just herself, nobody else. The girl thought she was too good to live here. She wanted something else out of life than just being a rancher's wife. Or a mother," Miss Joan added.

Anger furrowed her brow and Wynona could see that it was directed toward Clint's absent ex-wife.

"Clint's a smart man but he never saw it coming." Very thin shoulders rose and fell helplessly. "Guess some people just don't see what they don't want to."

Wynona only had one more question to ask. "Does he know where she is?"

"Nobody does." Miss Joan's voice all but shouted, "Good riddance."

"Last anyone heard," she continued, "Susan was on her way out to California. I have no idea if she ever got there." Miss Joan paused, a fisted hand on her hip as she looked at Wynona. "Why aren't you asking him these questions?"

"I'm just trying to satisfy my curiosity," Wynona answered. "As for Clint, he already thinks that I stuck my nose where it didn't belong when I managed to get him to come to Open School Night for Ryan's sake."

Listening, Miss Joan nodded her head in approval. "Gotta say that's pretty impressive, Wynona, getting Clint to do that. That man isn't the kind to be browbeaten or give in if he doesn't want to." She paused, appearing to size Wynona up. Wynona did her best to meet the woman's gaze head-on and not squirm. "Anything else you want to know?"

"No, not right now," Wynona told her. "But if I do," she added with a smile, "I know who to come to."

Miss Joan accepted the response. "Okay, then. And next time," she cautioned by way of a footnote, "don't be such a stranger. I remember you when you couldn't see over the counter."

That was the woman's way of reminding her that they had history, Wynona thought. "I can see over it now," Wynona replied cheerfully.

"All the more reason to come by," Miss Joan told her before she turned her attention to tend to another customer.

Wynona opened her purse, about to leave money on the counter to pay for her half-finished coffee.

As if sensing what she was doing, Miss Joan turned her head and gave her a sharp look over her shoulder.

"Did I say anything about paying?" she asked the younger woman.

"No, but—"

"Then put that away," the older woman ordered. With that, she went back to the other customer.

It was nice to know that there were some things that just didn't change, Wynona thought as she left the diner.

Once outside the diner, she went to her car. Miss Joan

hadn't told her anything that she didn't already know, thanks to Clint's brother. What she had decided to ascertain was that there wasn't anything else that had been omitted, like Clint trying to track his ex-wife down and bring her back.

If he *had* made the attempt to do that, Wynona was certain that Miss Joan would have known. It never occurred to Wynona to question that belief.

Or to question the information the woman gave her.

The confirmation of the information just succeeded in making Wynona more determined than ever to make sure that Clint became the father that Ryan needed.

What today also did was make her determined to make Clint come around and rejoin the land of the living. As far as she was concerned, Clint Washburn had been in solitary confinement much too long. Granted that his imprisonment had been of his own making, but that didn't change the fact that he needed to wake up. Not just for his son's sake, but for his own, as well.

Wynona set her mouth, making a decision. Clint Washburn had just become her newest project.

Clint was not so withdrawn from the immediate world that he didn't notice it. Notice that his son was becoming and acting more like a real boy with each day that passed. The evidence was blatant in everything he did.

When he came home from school, Ryan talked now. Talked about his day, about what had happened at school. He talked about the kids he interacted with in class. Nothing went unsaid.

It slowly dawned on Clint that his son sounded as if he actually had friends, other children whom he talked to and seemed to be getting along with.

Clint pretended it made no difference to him, but it did and eventually, he stopped pretending because the reality was he wasn't fooling himself.

He *liked* the fact that his once quiet, withdrawn son had friends.

Having Ryan chattering to him, to Roy, to Jake and to Lucia a good deal of the time—while he did chores, while at the table and just about anytime in between—was a little more difficult for him to finally wrap his head around and get used to, but he was getting there. Faster than he'd thought.

However, the part he found the hardest for him to get used to was when the boy talked about his teacher, the woman who had had such an effect on him and had, quite literally, changed the course of his life.

"And she has a dog," Ryan was saying this particular evening at the dinner table as he once again sang the praises of his teacher. He turned to look at his father. "Did you know she had a dog, Dad?"

Suddenly realizing that his son was waiting for an answer, Clint said, "No, I didn't know that."

"Well, she does," Ryan confided, launching into a further narrative. "It's a girl dog. Her name is Belle. And she's smart and pretty, like Miss Chee. Except she doesn't have fur," Ryan specified. "Miss Chee, not the dog," Ryan said quickly in case his father wasn't following him. "And she does tricks. Belle, not Miss Chee," he felt duty bound to distinguish.

"Did Miss Chee tell you the dog does tricks?" Roy asked, interjecting his two cents into the conversation.

"No, I saw Belle doing tricks," Ryan answered with excitement. "The whole class did. Miss Chee brought Belle to class today so we could all meet her." And just like that, he rerouted his conversation. "Can we get a dog, Dad?" he asked, looking at his father with the same hopeful eyes he'd turned on him when he'd asked his father to attend Open School Night.

"We've got horses and cattle," Clint said with a note of finality, as if that simple fact should be enough for his son.

But it was obvious that Ryan definitely had other ideas.

"And a dog could help us," Ryan told him. "If we got a dog like the one Miss Chee has, he could help herd the cattle. Maybe even the horses, too," the boy added.

He never took his eyes away from his father's face, as if confident that he could stare him down and make his father relent.

Clint wanted to say no. He had neither the time nor the inclination to add a dog to his household.

But the look on his son's face made the word *no* just impossible to utter, no matter how much Clint wanted to.

What the hell had that teacher done to him? Clint silently demanded. How had the woman managed to turn everything upside down and short-circuit his world in such a short space of time?

He wasn't himself.

Clint frowned. He needed to have it out with Wynona

Chee. Needed to tell her to stop putting ideas into his son's head. She needed to stick to educating her students and not finding ways to try to rearrange their lives the way she was obviously attempting to do with Ryan's.

Without warning, Ryan's high-pitched voice pierced through the thoughts that were building up in his head.

"Could we have her out here for dinner again, Dad?" his son asked out of the blue, managing to completely surprise him.

"Yeah, can we, Dad?" Roy asked, unable to hide his grin as he added his voice to his nephew's.

The rather knowing expression on Roy's face got under his skin.

In response, Clint gave his brother a look that silently ordered him to knock it off. But apparently, the message was not being received because Roy just went on grinning at him as he said, "I think it's a good idea."

"You want to see the woman," Clint snapped, "do it on your own time."

Out of the corner of his eye, he saw Ryan's face fall. The boy looked crushed. This time, when his son asked, the enthusiasm had left his voice. Instead, it was replaced with a serious, somewhat sorrowful note.

"Can't we have her here so that all three of us can see her, Dad?" he asked, never taking his eyes off his father's face.

And then Lucia added her voice to the conversation. "I could make her stew," the housekeeper volunteered. "She liked it the last time she was here."

"The *only* time she was here," Clint reminded the woman.

The words seemed to have no effect on his housekeeper. They certainly weren't registering with her, he thought darkly.

Neither were they registering with his brother or, more important, with his son. Clint felt like the ground under his feet was quickly turning into quicksand and despite all of his best efforts, he found himself sinking fast.

"I'll think about it, okay?" he finally said to his son, thinking that would be the end of it, at least for a while.

"Okay." Ryan paused for a moment, then in all innocence asked, "When will you be finished thinking about it so you can say yes?"

Roy laughed, tickled at the boy's response. "He's got you there."

When had all this happened? Clint wondered. A few months ago if he said no to something, whether to his son, his brother or the other two people at the ranch, it remained no. There were no attempts to get him to change his mind or reconsider. Certainly no hope of getting him to actually say yes to something like having a woman sit down at their table who wasn't Lucia.

How had things changed so quickly?

"Maybe she's too busy to come to dinner," Clint finally said to his son. "Remember, she's got a lot of students."

Ryan had an answer for that, too. "She told the class she'd never be too busy for us."

If his intention was to play fair, then he knew he was losing, Clint thought. Moreover, he had the feeling that

Ryan would only keep after him until he finally agreed to this fool notion.

He was never going to have any peace until then.

"I can ask her for you," Ryan volunteered. "Tomorrow, before class, I can—"

"If anyone is going to ask your Miss Chee to come to dinner, it'll be me," Clint said. He meant that to terminate the discussion.

Instead, it elicited a wide smile and a happy squeal. "Thanks, Dad!" Ryan cried.

Clint opened his mouth to protest that there was nothing to thank him for, but then he shut it again. He recalled something that Wynona had said to him. She'd said that Ryan saw him as his hero, or words to that effect. For now he decided to just bask in that light.

Maybe tomorrow he'd think of a reason not to invite the teacher to his table.

Chapter Twelve

Clint gave in. This invitation to the teacher seemed to mean a great deal to Ryan. And even if the boy didn't say anything, he knew that both his brother and the housekeeper would.

It wasn't a battle worth fighting.

Clint made up his mind. If he was going to extend the invitation to the teacher to have dinner at his ranch, he was not about to do it by phone. Though in the long run it was easier that way, it was, in his estimation, the coward's way out.

And having Ryan invite his teacher the way the boy had eagerly volunteered to do somehow just didn't seem right, either. It seemed to supersede his authority. So Clint went back to his initial conclusion on the matter.

The invitation needed to come from him, verbally, on a face-to-face basis.

Even so, Clint found himself coming up with spur-of-the-moment reasons not to go see her. But he could see his son becoming more antsy with each passing day. He knew it would only be a matter of time before the boy jumped the gun and did the asking himself, so finally, on Wednesday afternoon, Clint got behind the wheel of his truck and pointed the vehicle toward town.

"Hey," Roy called, coming up to the driver's side. "If you're going into town for something, I can go in your place." Unlike him, his brother looked for any excuse to drive into Forever.

"No," Clint answered, setting his jaw hard, "you can't."

And he drove away, terminating the discussion.

He'd come close, Clint thought, to handing over what he viewed as his "task" to his brother.

Even now, as he got closer to town, he couldn't believe that he was actually willingly doing this.

"It's just a dinner for the boy's sake," he muttered to himself. "That's all."

Under no circumstances could this be viewed as a date, he thought angrily. He'd sworn that he would never put himself into that sort of a situation again, a situation that allowed a woman the power to crush him into the ground the way Susan had ultimately wound up doing to him.

Besides, Clint reminded himself, he and the teacher weren't going to be alone at dinner. There was going to be a full house present. Ryan, Roy, his other ranch hand, Jake, and even Lucia would be there with them. Lucia might be making the dinner but he was going to insist that she sit down at the table with them. The more people there, the better.

No one in their right mind could possibly think of this as a "date."

He realized he was grinding his teeth and consciously made an effort to stop.

The refrain that this was *not a date* was still going through his head like a steady drumbeat when he pulled into Forever.

There seemed to be more people in town than usual, especially on a weekday. He scanned the area. A lot more, he observed. Rather than giving the impression that they were all about personal errands, he saw people gathering together, conferring intensely.

Something was up and Clint idly wondered what it was. Was there something he should be aware of? The sky looked too clear for there to be a storm coming.

Then what?

Reaching his destination, he parked his truck in front of the elementary school and got out. He stopped the first person who crossed his path, a man he vaguely recognized as being one of the people who worked in the general store.

If it hadn't been for the charged electricity in the air, Clint might have just ignored what was going on. But something seemed to be happening and he found he couldn't turn his back on it.

That had been Wynona's work.

The man he recognized from the general store had a bunch of flyers in his hands. Clint deliberately stopped him and asked, "What's going on?"

The man, Jason Rivers, looked at him as if he thought Clint had been living under a rock.

"Haven't you heard?" he asked with a look of disbelief on his craggy face. "Tyler Hale is missing."

The name meant nothing to Clint. But before he could ask Jason who Tyler was, the man pushed one of the flyers into his hands.

"We're putting together search parties to look for him." Jason paused only long enough to tap the page before moving on. "He's been gone since yesterday."

Clint scanned the page to fill in the rest of the information.

The boy, who was the same age as his son, seemed to have disappeared on his way home from school. The photo and description nudged forward no memories for him as he committed the former to memory.

Still holding the flyer in his hand, Clint walked into the school. He just wanted to get the invitation over with.

When he found Wynona, she was just leaving her classroom. Moving quickly, he got in front of her. She didn't look surprised to see him, which gave him pause until she said, "You've come to join the search."

The amount of relief and welcoming in her voice caught him totally off guard. For a second Clint didn't know how to respond. Saying no seemed rather heartless under the circumstances, but just saying yes was nothing short of a lie and he didn't believe in lying.

Torn, he fell back on what was, at best, a vaguely worded truth. "I just heard that the boy was missing."

Wynona took his answer in stride, thinking he was explaining why he hadn't been here sooner.

"Horrible, isn't it?" she asked as she walked out of the room. "His poor parents must be out of their minds with worry."

"People handle crises in different ways," Clint told her.

"True," she agreed, then said, "The way I handle it is I just have to do something about it."

He laughed softly. She really was a scrapper. There were worse things, he supposed. "I kind of figured that."

She didn't bother trying to figure out what Ryan's father meant by that. Instead, she just took charge of the situation. She did it without thinking.

"Why don't you come with me?" she suggested. "I'm not too bad when it comes to tracking." She'd had a friend, Tommy, on the reservation when she lived there and Tommy had taken delight in passing on what seemed to come naturally to him. He had taught her how to track. "And you're probably better."

Clint had no idea why she would think that. He'd never said anything to anyone about his abilities to follow a trail that was practically nonexistent. But it sounded as if there very well might be a life at stake. Making up his mind, he didn't bother with denials or refusals.

"Let's go." His response was the only testimony to the fact that he was willing to put his skills to work.

Sheriff Rick Santiago was in charge of the search parties. There was no shortage of volunteers. He didn't think that there would be. The residents of Forever could be counted on to look after their own.

Because the territory outside the town was vast, the sheriff divided the searchers into parties of twos and threes, and in a few cases, fours. His thinking was to use those who were inexperienced, putting them together with the more experienced trackers.

Despite the number of volunteers, there was still a great deal of area to cover.

"We'll meet back here in town right after sundown. It'll be too dark to continue the search then and I don't want to have extra people to look for." There was no humor attached to his words. "Hopefully by then one of us will have found Tyler."

Everyone got started, spreading out and calling Tyler's name. They also talked to one another in an effort to keep their spirits up as well as remain positive about the search's ultimate outcome.

Clint wasn't interested in uplifting spirits. He was focused on getting information that might help bring this search to a close faster.

"This kid ever run away before?" he asked Wynona matter-of-factly as they methodically conducted their search.

She spared him a look. "He didn't run away," she answered.

"How do you know that?" Clint challenged. He wasn't trying to be argumentative. In his mind, hunters needed to know their quarries.

"Because he's in my class," she informed him, a slight edge entering her voice. It was hard to tamp down her own concern. "He's a happy kid and his parents love him," she added as they made their way across terrain that was, for the most part, relatively flat.

There was a mountain range located in the distance. It was covered with trees and was the area where the town's annual Christmas tree came from. But the idea of Christmas seemed a million miles away.

"You never know what's going on in someone's home," Clint answered, looking straight ahead. "Families have secrets."

She looked at him again. "I'm well aware of that," she replied.

In his own way, he was trying to prepare her for the eventuality that they might never find the boy. "Maybe something happened and this kid—"

"Tyler," she interjected, not wanting the boy to be reduced to just a dehumanized, antiseptic term. "His name is Tyler."

"Tyler," Clint obliged as he continued to lead the way. "Tyler decided to run away. Maybe to teach his parents a lesson, maybe to just get away from them, or maybe—"

"Or maybe he just had a yen, went exploring and got lost. Boys do that," Wynona insisted with feeling.

He caught the inflection in her voice. "You believe that."

"Yes," Wynona said with such passion that he could only look at her for a long moment, almost won over by her spirit.

But his practical side resurfaced almost immediately. "Well, if that's the case, if he just 'went exploring,' why isn't he back?"

Wynona lifted her shoulders in a helpless shrug. She didn't have a definitive answer to give Clint and it frustrated her.

"He got lost, he tripped and got hurt," she said, enumerating all the different things that could have happened. "He wasn't looking where he was going and fell into a hole. Or maybe he somehow got trapped."

The last word caught Clint's attention. "Trapped?" he asked.

Desperate, Wynona was still fabricating excuses as fast as she could think of them. "A coyote crossed his path. Tyler started to cower, then he looks for someplace to hide."

Clint turned the suggestions over in his mind, reviewing them as quickly as Wynona was coming up with them. And then finally, he nodded, agreeing. "That might be a possibility."

"Thank you," Wynona replied in what sounded like a distant, emotionless voice.

Clint just assumed she was being sarcastic, but when he looked at Wynona's face, he realized that she wasn't. She was serious.

With a sigh, he signaled for her to follow him. They had a lot of territory to cover before sundown.

* * *

"We should be heading back," he told her, breaking the silence that had gone on for over the last fifteen minutes. Possibly even longer. He gestured at the sky. The sun was setting. "It's going to be dark soon."

She knew that and she was trying not to think about it or to allow panic to slither into her mind and slow her down.

"Just a little longer," Wynona urged. "Tyler's already been out here one night and he must really be scared by now. We need to find him," she emphasized.

So far, all the signs they thought they had picked up had led nowhere, or had faded away without yielding any results. There'd been no signal from any of the other searchers that they had found the missing boy, either. It felt as if they were no closer to locating Tyler now than when they started out.

"Aren't you afraid we'll get lost in the dark?" Clint asked her.

He was curious to hear her answer. As far as he was concerned, he could still find his way back, so being out here at this point presented no danger.

"Honestly, I'm more afraid that he's lost," she answered. She scanned the area, but it was getting harder and harder to make things out. "Are there any caves around here?" she asked.

"No." And then Clint rethought his answer. "But there're a couple of large burrows."

"Where?" Wynona pressed, her excitement mounting for the first time in hours.

Something was always in the last place a person

looked, she told herself. It was corny, but true. She glanced at Clint, waiting for him to answer her.

"It's been a while since I've been out around here," he told her.

She didn't want excuses; she wanted results. She could almost *feel* the boy's fear.

"Try," she stressed.

He looked at her. There was a full moon out, which helped to illuminate the area—and her. Moonlight became her, he caught himself thinking before he pushed the thought away.

Knowing that she had to have noticed him looking at her, he diverted her back to their lost boy. "You think he might be there?"

It made sense to her. "A burrow isn't very big, but neither is he. And it might be where he's hiding from the animals—and the cold. The temperature dropped when the sun went down," she reminded him. It worried her to think of the boy out here all night, cold and hungry.

Clint stood there for a long moment, scrutinizing the already progressively darker terrain. He was trying to remember the location of one of the burrows.

And then he pointed west. "I think there's a burrow over that way."

They began walking, picking up their pace. Once again Wynona began to call out the boy's name the way she had earlier. Her throat felt a bit raw but she forced herself to continue. This wasn't the time to think of her own comfort.

Nothing but night sounds answered her. There wasn't

anything remotely human in that mix. Tyler wasn't responding.

Frustrated, she turned toward Clint. "You said that there were a couple of burrows out here. Where's the other one?"

As far as he was concerned, this was a losing battle and they had stayed out a lot longer than they had initially agreed to. The sheriff might even be concerned about them by now.

"You ever give up, lady?" he asked her.

"Hasn't been known to happen yet," she told him crisply.

Clint sighed. Gesturing her onward, he muttered, "Let's go."

They searched for the second burrow. Finally finding it, Wynona began calling Tyler's name yet again. There was no answer.

"C'mon," Clint urged, taking her arm. "He's not here."

She pulled her arm away. "We don't know that yet. You can go back if you want to," she said, continuing to call Tyler's name.

Clint murmured a few choice words under his breath, but he stayed at her side. He joined his voice to hers, calling out to Tyler.

Several more minutes passed. And then a weak voice, more like a sob, was heard in the distance.

"Here. I'm here. Here!" The voice grew in strength, like a last-ditch attempt before total despair set in, silencing the boy.

Instantly alert, Wynona began running toward what

appeared to be another side of the burrow. She quickly cut the remaining distance down to nothing.

Clint was right beside her, his long legs eventually outdistancing her.

This part of the burrow was more like a hole in the ground that had all but caved in on itself, obscuring the opening from being seen by the casual eye.

Wynona was on her knees, calling down into the opening. "Tyler, are you in there?"

"I'm here, I'm here," the little boy cried. "I was looking for leprechauns. I thought I saw one and tried to follow, but then everything started coming down on me and I couldn't get out."

Clint was already digging, using his bare hands to get to the boy. Luckily, the dirt was soft.

Without a word to him, Wynona joined in, trying to dig the boy out, hoping their combined effort would enable them to get to Tyler faster.

"We're coming, Tyler," she called, doing her best to keep his spirits up. "Ryan's father and I are going to get you out of there. I promise."

Clint had realized something. "Hold still, Tyler," he ordered, for once trying to keep his voice gentle instead of stern. "The dirt's soft, but if you start moving around, you might make it shift on you."

He was phrasing it euphemistically not to frighten the boy. What he was really afraid of was that the remaining dirt would cave in on Tyler, burying the boy further. They had no tools to use in order to dig him out any quicker than they were doing.

"I'm scared," Tyler cried.

"Don't be scared," Wynona told the boy. She was worried that he might panic and that would just make matters worse. "We'll have you out in a few minutes, I promise. Just hold very still. Like a statue. Can you do that for me, Tyler? Can you pretend to be a statue?"

"Like the one you showed us in that picture?" he asked, his voice trembling.

"Yes, exactly like that," she encouraged.

"Okay, I can do that," he answered, but his voice was quaking.

Clint picked up his pace even though his arms were beginning to ache and it felt like his fingers were cramping up.

"You're doing great, Tyler," he encouraged. "Just hang in a little longer, cowboy. Just a few more minutes. And then you're going to have some story to tell your friends."

"I will?" he cried, desperately trying to remain brave.

"You bet," Clint told him. "All the other kids are going to be real jealous of you." More dirt flew to the side. His shoulders were aching. "Almost there, Tyler. Almost there."

The sound of his voice seemed to calm the boy down.

Chapter Thirteen

Painfully aware that this piece of nondescript clump of earth could have easily become Tyler's final resting place if they hadn't found him, after they carefully eased the boy out of the mound of crumbling dirt, Clint rose to his feet holding Tyler in his arms.

His first thought was to head back the way they had come. But he didn't know if Wynona was up to it after what they had just gone through to rescue the boy. By all rights she should have been exhausted by now, but he couldn't very well leave her behind.

"Can you make it back to town?" Clint asked, looking at the woman next to him. She had dirt in her hair as well as smudges on her face and clothes. He knew he didn't have any other options open to him. If she was too exhausted to undertake the journey, they'd have to wait here until morning.

Though he didn't want to, he made the proposal to her. "We can stay here and rest until morning if you feel that—"

But Wynona waved away his concern. "Don't worry about me," she told him. There was no way she wasn't going to make it back tonight, even if she had to crawl. "There's no signal out here," she said, reminding him that they couldn't call anyone. "Tyler's mom and dad need to know that he's safe." She smiled at the boy. "And I think that Tyler needs to get some dry clothes on him and some warm food *into* him, don't you, Tyler?" she asked the boy.

"Yes, ma'am," Tyler answered solemnly.

Polite even in dire circumstances, someone had raised this boy right, Wynona thought.

Clint nodded. "Then if you think you're up to walking," he told Wynona, "we'd better get started getting back."

Even as he said the words, he could feel Tyler clinging to him as if he was never going to let go. The boy had really been scared, he thought. "Hang in there, Tyler," he told the boy in his arms, "we're going to get you home."

They started walking back.

Both Clint and Wynona were prepared to walk all the way back to where they had first left their car, fairly certain that by now, given the hour, the other searchers had returned to town. So when a beam of light slashed through the darkness when they were a little more than halfway back, Clint stiffened. His mind immediately braced for the worst.

"Get behind me," he ordered Wynona.

She stubbornly disregarded the instruction and instead, picked up her pace so that she was in front of Clint and the boy he was carrying.

"Damn it, woman, listen to me!" Clint ordered.

The next moment the identity of the person wielding the flashlight and shining it at them was no longer a mystery.

Sheriff Santiago lowered the small, intense flashlight he was using. The grin on his face was almost as bright.

"Boy, am I damn happy to see you!" the sheriff declared. "All three of you," he added, smiling at Tyler. He ruffled the boy's hair. Tyler continued clinging to Clint. "You gave us quite a scare, Ty," the sheriff told the boy.

"I kinda scared me, too," Tyler admitted, his voice partially muffled against Clint's shoulder.

Nodding, the sheriff pulled out the walkie-talkie attached to his belt, pressing the button on the side. "We found them," he told the deputy on the other end. "The boy as well as Washburn and the teacher."

"We weren't lost," Wynona protested.

Santiago's eyes swept over the trio. "My mistake. We thought you were," he explained. He regarded them again. "You up to walking?" he asked.

"Just don't get in our way," Wynona told him.

The sheriff laughed, then gestured them on. "Then let's go."

They resumed walking back to the initial starting point, but this time, the journey was far from silent.

"A lot of people are going to be really glad to see you," the sheriff told Tyler.

Rather than look happy, the boy hung his head. "I'm sorry I caused so much trouble."

"Never mind that now. We found you and that's what matters," Clint told him.

Tyler hung on to him even harder.

Wynona saw Clint tighten his arms around the boy. She smiled to herself despite everything that they had gone through.

The man had a heart after all.

Alerted by the deputy, Tyler's parents were waiting for him before they had a chance to broach the perimeter of the town.

Donna Hale was sobbing as she embraced her son even while he was still in Clint's arms.

"I don't know how to thank you," Ed Hale told Clint and Wynona, his voice almost breaking as he choked back his own tears.

"No thanks necessary," Clint answered. Gratitude made him uncomfortable. He turned his small burden over to Tyler's father.

It took a moment for Tyler to release his hold on Clint. Before going to his father, the boy looked at the man who had helped to dig him out, his wide brown eyes saying everything that he was unable to convey to him in words.

Clint nodded in response, then took a step back as everyone who had come out to search for Tyler closed ranks, surrounding Donna and Ed Hale and their son.

"You did good."

The simple, three-word sentence of praise came from Miss Joan, who along with some of her waitresses, had set up a station with hot coffee and pastries in the town square for those searchers who had temporarily come back to town to refuel before setting out again. It was clear that no one felt right about calling it a day and going home until the boy was found.

And now they remained for another reason. Although Tyler had been found and returned to his parents, there was still a lot of wired energy ricocheting among the residents, needing a harmless way to be rechanneled and discharged.

"Celebration's on me," Miss Joan announced, raising her whiskey voice so that everyone could hear, "now that there's something to celebrate. C'mon." She gestured for everyone in the square to follow her to the diner. There was no question in her mind that they would.

As people began to leave the square and walk toward the diner, Wynona noticed Clint turning away.

He was going home, she thought. Moving fast, she stepped in front of him, blocking his path.

Clint raised one expressive brow. "You're in my way."

She didn't move. "Earlier today, before we started looking for Tyler, you came into the school. I got the impression you were looking for me and wanted to talk. Did you?"

All that seemed like a million years ago now, Clint

thought. Wynona was looking at him, waiting for him to give her an answer.

He shrugged. "Yeah, I did."

"About?" she asked, waiting.

He knew he couldn't just walk away without answering. For one thing, the woman would follow him. He was beginning to learn that she was as stubborn as they came. So he told her.

"Ryan wanted me to ask you to come to dinner at the ranch."

"Ryan wanted," Wynona repeated. She continued watching him, as if she was waiting for more.

"Yeah."

She waited a beat, but Washburn didn't say anything further. What did she expect?

Because he had been the reluctant hero today, she cut him some slack. "And what did *you* want?"

Clint shrugged. He didn't want to be put on the spot but he didn't see a way out. Between clenched teeth, he said, "To make the boy happy."

"Then I guess I can't disappoint him—and indirectly—you," she added, taking great pains to word her response carefully.

He shrugged, as if all this was a moot point. "It's a little late for dinner now," he told her.

"But not too late for a rain check," Wynona pointed out.

He frowned. "You never not have an answer for everything?" he asked, irritated that he couldn't just walk away from all this.

Wynona smiled, the teacher in her coming out. "That's a double negative, Clint."

He blew out a breath. "Yeah, well, I guess I'm kinda tired."

"Hey, you two, Miss Joan wants to know what's taking you so long," Angel Rodriquez, the diner's resident chef, asked. "And she said to tell you not to even *think* about begging off. You two are the official heroes of this thing, finding Tyler the way you did." The woman smiled understandingly at them. She knew that Miss Joan was a force to be reckoned with, same as they did. "This celebration's as much for you as it is for him."

Wynona could feel the man next to her bristling. She could guess what was going through his mind.

"If I remember my facts correctly," she told him, "nobody's ever crossed Miss Joan and lived to tell about it."

Clint considered saying that he would be the first, but then decided against it. After all, this afternoon he'd come to ask Wynona to come to the ranch for dinner, so in a way, the location of the meal had just been changed.

He shrugged, as if he was giving in. "Then I guess I'd better not."

"Smart man," Wynona told him with a wide smile.

They fell into step behind Angel and began walking to the diner.

"You know, you surprised me," Wynona confided to Clint in a whisper just before they reached their destination.

He was tempted to just let her remark go, but something goaded him to take this a step further. He supposed that his curiosity had gotten the better of him.

"How?" he asked.

She smiled at him. "You went on looking when I asked you to even though I know you wanted to go back the way the sheriff had instructed."

"What can I say? I guess you're just intimidating," he quipped.

He was close to a foot taller than she was. Even if he weren't, she couldn't visualize Clint being intimidated by anyone or anything. That just wasn't in the rancher's nature.

"Yeah, right," she laughed.

She saw a smile curve just the corners of his mouth a moment before she and Clint walked into the diner. "Well, you are," he told her matter-of-factly.

Wynona wasn't sure what came over her. Maybe it was the triumphant feeling that was all but vibrating through her because they had found Tyler and brought him back to his worried parents. Maybe it was that Clint's smile, unconsciously sexy, had struck a kindred chord deep within her.

Or maybe, just for the moment, she was responding to a man she'd done her very best *not* to respond to from the first moment she had climbed over his fence and walked straight toward him.

Whatever the reason behind her actions, Wynona didn't waste any time analyzing it. She just reacted.

Grabbing hold of the front of Clint's shirt, she stopped him in his tracks and then she turned him toward her.

Before he could ask her what the hell she thought she was doing, she did it.

She kissed him.

Kissed him with all the unbridled emotion that was currently throbbing in her veins.

Had the woman blasted him point-blank with a shotgun, Clint thought that she couldn't have surprised him any more than she did.

Stunned, Clint didn't have time to think about what was going down. Instead, he just reacted the same as she did. Reacted like a suffocating man who had suddenly been connected to a tank of oxygen just mere seconds before he was officially pronounced dead.

Instincts that he had thought had been laid to rest permanently cracked through the invisible walls that he had carefully kept around himself these past seven years and suddenly took over.

He pulled Wynona to him, his arms closing tightly around her as he kissed her back, deepening the unplanned contact.

Without giving it any thought, he lost himself in the heat that had suddenly ignited in his veins, very nearly setting him on fire.

Just as she almost did.

Clint wasn't sure just how long the kiss continued. The only thing he knew was that this woman had managed to awaken things within him that he'd talked himself into believing were dead and that he was better off because they were.

But they weren't dead.

And neither was he.

When Wynona finally drew back—because she was

the one who ended the kiss, not him—he found himself staring at her as if he had suddenly been struck mute. Clint struggled to get his bearings.

Struggled to appear unaffected even though he knew in his gut that he wasn't going to fool her. It didn't take a genius to know that she had to have felt him kissing her back.

Attack was always better than retreat. So he did. "What the hell was that?" he asked.

Rather than becoming defensive, he watched, almost in fascination, as a smile blossomed on her lips.

Not one of those self-satisfied or self-congratulating smiles that reeked of smugness, but a smile that radiated happiness. As if she was genuinely happy that he had felt something, the same as she did.

"If you have to ask, Clint," she told him, "then it's been even longer for you than it's been for me."

Clint cleared his throat. He didn't want her thinking that. "No, I just—"

The door to the diner reopened just then and this time it was Miss Joan who was on the top step, one fisted hand at her waist as she looked at them. The fact that she was there herself instead of one of her waitresses was not wasted on them.

"Just how much of a personal invitation do you two need?" Miss Joan asked. "Do I have to get the Murphy brothers to carry you into my establishment?" she asked, referring to the three men who were joint owners of the town's only saloon. "The only way I got them to come here in the first place was to say that this was going to be in your honor. They even donated beer for the occasion," she added.

It was a known fact that Miss Joan and the Murphys had agreed, years ago, that they wouldn't serve meals in their establishment and in return Miss Joan had said that she would not serve spirits in hers. Neither of them had ever violated that agreement.

"They donated beer?" Clint repeated.

He was stalling. Stalling as he desperately tried to clear his brain so that he could come up with a decent excuse why he couldn't attend this impromptu celebration Miss Joan was throwing.

Right now it felt to him like a fog had descended over his brain, completely blotting out his ability to think.

"That's what it says on the cases they brought with them."

Hazel-green eyes went from Wynona to Clint and then back again.

The knowing look on Miss Joan's face testified that she knew more about what was going on between them than she pretended to. The act was strictly for their benefit, not hers.

"So, are you two coming in or what?" she asked. She didn't bother hiding the impatience in her voice.

Wynona exchanged looks with Clint. Her heart was pounding so hard, she was afraid that Miss Joan would hear it. Most likely, the older woman would be able to see her throat throbbing.

She didn't know why the woman wasn't saying anything about what she had walked in on—Wynona was positive that the woman had seen them kissing—but she was really grateful to Miss Joan for choosing to refrain from making a comment.

Taking a breath, Wynona murmured, "Then I guess we'd better go in. Right, Clint?" It wasn't an order, but a request, asking him to agree with her.

Wynona held the breath she had just taken, hoping that Clint would follow her lead and just go into the diner. If he didn't, she had no doubt that Miss Joan *would* say something, not just to make Clint agree to come into the diner and join the others already there, but also to let him know that she had seen what they had just done. She also had no doubts that Miss Joan would comment on what she had seen.

She really didn't want that out there. At least, not tonight.

"Right," she heard Clint say. And then, as she watched, she saw him follow Miss Joan into the noisy diner.

Only then did Wynona release the breath she was holding.

She hardly felt her feet as she walked in behind Clint.

Chapter Fourteen

Because it looked as if the diner was going to be so crowded, Clint assumed that he could just slip in, and subsequently out again shortly thereafter totally unnoticed.

Instead, the moment he and Wynona walked into the place Miss Joan presided over like a somewhat benevolent empress, they instantly became the center of attention. All the people within the establishment stopped talking, as well as what they were doing, and within seconds a round of applause swept throughout the restaurant until it swelled, becoming a wave that quickly encompassed everyone.

"I guess there's no escaping now, Clint Washburn," Wynona said, smiling up at him.

If it was humanly possible, Clint looked even more

uncomfortable now than he had when he first began to cross the threshold.

He probably would have fled, except for the fact that every avenue of escape was blocked by at least two or more human obstacles. There was nowhere to go.

"Relax," Miss Joan whispered, coming up behind him. "There are worse things in life than being regarded as a hero."

Clint didn't want to be "regarded" at all. All he ever wanted to do was to continue going about his life unnoticed.

"How did you know where to find Tyler?" someone called out from within the crowd.

Sensing how very uncomfortable Clint was right now, Wynona answered for him.

"We really didn't know. We just continued searching through the quadrant of the area we were assigned." Seeing that the crowd wanted more, she elaborated. "We thought that Tyler might have looked for shelter in a cave or just about anywhere that would provide him with some kind of protection away from the elements."

She glanced toward the man next to her. "Clint remembered that there were burrows in the area, so we checked them out. And that's where we found Tyler, in the last burrow," she concluded with a smile just as someone pushed a mug of beer into her hands.

"Had to be more to it than that," Garrett Murphy insisted.

"Maybe a little more," Wynona allowed. "But right now I think we're both just too tired to remember the details." Her smile widened. "The point is, Tyler's back with his parents."

"But—" Another Forever resident protested, trying to get more of the story out of one or the other of the heroes.

That was when Miss Joan intervened, moving into the middle of the discussion. She eyed Liam Murphy, another one of the three brothers. "You heard them," the woman said authoritatively, "Wynona said they were tired. Back off, Murphy, or I'll cut you off from your own beer," she warned.

Liam inclined his head. "Yes, ma'am," he said, raising his hands to show that he was surrendering to the inevitable. There was no shame in that. Everyone knew that Miss Joan always won.

Clint appeared rather impressed that despite the legend that existed about her, the thin, at times downright fragile-looking woman could cast such a powerful, almost intimidating shadow.

At this point, Wynona took the opportunity to lean into him.

"You don't have to stay too long," she told Clint, her voice low as she whispered the words into his ear, not wanting to be overheard by anyone else. "You just have to stay long enough to let people thank you."

Clint was intrigued by her reasoning. She made it sound as if it was all him and they both knew that it wasn't.

"You were part of it, too," he told her. "You were *more* than part of it, really. If it weren't for you, I would have turned back," Clint informed her in a quiet voice.

"No, you wouldn't have," she countered knowingly.

He felt Wynona's breath skim along his neck and cheek as she spoke. Felt a shiver skimming through him in response that he had to consciously tamp down.

This was *not* the time to react to the woman. Actually, there *was* no right time to react to the woman. He'd sworn to himself that he was done with that sort of thing. Allowing himself to react only led to complications he wanted no part of.

"You claiming to know me better than I know myself?" he challenged. The woman hardly knew him at all.

Wynona's mouth curved and he felt her smile curling its way through his insides even as he struggled to try to block it.

"Maybe I do," Wynona answered.

Before he could say anything, Wynona's cousin descended on them, placing a hand on either of their shoulders. Shania's eyes were sparkling as she said, "I knew if anyone could find that boy, you would."

It wasn't clear to Clint if Shania was talking to just her cousin, or if her comment was meant for both of them. Whatever the case, he did what he could to shift the emphasis strictly onto Wynona.

"She insisted on going on even after it grew too dark to be able to see more than a few feet in front of us," he told Shania.

Shania nodded, pride evident in her voice as well as in her smile. "Wynona's always been pushy like that. I'd watch my step if I were you," she added, this time looking directly at him.

Clint frowned. Was she actually making some kind

of reference about them actually being a couple? His back went up.

"Why would I have to—"

Clint never got to finish his question, or to voice a denial.

Interrupting him again, Shania laughed as she winked at him. "Just know that forewarned is forearmed," she told him. "I'll leave you two to mingle with your adoring fans." And with that, Wynona's cousin quickly slipped away.

Wynona saw that Clint was frowning again. It struck her almost as odd that he looked rather cute when he did that.

"I don't want to mingle," he protested, although she noticed that he wasn't just walking out of the diner, either.

"I think that's been taken out of your hands," Wynona pointed out. But then she added once again, "Give this just a little longer."

As far as he was concerned, he'd already given this more time than he'd intended. But because he didn't want to cause a scene—or argue with Miss Joan—he resigned himself to remaining at the celebration "a little longer" as Wynona had suggested.

But *just* a little longer, Clint underscored in his mind.

The crowd gathered around them seemed to have other ideas.

Everyone wanted to buy them a drink, or at least share in the moment with them. Everyone, apparently, appeared to be flying high on a combination of good will and good feelings.

So they stayed longer.

* * *

It was only several hours later that Wynona finally offered up an exit excuse that was acceptable to the good citizens of Forever.

"Tomorrow is a school day and I need to get some sleep if I'm going to be of any use to my students," she declared, her words making the rounds in a general fashion. Specifically, Wynona's excuse provided Clint with a reason that allowed him to detach himself from the festivities, as well.

"I'll take you home." The words came out of Clint's mouth before he fully realized just what he was saying or the significance that others might very well wind up attaching to them.

The full import of his words was communicated when Wynona looked at him in surprise.

A beat later the surprised expression melted into a smile as she responded, "That's very nice of you."

He'd gotten caught in a trap inadvertently of his own making, Clint thought as he mumbled, "Yeah, sure." Then, because he couldn't think of anything else to say or any way to get out of this gracefully without looking like a complete idiot, he retorted, "You ready?"

She glanced over to where her cousin was standing. Shania was talking to one of the searchers, a Navajo. Will had come from the reservation when the call had gone out to look for Tyler.

Shania's eyes met hers for a brief moment. They'd always had their own way of communicating and now was no different. Shania nodded at her with a smile, then went back to talking to the native tracker.

"I'm ready," Wynona said, returning her attention back to Clint.

Resigned to playing the Boy Scout, Clint held the door open for her as she walked out of the diner. Wynona smiled at him.

But once they were outside and the door closed behind them, Wynona turned toward the rancher and said, "You don't really have to take me home."

Confusion creased his brow. "But you just said you wanted me to take you home."

"No," Wynona contradicted, "I was just providing you with an excuse to leave the celebration the way you've been *itching* to do since before we ever walked into the diner."

Clint regarded this puzzle of a woman as they went down the steps. Was she saying she didn't want him to take her home? No, that wasn't it. She actually did think she'd provided him with an excuse.

His car was still parked in front of the elementary school where he'd left it when he'd gone to invite her to dinner at the ranch. Taking hold of her elbow, he guided Wynona in that direction now.

"I can make my own excuses," he told her, then added firmly, "I said I was taking you home so I'm taking you home."

Wynona squared her shoulders. "I'm a big girl—" she began.

He thought of the way she'd turned and kissed him just before he'd walked into the diner. A wave of warmth washed over him.

"I'm well aware of that," he assured her.

His voice suddenly sounded silky, almost seductive,

Wynona thought. And she could feel him looking at her, his eyes moving over every inch of her very slowly.

It was all she could do not to react.

Forcing herself to focus, Wynona tried again. "What I'm trying to say is that I'm very capable of walking myself home."

He had set ideas when it came to certain things. He was the man and as such, the protector in this scenario. "It's dark." He assumed that was enough to get his point across.

"Very observant," Wynona remarked, the corners of her mouth curving.

He strove for patience. "What I'm saying," he told her, enunciating each word, "is that I'd feel better if I got you home safe."

Her brow furrowed just a little as she looked at him. "Why?"

Clint could feel the last of his patience flying out the window. "Damn it, woman, is everything up for debate with you?"

"I'm just trying to understand you." She wasn't being flippant, just giving an honest answer.

It wasn't an answer that he wanted. She was trying to get close to him and he didn't want that. The very idea scared him.

"Well, don't," he snapped. "Not everything has to be dissected, least of all me."

She looked into his eyes. "What are you afraid of, Clint?"

"That I'll strangle you and they'll convict me," he retorted.

Wynona laughed then. It was a light, silvery sound

that undid every single nerve ending in his body, leaving him defenseless.

They were right in front of the school now. He didn't really have any recollection of what came over him. All he knew was that one moment he was walking next to her, the next minute he had her in his arms with his lips pressed against hers.

For the first time in over two hours, he felt like he had come alive again.

Which was all wrong, he silently argued, because he shouldn't be feeling that way.

Shouldn't be doing this.

Shouldn't be *wanting* to do this. But yet, he couldn't stop.

So what he did was try to assure himself that this would never happen again. The only way he felt he could achieve that was to frighten her into keeping her distance. And that would have to involve kissing her so hard, so thoroughly, that the whole experience would wind up leaving an indelible mark on her soul and cause her to run from him. It would be the only way she could save herself.

The only way that *he* could save himself.

The only problem with his plan was that, within moments, he wound up falling into his own trap. Because he wound up kissing Wynona so completely that he was left gasping for air with his head spinning and his heart racing so hard, for a moment he was certain that it was going to burst right through his veins.

Wynona couldn't catch her breath, couldn't get her bearings. Within seconds of his lips covering hers with such feeling, she found that she had lost all orientation. She had no idea where she was.

All she knew was that she didn't want this to stop.

If the world would suddenly come to an end right at this very moment, this was exactly the way she would have wanted to die because this was truly the most wonderful thing she had *ever* experienced.

There was no improving on perfection.

When Clint finally drew back, looking, she thought, as overwhelmed and disoriented as she felt, neither one of them could speak.

And then, as the silence stretched out, underscored by the pounding of her heart echoing in her ears, Wynona heard herself saying breathlessly, "I don't live very far from here." She had to concentrate on breathing. "Would you like to come over?"

Was she asking what he thought she was asking—or was he just hoping that she was?

No, damn it, Clint silently argued, he didn't want this to happen, didn't want to sink into that quicksand again, feeling as if he had lost his very soul. His life was simple now. It was straightforward. He knew exactly what to expect from each day. No surprises. Feelings only complicated that.

And yet you're feeling really alive for the first time in years, a small voice in his head whispered.

His mouth felt almost dry as he finally answered her question. "I shouldn't."

Wynona shook her head. "That's not what I asked," she told him quietly. Her eyes on his as she repeated her question. "Do you *want* to come over?"

All he had to do was say no then turn on his heel

and walk away—after he brought her home. That was what he'd said he was going to do and he wasn't, as she had pointed out with great emphasis, a man who didn't honor his word.

But once he brought Wynona up to her door, he knew that he would go inside if she invited him. If she *asked* him to, he thought.

If.

The single word vibrated in his mind, almost mocking him.

"It's not that difficult a question," Wynona told him, her voice soft, almost seductive, as she waited for him to say something. "*Do* you want to?" she asked Clint for a third time.

It felt as if time had suddenly stood still.

He tried; he really tried to say the word. Tried to say no to her and with that at least temporarily put an end to his anguish.

After all, turning her down was the honorable thing to do. The *right* thing to do.

But as Clint looked down into her upturned face, Wynona's brilliant blue eyes all but mesmerizing him, he heard himself say the word that would, in all likelihood, wind up sealing his doom.

He said the word so quietly it was almost too quiet to be heard.

But she heard it anyway.

"Yes."

Chapter Fifteen

He really didn't remember the short drive to Wynona's house.

It felt like one moment he was opening the passenger door for her, waiting until she had seated herself and buckled up, the next moment he was pulling up his vehicle, bringing it to a stop before the modest house where she and her cousin currently lived. Everything in between had been just a big blur.

Clint made his way around the rear of his truck on legs that felt as if they were on loan from someone else. Coming to her side of the truck he put his hand on the passenger door handle.

Independent to a fault, Wynona had always felt that she was perfectly capable of getting out of the truck by herself. She nearly started to tell him as much.

But she sensed that all these steps were somehow important to Clint so she restrained her natural inclination to just climb out unaided and waited for him to open the door.

When he did, she was careful to take the hand he offered her before she stepped out. Her heart was beating wildly. Her eyes never left his face.

"We're here," he told her in a voice she couldn't quite fathom.

"We are," she agreed as if to rubber-stamp his words. She turned from him and unlocked her front door.

The sound of the lock clicking open seemed somehow magnified in the stillness.

She pushed the door open, then walked into the small, welcoming house.

Clint wasn't following her.

He wasn't debating the wisdom of coming into her house; he already knew that came under the heading of a foolish move even though he knew he was going to make it. What Clint was doing was attempting to reconcile himself with the consequences that he was certain were waiting for him once what he was about to do came to its logical conclusion.

Crossing the threshold, Wynona quickly moved about the living room, turning on lights, trying to make the house seem less intimate.

Once the room was sufficiently illuminated, she turned around to see if Clint had come in yet.

He hadn't.

Facing him, Wynona said nothing. She just stood there and waited in silence.

"It's warmer once you come in and close the door," she coaxed.

"Yeah," he agreed belatedly. Then taking in one more long breath, he walked into the house and closed the door behind him with his back.

Okay, Wynona thought. *Part one is over.* "Can I get you something to drink?" she asked.

For a second, Clint's mind went completely blank. Regaining the use of his tongue, he heard himself asking, "What do you have?"

Wynona moved toward the refrigerator. "Well, let's see." Opening the door she began to move things around to see what was available inside. "Looks like we have orange juice, beer, red wine and soda," she enumerated. "I can put up a pot of coffee if you like," she offered, straightening up and turning to look in his direction. "What's your pleasure?"

Only then did she realize that Clint had crossed the room over to her. He was now all but toe to toe with her, looking down into her face.

"You." The response was automatic without any deliberation or thought from him.

Trying to remember to breathe, Wynona released the refrigerator door, pushing it shut.

"Then I guess you're in luck," she answered. "I just happen to have some of that on hand."

Before she could berate herself for giving voice to a totally mindless answer, Clint had caught her up in his arms and brought his mouth down on hers.

The heat, the combustion between them, was instant,

firing her up and setting Wynona off like a flare shooting up into the darkened night sky.

She kissed him back as hard, and with as much feeling, as he had kissed her. This part of her life had been untapped for a very long time but there was no working her way up to passion. It was right there, waiting to be set off. One spark and it was engulfing her.

Desire took over.

Wynona couldn't just focus on any one area or on any one thing. Every part of her was responding. Every part of her was vibrating with excitement.

His lips roamed all over her face, her neck, branding every inch of skin as he came in contact with it.

Moving lower.

And just when she thought that there was no turning back, no stopping this runaway train that was barreling down the track, going full steam ahead, Clint pulled back, stunning her.

Wynona pressed her lips together to suppress the moan, the protest that had risen to her lips. Regaining her breath was a challenge as confusion ran rampant through her brain.

He couldn't be stopping now—could he?

"What's wrong?" she asked Clint, doing what she could to steady her breathing so that she wouldn't sound as if she was gasping for air.

"Your cousin," he responded, the two words just hanging in the air between them.

It was enough.

She understood.

It stunned her that he was that aware, that thoughtful of her at a time that was so fraught with emotion. In essence, he was thinking of the effect this would have on her reputation.

He was putting it—and thus her—ahead of his own needs.

"She won't be home for a few hours," Wynona assured him, praying that the momentary pause in the midst of all this wouldn't cause him to change his mind and make him go home.

Clint leaned in and kissed her again, but not with as much frenzied passion as he'd exhibited just a moment ago. She felt a sinking sensation in the pit of her stomach.

Had he had a change of heart? Was he leaving after all?

If he had an ounce of sense in his head, Clint would leave rather than allow this hollow longing within him to drive him this way.

But there *wasn't* enough sense and there was far too much hollow longing driving him onward—no, *begging* him to go onward.

"Where's your bedroom?" he asked Wynona in a raspy voice.

He wasn't leaving!

She almost cheered out loud as she took hold of his hand. Turning around, she led the way from the kitchen toward the two rooms that were beyond it.

Hers was the one on the right side.

The moment they were inside the room, closing the door on the rest of the world, Clint pulled her back into his arms again.

Kissed her again as if his very life depended on the action.

Clint had her up against the wall, kissing her with every shred of passion that had been totally unleashed within him.

She could feel his heart racing as his chest pressed up against hers.

This time there would be no turning back, no hesitation. She could *feel* it.

Her head was swimming as the depth of his kisses grew, engulfing her. Stealing away the very air out of her lungs.

She didn't care.

All she cared about was that Clint was here, with her. He was making everything within her sizzle with the force of a hundred suns.

Wynona struggled to make this taciturn man feel every single thing that she was feeling. She *needed* to make him feel what she was feeling.

Someone had ripped this man's heart out without a second thought, paralyzing all of his emotions. She was determined to bring him back among the living. And just as determined not to make him regret the fact that he could feel again.

Their lips sealed together, they tumbled onto her bed, caught up in absorbing every sensation, every nuance, that was being stirred and brought back to life.

She felt his hands on her body, caressing her, possessing her and pulling aside the cloth barriers that were in his way.

She felt her clothes being removed from her body,

being cast aside. As warm breath covered her body, it instantly prompted her to follow suit, undressing Clint with movements that were more jagged than fluid.

Even so, she still managed to do the job.

And then they were both nude.

Their bodies tangling together as if there was no question that this was what had been intended all along since the very beginning of time.

The voice of reason that Clint had cultivated over the years until it was almost all he was aware of had begun to fade from the first moment their lips had met. The voice was almost totally submerged now, melted in the bubbling waters of desire.

In a last-ditch attempt, he tried to summon it, to resurrect it. But it was completely out of reach, almost totally gone.

He didn't want to stop, didn't want to think. He just wanted this all-encompassing, addictive feeling shooting through his body to be allowed free rein until that was all there was within him.

The sensation was too overwhelming for him to release from his grip. It had been far too long since he had felt like an actual human being instead of just an empty shell.

Wynona twisted and turned beneath him, surrendering to Clint even as she held him captive. She moaned as his hot mouth skimmed along the length of her, leaving her almost completely mindless, a throbbing mass of hungry desire.

With her last shred of strength, she struggled to do the same to him. To make him *feel* the way she did.

Her pulse racing, she felt that she had succeeded, at least in part.

For a man who had withdrawn from the land of the living for so many years, he was unbelievably incredible, Wynona thought, making every single inch of her sing even as she longed for the final fulfilling moment, for the explosion that promised to rock her entire world.

Instinctively, she knew that it wasn't an empty promise. The only reason a part of her was still striving to hang back was because she wanted this feeling to go on for as long as possible.

But her self-control was splintering. Within moments she no longer had the strength to hold him—and herself—at bay.

She *needed* to feel that enormous final rush seizing her in its powerful grip.

Wynona arched her back, her body moving temptingly beneath his. With her eyes silently on his expression, she parted her legs, her invitation clear.

Clint's heart was pounding so hard, he could barely see straight.

Gathering her into his arms as she lay beneath him, his eyes never left her. Everything stood still as he entered her.

The instant he did, she began to move, her body urging him on to that one final place where they could complete each other.

With each passing moment, her tempo increased. Clint moved faster.

She upped the pace and he was right there, keeping up with her and then increasing the tempo until they were both so swept up in it, nothing else mattered.

This went on until they were both moving so fast, it was difficult to know who was outdistancing whom. Or if it even mattered.

The final gratifying explosion seized them simultaneously, enveloping them in a euphoria that defied description.

Clint realized that he was holding on to her tightly, not wanting this to end. Knowing that the moment he stopped holding her so close to him, it would.

The wild pounding of his heart lessened by increments until it was almost back to normal.

Normal was no longer a good thing, he thought. Normal was barren. Lonely. And he had no desire to move back into that stark prison.

Not yet.

He felt Wynona move against him, her torso radiating warmth as she shifted. In the next instant her body was partially over his.

And then she raised her head, the smile on her lips somehow leeching into his very consciousness. That he was aware of it surprised him. That he liked it surprised him even more.

"Bet when you came to school to invite me to the ranch for dinner you never thought we'd wind up like this at the end of the day," she said.

He had no idea why that struck him so funny, but

it did and he laughed. At first, a little and then wholeheartedly.

The laughter in his chest transferred itself to her, turning into something they felt jointly.

"No," he agreed, stroking her hair as he finally caught his breath, "I can't say that I did."

Wynona shifted again. He felt her breasts moving against his chest. Felt himself getting aroused all over again. Despite the vigorous, all but draining, lovemaking they had just experienced, somehow he found himself wanting her all over again.

He had to be losing his mind. But it wasn't his mind that was causing his body to respond this way.

He could feel her smile on his skin as it spread along her lips. The next second she was raising her head again.

"Again?" she asked.

Considering their state of undress, there was no hiding his reaction to her. But he didn't want her thinking that he was some insatiable creature who would demand satisfaction from her whether she was up to it or not.

"No, I—"

He didn't get a chance to finish. Wynona wiggled her body even closer to his, her eyes sparkling with humor and laughter.

"Again," she repeated.

This time he didn't hear it as a question. This time, he realized, she was telling him what *she* wanted.

But was she just saying that to go along with what she could tell he wanted? He shifted farther in order to be able to squarely face her.

"You sure?"

As she leaned in to kiss him, Clint could feel the laughter on her lips. When she moved her head back, creating a small space, her smile had widened, spreading from ear to ear.

"What do you think?"

"I think the best is yet to come," he answered, the words all but vibrating within him as they emerged on his lips.

"My thoughts exactly." Her eyes were bright with laughter as she raised her lips to his.

Chapter Sixteen

Had she made a mistake?

Had leaving the celebration at Miss Joan's diner and bringing Clint home with her been ultimately a mistake on her part?

Wynona didn't want to believe that, but as each day passed, fading into the next, she began to grow more and more certain that, no matter what was in her heart, she had made a mistake.

Making love with Clint had felt so right when it was happening. She had been sure that deep down inside him, he was feeling the exact same thing that she was. Moreover, that Clint had feelings for her just the way she had for him.

But after they'd made love—*twice*—he had quickly

gotten dressed and left, making a point of leaving before Shania came home.

At the time she had thought that Clint was just being protective of her. That he didn't want her cousin to know that they had slept together until and unless she was the one who wanted to tell Shania about them.

But she was beginning to think that maybe he hadn't wanted Shania to know—hadn't wanted *anyone* to know—not because he was protecting her but because making love with her hadn't really meant anything to him. That what had happened was all just part of an age-old cliché.

Now that Clint had gotten what he'd wanted from her, she no longer mattered to him.

With all her heart, Wynona didn't want to believe that, but what other explanation was there for his disappearing act?

Two weeks had gone by and she hadn't heard a word from Clint. He had made no attempt to get in contact with her in order to finalize any plans regarding having dinner at the ranch. He hadn't called, hadn't even sent a message to her via his son.

Nothing.

It was as if now that he'd slept with her, he no longer wanted any part of her.

Had she just imagined the whole thing? Imagined that he cared?

Wynona had no idea what to think. All she knew was that her heart ached and it was all because of Clint.

She was able to keep up a brave face in class, but it was getting a little more difficult with each day that passed.

* * *

"When is Miss Chee going to come over for dinner?" Ryan asked his father.

The boy had waylaid him by the corral to ask the question.

This time.

The boy had asked him the same question every day for over two weeks ever since the afternoon that he had gone into town to extend the invitation to Wynona and gotten caught up in the search for Tyler.

Gotten caught up in Wynona, Clint thought almost unwillingly.

Making love with the woman had been nothing short of exquisite. It also showed him how very susceptible he was to her. Showed him in no uncertain terms how extremely *vulnerable* he was when it came to anything that had to do with Wynona.

And that scared him.

Scared him because since he felt the way he did about her, it gave the woman power over him. The kind of power that could, so very easily, completely undo him.

Completely destroy him.

The last time that had happened, he had managed, through sheer grit, to pull himself together. To resurrect himself out of the ashes that Susan had reduced his soul to when she had coldly walked out on him and their son without so much as a word. Without any kind of warning.

But he instinctively knew that if that happened to him again, there wouldn't be anything left of him to rise up again.

His gut told him that he wouldn't be able to survive a death blow like that.

So for his son's sake, as well as his own, Clint decided that he needed to cut off all ties with Wynona *now* before his inner constitution dissolved to the point that he didn't have the strength to walk away. Because if he didn't cut off all ties, if he wound up convincing himself that he could maintain at least minimal contact with her and still be able to keep his distance emotionally, then he was utterly doomed.

No, cutting off all connection with the woman was the only way that he had even a prayer of remaining whole and sane.

Knowing that didn't make its execution easy. If anything, the complete opposite was true.

And having Ryan constantly asking him about the invitation, about when Wynona was coming over to the house, really didn't help.

"I don't know," Clint finally said when he felt his son's eyes all but boring into him.

"But you said you were gonna ask her," Ryan reminded him innocently. "That was two weeks ago," the boy pointed out, then paused as he thought about it. "More," he corrected. He looked at his father hopefully, obviously trying to push him along without coming right out saying as much. "Miss Chee said yesterday that it's never polite to keep anyone waiting."

Clint's eyes narrowed as he looked up from the repair work he was doing.

"Oh she did, did she?" He could feel his walls going up, bent on securing his heart in place so that it would be safe from the painful consequences of any verbal assault.

Had he been right in his estimation of the woman? Was she fighting dirty by using his own son against him? "Did she say that to you specifically?"

Ryan looked at him in confusion. "No, she said that to the class, but—"

"So she was just talking in general," Clint retorted curtly, terminating the conversation. His cold, stern tone warned his son not to say anything further on the subject.

The message was not received. Except for the bottom line, which told Ryan that the invitation hadn't been delivered.

"But, Dad, why can't she come to our house?" Ryan asked plaintively.

This new stubborn streak Ryan was displaying was a revelation to him. Where was this coming from? Clint wondered, irritated.

Exasperated and at a loss how to answer Ryan, Clint fell back on an old stand-by.

"Don't you have some homework to do?" he asked.

Ryan's face fell. "Yes, but—"

"Then go do it," Clint snapped at his son, turning back to his work.

Ryan made one more attempt to get his father to see things his way. "But, Dad—"

He got no further.

Clint's eyes darkened as he looked sternly at his son. "Now," he ordered.

Ryan dropped his head and walked slowly back to

the house, taking baby steps as if he were part of a funeral procession.

Only once the boy was out of earshot did Roy step out of the stable and cross over to where his brother was standing.

"A little hard on the boy, weren't you, Clint?" he asked.

Clint was in no mood to be on the receiving end of a lecture, especially not from his brother. Roy had never been in any kind of a serious relationship and had no idea what he was going through.

With a careless shrug, Clint looked back at his work. "He's got to learn."

Roy moved around until he was right in front of his brother. "Learn what?" he asked. "That his father, the hero, is as unapproachable as ever?"

Clint glared at his brother. "I'm not a hero," he snapped.

"Keep shutting Ryan out like that and you damn well won't be," Roy agreed. Clint made no attempt to explain his actions, leaving Roy no choice but to demand, "What the hell's come over you?"

"Nothing," Clint retorted. He just wanted everyone to leave him alone. But apparently, Roy wasn't taking the hint. Glaring at his younger brother, Clint told him, "Look, if you don't have anything to do, I can find work for you."

Roy ignored the offer, seeing it as nothing but an attempt to divert him from what was really wrong with his brother. "You've been behaving like a wounded bear ever since the night you and Wynona found that boy and brought him back." Roy's eyes widened as a thought suddenly occurred to him. "Something happened between you and that teacher, didn't it?"

"No!" Clint shouted.

The sound of his voice registered and Clint abruptly closed his mouth, moving over to another section of the corral.

Roy refused to let him walk away. "Yes, it did," he insisted, the pieces finally all coming together for him. "Hot damn, you came back to the world of the living and made love with Wynona, didn't you?"

His hand tightening on his hammer, Clint shot his brother a dirty look as he drove the nail into the post with far more vigor than was required. All the while he kept his mouth shut.

But Roy wouldn't give up or be put off. Grinning, he clamped his hand on his older brother's shoulder, taking Clint's silence as affirmation. "Wow, that's wonderful, Clint."

Clint's look grew even darker. "What's so wonderful about it?" he demanded angrily.

"It means you can feel," Roy emphasized, still rejoicing in what he took to be his brother's reawakening.

Clint was quick to set him straight. "Well, I don't want to feel," he ground out between clenched teeth.

Momentarily taken aback, Roy could only look at his older brother in confusion. And then his confusion slowly receded as he smiled again. "I think it's too late, Clint. You already do."

Clint had had just about enough of his brother's babbling. "You have no idea what you're talking about.

And no, I don't." He paused for a second, then told his brother with even more feeling, "I *won't.*"

"Why?" Roy asked.

"Because I am not going to go through that again," Clint insisted even more angrily, walking away from his brother again.

"Go through what again?" Roy asked, following him. He refused to just give up and walk away from Clint. This was far too important; Clint had to realize that, he thought. "Being in love?"

Clint whirled around. "No! Being ripped to shreds," he snapped.

"Who's ripping you to shreds?" Roy asked in all innocence. "Wynona?" he guessed, then asked in disbelief, "Has she done something to you?"

Another man would have said yes and been done with it. But he had to be honest even though he just wanted Roy to go away and leave him alone. "Not yet."

"Oh. Then all this—" he circled his hand around in front of Clint "—this building up of walls around yourself again, that's just you taking preventative measures, is that it?"

The last shred of his temper went up in smoke. "Back off! It's none of your damn business," Clint shouted.

But Roy wasn't about to back off, not this time. Clint was hurting and it was time to put a stop to it.

"You're my brother. It damn well *is* my business. And this my-heart's-made-of-stone act of yours is hurting your son, so that would make it my business even if I *wasn't* your brother, understand?" Roy demanded. He was close to losing his own temper because he couldn't seem to knock any sense into his brother's thick head.

"How?" Clint demanded. "How is this hurting my son? This is between Wynona and me."

Roy laughed drily as he shook his head. "You keep telling yourself that."

"Why?" Clint repeated. He didn't see how this could have any repercussions on his son, unless Roy meant Wynona would retaliate as Ryan's teacher. "She wouldn't take this out on him," he protested. Wynona wasn't like that, Clint thought.

"No, she wouldn't and she isn't," Roy agreed. "But you are."

Roy had lost him again. Clint had no idea what his brother was talking about. "No, I'm not."

"Oh no?" Roy questioned, then proceeded to give Clint examples. "You're pushing him away, snarling at him like a wounded bear. No wonder Ryan thinks he's done something wrong."

Clint was stunned. How could Roy say that? "I never said that to him," Clint insisted.

"Maybe not in so many words," Roy allowed, "but Ryan's filling in the blanks. Kids always think they've done something wrong when their parent snaps at them."

Roy stood studying his brother, waiting to see if he'd gotten through the thick shields that Clint had constructed around himself.

When Clint continued to remain silent, saying nothing in response, Roy tried again. This time, in a quiet voice, he said, "She's not going to do it, you know."

Clint's head snapped up. He didn't have to ask who the "she" was that Roy was referring to. He knew. "Do what?"

"If you're waiting for Wynona to walk out on you because she's looking for something more fulfilling in her life, she's not going to do it," Roy told him.

Clint scowled. "You don't know what you're talking about."

Roy continued looking at him. "Did you even take any time to find things out about this woman?" he asked. Not waiting for an answer, he continued, telling his brother what *he* had found out about Wynona. "She grew up on the reservation right outside Forever. While she was in a strong community, life was hard. She never knew her father and lost her mother young. Her uncle and aunt took her in. Things were good for a year and then she lost them, too. The uncle in a car accident and the aunt to pneumonia.

"She and her cousin were minutes away from being swallowed up into the foster care system when her great-aunt suddenly came on the scene and took them both with her to Houston where she lived. She paid for both their college educations. Wynona could have done anything she wanted once she got her teaching degree and all she wanted to do was come back here to show kids that it was possible to become something if they worked hard at it."

Clint said nothing. Frustrated, Roy shouted at his brother. "Don't you get it? Wynona isn't anything like Susan. Susan was the center of her own universe. Wynona is a selfless woman who only wants to help people. She's a rare human being," Roy said with feeling. "So if you don't come to your senses and start acting more like the grown-up you were when you were eighteen instead of the cowering, scared kid that Susan turned you into, then you are *not* the brother I know and I'm ashamed of you."

Clint frowned, although the anger had been all but totally leeched out of him.

"You think you have all the answers, don't you?" he asked.

"No, you do," Roy told him.

This time Clint could only wave a hand dismissively. "Yeah, right."

But Roy wasn't about to be put off. "You do. You just have to look a little harder into yourself. And remember, Wynona isn't Susan. Susan wasn't good enough to even clean Wynona's shoes," he insisted. "Now, I can't tell you what to do—"

"Doesn't seem to be stopping you," Clint commented, the fire having entirely left his voice.

"But if I were you," Roy continued as if he hadn't been interrupted, "I'd run, not walk, to that teacher's house, fall on my knees in front of her and *beg* her to forgive me."

"I can't do that." He'd done too much damage by staying away. It was already too late for any apologies.

"Yeah, you can," Roy insisted. "You can tell her you'd taken temporary leave of your senses, but you're all better now and you will do *anything* to make it up to her if she would just give you another chance."

Clint laughed drily. "You have this whole thing worked out, don't you?"

Roy became serious as he answered, "All except the part where I get you to listen to reason and try to win her back."

"It's too late for that," Clint repeated. "The damage is done."

"You don't know that," Roy insisted.

"Yeah, I do," Clint answered flatly.

"No, you don't," Roy countered. He could guess what his brother was thinking. "You're afraid she'll turn you down but you don't know for sure. And my money is on Wynona. The woman has a great capacity to overlook people's flaws."

"How do you know that?"

"She was willing to go out with you, wasn't she?" Roy pointed out.

He hadn't told Roy that he'd told Wynona on the night of the search that he had initially sought her out at the school to ask her to come to dinner. "How would you know that?"

"Simple. You don't share anything with me so I make it my job to find things out," Roy explained, adding, "I was never the kind of guy who was content staying in the dark. Now, for the love of Pete, stop stalling! Get into your truck and drive over to her place before someone else in town realizes what a catch that woman is and aces you out of what could have been the best thing that ever happened to you—outside of me and the kid."

The last words were addressed to Clint's back as

his brother turned on his heel and began to run toward his truck.

Roy smiled. *Finally!*

There was hope for his brother after all.

Chapter Seventeen

Clint kept going over what he wanted to say to Wynona the entire trip from his ranch to her doorstep. Rehearsing, he used different words each time, predominantly because he couldn't remember the words he'd used only minutes before.

Nothing he said sounded right.

Clint swore under his breath. He'd blown it; he was certain of it. Wynona was never going to give him a second chance, he thought.

And why should she? If he'd been in her place, he certainly wouldn't give him a second chance.

"If you had half a brain in your head, Washburn, you'd just turn around and go home," he told himself in hopeless disgust.

Clint's frown deepened. If he did just turn around

and go home, he knew that Roy would give him hell. But that didn't matter to him. Maybe he even deserved it, he thought. But what *had* gotten to him, what kept him driving to town rather than just giving up, turning around and heading back home, was the look he had seen on Ryan's face earlier.

The look he would see again if he returned without having even *tried* to get Wynona to understand why he had done what he'd done.

The look of complete, total disappointment.

Clint sighed. He had finally seen his son coming around, finally becoming lively and animated. He didn't want to be the one responsible for making Ryan revert back to the withdrawn shell of a boy he had been before Wynona had come into their lives.

So he kept driving, ready to take his medicine and whatever else he had to do in order to, as Roy had pointed out, rejoin the forces of the living.

He still didn't know what to say or how to begin.

All the words he had rehearsed on the drive here completely deserted him as he brought his truck to a halt in front of Wynona's house. Deserted him and scurried away like rats fleeing a sinking ship.

He could far more easily face down a wild, bucking mustang than do what he was about to do.

He *knew* what to do when it came to taming a wild horse. He was good at it. But as far as baring his soul to a woman he knew he was guilty of treating badly—a woman who deserved so much better than him—he had no idea what to say or what to do.

Completely clueless, he had no idea how to make her forgive him. All he knew was that he *wanted* her to forgive him.

Steeling himself off, he finally raised his hand and knocked on the door.

There was no answer at first and he knocked again. Was Wynona still at the school?

Or had she gone out? Maybe she was at Miss Joan's, or—

A number of places crossed his mind and he thought about looking for her, then decided that eventually, the woman who had taught him that he still had a heart had to come home.

Right?

He finally decided he was going to wait for her in his truck no matter how long it took.

Reluctantly turning away from the front of the house, he had just begun to walk to his truck when he heard the door behind him opening.

Clint whirled around immediately, prepared to launch into a disjointed, jumbled apology in order to break down any walls that Wynona might have constructed around herself.

But the words he began to say froze on his lips. He wasn't looking at Wynona. He was looking into the disapproving face of her cousin, Shania.

"Are you lost?" Shania asked him coldly. "The feed store is on the next street," she told him, pointing in the store's general direction.

He wasn't in the habit of making anyone privy to his business, but he knew that wasn't going to cut it right now. Forcing himself to put his personal feelings aside, he told the young woman in the doorway, "I want to talk to Wynona."

Shania remained planted right where she was, blocking any access into the house. She even put her hands on opposite sides of the doorsill to form even more of a barrier.

"Well, she doesn't want to talk to you so why don't you just go back where you came from?" Shania suggested with a smile that was cold enough to freeze a medium-size lake.

He'd come this far; Clint decided to push a little further. "I want to hear Wynona tell me to go."

Shania's face darkened. "You are not in any position to make any demands, Washburn."

"But—" Clint protested.

Shania wasn't about to hear him out. "You lost that right," Shania informed him angrily, "when you treated my cousin as if she didn't matter."

"I need to talk to her, to explain," Clint insisted, refusing to be put off. "Wynona needs to understand that I didn't mean to hurt her."

Shania wasn't budging. "Talk is cheap, Washburn," she retorted.

"Please," Clint said. His eyes said things to Wynona's cousin that he couldn't.

"It's all right, Shania," Wynona said quietly, coming up behind her cousin. She placed a hand on Shania's shoulder. "Let him come in."

Shania frowned. If it was up to her, she'd toss Washburn out on his ear, but ultimately this was Wynona's call.

"Fine," she relented, stepping aside. "I'll go get a broom and a dustpan so I can sweep up the pieces that'll be left behind once he's had his say."

Clint walked in as Shania left the room. The latter paused to shoot a warning look at him over her shoulder before leaving the area.

"She hates me, doesn't she?" Clint said to Wynona as he closed the door.

Rather than agree with or deny the assessment, Wynona merely said, "She's being protective of me." Hoping she wasn't going to regret this, Wynona led the way into the living room. "Would you like some coffee?" she asked him, turning around.

He had no desire to drink coffee or anything else, but it was a way of stalling for a few minutes, so he said, "Sure, why not?"

"I'll be right back," Wynona replied, then walked into the kitchen.

Shania had put up a pot of fresh coffee when she'd come home earlier and there was still about half a pot left. Wynona poured a cup and returned with it to the living room.

He saw the single cup. "You're not having any?" he questioned.

She shook her head. "If I have coffee past a certain hour, it keeps me up at night."

"Oh." Clint put the cup she had brought him down on the small coffee table, untouched.

"Not to your liking?" she questioned.

The smile on his lips was forced. "I'm sure it's fine."

This whole situation was so awkward, it was downright painful, Wynona thought. It was time to put both of them out of their misery.

"Why are you here, Clint?" she asked him.

Picking up on her tone, he read into it. "Do you want me to leave?"

Wynona didn't say yes or no. Instead, frustrated, she said, "What I want is for you to tell me why you left your ranch, drove all the way here and asked me for a cup of coffee you had no intention of drinking."

"Well, technically," he told her, "I didn't ask for the coffee. You offered it."

Wynona's eyes widened. He was going to lecture her about *technicalities*? Wynona felt her temper spiking. "And 'technically,'" she retorted, "no court in the world would convict me if I threw the cup of coffee straight at your head."

Clint took a breath. "I'm sorry."

"Not as sorry as you're going to be once that cup grazes your skull," she informed him angrily.

She had kept her temper under wraps for the past two and a half weeks, struggling not to allow anyone to glimpse the pain she was going through. Now that she had allowed her temper to finally erupt, she was having trouble getting it back under control.

But Clint didn't let himself get distracted, didn't extrapolate on any sidebars that had come up. Now that he had finally said the words to her, all he could do was repeat them until their meaning sank in with her.

"I'm sorry," he said to Wynona again.

"Well, you just—"

About to make another comment, this one about the

way his vanishing act had affected her, Wynona stopped midword and stared at him, her eyes wide. She was reading into this; she just knew it.

But even so, Wynona heard herself asking, "You're what?"

"I'm sorry," Clint repeated a third time with sincerity. "Very, very sorry."

Afraid that she was interpreting his words in her own way, Wynona wanted this apology spelled out.

"For?" she asked him, waiting.

He took in a deep breath as if to fortify himself. And then he said, "For not getting back to you. For acting like a coward. For allowing a ghost from the past to do a number on me and scare me off." Revved up, his words took on strength as he continued. "For very possibly losing the best thing that's happened to me. I've lost sight of the last time I felt so happy. I'm sorry for—"

Wynona put her index finger against his lips, stilling them. Despite everything, she could feel her mouth curving.

"You can stop now. You've answered my question," she told him.

But he had only gotten started. "I know this isn't something a man's supposed to admit," he told Wynona, his voice softening, "but making love with you woke up so many things inside me, things I wanted to feel, I was afraid that you'd use that against me somehow."

She looked at him, feeling both hurt and mystified at his reasoning. "I think that maybe we need to go back to the beginning so that you can get to know me, get to know the kind of person I am."

"I already know you," Clint told her.

But Wynona shook her head. "No, you don't. If you did, you wouldn't have harbored those kinds of thoughts about me. You would have known better."

"That didn't have anything to do with you," he told her with feeling. "All those thoughts had to do with Ryan's mother. When we started out, I had those kinds of feeling about her. She used them to twist my heart right out of my chest like it was some kind of a living corkscrew."

Reliving these memories was incredibly painful, but if he had a prayer of making Wynona stay, he had to share them with her so she could understand what had driven him to do what he'd done.

"When I found that Susan had just up and left me without warning, I thought I'd never recover. Eventually, I learned to live with the pain and I made my peace with that, but I wanted to make sure that it never was going to happen to me again."

She saw it differently. "You were a man with no heart, no feelings, who couldn't even relate to his own son. That's not making your peace with anything, Clint." Couldn't he see that? "That's resigning from life altogether."

He looked at Wynona, looked into her eyes as she spoke. He felt her passion. Moreover, he knew she didn't just have a point; she was completely right.

So he told her as much.

"You're right," Clint said out loud.

Wynona had revved herself up to deliver a full-fledged lecture to him. To have Clint immediately agree took away some of her thunder, leaving her with nothing to add.

She blinked. "I am?"

"Yes," Clint answered. "You are."

"Well, I guess I can't argue with that," Wynona murmured.

A hint of a smile slipped over his lips. Why had he run from this? What kind of an idiot did that make him? "You can if you want to," he told her.

"What I want," she told him, "is to just forget the past two and a half weeks ever happened."

"But not the lovemaking," Clint quickly interjected, looking at her hopefully.

"No," Wynona agreed, smiling at him, "not the lovemaking. Not if it's the part that you *want* to remember." She held her breath, waiting to see what he would say to that.

Her stipulation puzzled him. "Why wouldn't I want to remember coming to life for the first time in over seven years?" he asked her.

She just wanted to be sure that it was as important to him as it was to her. "I have no idea," she told him honestly. "I never claimed to be able to understand the male mind."

Relieved beyond words that it looked as if it was going to work out after all, Clint put his arms around her. "I could give you a quick course. If you're interested, that is."

"I guess I have to be. That is, if I'm going to survive this relationship." And then, just to make sure she hadn't jumped to conclusions, she asked, "This *is* a relationship, right?"

Clint nodded. "That's one way to describe it," he answered.

She wasn't sure what to make of his response. "What's another way?" she asked, looking at him uncertainly, bracing herself for anything.

He took a breath to fortify himself. "How about 'an engagement?'"

Had she had any of the coffee she had offered him, she would have undoubtedly been choking on it at this point.

As it was, she found herself coughing as she tried to catch her breath. "What did you just say?"

"An engagement," he repeated, then quickly backtracked, afraid he'd taken too much for granted. "No, I'm sorry, that was too soon. I shouldn't have just thrown you into the deep end of the pool like that. I didn't mean to—"

Wynona put her hands on either side of his face, symbolically capturing his words so that he could catch his breath.

"I think you missed a few steps, Clint. Do you want to start from the beginning?" she asked.

"The beginning?" he asked. Then, as she nodded her head, he said, "Right, the beginning. Do you think that maybe you might, maybe someday, be willing to maybe think about, um, well, marrying me?"

Not exactly the eloquent proposal she was hoping for, Wynona thought. But it would do.

"Someday?" she questioned.

He took that to mean that she thought it was the right word to use in this case.

"Yes, like maybe a long time from now," he added quickly.

"Why?" she asked. She needed to hear reasons, *his* reasons, before she answered the all-important question that was making her heart flutter.

"Why?" he repeated, not sure what she wanted to hear him say.

So she explained it to him. "*Why* are you asking me to marry you?"

"Because I love you," he said, blurting out the answer before he had time to stop himself.

Wynona smiled. Finally. "That's all I wanted to hear," she informed him.

"So does that mean you'll think about it?" he asked hopefully.

Her eyes were dancing as she answered, "Think about it?"

She managed to suppress the laugh that rose up in her throat. The man was going to really have to work on his confidence, she thought. Couldn't he see that she loved him?

"No, I'm not going to think about it. I'm going to say yes, you big, thick-headed cowboy. Because I love you," she told him before he could ask.

Relieved beyond words, Clint pulled her into his arms. Lord, but she felt good, he couldn't help thinking. A part of him had been convinced that he'd lost her. He had never been so happy to be wrong.

"I love you, too," he said, lowering his mouth to hers.

The rest of what happened after that was a blur, but that was all right with them. After all, they had the rest of their lives to sort it all out.

Epilogue

Clint was standing in one of the two tiny rooms located at the rear of the church. The rooms were reserved for brides and bridegrooms spending their final moments as single people just before they exchanged the vows that would bind them to each other.

At the moment, he was looking into the full-length mirror and doing his best to get his tie straight. In his opinion, the gunmetal-gray suit he was wearing made him look as if he had just fallen off the top of a wedding cake, but he wasn't doing this for himself. He was doing this for Wynona. She deserved to have the wedding that she'd admitted she had dreamed about.

It was because Clint was looking into the mirror in order to get his tie just right that he caught a glimpse of his son peering into the room. The moment Ryan realized that he'd been seen, the boy quickly stepped back, out of sight.

Clint stopped fumbling with the black fabric. The two sides of the tie hung on either side of his neck, silently mocking him.

"C'mon in, Ryan," Clint called out. "You're just the person I want to see."

"I am?" Ryan asked in unabashed surprise. The boy slowly crossed the threshold into the room and then took hesitant steps to draw closer to his father.

"Absolutely," Clint replied. He turned away from the mirror, temporarily abandoning his efforts to tie a reasonable-looking tie, and looked down at his son. "Come on over here and sit down with me, Ryan."

"Yes, sir." Ryan obediently followed him to the single small sofa in the room and sat down beside his father once the latter had taken a seat.

It occurred to Clint that the events in the past few weeks had happened very fast. When Wynona had said yes to him, he didn't want to waste any more time with things like long, formal engagements. Afraid she might change her mind or come to her senses, he was anxious to make Wynona his wife as soon as possible.

The sped-up pace was fine for him, but maybe it was a little difficult for his son to accept.

Maybe Ryan would have needed some time to adjust to what was going on. He didn't want the boy to feel as if the rug had just been pulled out from under his feet. He was finally making amends for having ignored Ryan for all these years and he didn't want to mess it up now.

Clint put his hand on his son's shoulder and felt a twinge of guilt when he felt Ryan stiffen. The boy had turned out really well, considering how he had neglected him.

Wynona had come into *both* their lives just in time, he couldn't help thinking.

Clint left his hand on the boy's shoulder. "You okay with this?" Clint asked.

"With what?" Ryan asked almost timidly.

It occurred to Clint that he and Ryan hadn't had any father-son talks or even moments together.

He was going to have to change that. Starting now.

"With my marrying your teacher. Ms. Chee."

They were going to have to come up with a way to refer to her, Clint thought. Wynona wasn't going to just be his teacher, and calling her Mom would probably be difficult for Ryan, at least at first.

Later, Clint told himself. He'd deal with that after the wedding, not now.

"Sure," Ryan answered cheerfully. "She's great. She already told me I could call her Mom if I wanted to. And I do." He looked at his father. "Is that okay with you? 'Cause I won't if it's not," Ryan assured him quickly.

Clint slipped his arm around his son's shoulder, pulling the boy to him in a quick, impromptu hug. "It's okay with me." He felt as if he was suddenly going to choke up. "Well," he continued, taking a breath and releasing the boy, "I'd better get back to wrestling with this tie if I'm going to look presentable for this wedding."

"I can help you if you want," Ryan offered.

Clint looked at him, astonished. "You know how to tie one of these things?"

Ryan bobbed his head up and down. "Uh-huh."

"How did you learn how to do that?" Clint wanted

to know, still rather skeptical that Ryan could actually live up to his claim.

"You've gotta stay sitting down or I can't reach you," Ryan said as his father began to get up. When Clint lowered himself back on the sofa, Ryan got to work. Staring intently at the tie, he quickly brought the two ends together. "Lucia taught me."

"Lucia," Clint repeated, surprised. "And why would she do that?"

"She said you never knew when something like that could come in handy." Finished, the boy beamed as he looked at his handiwork. "I guess she was right."

"I guess she was at that." Clint rose from the sofa and surveyed himself in the mirror. "Perfect," he proclaimed to his son. "So, are you ready to get married?"

Ryan beamed. "Me, too?"

"You, too," Clint answered.

Ryan slipped his small hand into his father's, his eagerness barely contained. "Let's go!"

And they did.

* * * * *

MILLS & BOON

Coming next month

SURPRISE BABY FOR THE HEIR
Ellie Darkins

'I'm pregnant.'

The words hit Fraser like a bus, rendering him mute and paralysed. He sat in silence for long, still moments, letting the words reverberate through his ears, his brain. The full meaning of them fell upon him slowly, gradually. Like being crushed to death under a pile of small rocks. Each one so insignificant that you didn't feel the difference, but collectively, they stole his breath, and could break his body.

'Are you going to say anything?' Elspeth asked, breaking into his thoughts at last. He met her gaze and saw that it had hardened even further – he hadn't thought that that would be possible. And he could understand why. He'd barely said a word since she'd dropped her bombshell. But he needed time to take this in. Surely she could understand that. 'I'm sorry. I'm in shock,' he said. Following it up with the first thing that popped into his head. 'We were careful.'

'Not careful enough, it seems.' Her voice was like ice, cutting into him, and he knew that it was the wrong thing to say. He wasn't telling her anything she didn't know.

Fraser shook his head.

'What do you want to do?' he asked, his voice tentative,

aware that they had options. Equally aware that discussing them could be a minefield if they weren't on the same page.

'I want to have the baby,' Elspeth said with the same firmness and lack of equivocation that she had told him that she was pregnant. How someone so slight could sound so immovably solid was beyond him, and a huge part of her appeal, he realised. Something that he should be wary of…